What We
Could
Have Been

What We Could Have Been

◆ *A NOVEL* ◆

JESS SINCLAIR

alcove
press

Published in the United States by Alcove Press, an imprint of The Quick Brown Fox & Company LLC.

Alcove Press and its logo are trademarks of The Quick Brown Fox & Company LLC.

Library of Congress Catalog-in-Publication data available upon request.

ISBN (paperback): 978-1-63910-471-0
ISBN (ebook): 978-1-63910-472-7

Cover design by Nicole Lecht

Printed in the United States.

www.alcovepress.com

Alcove Press
34 West 27th St., 10th Floor
New York, NY 10001

First Edition: October 2023

10 9 8 7 6 5 4 3 2 1

For Joe, my Enzo from age six at the A&P
until the final page

♦ 1 ♦

BLUE'S MOTHER WAS DEAD. Her pale legs hung limply over her father's arm as he carried her, his wide shoulders and back rigid. Blue followed her parents home from Enzo Castellari's house, the midnight sand still warm under her bare feet, shoes left behind in haste. She was afraid to speak. Approaching their cottage, her father shifted his hold on Ella and she cried out, the sound knocking the air from Blue's chest in her own choked sob. *Mum.* She'd stood in the bedroom doorway, invisible, while her dad settled her mother in bed, bending to press his cheek against his wife's.

Years later, her mother's cry still echoed in her ears whenever the memory jabbed at her, a distorted, incomplete snapshot. Her mum had eventually recovered; they hadn't lost her, not that night anyway. Standing here now, facing the gray, peeling paint of the door to her childhood home, Bluebelle Shea squeezed her eyes shut against the memory, only to have others tumble forward. Her world had been upended that night she'd trailed along the beach behind her parents, sick with fear, but it was nothing compared to actually losing her mum, and everyone else she loved all at once, two years later.

"Mom?" From behind her on the porch, Murphy's voice jarred her from her thoughts. "I'm hungry. Do you think Grandpa will have lunch for us?"

Her son's eyes were so dark they were nearly black, a stark contrast to his sandy blonde hair. He'd put his backpack on before getting out of the minivan. Just to walk from the gravel drive-way up the broken front steps to the porch. His stuffed sea turtle Sammy endured the twisting, squeezing motions of his hands in front of him.

She rested a hand lightly atop Murphy's head, feeling every bit as anxious as he looked. She faked as much grown-up confi-dence as she could summon. "Well, even if he's already had his lunch, I'll make you something. Sound good?"

He ducked away, rolling his eyes. "Okay. Stop."

Blue dropped her hand to her side. Stuffed turtle or not, nine-year-old Murph kept reminding her he wasn't a little kid anymore. She'd hoped his attitude would improve on the way here, but so far it hadn't.

"You have to knock if you want him to know we're here, Mom."

She gritted her teeth against a retort she'd regret and knocked. She waited, turning away from the door to gaze out over the blue water beyond the seawall to breathe in the ocean air, that soothing hint of Florida Gulf Coast salt and balmy dampness that marked the beginning of summer in Bliss. The shrimp trawler and the large, center console vessel her dad used to catch mack-erel were at the docks, exactly as they had been Blue's whole life.

"Maybe he forgot we were coming," Murphy said.

She smoothed a hand over her wavy blonde hair, wishing the cowlick at her left temple would relax; she'd inherited it from her mother. He wouldn't have forgotten they were coming. She'd phoned and asked to see him, leaving out the fact that all of their worldly belongings were with them because there wasn't a place for them in Tallahassee anymore. She'd made sure to say she'd be bringing along his grandson. Her dad's tone over the phone had been gruff and unreadable, but he'd agreed to the visit. Had he already known about Murphy? When Blue ran away ten years ago, a week into her senior year of high school, she'd left without a plan, but had ended up with Aunt Eva, her mum's sister up in the Florida Panhandle. Eva had hated Mitch Shea. Blue doubted her aunt would've told her father anything.

There was no running away now. She knocked again, louder this time, and footsteps sounded somewhere inside the house. Her dad was on the other side of that door, not answering. She took a couple of steps back from the door and nearly fell through a rotted wooden plank. Her arms flailed and Murphy reached out, helping her regain her footing. Blue's pulse pounded in her temples. This was a mistake.

"I think, um . . . Murph, let's go. We'll get a room at that motel we passed before the turn off. I think I saw a pool." She let her tone rise at the end, trying to make it sound fun.

She'd spent the last few days hearing her own false cheery tone and hating it. Her son hadn't wanted to leave Tallahassee. He didn't want to leave his friends or his school, and she didn't blame him. Brent hadn't even bothered to argue when she told him she was taking Murphy and going home to her dad's. She'd thought Murph was upset with both of them for their family falling apart. But on the way here, he'd made it clear he was only mad at Blue. *You could've let me stay with Dad,* he'd said, sullen and sniffling in the back seat after crying for the first hour of the trip. He didn't mean it. He was hitting her where it hurt because he hurt; even at nine, he had to know on some level that his stepdad didn't want that.

Mitch Shea opened the door. His ruddy cheeks were flushed under a beard that had grown bushy and gray, though the hair he smoothed a hand over was still dark red. Deep lines were etched between his unkempt brows, pale blue eyes regarding her and then coming to rest on Murphy. "Good Lord," he uttered.

"Hi, Dad."

"Bluebelle." He pushed the screen door open for them and stepped back. "Come in."

The three of them stood in the small living room, dust floating in the scattered rays of sunlight. Decaying grief gripped her, squeezing her around the chest; everything was exactly as it had been when she'd left. The blanket her mother had knitted lay folded over the back of the couch, same as always, the rich earth tones now faded from the afternoon sun streaming through the curtainless picture window. Ella's favorite books were still stacked on the end table near the couch. It was as if she'd just stepped out to the store, rather than drowned.

"Christ but you look like your mum," Mitch said, his normally mild Irish accent heavier than she remembered. He was staring at her as if he'd seen a ghost.

"Do I?" she asked. "I hope so . . . Dad, this is Murphy, your grandson. Murph, meet your Grandpa Mitch." She sucked in air. She stared at her father, wide-eyed. Was he ready for this? Was she?

Mitch looked down at her small son. Blue glimpsed a portion of white fluff emerging from the green cloth of Sammy's shoulder joint, twisting in the boy's grasp. Her father extended his hand. "Murphy's a fine name," he said, his voice gravelly, as if from disuse. "Good to meet you, son."

Murph's hand was completely eclipsed by her father's. "Hi, Grandpa."

"Dad. I'm so sorry," Blue blurted. She reached out, wanting to hug him, wanting him to know this was hard for her too. Something in his expression stopped her. She shoved her hand in her pocket. "I, uh—"

He looked down. "All right." He turned and walked away from them.

She followed him to the kitchen, the breakfast nook countertop and a million miles between them. Two of the four stools that had occupied this space were gone, and the cushions on the other two were gray and threadbare. Three place settings were arranged on the counter, with paper plates and napkins, a large platter of homemade ham and cheese sandwiches between them. "I thought you might be hungry after the drive."

"I'm starving!" Murphy climbed onto a stool and plunked Sammy on the counter. "Mom didn't pack enough car snacks."

"I'm sorry, Dad," Blue said again. "I know they're just words and they don't undo me staying gone so long, but I'm just so sorry. When Mum died—"

His hands froze and he met her gaze, his imposing eyebrows scrunched together, narrowing the blue of his eyes to slits. "No."

"But I—"

"We're not speaking about that. I won't." His words were clipped, sharp.

"Okay," she said, biting the inside of her cheek. They'd have to talk about it eventually.

Mitch pushed the sandwich plate across the counter to Murphy. "I've got water or Coke, which'll it be?"

"We don't give him soda," Blue said reflexively, at the same time Murphy replied, "Coke, please."

Her father poured a glass of cold water from a pitcher in the refrigerator and set it in front of her son. "I'll not help you break the rules, son. At least not while your mum's watching."

Murphy giggled. Blue caught Mitch tossing a quick wink to her kid. Her eyes flooded with tears, startling her. Maybe this wasn't a mistake. Maybe it was the first thing she'd done right in a long time.

When they'd finished their sandwiches, Mitch straightened up from his leaning position on the counter. "Why are you here, Bluebelle?"

This was the question she had been dreading. She'd rehearsed what she would say, but now her mind was blank.

Murphy spoke up. "Dad moved out and then Aunt Eva died and Mom says we don't have anyone anymore. Which isn't true. I still have lots of friends."

"Murph—" Blue didn't bother finishing her sentence. He wasn't wrong. She hadn't been happy with Brent, but since he'd left, she'd become acutely aware of how small her and Murphy's world was. And then the one person she'd always been able to count on—aunt, friend, babysitter, advice giver Eva—had died suddenly of an aneurysm.

"I didn't know your aunt passed," Mitch said. "I'm sorry. I know you loved her."

"Thank you. Um. I'm not sure what Aunt Eva told you?"

"Not much." Her father's shoulders slumped, and all at once he looked old, much older than when they'd arrived, so much older than when she'd left. "Eva told me next to nothing. She called me once a year on your mum's birthday to say you were fine. I don't know why. I know she blamed me. But—" Mitch exhaled forcefully and braced a hand on the chipped tile of the countertop. "I suppose she called so I'd leave her alone. She got tired of hearing from me, I'm sure."

Blue's arms ached to hug him. She moved toward him, the smallest step, but he turned and ran water onto dishes piled up in the sink, adding soap and grabbing a stained dishcloth. She stayed where she was, glancing at Murphy. He'd discovered the long, curly phone cord on the ancient wall-mounted telephone and was winding it around and around his fingers and up his arms. He'd gotten good at tuning out adult conflict in his short life.

She dove in. "Aunt Eva helped me get my GED and then get through the nursing program when Murphy was little. She helped me get a job at the hospital where she worked. My husband, Brent, is filing for divorce. I've missed you for a long time, Dad. I wanted to come home. But I didn't know how." Her dad's dishwashing motions had slowed. She kept going, addressing his back. "After Brent moved out, Aunt Eva was the only family we had up there—the only family Murphy knew, besides me. I've always wished he could meet you."

Her dad turned around. He listened, drying his hands on a towel that had once been yellow.

"I don't think we're going back," she said, her words hesitant. "I start my new job tomorrow; I was able to transfer from the county hospital in Tallahassee to Collier County ER. Murph and I can find a motel to stay in for a while, if you want, but maybe we wouldn't need to? I have enough saved to help with your bills here. If, uh, I don't know, maybe while we look for a place."

She winced at her offer. She had a little money left with the vacation time she'd cashed out, but not much. Brent had warned her not to touch their joint account, or his lawyer would—well, his lawyer would do something to her, she didn't fully understand all the legalities of divorce proceedings. She didn't have a lawyer.

"You want to stay here? With me?" her dad asked.

She'd never hated her father's unruly beard before this moment. His expression was completely unreadable. Her heart raced as she tried to steel herself against his rejection, his hurt over her staying away so long manifesting as anger. "If you'd let us."

He nodded. "All right." He bent at the waist suddenly, ducking down to peer out the front window over the Gulf to the west. "Getting late, I've still got work to do before my shrimp run."

Murphy jerked to attention, accidentally pulling the handset off the receiver as the cord around his arms moved with him. "What's a shrimp run? Can I come?"

"No," Blue answered before her dad could.

Mitch opened the refrigerator and grabbed a soda. "Blue-belle, I—" He stopped, mid-stride toward the back door, looking at her. His brow was furrowed, his expression conflicted. He opened his mouth to say something and then seemed to think better of it. He scowled at the floor and shrugged, as if trying to shake off the emotion she could feel emanating from him. "There's your old room and the sunroom. Sunroom's full of boxes and crap. I'll get it cleared out tonight so one of you can use that." He walked abruptly through the side door outside, the wooden screen door bouncing against the frame.

Murphy climbed down from his stool and moved around the counter. "Does he have some cookies or chips or something?"

"Let's see." Blue went for the refrigerator first, giving in to her curiosity. Sierra had said her dad wasn't drinking. Her dad had always maintained that the last drink he'd had was two years before losing Ella, despite the Breathalyzer results used against him in the trial. She had never really understood why he'd continued to refute the evidence, even after his conviction. Blue saw that he'd been truthful, at least today: other than the water pitcher and soda, there were no other beverages. No alcohol in sight. She rifled through the narrow pantry, where dry goods and staples were randomly strewn over the shelves. No bottles stashed in here either.

She pulled out a box of Saltines and handed it to her son. "This is as close as you're gonna get to chips or cookies," she said, laughing as he wrinkled his nose. "We'll go shopping tomorrow after work when I pick you up. I promise. We'll get all kinds of good snacks." She was on guard, ready for him to complain about having to go to the day camp she'd arranged for him for childcare, but maybe he'd give her a break on that one.

Murphy plucked a cracker from the box. "Grandpa's kind of crabby."

She sat on a stool and leaned on the counter. "He's not usually, I promise. He's just out of sorts. I'm his only child, just like you're mine, and it's been a long time since he's seen me. But he's glad we're here. He likes you. Oh!" Blue arched back as a big gray tabby cat landed on the counter between her and Murphy. "Oh my goodness, Hook," she said, running a hand over the cat's back and smiling. "Who'd have thought you'd still be around?"

"He's gnarly looking, Mom. He's gotta be old. You had him before you left here? Cats live that long?" He stood a couple of feet back, assessing the cat.

Blue frowned at her son and put her head down as the cat turned around and came back to her, sniffing her hair. Hook had half a left ear, and a long scar ran from the cat's mouth up to just above his right eye where the fur had never grown back. "Sure, some do. Murphy, meet Hook. He's nicer than he looks, once he gets to know you. Same as Grandpa," she said, grinning at her son. "He'd always go out on the fishing boat. He never minded the water. The perks were probably worth it, weren't they?" She scratched the cat behind one ear, and he purred loudly, leaning into her hand.

"He missed you."

"I've missed him too. Your grandpa found him caught in some wire mesh under a shrimp trap when he was a kitten. He saved him. That's what the scar is from. He lost a toe off his back foot too," she said, pointing. "I remember us taking him to the vet so many times at first. He must be seventeen or eighteen now. He's a tough old guy."

"He's kind of cute, in a Halloween-y sort of way," Murphy said, tipping his head. He put a hand out to pet the cat and the tabby faced him and hissed, teeth bared, ears laid back and tail puffed up. "Dang, cat, okay." Murphy put his hands up and stepped back.

"He'll get used to you. He's like that at first with everyone; he hasn't changed, apparently." Blue was suddenly disproportionately sad. This place was just so unwelcoming; when she'd seen Hook, she'd actually thought for a second that it'd be nice for her son to have a cat. He'd never been allowed to before. But then, of course, Hook had to go and act like his jerky self. The cat rubbed against Blue and jumped down off the counter and they heard him let himself out the screen door.

"Can I see my room?" Murph asked.

She and Murphy hadn't packed a lot into the minivan. She still couldn't really wrap her head around her marriage being over. In the two months she'd been alone in her house with Murphy, it was often a peaceful feeling, knowing Brent wouldn't be walking in the door at the end of the day. It hurt to admit that, but it was true. But sometimes, her quiet, peaceful house was glaring proof that she messed up everything she touched. She'd never expected to end up divorced. She'd also never expected to end up pregnant at seventeen, hundreds of miles from home. If she'd known then that she'd be carrying her and her son's suitcases around the hole in her father's front porch to move back into her childhood bedroom at the age of twenty-seven, would she have found a way to come home years ago? Would she have ever left?

She thought back to seventeen-year-old Blue, the dreamlike bliss of an afternoon with Enzo Castellari abruptly replaced with sickening dread at seeing two county Sheriff's Department cruisers pulling into her driveway. Her mum was gone from the world by then, taken by the Coast Guard to Collier County Hospital, where they'd list her time of death as over an hour before she arrived. Ella had gone overboard, tangled in the outrigger lines.

Her dad had been too incoherent with grief that night to explain anything. The sheriff had given up on getting a formal statement from him until the next day and left them reeling in shock. Their neighbor Dale, a deputy for the county and Mitch's friend, had stayed behind, setting out food for them that got cold and then washing the dishes. Before leaving, he covered a fitfully snoring Mitch up on the couch with Ella's blanket while Blue stared, unseeing, at the television, promising she'd go to bed soon. She'd ended up in the fairy garden with Enzo at two in the morning instead.

Only twenty-four hours earlier, Blue and Enzo were hanging their legs off the docks as the sun set across the water. Blue tucked one bare foot behind Enzo's ankle, pushing his leg upward until he swung it back, sliding his much larger foot behind her ankle and flinging Blue's leg into the air. She'd tipped backward on the dock, laughing. She remembered the feel of the hair on his leg, his muscled calf, the little zings through her skin where their legs touched, stirrings in the pit of her belly that compelled her to touch him, feel his skin on hers, as often as she could, in any way possible. She'd told him she loved him that night on the docks under the moon. He'd promised her his future then, before everything changed.

They'd been friends since they were two. The Castellari family had moved in across the vacant lot next door, and Blue's mum Ella and Enzo's mother Sofia had met bringing their toddlers to the beach to play. Bluebelle was Mitch and Ella Shea's only child, though they had tried for more. Enzo was the firstborn of five boys. The families had quickly become friends, sharing recipes and wine and evenings spent laughing around firepits next door before the vacant land between them was bought by a real estate developer and filled with condos. After that, Blue and Enzo had taken turns cutting across the beachfront between houses to spend evenings and lazy Sunday afternoons together.

Enzo had been her best friend her whole life. But something shifted the summer before high school began. He was still her best friend, still her person, but he was suddenly so much more; they were more. It was as if someone had turned the light on in another room that neither of them knew was there. For a solid year, until the night her dad carried her crying mum home, the dinners and game nights and bonfires between the Sheas and Castellaris had taken on an evolving, exciting new dimension. Enzo shoving a younger brother out of the way so he could be closer to her, Blue pretending to fall asleep with her head on his shoulder—everything became about being together. By the time he kissed her, she'd imagined it so many times in her head, the real thing was startling. Tentative, gentle, wanting. A promise of things to come.

Blue leaned into the minivan in her dad's driveway and hoisted the heavy plastic bin that held remnants of her life in Tallahassee, Murphy's baby books, photo albums documenting nine years of birthdays and holidays and vacations with just her and her son at first, and then with her new husband. When Murph was three, she'd married Brent, a police officer with the city who'd persistently asked her out every time he was in the ER until she'd finally gone on a date with him. For six years, he'd been Murphy's dad; he was in the father–son photos for softball, soccer, Cub Scouts, and had stood by the boy's side for trophy pictures. He was also the man who'd spat the worst, most hurtful words at his stepson in the midst of their final argument, the day he'd stormed out. Murphy had gotten in the middle, trying to calm them both down. Brent had lashed out: *It's your fault I'm leaving. Your mother raised a brat—I can't stand being around you.* She squeezed her eyes shut now, remembering. Brent had slammed the door so hard the windows shook. The sound of his tires squealing down the street was followed by deafening silence. Murph's eyes were saucers in his stricken face.

Now, she jerked the heavy bin up, shoving the painful memory behind tonight's mile-long to-do list, and wrestled it up the walk, careful to avoid tripping on the broken and overgrown paving stones. The whole yard looked as if it hadn't been touched in years. When they'd pulled in, she'd glimpsed the wild and unkempt backyard, vines climbing the fence and willow branches tangled in ground weeds where her fairy garden used to be.

Murphy came sprinting out and took a side of the bin from her. "Mom, I said I'd be right back out to help with the heavy stuff," he said.

She watched him struggle with his end in determination to be strong and help her, dropping the bin in the living room and going back for more. He was getting tall already, the way she'd been at his age. As much as she saw him as her baby boy, her son thought he was so grown up. Maybe he felt like he had to be. When Brent left, he'd really left, not just Blue or the marriage but their entire family. She'd thought it would be temporary, he was going through something, he'd change his mind. But her husband's things were already loaded into the new black Mustang he'd bought himself the week before. Even in the face of the knowledge that he'd been planning this, Blue had argued and begged him to stay, they'd get counseling, she'd do better. Murphy ran down the driveway after his stepdad's car while Blue stood crying in the front yard. She'd expected him to turn around, at least to say goodbye to Murphy. But he hadn't. She'd been served the divorce papers two days later.

And she'd come back here with no clue what she was going to do about Enzo. She hadn't spoken to him in ten years, but didn't he deserve the truth? Murph knew Brent wasn't his biological dad, but until Brent left them, she'd believed it didn't matter. She abruptly sat down on the last bin she was dragging across the driveway, cradling her head in her hands. Enzo had made it clear how he felt the night she left. But she'd never meant for Murph to pay the price for her mistakes.

It was nearly dark by the time she and Murphy cleared out the sunroom. The large room on the side of the house had once been a lanai, screened in but not a real room, until Blue's mum and dad had spent an entire spring out here painting, laying ceramic tile, and replacing the screened walls with glass. It had become the favorite room in the house, perfect for lazing about, working on a puzzle, listening to music, or making beaded necklaces and bracelets with her mum. Since Blue had been gone, the sunroom had become a catchall, cluttered with empty flower pots, patio chairs, and dozens of other things that had to be taken to the garage or basement or curb.

Blue cleaned the cabinet that would serve as Murphy's dresser for now and attacked every pane of glass with Windex and towels and finished by washing the floor. She and Murphy carried the daybed in from the family room, and she made it up with his Star Wars comforter set along with his matching bedside lamp. She would make sure to set aside part of what she had saved so she could get him a real bed and dresser.

Murphy stood with his back to her, looking out over the Intracoastal Waterway that ran between Bliss and the mainland. The sunset to the west had streaked the sky with a blend of pinks and purples over the Sheas' docks. Blue joined Murph, careful not to hug him or do any of the mom stuff that always seemed to make him mad lately. She didn't speak. The light from her father's shrimp boat came into view, its mirrored reflection wavering on the dark water. He seemed the same, except surlier. Mitch was still working sunup to sundown to keep himself in business, and without Ella's extra set of hands. As angry and upset as Blue had been when she'd left, she'd worried over what would happen to her dad's fishing business while he was in jail. Aunt Eva had finally given in and found out that Dale was taking care of the boats and covering the bills during Mitch's six-month sentence. At seventeen, Blue hadn't wondered how her dad's friend had been able to afford that. Now, having come to terms with the fact that she couldn't afford her mortgage on her own, she had no clue how he'd done it.

"Is that a crab boat?"

"It's a shrimp trawler. Close but different. There's too much competition around here for crabs, so he switched to shrimp years ago."

"Oh. Too bad. A crab boat would be perfect for the old crab."

Blue laughed, a loud, gleeful burst. "Oh, Murph." She gave him a sideways glance. "That's so bad."

"I mean, shrimp boat doesn't really work. He's a big guy. I'll add the crab joke to the book." She and Murphy had started a bad joke notebook a couple of years ago. It was full of mediocre jokes and puns, collected from everyday moments with his friends, her friends, even his stepdad, though Brent had no idea his occasional jokes were now preserved in the pages of their bad joke book. Blue thought someday she'd take the spiral notebook somewhere to have it made into a real book, maybe when Murphy eventually outgrew the desire to keep adding to it.

Blue sighed. "I'm sorry this is how you're meeting your grandfather. He's upset with me. And that's my fault." She'd never told Murphy much about her life before him, and he'd never asked.

She probably should have said more than she had, at least at this point. Her son only knew that she'd left Bliss years ago and that she and her dad had been out of touch since before he was born.

Murphy rested his forehead on the glass, watching his grandfather tuck the boat in for the night. "Mom. You gotta stop apologizing all the time."

"Sorry," she said before she could stop herself. She pressed her lips together.

He smiled and shook his head. "See?"

"I *am* sorry I made us leave home. We'll bring Cooper and Josh down to visit soon, I promise. Even if we have to do all the driving. I'll talk to their parents; maybe they could stay a week or so."

He left his head on the cool glass and turned, looking at her sideways. "It's okay."

She didn't know what else to say. It wasn't an empty promise. He needed his friends, and Murphy had never made friends easily. She'd make the drive if it meant him being happy here.

"What if Dad changes his mind? Then can we go home?"

"Murph." She sighed. "I don't think that's going to happen."

◆ 2 ◆

Enzo Castellari was having an off day. He scrubbed his grease-covered hands hard with a rough work towel, growling as he ducked under the hull of the *Feelin' Crabby* in the warehouse. He'd been working on the crab boat's temperamental motor since that morning and he'd had it. He pushed through the door to the marina offices using his forearm, and his brother looked up from his desk.

"Who kicked your puppy?" Marcello asked.

Enzo shook his head, bending over the sink to finish getting the grease off his hands. "The engine's done on that crabber. Pretty sure it needs a rebuild, which means it'll be off the water at least a week by the time I get parts in and get her taken care of." He glanced over his shoulder at Marcello. "You can tell Pops."

His brother leaned back in his chair, tipping his head at Enzo and frowning. "That's a big negatory. I'm not telling him she's out of commission. We can stall, say you're still looking at it and buy us time to order the parts. By the time he knows it's a whole rebuild, you'll be halfway done. You sure you don't want to just send her out?"

"Are you crazy? That'd cost triple."

Marcello nodded. "You're right. But you doing the rebuild will mean you're off the water too. It's your call."

He sat in the chair opposite the desk. At twenty-six, Marcello was a year younger than Enzo and handled the financials as CFO for Castellari and Sons. He'd gotten his CPA after Enzo finished his mechanical engineering degree. Their father had covered the cost of each of their degrees with the understanding they'd be putting them to use within the company afterward. Most of Gino Castellari's sons had no problem with that, though their younger brother Matteo hated the fishing business as much as Enzo loved it.

"If it's my call, then say I think it's a fuel injection issue but I'm not sure yet," Enzo said. "Meantime, I'll send you a list of what to order so we can get going on the rebuild. She should be back in the fleet by next week at the latest."

"All right, good plan. I'll tell him."

Enzo stood. He ran a hand through his thick black waves, the sides cropped close. "Thanks, man. Jillian's got us checking another spot for the reception. Because the nine we've seen so far aren't good enough. I need to go change before I pick her up."

"Hey. You should be grateful she cares so much about finding a great place. Is Ma going again too?"

"No, she's at Aunt Lorna's. And I am grateful," he said over his shoulder, one hand on the door. "The wedding will be perfect because of her."

Gino Castellari was climbing out of his sedan as Enzo exited the office. Cell phone to one ear, he nodded in his son's direction. He was shorter than Enzo by an inch or two and still as fit as a man half his age. High-end Rolex, linen trousers, and wide, callused hands conveyed the impression of a wealthy man who wasn't afraid to get his hands dirty.

Enzo opened the door to his truck, catching his father motioning for him to wait.

Gino approached as he finished the call, dropping the phone into his pocket. "Cutting out early? Got that crabber all squared away then?"

"Not yet, but no worries. Hey," Enzo said, tossing some distraction his father's way, "what's the update on the Pelican Alley contract? Did they decide to go with us?"

"We'll get 'em. I've got a dinner meeting set up tomorrow, and your brother's pulling numbers for me. If they think they're gonna get a better deal anywhere else, they're crazy. I'm not—" Gino's phone rang again, and Enzo used the distraction to make his exit.

Enzo's black Lab mix greeted him at the door, fluffy tail wagging so hard it wagged his whole body. He dropped his keys on the entry table so he could scratch the dog behind both ears, making the wiggling dog even happier. "Okay, buddy. I'm only home for a minute, but we'll play as soon as I'm back." Moon already had a tennis ball in his mouth, waiting excitedly.

He moved past him to the stairway, checking his watch. He sprinted up the steps, took a quick shower, slapped some aftershave on his face in lieu of shaving, and came back to the top of the stairs in record time. The dog was right where he'd left him, yellow ball still clenched in his jaws.

He spent a good ten minutes throwing the ball for Moon in the yard. Every time the dog brought the ball back to Enzo, it was a little farther from his master and a little closer to where the crabgrass turned to sand. Ugh. He knew his dog wanted him to throw the ball the extra couple hundred yards to the beach and the waves crashing onto the sand, but there was just no time for that today. Enzo truly felt bad, coming home and leaving again right away.

His beach house sat about a half mile south of the Castellari estate. The elegant, sprawling compound where his parents and his baby brother Luca lived wasn't the house they'd all grown up in. Almost a decade ago, his father had moved the family temporarily into the old carriage house and bulldozed their home. Gino Castellari had always had this plan; Enzo and his brothers had heard it their whole life. When he'd bought the tiny beachfront cottage for his bride Sofia, he'd bought it for the land, knowing he'd need plenty of space to build their mansion one day. He just needed a boom in business. The expansion of the family business during Enzo's senior year of high school was that boom—Castellari and Sons acquired over a dozen new supply contracts with major Gulf Coast seafood markets and restaurants. Money followed, and the massive estate was built.

Enzo loved Bliss, loved the stretch of shoreline he'd grown up on. So when a modest beach house with an open floor plan and plenty of wide windows had gone on the market down the coast a bit, Enzo had snapped it up. He backed out of his driveway and glanced in the rearview mirror. Moon's happy, furry face looked at him in the rearview mirror from the back seat. Jillian would have to understand.

He pulled onto the road. The Collier County coastline was populated with gorgeous villas, vacation homes, and condos interspersed with the occasional small cottage, usually occupied by year-round residents who'd been there forever. He drove past his parents' place, then the condos next door, and then the Shea cottage before making the turn onto Highway 41. He wondered, not for the first time, about Blue.

Enzo wondered every day. It was impossible not to, driving past that run-down cottage anytime he left the peninsula. Sometimes, she'd appear in his thoughts as a fleeting wisp, the pale skin of her neck, her soft, wavy hair conjuring sensation in the pads of his fingers. He could still hear the lift in her voice when she said his name. She'd drift through his mind like a faint smoke trail of a long-ago fire and be gone before he could even notice noticing. But other times, images of her that final night, first begging him to go with her, then recoiling from him, yelling, crying, fleeing, would appear in his head and stick, causing the pain of losing her to course right through him, still fresh. But those times hardly happened anymore. He turned onto the highway and put her cottage behind him.

Ten minutes later, Enzo turned into the Suncoast Law parking lot and spotted Jillian already outside, waiting for him. He hurried around to her side, opening the back door for her to set her things down; her arms were overflowing with her briefcase, files that apparently wouldn't fit in the briefcase, purse, gym bag, and a coffee. Moon greeted her with more of his wiggling enthusiasm and she laughed, obliging him with pats on his head. She turned toward Enzo and he slid an arm around her waist and pulled her into him for a kiss before she could ask why the dog was in the car.

"Moon wanted to see Gulfscape Gardens, too, huh?" She raised one perfectly shaped eyebrow at Enzo as she climbed into the front seat.

"He made me feel guilty. I had to bring him." He detected irritation under her playful tone and chose to ignore it. Once they were on the highway, he glanced over at her. Jillian's straight blonde hair was pulled into a sleek low ponytail swept over the shoulder closest to him, falling over her breast. The tailored suit with slim black pencil skirt and pink blouse was the same outfit she wore on the Suncoast Law billboards. They featured Jillian and two other partners, all looking smart and attractive and ready to win any case, big or small. But mostly big. At thirty, Enzo's fiancée was three years older than he was and the youngest attorney to ever make partner in the multicity corporation's history. Sure, it helped that her father was a Suncoast founder, but Jillian hadn't taken any shortcuts climbing the ladder; her win rate spoke for itself.

She turned in her seat so she could pet Moon. "Did you figure out what's wrong with the skiff?"

That was another thing about Jillian. She never forgot a single thing he told her. She'd spent the morning in court—at least he was pretty sure she had—and she wanted to know about the crab boat. He nodded. "She needs an engine rebuild. But the other three are fine so it won't hurt us much having her drydocked for the week. How was your case? Was today the custody hearing?"

She poked his arm. "Yes! Good memory. We had Judge Brock, who's actually good about requiring documentation of therapy time, so it went the way we wanted it to." Jillian couldn't share any real details about her cases because of confidentiality, but they'd gotten good at speaking in generalities during the years they'd been together. She pulled a brochure from her purse. "So, Gulfscape Gardens is the newest indoor-outdoor wedding reception venue in Collier County. I mapped it, and it's only twenty minutes from the church, and so far it's available on our date. It's so pretty, Enzo." She turned the brochure toward him.

"It looks really nice."

"Did you get the link I sent you? Did you check it out?"

Shit. "I did." He had not. He'd meant to, but Jillian knew this stuff better than he did. She'd made planning their wedding into her side hustle. She had charts and spreadsheets and a map with pins on it for all the places they'd looked at. She knew what'd be best for them. He glanced at her. "It looks awesome."

Jillian was scrolling through messages on her phone. "We're doing a tour of the package that includes the banquet hall in addition to the outdoor patio we think we want. Just in case—you never know if it might rain. And I've already requested the complimentary flash drive with clips of the house band."

He felt his jaw tighten. The house band that wouldn't be his band. He knew it was a silly point to be fixated on. Enzo, his brother Salvi, and two of their friends played a couple of times a month at Captain Crab's in the village. They just played for fun, and they were obviously good enough for the Captain Crab's crowd. When Jillian had started planning their wedding, he'd floated the idea of having his band play, minus Enzo of course. He knew one of his bass player friends would gladly fill in for him. It hadn't even been his idea. His brother, their guitarist, had suggested it, a way for their band to pay tribute to Enzo and Jillian. She hadn't said no . . . but she hadn't said yes either. And almost every venue they'd considered so far had the option of a house band.

She had an uncanny way of reading his mind. "I'll trust your judgment on the band. You and Salvatore have a listen and let me know if you think they're good enough. You know we could still have your band play, right?"

He reached over and took her hand. She didn't mean that, but it was a nice gesture. "I appreciate that. I'm sure the house band is great." He understood. Even while it needled him, he did understand. She wanted their night to be perfect. And with Jillian at the helm, he knew it would be.

Moon waited in the car for them, with the windows halfway down. He was accustomed to riding along and waiting on Enzo's runs up and down the coast for work; he was always happier tagging along until the weather turned too warm to bring him. The dog had never met a person or another dog he didn't love instantly.

He and Jillian followed the event planner across the lawn to the pavilion, the last stop on their walking tour of all Gulfscape Gardens had to offer. With a gorgeous view of the ocean, the structure was distressed wood with thousands of small fairy lights strung across the ceiling. Enzo noticed two rows that were out. The event planner was chatting with Jillian about caterers. He listened with one ear while moving to the circuit box mounted on the end post. Nope, it wasn't a flipped circuit. He crossed to the other side and found the defective strand, the portion nearest him still lit. Enzo gave it a tug, and those lights flickered out as well. Then he saw the problem. A bird had made her nest where the strand of lights wrapped around the corner post. A two-inch spot along the strand had been shredded, the white plastic wire frayed.

He reached up, almost close enough to grab it. If the electricity was still live and the bird happened to land slightly to the left side of the nest, she'd be in for a shock. Literally. He glanced back at his fiancée. She was in her element, grilling the event planner on references and menu details.

Enzo pulled a chair over and stepped on it, now plenty tall enough to reach. He unplugged the strand and used his pocket knife to remove the section of bad cord. He was careful not to jar the nest, in case the babies were still in it. He made sure the opposite end of the now useless light strand was also cut short and tucked back underneath itself. Before stepping down, he slowly, carefully peered over the edge of the nest; he'd never seen a bird's nest this close before.

A baby bird popped up, its long neck stretching its head and open beak toward Enzo's face. Startled, his hand went up reflexively, and the bits of shredded wire and plastic he'd been collecting to discard flew into the air as Enzo suddenly felt as if he'd been stabbed with a hot poker in his right eye. He bellowed, slapping his hand over his eye. Jillian rushed to his side, helping him off the chair.

"What happened? What were you doing?" She looked up. "Are there birds in there? Did one get your eye??" She pulled on his forearm, trying to get him to move his hand, but he couldn't.

As long as he kept his eye closed and his hand over it, it only hurt a little. He shook his head. "No, I was getting rid of the bad wire—"

"Oh my God, Enzo! Why? Can't you just—ugh. Never mind. Let me see, come on. It's okay, move your hand."

"I can't. It's sharp, I think it's a piece of the wire. It's all right, I'll just keep it closed." There was an eye patch in the first aid kit under his bathroom sink; he'd noticed it when he moved in last year and his mother made him promise to keep the kit she'd made him stocked. It was a white gauze oval, and he'd even seen a cover for it, a black cotton eye patch with elastic. He already worked on boats, so what if he looked like a pirate for a day or two while the offending piece of wire worked its way out.

"Sure," Jillian said, guiding him down the path toward the exit and parking lot. "Just keep your eye closed from now on. Good thing you don't need it to see." He could hear the snark in her tone.

"It'll be fine, I'm sure it will come out on its own," he said, calmer now. Once he put the patch on it'd be fine. It didn't hurt that bad. "Ow!" he shrieked, tripping and stumbling on the curb at the edge of the parking lot. His hand had raked across his face, pressing the sharp object that felt as big as a boulder deeper into his eye.

"All right, I've got you. Hold onto me and do not take your one good eye from where you're walking, okay?" Jillian kept one arm around his waist.

He let her talk him into a quick trip to the ER to get the blasted thing out of his eye. Enzo made Jillian stop at his parents' place and drop off Moon, who'd have happily gone along to the hospital. But they could be stuck there waiting for hours. His dad was always out on the water at this time of evening, and his mother wasn't home, thank goodness. His baby brother Luca informed them she was still at their aunt's house up in Orangetree. Enzo warned Luca not to say a word about him going to the emergency room, in case Sofia got home and wondered why his dog was visiting without him.

"You know I can't lie to Ma," Luca said, eyes wide. At twenty-one, he was the youngest, and he looked it. He still couldn't grow anything but a patchy beard, and his uber-trendy haircut had his dark hair several inches long on top and gathered with a hair tie and shaved on the sides.

"You don't have to lie," Jillian said, leaning across Enzo to peer out the passenger side window at her fiancé's brother. "Just don't tell her the details. Do a little dance *around* the truth without actually saying it. Like this. 'Luca, why is your brother's dog here? Have you seen him?'" She deepened her voice. "'Yeah, Ma, I saw him, he'll be back soon.' See? Easy."

Luca scoffed. "It's never that easy. She asks a hundred questions."

Enzo groaned, turning his one good eye on him. "Figure it out. If you tell her I'm at the hospital, I'm telling her you spent the night at Christina's Saturday when you said you were with Matty."

Luca fell silent. He crossed and uncrossed his arms. "You suck." He nodded at Enzo's eye. "Maybe they'll have to use the big scalpel on that."

A wave of nausea hit him. "*You* suck. Go throw a ball on the beach for Moon, would you? He's been waiting."

Jillian ushered Enzo into Collier County Hospital through the emergency room entrance. He handed over his insurance card to the front desk, and Jillian answered questions about what had happened until the triage nurse politely asked her to stop. The patient needed to be the one providing information. He repeated basically the same information Jillian had covered.

He was shown to his own curtained cubicle and they waited. Enzo's arm was starting to twitch, the bicep trying to spasm from being held in the same position for almost an hour. Jillian disappeared and came back moments later with pillows piled up to her chin. She stacked them on the bed under his elbow, gently moving his arm to rest on the pile of pillows.

"Thank you," he said. His right upper arm already felt better.

Jillian pulled the chair over to the bed beside him. "I'm sure the doctor will be in soon, they know it hurts."

He didn't answer. He must have jarred the bit of wire or debris when he'd tripped on the curb. It hurt a whole lot worse now than it had at first.

By the time the curtains were pulled back again, Enzo had shifted his position again and was lying down, elbow jutting out to the side as he kept his hand cupped over his eye. He'd figured out that keeping both eyes shut worked better for keeping the bad eye still. He briefly opened the good eye and closed it again on a scrubs-clad woman moving about, gathering gloves, gauze, and a bottle of something with a long, bent straw coming out the top. She set a blue paper-wrapped rectangle on the stainless-steel tray beside the bed.

"Doctor, is it possible to get him something for pain?" Jillian asked. "He doesn't say much, but I know it hurts."

"I'm the nurse, sorry. Doctor Patel will be in soon, I'm just setting up for her. I'll ask for a pain pill, but the computers are down for the moment so I'm still waiting on the chart. Can you tell me your name and date of birth, sir?"

"Enzo Castellari. October 24th, 1994."

"Oh," Jillian spoke up. "Vincenzo. He always forgets to give his full name."

The nurse hesitated, blue latex gloves half on.

"It's C-A-S-T-E-L-L-A-R-I," Jillian said.

The nurse resumed pulling on her gloves. She slowly moved to the head of the bed over Enzo. "I do need to know what we're dealing with here, all right? Can you let me see?"

Enzo's brow was furrowed in pain. He finally let his hand fall away from his face and carefully, painfully looked up. From above, the sea blue eyes of Bluebelle Shea gazed into his.

3

Enzo was suddenly no longer in the emergency room. He was eleven years old on Bliss Beach, grains of sand in his nose and eyes, still choking from being swept out with the undertow of high tide, reeling from the disorienting pummeling and pulling of the waves until hands had grabbed his arms, dragging him upright and onto the safety of the beach before he drowned. Blue staring down at him, the clear blue sky behind her pale blonde halo of hair, was permanently seared into his memory.

He blinked, and the stab of pain jerked him back to the present in Collier County ER. Her hair was longer and she was taller. There was something different about her eyes. But it was her. "Blue," he murmured, and her eyebrows furrowed, a wince.

"What's that, Babe?" Jillian put a hand on his thigh, leaning forward. When he didn't answer, she looked up at Blue. "I don't know if the other nurse told you anything yet, but we think he's got a little scrap of plastic or plastic-covered wire in his eye. We were at Gulfscape Gardens checking out—"

"I was trying to move some crumbling wire away from a bird's nest," Enzo interjected. "I uh, my hand jerked and the pieces of plastic flew into the air." Blue didn't need to know he'd done this to himself when a baby bird scared him. Or that they'd been checking out wedding reception venues.

"Okay," Blue said. "I'm going to take a look with the light now." She applied gentle pressure to keep his eye open while she shone the light into his eye.

Enzo's heart was thrumming triple time in his chest. He jerked and squeezed his eye shut without meaning to. *Goddamn that hurt*, and she'd barely touched him. And—Bluebelle Shea was touching him.

Blue stepped back. "I'm sorry," she said. She moved to the sink, her back to him as she removed her gloves and washed her hands. "Let me get Dr. Patel. I don't see anything, but we have a dye we can use to help mark foreign bodies. Dr. Patel will order some numbing eye drops too, as soon as she's taken a look." She disappeared between the curtains before he could say anything.

"I don't know why she can't just do that herself," Jillian said. "I'm going to find someone else who will actually help you."

He grabbed her hand as she stood. "No."

She frowned at him. "Why not? You're lying here in pain. This is ridiculous."

"I'm all right." He squeezed her hand, pulling her toward him. "I am. Let's give them a minute. I'm sure the doctor will be in."

Jillian gave up and sat back down, covering their linked hands with her other one. "You're nicer than I am."

Enzo closed his eyes. "That's not true. You're just trying to help." It didn't surprise him that she wanted to march out to the nurses' desk and demand immediate treatment on his behalf. But Blue was only doing her job. Blue. His Blue.

The gurney tilted under him, spinning, though he knew it was perfectly still. Enzo sat up, eyes open wide—he was going to be sick. He bolted off the thin mattress and lurched to the wastebasket in the corner, crying out from the pain in his eye and losing his lunch at the same time. "Oh fuck," he muttered, wiping the back of one hand across his mouth, still bent at the waist. The floor under his feet was reeling like he was a greenhorn out on one of his boats.

Jillian was at his side, gently stroking his back. "Babe? Here," she dabbed at his forehead with a cold, wet paper towel. He took it from her and pressed it over his face, leaving his palm open. The movement in the floor was slowing. But he might throw up again. He moved the towel to the back of his neck, the white-hot jabbing pain in his eye nothing next to the vise grip around his chest.

Jillian crouched low, on his level. "Enzo," she said, her tone soft, "come lie down. I'll get the doctor. Are you okay?"

Enzo sucked in air, breathing deep, in through his nose, out through his mouth. In. Out. Blue had been his best friend his entire childhood—until she had become his everything. In. Out. For ten years he'd regretted letting her leave without him. In. Out. She was not *his* Blue, was she? Her father had wrecked that. But he and Blue had done a great job ruining things on their own as well. He slowly straightened up.

"I knew that pork was bad," Jillian said. "You've got food poisoning. I knew we shouldn't have stopped at that food truck last night, Enzo. Ugh! I hope the chicken I had was okay!"

Enzo moved carefully back to the gurney to lie down. He still felt slightly queasy but didn't think there was anything left for him to throw up.

He heard Jillian opening and closing cupboard drawers, rifling around for something, but he didn't turn his head to look. His eye was throbbing and he felt shaky, off balance.

She returned to his side. "Nothing. No actual towels, no mouthwash, they need to stock these places better. I'm getting the doctor—if you're okay for me to step out? I'll be two seconds."

"Sure," he said. The curtains swished as she left. He couldn't believe Blue was back. She was a nurse. She was probably an amazing nurse. How long had she been home? Why had no one told him? Had she ever planned to tell him herself?

He'd been devastated when she'd left. They'd never gone more than a day or two their whole lives without seeing each other or talking. In the last two years before she ran away, they'd grown closer than he'd ever been to anyone since, all while keeping both their families in the dark. They'd found ways around the rule. The first time he'd kissed her was under the fairy garden lights in her backyard. Enzo had loved her since before he could remember.

He'd thought she would come home. When days passed, then a week, and she wasn't back, Sierra told him she was safe, but that was all. He'd stopped eating. He couldn't sleep. He missed nearly a month of school during the fall of his senior year until his mother had gotten tough and hauled him out of his bedroom and forced him to participate in his life again. By then, he'd lost twenty pounds he didn't have to lose in the first place, tanked his high-school football career, and was on the verge of failing until the acceptance letter from the University of Miami had come in the mail and forced him to catch up with his classes.

He'd tried once to see her. He finally convinced Sierra to tell him where she was, and he'd driven the seven hours up to Tallahassee. Blue wouldn't even come to the door. He'd stood on her aunt's porch, begging, probably while she listened, and for nothing. He'd tried to hate her after that.

Now his fiancée was about to get her in trouble or worse. Maybe she'd introduce herself as his fiancée. Which she had every right to do. He swung his legs over the edge of the hospital bed and stood up. He was fine. The thing in his eye would work its way out eventually, wouldn't it? If it didn't, he'd go to the urgent care up in Naples. He tried opening his good eye, which was impossible to do without moving the skewered eye—it felt like someone had stabbed him with a hot marshmallow roasting stick.

Jillian came through the curtain followed by a mid-dle-aged woman in a white lab coat. "I found the doctor," she stage-whispered, tipping her head toward the woman.

"Mr. Castellari, I'm Dr. Patel. Let's have a look. Hop up here." Dr. Patel patted the gurney, locking eyes with him. She had to have seen his type before, scared and ready to bolt. She waited while he hesitated, still wanting to follow his impulse and get the hell out of there. The doctor staring up at him couldn't be more than five feet tall. Her demeanor immediately reminded Enzo of his mother. You didn't argue with Sofia Castellari, and Enzo suspected Dr. Patel was the same way.

He did as he was told. The doctor added drops to numb his eye. She donned a headband with a magnifier on it. "Mmm hmm. It's hard to see, but there's one . . . maybe more. No wonder it hurts." Dr. Patel straightened up and took off the headgear. "I'm going to send the nurse in to make you glow and get these taken care of, and we'll get you a dose of pain medication. Do you prefer pills or a shot?"

Normally, Enzo would've seized the opportunity at a joke there, asked for a shot of whiskey or something. But he was fixated on the part where she'd said the nurse was coming back in. He needed to see her again but didn't think he could handle seeing her again. "Pills are fine."

Five minutes after Dr. Patel left, another nurse came through the curtains.

"Hey Enzo, Jillian." Maggie Trudell, his brother Salvi's girlfriend, crossed to the bed and handed him a little plastic cup with two white pills.

"Are you taking over as my nurse?" Enzo knew he should be relieved. He needed to not see Blue again, he was already a basket case from the thirty seconds she'd spent in here with him. Maggie fixing his eye was perfect. So why did he feel so deflated?

"Your nurse and I were going to trade patients, but I've got to go tell her we can't. I'm just here with your meds. We're not supposed to work on friends or family unless there's no other choice, sorry. I'm sure that hurts," she said, pointing at his eye. She handed him a tiny apple juice to wash his pills down.

"It's pretty numb now." So Blue was so over him, over them, that she'd tried to pawn him off on someone else? "How're you doing?"

"Great! Better than you, anyway." She turned to Jillian. "Have you picked out your dress yet?"

"Oh my gosh," Jillian said. "I've been to so many places, and my mom and I finally found this little shop that has the designer I really wanted. So now, after not being able to find a dress I liked at all, I've got to narrow it down between three! It's so hard!"

Maggie chuckled. "Sounds like a good problem to have. I'm going to grab the other nurse so you two can get out of here. I hope your eye feels better, Enzo."

Jillian nodded. "Right! Thank you. We're overdue for dinner with you and Salvi, call me and we'll find a day that works."

Blue returned, switching off the overhead light as she entered. "All right, Mr. Castellari, this will only take a few minutes." She moved to the head of the bed and switched on a blue light extending out from the wall. She positioned the rolling metal table nearby and opened some kind of sterile kit Enzo was glad he couldn't see. "Can I have you move up a few inches, please? A little more."

Enzo scooted upward, lying back down and feeling Blue's hands cradling the back of his head as she took the pillow away and tucked a towel beneath him. She pulled on gloves and handed him a tissue and finally looked into his eyes, upside down. He searched her gaze, looking for something, some acknowledgment that she'd thought about him. One long blonde strand of hair had come loose from her ponytail and curved down over her jaw, just touching the pale skin of her neck. Enzo's hand involuntarily twitched as he thought of brushing it back. He clenched his fists.

"This might sting a little." She gently pulled his lower eyelid down and dabbed with a thin strip of paper. She let go. "Go ahead and blink a few times please to distribute the dye."

He did as she said. It stung more than a little.

"There are two fragments," she said. "Try to lie still." Blue picked up an instrument and brought her face closer to his, concentrating.

Enzo's heart pounded in his throat. She smelled exactly the same, how was that even possible? He inhaled, breathing in the scent of sweet pea flowers, a heartrending assault on his senses and memory. His eyes filled with tears and he swallowed hard, trying not to blink.

"I'm sorry," she whispered, and his throat closed, a hot tear streaking toward his temple. "I know this is uncomfortable. You're doing a great job at staying still."

He gulped air, knowing he was doing a shitty job at hiding what she had apparently misread as physical pain. Unable to escape the scent of sweet peas, images flooded his mind: Blue hopping the backyard fence in her junior prom dress, waves of pink fluffing out around her as he caught her; her pale, arched neck as his lips brushed her collarbone, every curve of her body pressed against his; her palms flat on his chest, shoving him away that last night, when she'd broken his heart.

He dimly registered Jillian speaking, her hand on his knee. "Hang in there, Babe. It's almost over."

Blue straightened up. "All set, got them both." She turned away, busying herself with changing her gloves. She turned toward him, holding a small plastic bottle. "Just an eye flush now. Tip your head back, please."

Cooling saline washed over his eye, providing immediate relief from the stinging and covering the evidence that she'd made him cry. Jillian touched his clenched fist and he opened it, palm up, letting her interlace her fingers with his. She squeezed, reminding him how lucky he was to have someone who was always concerned for his well-being.

Blue patted his face dry with a fresh towel. "It's going to be sore for a while, but you didn't scratch the cornea. You'll need to keep this patch on," she said, opening a package of gauze and covering his eye, "until tonight, or longer if needed, until the pain is gone. You shouldn't drive for at least six hours since your pupils are dilated. And that's it."

He sat up. She was nothing if not professional—but that was all. Cool; cold even, starkly different than his own reaction to seeing her. He watched with his good eye as she cleared away the medical wrappings and avoided eye contact with him. "Thank you."

"I'll be back with your discharge papers." She ducked through the curtains.

Enzo hopped off the hospital bed. "Let's go."

Jillian stared at him, not moving from her chair. "We have to wait for your paperwork."

"No, we don't." He pulled the curtain open and poked his head out. The hallway was clear. "Come on." He held out a hand and she slung her purse over one shoulder and went with him.

In his car, Jillian faced him before backing out of the parking space, her hand on the steering wheel. "Are you all right?" She was frowning, her expression worried.

"I'm great. Really," he added when she continued to stare at him. He should have waited, but he had to get out of there, as far away from Blue as possible. He used to believe they were meant for each other. She'd been part of him, his heartbeat, the air he breathed; he'd nearly died learning to breathe without her. But Blue seemed to be doing just fine without him.

4

BLUE STOOD IN THE empty exam room, half crushed, half relieved. He was gone. Clutching his discharge papers in one hand, she backed out into the hallway and looked in both directions. He was really gone. Her legs suddenly went weak, her head woozy, heartbeat racing. She shoved through the supply room door to her left and lurched to the row at the back, sliding down the cool painted brick wall and tucking her head down onto her drawn-up knees. She was shaking, freezing. The room was spinning. She forced herself to take deep breaths, eyes squeezed shut.

She'd gotten through it, she'd done her job, as she had on hundreds of other tough cases, maintaining her objective, professional exterior. She'd never imagined having to see Enzo for the first time after all these years away, like this, on the second day of her new job. She'd hoped to find a way to reach out to him before she ran into him in town.

Transferring within the same hospital system and having a position lined up in Bliss had eliminated the worry of looking for a new job. Collier County Hospital was the largest in the area. The ER wasn't very different from the one in Leon County. She'd spent her first shift yesterday shadowing a preceptor and learning the routine from triage to discharge. Today, she was being given one patient at a time while being trained in processes for medical supplies and pharmacy orders. Since this morning, she'd only had three patients. Enzo was the fourth.

His voice was unmistakable. Blue had frozen when she heard it, the last time they'd seen each other instantly rushing back to her. The night she'd run away, she'd run first to him. She'd been crazy to think he'd just drop everything and leave with her. But she hadn't expected Enzo to echo the awful things the town was saying about her dad. And now the skinny seventeen-year-old boy she'd last seen was an actual grown man. His shoulders were broader, his chest and arms muscled. His jawline had squared and held the hint of five o'clock shadow. His black hair was shorter, more wavy now than curly.

She remembered hearing the woman with him spell his name. As if Blue wouldn't have known him anywhere. As if the Castellari name even needed to be spelled. A stab of irrational anger interrupted her subdued shock at seeing Enzo. Was that pretty, condescending woman with him his wife? Was he married now? Wouldn't Sierra have told her about something as big as Enzo getting married? Maybe not, maybe Sierra would have kept that from her.

What must he think of her? Did he know about Murphy? Did he hate her now? Had he even recognized her? Blue had given in to curiosity a few times and looked him up on social media, after steeling herself for what she might see, but most of his posts were in relation to Castellari and Sons; she hadn't been able to glean many personal details. Certainly no wedding photos. She couldn't believe she had been mere inches away from him after dreaming about him, about them, for the last ten years. It seemed horribly, painfully perfect that she hadn't been able to touch him except with her gloved hands; that the few sparse moments she had spent with him were shared with his new love. Blue tipped her head back now against the cool supply room wall, blinking fast, her eyes hot with tears she did not have time to cry. She clapped a hand over her mouth as a sob escaped her. She'd made so many mistakes. Leaving Enzo was her worst.

The supply room door swung open at the same time her work phone rang. She was on her feet and rushing out the door before the patient care tech could ask if she was okay, wiping roughly at her eyes as she headed toward the nurses' station. She had to get into the next case before she ended up a sad puddle on the supply room floor.

*   *   *

Sierra was the only thing on Blue's mind when she clocked out for the day and picked up Murphy. They had been invited over for a late dinner. She couldn't wait to see her friend again, and was so excited to meet Chloe. But more than that, she needed to know about Enzo and if he was married. She'd asked no questions at all before coming home, her own fault. But for Murphy's sake, now she needed to know everything.

Laughter drifted through the front door when she stopped at her dad's to change out of her scrubs. She and Murphy found Mitch sitting in the kitchen with a pretty, middle-aged redhead Blue recognized from town. The remains of a baked lasagna and garlic bread sat on the table between them. Mitch stood up quickly upon seeing her in the doorway, like he'd been caught misbehaving.

Rita was next out of her chair, smiling widely, a hand fluttering to her neck. "Oh my goodness, Blue, you're so grown up. And a nurse, your mother would be so proud. And this must be young Murphy! We, ah, thought you had dinner plans, I'm so sorry. There's still plenty! Let me grab more plates."

Blue knew Rita indirectly, simply from being raised in Bliss and shopping at Rita's little boutique shop, Rita's Roses, with her mum on occasion. The woman's cheeks were flushed. The kitchen smelled divine. Her dad looked happy, right through his beard all the way up to his eyes. Her dad and Rita were staring at her, waiting for some kind of reaction.

She crossed to the table and gave the woman a quick hug. "Thank you, but no, we've got dinner plans with my friend.

And . . . this is so nice. I'm so—um—never mind. I'm sorry we interrupted." She wanted to say so much more, to thank this kind woman for being her dad's ally in an unfriendly majority, but she'd probably already embarrassed him enough.

She changed and hustled herself and Murphy out of there in record time. She was overcome with the warm fuzzies for Rita, whatever her intentions were.

"Mom! It's not fair, why do I have to go?" Murphy jarred her from her thoughts from the passenger seat beside her.

"Sierra was my best friend. Is my best friend," Blue said. "I told you, she invited us for dinner. I want you to meet her, Murph, and her to meet you. I'm not sure where I'd be without her."

He scoffed. "Maybe back home with Dad, instead of in this stupid town?"

She scowled at her rude, disrespectful son. "Stop it! You can't keep talking to me like this. There's too much you don't understand. Sierra helped me through the hardest time of my life. I know you're mad at me, but could you please just give this a chance?"

He twisted in the front seat, facing her, defiant. "Why'd you make us come back here? Grandpa's crabby, his cat's mean, and you just dump me in camp all day! I wanna go home. I hate it here."

Blue's eyes stung, and the road beyond the windshield blurred. This was their home for now. He was nine; how was she supposed to make him understand? They'd only been here for three days. Every single day, she worried she'd made a mistake. Murph sure thought she had.

They rode the rest of the way in silence. She wanted Murphy with her tonight because she wanted Sierra to see the best thing she'd ever done—though she was over his attitude. Sierra had been her lifeline when she'd fled this *stupid* town right after her dad was arrested. She'd had no plan other than escaping; she couldn't stand the whispers at school, in town, even her so-called friends were saying her dad was a drunk who couldn't save her mum. She didn't know what to believe, not with Enzo's words ringing in her ears. Six long days after she'd left, when Aunt Eva had rescued her near Gainesville, Eva had told Blue the police couldn't have arrested and brought charges against her dad without proper evidence. The arraignment was over. Mitch was going to trial for second-degree manslaughter while intoxicated. Her dad had lied to her; he'd been drunk the night her mum drowned.

There were so many things she wished she could forget. The bus stations. Vending machine dinners. Wishing for a real shower rather than a dirty gas station bathroom sink to wash her hair in. The creepy man who wouldn't stop talking to her on the last bus she took. Blue imagined returning to Bliss as soon as her father was found innocent and released. But learning she was three months pregnant on the heels of agreeing to stay with Aunt Eva changed that—changed everything. Through it all, Sierra had never wavered in her support, always there on the other end of the phone line, doing what little she could to help.

Now, the minivan's navigation system instructed her to turn left onto the palm tree–lined side street where her friend lived. She slowed to a crawl, reading addresses until she found it and pulled into the driveway. "Listen, Murph, Sierra is engaged. She's getting married next month."

"Okay." He was quiet and sullen now instead of loud and obnoxious, a small improvement.

"Her fiancée's name is Chloe. She's a woman."

He glanced at her. "Okay?"

Blue raised her eyebrows. "That's all. I'm just telling you." Brent hadn't been accepting of Sierra. Not that she'd ever invited her to come visit them in Tallahassee; she wouldn't have. She wouldn't subject her friend to her husband's bigoted attitude. But Blue was thrilled for Sierra; she sounded as if she was madly in love with Chloe.

"Josh has two dads," Murphy said. "We had dinner over there, remember? What's the big deal? You don't have to tell me how wrong it is. Dad's already covered that."

Blue closed her eyes and rested her forehead on the steering wheel. "Murph."

"What?" His tone challenged her.

She looked at him from the corner of her eye. "I can't believe all the ways I've messed up."

Her son was quiet.

"I hope you know he's wrong. He's wrong about a lot of things, and I've been wrong too, for not speaking up about it. I'm sorry. I'm trying to do better. You . . . you know there's nothing wrong with Josh's two dads or Sierra marrying Chloe. Right? Love is love." She had so much to fix. The weight of it was overwhelming. And she was trying to let her son's anger roll off, but it was getting to her.

"God, Mom. Stop treating me like I'm a little kid," Murphy said. "Are we going in or are we just going to stay in the driveway all night?"

Sierra and Chloe's house was a pretty ranch with coral trim. The couple stood in the open doorway as Blue and Murphy came up the walk. Sierra reached out and grabbed her impatiently on the porch, wrapping her in a long overdue hug. Blue's eyes unexpectedly overflowed with tears that hadn't been there a moment earlier. She held on, hugging Sierra tightly and laughing while more tears rolled down her cheeks. Sierra's small frame shook with laughter too.

When they broke apart, Blue spoke first. "This is Murphy, my son."

Sierra held out a hand and he shook it. "Murphy," she said. "A good Irish name. Your Grandma Ella would be proud."

Blue's throat swelled with more tears. There it was, rip the Band-Aid right off with no warning. Sierra had never had much of a filter.

Sierra took Chloe's hand, pulling her closer. "Murphy, Blue, this is my fiancée Chloe."

Chloe was the polar opposite of Sierra, at least in appearance. Tall, with straight, shoulder-length auburn hair and bright green eyes, she wore no makeup and was absolutely gorgeous. By contrast, Sierra Jones was just a smidge over five feet. Her dark hair fell in shiny waves to her small waist, which was accentuated by the red floral wrap dress she wore with jingly ankle bracelets and bare feet.

After introductions were made, they followed Sierra and Chloe on a brief tour of the house, ending in the most beautiful backyard Blue had ever seen. Surrounding a large free-form in-ground pool were lush bird of paradise flowers, pink hibiscus, and green hostas. Soft white lights lit the entire area, and there were at least a dozen multicolored candles scattered over the dual-level patio, the upper tier of which was filled by a large table that was already set, while the lower tier held a stone firepit and seating.

Sierra and Chloe went back inside to bring drinks out while Murphy inspected the pool. "Are you still mad I made you come?" Blue asked when he'd walked all the way around it. The end closest to the patio even had a small jacuzzi.

"I didn't bring my suit."

"I'm sure it's fine if you just swim in your shorts," Blue said.

Chloe came through the doors and handed her a pink and orange cocktail with a pineapple slice on the edge of the glass. "That's totally cool," she called. "But—well, hold on just a second. We have a little welcome-to-Bliss gift for you two." She went back inside, reappearing momentarily with Sierra carrying a large gift bag.

Blue shook her head. "You didn't need to do this."

Sierra bounced on the balls of her feet, hands clasped in front of her chest. "Of course not. Go on, open it!"

They'd thought of everything. Blue set each item on the table as Murphy pulled things from the bag: a beach ball, sunscreen, two huge, plush beach towels, a snorkeling set with fins and a shark-patterned set of swim trunks for Murphy, pretty tortoise-shell sunglasses for Blue, chocolate candies, flavored coffee, and a collection of hand-me-down paperbacks. She picked up a worn, dog-eared book with a bright beach umbrella on the cover, turning it over to read the back.

"Our favorite beach reads," Chloe said, nodding at the books. "We're hoping you'll find time to relax, here or at your beach or wherever you can."

"Thank you," Murphy spoke up. "You guys are awesome." He had the swim trunks and fins in hand.

"Come on," Chloe said, "I'll show you where to change."

When they'd gone inside, Sierra reached across the table and wrapped her hands around Blue's forearms. "I've missed you so much, Bluebelle Shea."

"I can't believe I'm here. I love your wife-to-be. She's great. And you . . ." She tipped her head, scrutinizing her friend. "You're positively radiant."

Sierra nodded. "I feel it. I'm lucky to have found Chloe. You'll love her even more when you get to know her. We wanted to ask you something. A favor."

Blue raised her eyebrows. "Anything. You know that. I owe you so much."

"All right then. Be my maid of honor. And help me convince Murphy to be an usher. Please?"

"Um. I, uh, wow. I'm honored that you'd ask." Her mind raced. The wedding was over a month away. She'd taken a huge leap, coming home to Bliss and leaving her old life behind. Committing to be in the wedding would be—

Sierra interrupted her train of thought. "But? I can see a but brewing in there."

Blue pursed her lips, looking up toward the house to make sure Murphy wasn't on his way out. "I'm not so sure what our plans are," she said softly. "Yet." She kept trying to see this as more than a temporary move, but so much had changed in such a short time. Murphy's reaction on the way over was causing her doubt. She still couldn't imagine any kind of future for her and Murphy, in Bliss or in Tallahassee.

"No." Sierra moved her chair closer to Blue's and peered into her eyes. "Oh no. No goddamned way. You are not thinking of going back, I know you're smarter than that."

Chloe and Murphy returned at that moment, Chloe carrying a delicious-looking charcuterie tray and saying something to the boy about pulling teeth on horses.

Sierra spoke to Murphy as he passed. "Don't get her started talking about work unless you want to hear all the gory details. She'll never shut up."

"You're not getting a horse," Blue called out, right before he jumped into the deep end.

Chloe set the tray down along with a stack of small plates and joined them. "He wants a horse?"

"I think he just wants any kind of pet, but he's playing me. He's too smart for his own good. He figures I'll say yes eventually to a dog because at least it's not a horse—he's been working on his angle since his friend back home got one. An actual horse," she added, to clarify.

Chloe laughed, a throaty, pleasant sound. "I love horses, but they can be a lot of work. If you ever do cave and decide to get him a cat or dog, talk to me first. We're connected with some good rescue organizations at the clinic."

Chloe was a veterinarian up in Bonita Springs, about a half hour north of Bliss, and Sierra sold her own artistic creations online and in local shops. Hair jewelry was her specialty, but she sold a little of everything, whatever medium and item she was working on at the moment.

Sierra didn't return to the sensitive topic at hand until they'd finished with dinner and were gathered around the firepit. Chloe had set Murphy up inside with her X-Box and her collection of games, and Sierra had made the three of them decaf iced lattes, perfect for the warm evening.

"You can't go back to him." She picked up where she'd left off.

"I wasn't planning to. But I don't know if—"

"You don't know what? If Brent will come to his senses and realize he misses you and wants you back? He might. He may even promise he'll treat you better. Or maybe he'll just keep making you think it's your fault he left. I predict a combination of all three." Sierra's voice was cutting and brusque.

"That's not fair," Blue said quietly. Her gaze strayed to Chloe.

Sierra also looked at Chloe and then back at Blue. "Oh, don't worry, she knows everything. We've been together three years. Chloe missed the fun parts when your son was young and your husband's hobby was shouting at both of you for smudges and fingerprints on the walls and tracked-in mud and too much noise all the time, but we both remember you calling when he threw you into the wall and dislocated your shoulder. I remember the lie you made up for your Aunt Eva."

"That wasn't—"

"Wasn't what? Brent's fault? It was an accident? Or maybe you made him mad, so it was your fault? Every time he got mad it was your fault, right? What's it going to take? How long before he hurts Murphy?"

Blue sank into her chair. She stared into the embers, determined not to cry again. She'd already cried way too much. "I probably made it sound worse than it was." Her voice was small. "He's not that bad."

Sierra leaned forward, elbows on knees, and dropped her head into her hands, letting out a groan. She gripped the sides of her head through her hair, finally looking up, but not at Blue. "You see?" she said to Chloe.

"I'm sorry," Blue said. "Maybe I made too much of our arguments. He really never meant to hurt me. I wish you knew him.

Everyone likes him. I think if I'd tried harder, maybe none of this would have happened."

"Oh my God. Are you really saying you and Murphy deserved to be treated that way?" Sierra was nearly yelling, her tone exasperated.

"Stop it." Chloe snapped the words abruptly. She leaned forward, one hand lightly capturing Sierra's. "Stop it right now. She's not ready for this."

Sierra jerked her hand away and stormed inside without another word.

Chloe sat back and crossed her legs, watching the fire. "She loves you a lot. This has been hard for her too."

Blue didn't know what to say.

"So," Chloe began. "How about this? You tentatively plan for you and your son to be in our wedding, but nothing's set in stone. If things change, then they change. I understand it seems like a long time from now, especially with all you and Murphy have been through recently. Let's play it by ear."

She nodded. "That sounds good." It sounded unpredictable and difficult to plan around, but Chloe was being generous and kind.

Chloe stood. "I'm going to see if he's beaten my scores yet." Blue began to stand, and Chloe motioned for her to stay. She inclined her head toward the house, where they could see Sierra standing in the kitchen window, looking out at them. The two women crossed paths as Chloe went inside and Sierra came out.

She walked past Blue to the jacuzzi and sat on the edge, pulling her dress up around her thighs so she could let her legs hang down into the water. Blue joined her. The bubbly water was almost unbearably warm, but so soothing. Sierra slid over to her, closing the gap between them, and rested her head on Blue's shoulder. She took a deep breath, about to say something, and Blue stopped her.

"I don't want to talk about my marriage."

"Okay. Me neither."

Blue said the words she'd been dying to say all evening, but had been too embarrassed to speak in front of Chloe. "I saw Enzo."

Sierra sucked her breath through her teeth. "You already did it? Oh my God. How did it go? What was his reaction?"

"No, no. I didn't—I haven't actually talked to him. I mean not really, not about Murph." The thought of that hurdle made her pulse pound in her temples. "I ran into him at the hospital. He came into the ER."

Sierra's eyes widened. "Oh. Is he all right? What happened?"

"I can't really say. It was just something minor. I wasn't prepared to see him there. He looks . . ." Blue peered down into the roiling water. She paddled her feet and bit her lip. "He's so . . ."

"Freaking hot," Sierra finished for her. "I know. I'm not blind. He grew up well. Was he shocked to see you? What did you even say to him?"

"Nothing."

Sierra smacked Blue's leg. "Bullshit. Tell me."

"Nothing!" she repeated. "I couldn't. What could I have said? I'm really sorry I ran away and never spoke to you again even though I've loved you since I was two and I'm raising your son?"

"That'd be perfect," Sierra said quietly. "You have to tell him, Blue."

"I know; I will. Why didn't you tell me he's married?"

Her friend looked down. "Not married; not yet. So she was with him?"

Blue nodded. "Yeah."

"Jillian Josephson," Sierra said. "Fiancée." She wrinkled her nose.

"What's that look? You don't like her? What's wrong with her?"

"Literally nothing. You saw her. It's not even like she's just pretty, she's a lawyer—a good one, supposedly. She's too perfect." She hesitated. "Or at least she seems like it. But she's not you."

"It doesn't matter," Blue said, trying to convince herself. "She doted on him—she obviously loves him. He seems happy. He's almost married, and I still am. It's fine." It wasn't. She'd nearly fainted upon realizing he was her patient. Being inches from his face, breathing in his clean, masculine scent, had nearly brought her to her knees. She'd struggled to focus on anything other than the little flecks of green in his golden-brown eyes, stars in the constellation of her past; but they were different people now. She had no choice but to leave the past where it belonged.

★ ★ ★

Blue unlocked the cottage door and carefully, quietly ushered a groggy Murphy around the broken board on the porch and inside to his room. He was always sweet when he was sleepy. She tucked his Star Wars comforter around him and kissed his forehead. He smelled of chlorine and roasted marshmallows and she loved it. This was a good night.

She tiptoed through the house toward her own room. Tomorrow was Saturday, which didn't matter in the life of a commercial fisherman like her dad. He was always up at five AM. So she was surprised to see his bedroom door standing open, his room empty, as she passed.

She found him in the backyard, on her bench under the willow tree. Her father had built it for her. She and her mother had painted it white, and Ella had helped Blue use stencils to add a sweeping pattern of bluebell flowers in a curve across the back rest. Her father had finished it with three coats of glossy lacquer. She joined him on the still pretty bench, a bright spot in a yard that was now overrun with weeds and old palm fronds. Faithful Hook was at her heels. He purred and snaked his body between and around her ankles once she sat. She reached down and scratched around his ears.

Mitch was smoking. He'd started back up the night her mum died, and it must've stuck. He brushed the embers off the tip of the cigarette with a thumb, putting it out. She still didn't know how he did that without burning himself. "Sorry. Bad habit."

The path through their small grove of trees began ten feet from where they sat. She squinted, looking for any sign at all of the fairy village she and her mother had so painstakingly created and tended, but the trail was completely overgrown with vines and bluebell flowers.

"How's the job?"

"It's good. I like my coworkers so far, and the work is about the same as my old job." She couldn't say a word about seeing Enzo. Her dad was a kind man, despite his gruff demeanor. But he hated the Castellari family with an angry dedication that Blue had never openly crossed. Mitch hated Gino Castellari in particular, though he'd made it crystal clear that he viewed the five boys as extensions of their father, all destined to become just like Gino or worse, whatever that meant. She was fifteen the night he'd dragged her away from her cozy spot by the bonfire with Enzo. Mitch had exhaled the sickly-sweet stench of liquor into her face when he spoke, and she hated him, started to say so—to shout it at him—when her gaze caught on her mum, crumpled on the sand behind him.

The sharp crack of a gunshot had woken Blue the next morning. She'd sprinted to the front door startled awake, her groggy mind struggling against her panicked body. On the porch, her dad lowered his shotgun, pointing it straight at Enzo's parents. Mr. and Mrs. Castellari were frozen in place on the lawn, frightened, this couple who were like family. Blue screamed. Sofia took her husband's arm and coerced him back to their car. Ella never spoke a word about any of it. In the silence that followed, the still, malignant quiet that pervaded every speck of air in her house, Blue felt her world closing in on her. She'd learned the only way around her parents' abrupt hatred of the Castellari family was to lie.

"Bluebelle." Her dad pulled his black cap lower, staring straight ahead now.

She turned on the bench and faced him but he didn't look at her. Hook purred at her feet.

"Your, uh, husband. Is he why—did he—are you home because he hurt you?"

"No," she said reflexively. "I mean, he . . . not exactly. It's a long story."

He met her gaze. "I've got time." She must have looked taken aback because he added, "Whenever you're ready."

She nodded. "Thank you. Dad—" She faltered, sucking in a deep breath. Shit. She couldn't imagine a day when she'd be ready to talk to her dad about Brent, but she'd been trying to work up the nerve to talk to him about Murphy since she'd arrived. Since she knew she was leaving Tallahassee. Hell, since she'd learned she was pregnant.

He watched her, eyebrows raised expectantly.

"Murphy is Enzo Castellari's son."

Mitch nodded slowly. "Right. Makes sense."

"But—did you know?" She didn't know what kind of reaction she'd expected, but this subdued, calm response threw her.

"Blue. We knew we couldn't keep you two apart. I'm not surprised. And anyone can see your boy is a Castellari. He may have your mum's hair, but he looks just like Enzo at that age."

Blue clapped a hand over her mouth, stifling a sob as her tears overflowed. All this time, all these years, she'd feared her dad would hate her—hate Murphy by extension. He'd suspected this whole time. Mitch wrapped one arm around her and pulled her into him, and she closed her eyes, face pressed against the rough fabric of his jacket. He smelled of sunbaked seawater, fish, cigarettes, Old Spice; the same as ever, minus the stink of booze. She squeezed her eyes shut against a rush of memories—her mum dabbing her face with sunscreen while her dad tightened the straps on her pink unicorn life jacket; fishing line wrapped around Mitch's rough hands and her smaller ones while he patiently helped her respool a spinning reel; the way he'd dipped his head and rested it atop hers when he couldn't hug her back, right in this same spot, the day the sheriff's deputy had placed him in handcuffs.

She believed him. It was beyond her how he could have served a manslaughter sentence due to intoxication, but her dad had steadfastly maintained he hadn't had a drink since the night he'd carried her mum home along the beach that night when Blue was fifteen. He'd promised her mum he was finished with it. Blue believed he'd kept his promise.

"All right now?" Her dad's voice was low, concerned.

She nodded, sniffling. "I'm sorry. For everything."

"No need for that. You and the lad are home now, I'm glad for the blessing. It'll all be all right. "

She took a deep, hitching breath, a wave of shame washing over her. She hadn't realized until this very moment that she'd still held so much doubt in her heart about the truth of the night her mum had drowned. She seized the moment, her words coming quickly before he could stop her. "I should've believed you. I never should've left. I know that now. You really haven't had a drink since that night at the Castellaris'." She wasn't asking; but finally wrapping her head around accepting that truth despite hearing an entirely different narrative all these years.

"No, I haven't."

She felt like she was seeing things clearly for the first time, the way she should have since the moment her father had been arrested, if she'd only been older, or smarter, or had someone to help her believe what she'd already known in her heart. Enzo should have been that person. But that wasn't fair either; the only person responsible for her lack of faith in her father was her. "I don't get it."

Her dad was silent.

"How could they have proven anything? I know you tried to save her. I know you were sober. Did you ever try to fight the conviction? Maybe we can talk to a lawyer, find out—"

"No. It's over."

She pushed on. "But why not? I'm sure there are people who could testify that you hadn't had a drink in two years. More than just me and mum knew you'd quit. What about Dale? You must've talked with him about it. Maybe he was even there at the Castellaris' that night for whatever made you decide to quit? He could go on record saying you'd been sober since then. Don't you care what the town thinks? Why wouldn't you want—"

Mitch cut her off, standing up. "I don't care what anyone thinks of me but you. It's over," he repeated. "We've got no power over some things. Leave it alone."

She pressed her lips together; she didn't agree. Maybe she'd simply start by talking to their neighbor Dale. He'd been her dad's friend forever, and he worked at the county Sheriff's Department. She followed her dad across the lawn.

At the screen door, he turned to face her. "I need you to promise me something." His eyes were hidden in deep shadows, his tone serious.

"Okay, sure. Anything."

"Stay away from Gino Castellari." He scowled, putting a hand up as she began to interrupt. "I'm not asking you to keep your son from his father."

"Dad—"

"Bluebelle, stop," he said, his voice gruff. "Ain't no need for you two to be over there, part of all that. You're all I have. You and the boy. You understand?"

No, she started to say. *Help me understand.* She swallowed the words. "Yeah." Even in shadow, her father's features were twisted with concern. She followed him inside, waiting until he reached his bedroom door to speak again. "I was thinking we could come out on the water with you sometime." She wasn't sure she was ready, but it was time.

"How about Sunday? If Murphy wants to."

Well, it was done. She couldn't take it back now. Her dad had agreed so quickly, maybe he wanted to find a way back to normal as much as she did. "I'll talk to him tomorrow. We'd love that."

✦ 5 ✦

BLUE PUT MURPHY TO work on Saturday. She'd only been back home in Bliss a few days and the broken boards on the front porch were making her crazy. She kept imagining her dad or Murphy stepping in just the wrong spot and going all the way through. It was a broken ankle waiting to happen. She'd waited until Mitch was out on the boat that morning and then she took measurements and went to the hardware store in town for supplies. She was hoping it was only the boards and not the supports underneath. If the struts were also bad, the whole porch would have to be replaced.

Needing something better than her flimsy flip-flops or sneakers to work outside, she scrounged her old pink rainboots from the back of the coat closet, still tucked away after all these years. "Here," she said, handing Murphy the hammer. "Use the claw side and try to pry that board up from that end."

He did as she said, leaning in and putting his weight into getting it all the way up. The board came free easily, as the opposite end was splintered and hanging, only partially attached. Murphy moved to the next board without being told, while Blue worked on getting the debris cleared and the old nails pulled out. They'd become a good team back in Tallahassee on projects like this around the house. Brent had been great at starting things but not at finishing them. Blue had taught herself how to do almost any kind of repair, and then she'd taught Murphy. There were You-Tube videos for everything.

By noon, she and Murphy had cleared away the four boards in the center of the porch that were broken or crumbling. She lay on her belly and hung her head down through the hole, tapping the supporting beams with the hammer from the ground to the planks she was lying on while Murphy held the flashlight. They all seemed sound. In another hour, the new boards she'd had cut this morning at the store were nailed down. She stood back, admiring their work.

"So are we painting now?" Murphy asked.

"Not yet . . . we'll have to sand all the chipping paint and then scrub the porch down really well. And then it'll need a solid day in the sun to dry before we can paint it. But it's safe now and looks so much better already!"

"'Kay," he said and trotted up the porch steps to go inside.

"Where are you going?"

"Back to my video game."

"We're not done, Murph. I'm sorry, there was one more thing I needed your help with."

"Ugh, Mom," he whined. "You said I had to help. You didn't say it was gonna take all day. I hate it here!"

She stared at him. Had he been this disrespectful in Tallahassee and she just hadn't noticed? "Fine," Blue said through her teeth.

"Fine? What does that even mean?" Her son held the front door open, his face scrunched into a furious scowl as he looked down at her.

It hit her hard: he sounded exactly like Brent. She took an involuntary step back, her heart pounding in her ears. She shook her head. "It means you're done." She walked around the side of the house as fast as she could without running, trying to maintain her composure. She heard the screen door slap shut against the wood frame, and then the heavy front door slam hard behind it, rattling the windows.

Blue stood under the willow at the vine and palm frond covered path through their grove of trees, breathing hard. She dropped to her knees on the soft, mossy ground, the earth cool on her legs above her boots. She didn't know how to fix any of this.

She closed her eyes and breathed in the sweet scent of blue-bells. They ran wild through the grove, spreading along the path and out to the fence line and anywhere they found shade. Aside from the bluish-purple flowers and her bench next to her, the whole backyard was brown and neglected. Vines covered the fencing, what was once her parents' vegetable garden, even a portion of the bench. The lawn had become crabgrass, the green of it only visible in patches underneath dead palm leaves accumulated from years of inattention.

She scooted forward on her knees, carefully moving dead vegetation away from the path. She and her mother had painted a pretty sign at the entrance to the fairy village when she was ten. It was made of wood, a notebook-sized piece that Mitch had affixed to two wooden spikes. Blue felt the edge of it and began digging through the debris in earnest. She gripped the bottom edge, afraid she might snap it off its spikes before it came loose, and pulled straight up.

Here Be Fairies

It was gray with age and weathering, the words only dimly visible. There was no color left on the once vibrant pink and yellow sign.

She stood, brushing off her knees. She couldn't fix Murphy or her marriage or even herself. But she could restore something of her mother's. They'd worked out here for hours, for years, always adding more, rearranging, repainting, adorning. She'd wanted to show her son the fairy houses today and tell him the stories her mother had told her, folklore gathered from her own mother in

Ireland about fairies and bluebells. But she wasn't going to force it. She set the sign on her bench so she'd remember to bring it in and went to get a rake. She'd have to be careful not to crush the flowers, but she'd start by clearing the path and see what else she uncovered. Before she knew it, she'd lost herself in the garden just like she had when she'd work here with her mum. She was surprised when her dad called hello on his way across the yard from his day spent fishing—she'd had no sense of the hours passing and had gotten a good start.

★   ★   ★

Blue knocked softly on Murphy's bedroom door Sunday morning. The sun wasn't quite up yet. "Murph," she whispered.

He slept burrowed under the covers. They were pulled right up over his head. All she could see of him was part of one hand, fingers curled around the edge of his pillow. He didn't stir.

The coffee maker came on in the kitchen, the sound of cupboards opening—her dad would be ready to go soon. "Hey, Murph," she said again. "Time for school. You'll miss the bus."

The lump under the Star Wars comforter shifted and he bolted upright, looking around wild-eyed. His brown hair stuck out in crazy directions. The too-large Florida Gators shirt he wore hung down off one shoulder; her dad had given it to him that first night, when none of their things were unpacked yet.

Blue sat on the edge of his bed. "Just kidding, bud. No school for two more months."

He blinked at her, groggy. "Okay," he murmured. He began to lie back down and she put a hand on his ankle through the comforter.

"We're almost ready to go out on Grandpa's boat, though. It's a lot of fun, I promise. Wear your swimsuit."

Murphy rubbed his eyes and yawned. "Okay." He swung his legs over the edge of the bed and padded to his makeshift dresser.

Blue left him and went to the kitchen to pack some food for the day. Mitch stood at the counter spooning cat food into a bowl for Hook. He'd already poured Blue a cup of coffee with his own.

She smiled at him; he hadn't done that before. "Good morning. Thanks for the coffee."

He nodded once. "Wasn't sure what you take in it." He set the cat's dish on the floor for him.

"Usually just cream. Does Hook still come out on the boat?" She was counting on him coming. Hopefully grumpy old Hook was still a fishing cat.

"Sure does." He tipped his coffee cup back, finishing it.

"That's pretty impressive for a seventeen-year-old cat." Hook was scarfing down his food near Blue's feet. He was one of the biggest cats she'd ever known, even now in his old age.

Her dad looked offended. "Don't talk about it," Mitch grumbled. "He's young at heart."

Blue smiled to herself while she packed the small cooler she'd brought from Tallahassee, filling it with sandwiches, cut-up cantaloupe and strawberries, iced tea, and the cookies Murphy had chosen at Gulfside Grocery. When they let Hook lead the way out to the docks, she was surprised to find a familiar figure waiting by the fishing boat.

Dale Bryant was in full gray uniform this morning, Collier County Sheriff's Department badge pinned over his heart. He hadn't aged well since she'd last seen him. His leathery skin was deeply etched with smile and frown lines, and he'd grown even skinnier than Blue remembered him. She hoped he had the sense not to say anything in front of Mitch about the message she'd left him yesterday. She'd found his house phone number in her dad's old county phone book and had been surprised to find it was still active. She'd left a message asking him to call her. She intended to find a way to clear Mitch's name—but she hadn't meant for Dale to just show up over here.

"Mr. Bryant! Oh my, it's good to see you after all this time," she said.

"Bluebelle Shea. Good Lord, girl. I woulda thought you was your mama if I didn't know better."

Her throat swelled and tears rushed to her eyes. God. Was this normal, this reaction, every time someone mentioned her mum? She met Dale's gaze, trying a smile, and was shocked to find him with tears in his eyes too.

"Shit, I'm sorry," he muttered. "Didn't mean to—"

"It's okay," she said. She hugged him, the scent of too much aftershave and stale pipe smoke enveloping her. "Thank you. It's nice to hear. You doing okay?"

He nodded, swiping at one eye when they let go. "'Course. Oh! Almost forgot why I stopped by."

Her heart jumped in her chest. She didn't need to spend today arguing with her dad out on the water about letting sleeping dogs lie.

"Your dad asked for a couple of life jackets—the Yellowfin's dry rotted years ago." He grabbed the two vests he'd hung on the dock post and handed them onboard to Mitch before facing Blue again. "Hope they'll fit. I'll need the small one back, it's my grandson's. You can keep the other one, it's Missy's; she doesn't need it. This your boy?"

Dale's daughter Missy was a few years older than Blue. As far as she knew, she was an only child, which meant she'd had a baby. She looked down at her own son. "Yes, this is Murphy. Murphy, this is Mr. Bryant. He and Grandpa have been friends since . . . well, I don't know."

Dale shook Murphy's hand. "Since way before your ma was born. I was in your grandad's wedding," he said, leaning in a bit toward Murphy and Blue. "And he's older 'n dirt so y'know that's a long while."

"Younger than you." Mitch spoke from the bow of the fishing vessel, in the process of looping a line around his arm.

Blue laughed. "Thank you for the life vests. Um. Hey, Murph, go ahead on board with Grandpa and Hook. I forgot my sunglasses." She helped hand him off to her dad, feeling better immediately once he'd buckled on the life jacket.

Dale walked with her back toward the house.

"How's Missy doing? And you mentioned a grandson?" Blue asked.

He nodded once, curtly. "Caleb's eleven going on sixteen. They keep you running, don't they?" He was poker faced, jaw jutted forward, the fact that he'd failed to say a word about his daughter just hanging out there like a dare between them.

She was not about to take it. Her quick math meant that Missy must've had her son in her teens, like Blue.

When they reached the seawall where he'd separate to head toward his place, he said, "Mitch needs you here. Hope you're staying."

"I plan to. I think so, anyway."

"Glad to hear it. You said you got questions? Probably best to use my personal cell. Here, it's written on the back." He handed her his card. "It's been years. Not sure there's anything I can do to help, but if there is, I will."

Her attention was pulled away as the fishing vessel's engine came to life at the end of the dock. Dale was already retreating when she looked back. "Thank you, Mr. Bryant," she said.

"Dale," he called back, correcting her. "Tight lines. See ya' around."

She smiled heading back to the boat. It'd been years since she'd heard that—*tight lines* was fisherman jargon to wish a person success while fishing. She'd heard it a thousand times growing up, especially between here and Enzo's house. She climbed aboard, meaning to ask her dad about Missy Bryant, but the day took over. God, she'd missed this. The sun glowed through the trees to the east against a pink sky as Mitch's fishing boat motored due west out onto the Gulf, the bow cutting through water that was like glass. The boat was a 55-foot Yellowfin center console vessel that her dad had financed years ago. Unlike his house and yard, it was still in beautiful shape, clean and kept up. There were outrigger poles mounted at both sides of the vessel, on each side of the steering console where Mitch stood, one hand on the wheel. He used the boat for longline fishing too, though that required some setup and was typically done to yield larger quantities of smaller fish, not what he'd planned for them today. Blue was surprised to find herself anticipating each motion her dad made before he made it. She remembered everything; she'd been fishing with him since she was younger than her son was now. Navigating, reading the wind, handling the outriggers and longline intricacies—it was as natural to her as breathing.

She sat back and watched as Murphy drifted to his grandfather's side; she'd hoped coming out on the boat might help them get to know each other better. Her dad wasn't one for words, but now, once Murph began asking questions, Mitch talked the boy's ear off, covering types of fishing, different kinds of boats and what they were used for, how he'd already gotten their stockpile of baitfish that morning with a casting net, and how he knew where to look for fish.

"Kingfish—king mackerel that is—like to hang out around reefs and wrecks," Mitch said. He tapped the edge of the navigation screen over the wheel. "GPS and sonar help us figure out where those spots are. And then once we think we've got a good location, we can see if there's any activity in the area."

"Do you ever catch sharks?"

Mitch chuckled, and the foreign sound pinged around in Blue's chest, warming her. She hadn't heard her dad laugh since . . . she wasn't even sure when. "I try not to catch sharks," he said. "Sometimes they'll grab a hook if I have the longlines set up, not fun for me out here by myself."

Murphy listened with interest, looking up at his grandpa. "Then what do you try to catch? Grouper? That's what Mom usually eats, that or shrimp."

"Sometimes grouper. Getting a hefty kingfish on the line is the goal. But we've got all kinds of fish out here. Marlin, snapper, swordfish, tuna. And I always get shrimp, that's what the trawling boat is for. That's usually an evening job. I've got a guy who skippers for me sometimes. You could come out sometime when I go." Mitch frowned at the boy. "What do you mean, your mum eats grouper and shrimp? What about you?"

"No way." He made a face. "I don't like fish."

He might as well have said there was no salt in the ocean, the way Mitch looked at him. Blue was sure he'd tell her son he had to try something before saying he didn't like it, or something along the lines of everything she had heard throughout her own childhood. "We'll see," he simply said.

Her father let Murphy take the wheel for a bit, showing him how to stay on course with the Nav system. Then Mitch took over again so they could find the perfect spot. He cut the engine and got to work, demonstrating each step for his grandson as he set up the starboard outrigger with a metal lure and the mullet fish bait he'd netted that morning. Putting Blue in charge of the outrigger—the large, mounted fishing pole attached to the boat— he chose a handheld rod and reel and baited the hook, casting it and handing it to Murphy. "Go ahead and put that in the rod holder," he said, tapping the side-mounted device used to stabilize the fishing rod when reeling in larger catch. "Keep an eye on the end of the pole for bites or drags. And mind Hook up there when you cast, he likes to get in the way if the baitfish smells good," he told him, jerking his head toward the big tabby on the bow.

"I don't know how to cast," Murphy said.

Mitch looked up and met Blue's gaze. She could read his mind. Her son should know something about the trade that had supported their family for thirty-odd years. She'd purposely avoided nurturing any interest in fishing or boating in Murphy. Until today, which she'd done as a means to bring them all together.

"I'll teach you," her dad told her son.

This had been a terrible idea. Why had she opened her big mouth and said she wanted to go out on his boat? Her dad had taught her all these things too, how to handle a boat, navigate, choose a prime location, set the lines, until the sea had given them both a stark reminder that being in control on a boat was an illusion.

Before she could completely lose her cool, Blue stood and went down into the cabin, pulling the hatch door closed behind her. The Yellowfin's cabin slept three comfortably and held a tiny kitchenette and table, the bench seating converting to another sleeping space for the occasional overnight fishing trip. Like the one her mum had never come home from. Blue gripped the edge of the countertop, fighting the anxiety that clawed at the edges of her nerves. She finally forced herself to begin taking their lunch items from the ice box storage and setting everything up, her hands shaking.

Blue had argued with Ella the morning before she died. Her mother didn't always accompany Mitch on his fishing excursions, but she'd loved the overnights. She'd asked Blue to come. *The night sky from the middle of the sea, Bluebelle. We all need that. It's been too long since you've come with us.*

She was right; it had been over a year since she'd gone with them. But the overnight trips provided her best opportunity for time alone with Enzo—real time, not stolen moments after school or late at night, but long, blissful stretches of time together, inside their world of two, murmuring wishes and dreams of a possible future, drifting through sensation in his arms, where she'd always belonged.

At seventeen, she'd always chosen Enzo over her parents. She'd wormed her way out of going on the overnight excursion and even offered to keep Hook home with her, so they wouldn't have to worry about the cat. Looking back, her mother had probably seen right through her feigned selflessness. She should have gone. If she had, her mother might still be alive. Her father hadn't been able to save Ella, but maybe the two of them could have pulled her from the water. There'd have been no arrest, no accusations, she'd never have run away. She and Enzo might have been able to somehow repair the rift between their families and be together. Murphy might have grown up with his own loving father. The back corners of her mouth stung, tightening her jaw and bringing tears to her eyes as she imagined her mum as doting grandma to Murph.

"Mom!" Murphy's voice yanked her into the present and she darted from the cabin, panicked. She knew this was a bad idea.

On deck, her son stood grinning from ear to ear holding an enormous king mackerel across both forearms.

"Murph! Holy jeez, look at that big guy!" Tight lines indeed.

"He's a natural," her dad said. "Just like you."

"What's this kind called again?" Murphy looked up at Mitch.

"I'd call it a perfect homecoming dinner," Blue said.

6

E NZO'S JARRING EXPERIENCE IN the emergency room had been exactly one week ago. He knew because his phone dinged with a calendar reminder—*Recheck for eye injury today*—while he was waiting for everyone to finish filling their breakfast plates and take their seats in the Castellari and Sons' large conference room. The company's all staff meetings were held the second Friday of each month.

Jillian liked to put reminders in his phone calendar so he never missed anything important. She'd convinced the Collier County emergency room to fax his discharge instructions to her office after getting Enzo to sign a release. He'd skimmed them, seeing where Jillian had highlighted the section saying if his eye still bothered him at the one-week mark, he was to return to have it checked.

His eye felt fine. It had stopped hurting the day after Blue had taken care of him. He had no reason to go back for a recheck. Other than to see her.

Which would be a terrible idea. He wanted to see her so badly, but he also couldn't bear it. And even admitting that to himself made him feel like he was betraying Jillian.

So he would not be stopping by the hospital on his way home from fishing today. He'd made up his mind and he was sticking to it. His reaction to seeing Blue last Friday had been so extreme, mainly because it was unexpected, and he had been in pain; that was all.

The conference room at Castellari and Sons was filled with the aroma of pancake syrup and bacon. The monthly meetings Gino held meant his five sons and the dozen or so other employees came for breakfast and stayed for updates on productivity, policies, weather predictions, fishing trade fluctuations, and the like. Enzo and Marcello attended every single month, no matter what; Gino expected it of them as the two eldest. Salvi, the middle son, and Luca, the youngest, were also in attendance today, but Matteo was missing.

"Wait, that's not nearly enough for you," Enzo's mother Sofia called one of the seafood processors back, adding another pancake to his already heaping plate.

"Thanks, Mrs. C." The young man knew better than to argue.

Enzo chose the made-to-order omelet instead, though he'd probably end up coming back for pancakes too. Gino never skimped on food. He provided an omelet bar, a fruit bar, pancakes, bacon, sausage, juice, and coffee every month for his staff. Sofia always ended up helping the catering company, unable to sit idly by while they prepared and served food. Collier Catering had also learned not to argue with her.

When everyone had a plate in front of them and was seated, Luca opened the meeting with three pieces of good news. Today, that involved a new contract with a popular restaurant in St. James City, news that the *Feelin' Crabby* was back on the water thanks to Enzo, and the happy announcement that one of their fishermen had welcomed a healthy baby girl to his family last night.

Luca handed things over to Marcello, who reviewed the company's growth and future expansion goals, and then passed the baton to Enzo, who brought everyone up to speed on what was happening out in the Gulf. The missing Matteo should have gone next, but Gino pushed that agenda toward the end, letting Salvi go over updates on the processing and transportation end of the business.

Gino was always last. He shared the information that Matteo should have, with a new safety item to be implemented on the trawling vessels. He followed with the announcement that his legal team at Suncoast Law was drawing up the exclusive contract today for Pelican Alley, a popular waterfront restaurant and sushi bar, wrapping it all up with praise for his employees' hard work and commitment. The monthly meetings were a flurry of food, updates, policy, and pep talk packed into a tight hour, so as not to cut into the day's productivity too much. The family stayed behind after everyone else had filtered out.

"What's up with Matteo?" Gino asked. He poured himself more coffee, leaving it black.

Enzo side-eyed Salvi, who glanced at Marcello.

"He's fighting a bad cold," Luca said.

"Since when? I'll take him some food," Sofia said. "Does he have a fever? When did you see him?"

"I don't think he has a fever. I saw him yesterday and he wasn't feeling great. He probably just needs to sleep."

For a moment, Enzo believed his little brother, until he caught the look he was trying to shoot at Salvi.

"It's my fault," Enzo lied, holding up his phone. "He texted early this morning to say he'd have to miss the meeting and I didn't see it until now." He turned the phone back toward himself and tapped the screen. There were no messages. Moon's wide, toothy grin appeared, one ear up and one ear down. "He says he's going back to bed. I'm sure he'll feel better with some rest."

His mother's worried expression relaxed slightly. "Good. I'm glad he's being smart. I'll take him dinner later tonight; he's got to eat."

Enzo and Luca exchanged looks. They'd just bought Matty another full day off, though none of them knew why. Enzo made a mental note to text him later and make sure he was fine. Of the five of them, Matteo was the only one who'd joined the business reluctantly. But Gino could be pretty persuasive.

"All right, boys," their father said, smacking his palms on the table and standing. "Anything else I should know? I'm headed up to Fort Myers, got to see a man about a fish." Gino stopped at the pancake table and kissed Sofia goodbye before he left, turning down her offer of a second serving. Their mother watched him go and took off her apron.

Gino and Sofia Castellari were basically royalty in Bliss. The town looked up to them, the working-class immigrant couple who'd created an empire from a dream and a fishing boat. Enzo had noticed little things lately that he wished he hadn't, part of a pattern with his father that he'd hoped was behind them. He doubted very much that Gino was really heading to Fort Myers for work today.

Out on the water with Salvi, his frequent fishing partner, Enzo chewed on the pros and cons of bringing up his suspicions to his brother. They were running a longline vessel today, and the fishing all morning was excellent. They began securing the lines to head back to the docks around three, with the sun at its hottest and no bites the last hour.

"I think Pop's cheating on Ma." Enzo couldn't keep it in any longer. There was way too much going on his head right now, what with Blue being home and the wedding and now worrying about his mother.

Salvi turned away from the large fishing pole he was working on respooling and scowled at Enzo. "Again?"

He nodded. "I think so. I can't be sure."

"God dammit," Salvi spat. His cheeks were red and his dark eyes furious below his faded red bandana. Salvi's hair was an untamed mass of wild curls that grew wilder and curlier out on the water. He'd taken to covering it with bandanas when he was fishing to keep it out of his eyes. It drove their mother crazy, but it suited him, especially onstage with Enzo at Captain Crab's. He resumed what he was doing, attacking the reel with a new viciousness. "Son of a bitch!" The reel locked up, thick nylon line tangled in the line spool, and would go no further. He bent over it, trying to work through the mess of 800-pound test fishing line.

Enzo handed him his knife. "Sorry, my timing's always sucked."

Salvi cut the line. "He promised her it was over."

Enzo started the engine. "I think it is over with Nadine. I think he's got something going on in Fort Myers now with someone new."

"Why? What makes you think that?" Salvi raised his voice to be heard over the engine as the vessel sliced through the waves.

"A lot of things. He's lost weight again. He's extra cheerful lately. And I followed him yesterday and saw her."

Salvi hit the steering wheel. "Goddamned Gino! Why does he do this?"

Enzo shook his head. "Ego? Total disregard for Ma? I hope she doesn't know." Their mother deserved so much better.

"I bet she suspects. I don't get why she stays."

"Me neither," he agreed. "We've got to be idiots for thinking he'd ever change. Y'know, I've always wondered—" He caught himself and stopped short. Shit. He was thinking aloud, but he couldn't finish the thought—*whether he maybe had something going on with Mrs. Shea years ago.* It'd explain so much: why Blue's distraught dad and mother had dragged her away that night at the beach, why Mitch had cut off all contact between his family and Enzo's.

"Wondered what?" Salvi asked.

"Huh? Um." Enzo hadn't spoken of Blue or her family in ten years. If he brought up the subject, he'd end up spilling everything to Salvi, seeing her in the ER, his instant gut reaction, his failure to get her out of his damn head in days—years, if he was honest. He shrugged. "I don't know. Forgot what I was gonna say."

His brother shook his head. "I haven't forgotten anything. I'm gonna kick Pop's ass," he vowed.

Enzo stared at Salvi, poker faced. "You can't beat up our father. No matter how much I'd love to help you. Let me talk to him."

"That's not going to accomplish shit."

"We have to try. Besides, how do you think that'll go, if you punch him in the face and Ma sees it?"

"Okay," Salvi said. "You're right. So we'll talk to him. If that doesn't make him knock it off, I'll rat him out to Ma, I swear."

"Marriage is awesome," Enzo said. His tone dripped with sarcasm. "And Jillian wonders why it took six years before we got engaged."

Salvi dropped onto the bench behind the steering column, letting Enzo take over. "You have to tell her you've got cold feet, Zo."

He shook his head. "I can't. She'll freak out. I'm just not a fan of marriage. It's a great way to ruin a good thing. But maybe we'll be different." He knew how much Salvi liked Jillian—everyone did. Their girlfriends were friends, they all hung out and had fun, it was just easy.

His brother's words needled him on his short drive home; he didn't have cold feet, exactly. It was more like approaching the finish line of a race he hadn't meant to run.

The road back to Live Oak Way and his house took him directly past Collier County Hospital. Enzo's pulse sped up as his car did, and he avoided scanning the hospital parking lot for the first couple of seconds, until he got stopped at the light. Fan-fucking-tastic. He'd spotted the gray minivan at Mitch Shea's cottage in the evenings, so he knew what she drove, but it was such a generic vehicle there was no way he could tell by looking whether Blue was working tonight or not.

Enzo blinked, suddenly acutely aware of his right eye. It felt dry and achy. Maybe it wasn't fully healed. Was he being too stubborn, avoiding getting it rechecked? He could walk in and show them the downloads of the faxed discharge instructions from Jillian; they probably wouldn't make him wait too long.

He shook his head. "No." He said it too loudly, alone in his SUV. If it really was still bothering him by tomorrow, he'd consider getting checked out. He had to get past this, get over her.

A car horn blared behind him and made him jump. He looked up at the green traffic light overhead and lurched forward, no idea how long he'd made the line of cars behind him wait. He glanced out the window one more time as he drove past the hospital entrance and kept going.

On Live Oak Way, Enzo's gaze went automatically to the Shea cottage before he could stop himself. Blue's minivan was in the driveway, and someone was in the yard. He craned his neck, trying to get a better look, mindful of not holding up traffic this time. There was a young boy with a rake working in the yard and, as he watched, Blue came around the corner of the house.

Enzo made a hard right onto the beach access lane that ran just the other side of the Shea property. He let his car roll to a stop behind a stand of oak trees in the small parking area, heart pounding in his ears as he stared at Blue and the boy. He was young, maybe eight? But maybe older, closer to nine or ten.

He leaned forward, pressed against the steering wheel as he narrowed his eyes, trying to get a better look. The child's light blonde hair was the same color as Blue's, his features enough like hers that he must be her son. Enzo's throat swelled, his heart lifting, buoyant in his chest. What if . . . it couldn't be. Could it? His neck prickled with the implications of allowing the possibility. Was he crazy to wonder? To *hope*?

His gaze darted between the child and Blue. Her hair was in a high, messy ponytail; pink tank and rain boots and denim shorts that rode low on her hips highlighted willowy arms and

legs she'd never fully grown into. She moved with an uncon-
scious grace. She wore work gloves, holding a lawn bag for the
boy to scoop yard waste into, and swiped a hand across her forehead, leaving a smear of dirt. Her son tossed a huge armful of
leaves and palm fronds into the bag and missed, scattering them
over their feet instead. Blue laughed, kicking up the dry leaves
and making her son shout and duck away before flinging more
back at her.

Enzo didn't know how long he sat there, watching them
work. He'd never seen anything so perfect. It took every ounce
of his strength to turn around and drive away.

Blue was enjoying Murphy's momentary good mood Friday afternoon. They'd spoken to Josh's parents and Cooper's mom that morning and made plans for the boys to visit in July. There were details still to be worked out, but it had made her son's day knowing he'd see his friends soon. Blue hadn't even had to twist her son's arm to get him to come help her outside after they'd hung up with Cooper's mom. In the ten days since she'd been back, the front porch was now repaired, painted and presentable, and the backyard was starting to look as if someone actually lived here again. With all the palm fronds and dead vegetation cleared out, maybe she could even plant some flowers along the side of the house and out front.

She leaned her rake against the tree and headed over to the path under the willow tree. "Murph."

He was tossing old maple helicopter seeds in the air and watching Hook swipe at them as they spiraled down. "Yeah?" He joined her, the cat following him.

"I wanted to get all of this fixed up before showing you, but it's taking longer than I thought. Your Grandma Ella and I created this garden through the trees when I was a kid, from when I was six or seven all the way until—well, until I was in high school." She'd worked on the garden with her mum the day

before she died. "I'll bet there's still some cool stuff hidden here."
She stooped down and brushed off the first fairy house along the
path, a lattice roof style cottage that had once been yellow and
orange and was now mostly gray with age and dirt. She'd gotten
all the big vines and overgrowth off the trail, but the smaller
structures, like the tiny lounge chairs and the archway leading
to the first house, were still half hidden. She and her mother had
painted pretty little homes and added small wishing ponds filled
with blue glass, swing sets, dining tables, and similar items along
the edge of the trail through the trees.

Her son hung back. "A fairy garden?"

She straightened up, brushing her hands off on her shorts.
"Sort of a winding fairy village or town. It goes all the way
through to the other side by the fence," she said, pointing into
the trees.

"Oh." He looked beyond her but made no move to go see.

She'd worried about this, that Murph would act too cool to
care. She moved along the path, the cat pouncing ahead of her.
"Your grandma was funny, she wanted the fairies to have things
to do, hobbies. There's a fishing boat somewhere up ahead, on a
real miniature lake we made. There's even a campsite with a couple of tents, I think it's on the left side of the path here." Blue bent
down and plucked a rounded rectangular-shaped item from the
scattered leaves. "And a camper! I'd almost forgotten about this."

He was right behind her. "Let me see. Fairy gardens have
tents and campers?" He took the faded camper from her, turning
it around in his hands.

She laughed. "I'd like to get it all cleaned up, maybe even
add a bit of fresh paint to some of this. It might be a fun summer
project."

"Where are the fairies? Don't you have like, action figures of
fairies or something?"

She smiled at his verbiage. She'd had this exact conversation
with her mum. "Well, some people believe that we only have

to provide what the fairies will need, and they come when we aren't looking. When I was little, I fought with my mum about that."

Murph's eyebrows went up. "You fought with her?"

Blue nodded. "I was insistent that we should add our own. You know, mini fairy figurines. How else are other fairies supposed to know they can come here? She finally gave in and let me add a couple." They were about halfway down the path now. "I haven't seen them since I've been cleaning, though. They're probably lost under the bluebell flowers."

"Huh." He handed the camper back to her. "Wait. That's what you're named for? These flowers?" He toed a cluster of purplish-blue flowers at the edge of the path.

An involuntary gasp escaped her. "Careful."

Murph frowned at her. "What? I didn't do anything."

"I know. That's a Grandma Ella thing. Bluebell flowers should never be crushed."

"I wasn't going to step on them!" His voice cracked and he scowled down at the flowers near their feet.

Blue put a hand on her son's shoulder. "I know, Murph," she repeated. "I'm sorry. Your grandmother always said the fairies use them. In Irish folklore—"

Murphy turned and pulled away from her. "Whatever. I'm too old for stupid fairies." He retreated across the yard to the house. She cringed. They'd been doing so well. She'd only tried to caution him against stepping on the flowers. He'd grown so accustomed to Brent's criticism, he'd come to expect it, and not only from his stepdad.

Hook passed her on the path and took off running after Murph. The traitor tabby had sure warmed up to him fast. He slept in Murph's room every night now and was by the boy's side whenever he wasn't playing fishing cat with her dad.

★ ★ ★

Later that evening, Blue's phone rang in the middle of dinner. She glanced over at it on the counter, meaning to silence it. Her husband's picture filled the screen. Murphy jumped up from the table and grabbed it before she could stop him, taking it out of the room. She gritted her teeth, closing her eyes. Brent hadn't called her once since they'd left. She suddenly had no appetite. What did he want? It couldn't be good. She didn't want to talk to him. Her dad's voice jolted her from her thoughts.

"You okay?"

She nodded. She'd made this mess. And she couldn't voice any of her angst to her dad.

Murphy came back in and handed her the phone. "He wants you, not me." His expression was stony. He spun and went out to the yard, deliberately slamming the screen door behind him.

Blue swallowed hard and put the phone to her ear. Her dad nodded at her and left the room, giving her privacy.

"He's back in his door-slamming phase I see," Brent said.

"Yeah, he's perfecting his technique." Her response was automatic and she immediately bit down on the insides of her cheeks, angry with herself for her mindless volley with him. What the hell was wrong with her?

"He's just going to get worse if you don't shut that shit down, Blue. I've told you before."

She kept her mouth clamped closed to avoid another knee-jerk reply. In spite of the pediatrician's more humane suggestions, like deducting allowance for each door slam, which wasn't an option as Brent didn't believe in allowances, her husband's solution to Murphy taking his anger out on their doors had been to remove them from their hinges. He'd started with Murphy's bedroom door. Her defiant, then eight-year-old son had risen to the challenge and slammed his bathroom door next, and Brent took that one off too, making it clear that he was not to use their master bathroom. The result was Blue ending up in the emergency room with Murph, trying to explain to one of the docs she worked with why her young son was constipated and had a bladder infection.

She squeezed her eyes shut. It hurt to think about. Had she really supported her husband in disciplining Murphy like that? Why did it seem so much worse now, looking back? "What do you want, Brent?"

His forceful exhalation came through to her ear. "I'm calling to check on you. You always said you'd never go back to your dad's. You shouldn't be there. Are you all right?"

Blue sank into the kitchen chair, resting her forehead in one hand. "I'm fine. That's why you're calling? You're concerned about me?"

The line was silent. She waited, but he didn't speak.

Maybe she'd lost him. "Brent?"

"I'm here."

"I don't understand," she said softly. He was so confusing.

"I should have been a better husband. I'm sorry," he said.

Her eyes flooded with tears. She tried to speak but she couldn't get the words around the thick lump in her throat.

"I've had a little time to think now, with you gone. Work's still a pressure cooker. But I think between that and then dealing with yours and Murphy's crap—"

"Brent," she interrupted. She tried to make her voice steady, tried to sound stronger than she felt. "I don't want to go through this again. Can we just . . . leave it?" She really didn't need to hear again the multitude of things she couldn't do right. She'd made Brent angry or exasperated with her nearly every day of their marriage.

"I miss you," he said.

She covered her eyes, silent tears spilling over her cheeks. Hearing those words from him was everything she'd been afraid to hope for. She wanted to hate him.

"Do you miss me?" His voice was small, quiet. Conciliatory.

She sucked in a breath, sniffling. *I miss you too.* The words were on her tongue, ready, but she bit them back.

"I'm not sure you've thought this whole thing through," he said. "Neither of us did. I don't like thinking of you there, on your own, having to support yourself and Murphy and now your dad. How long do you really think you'll be able to handle all that?"

She wished he'd just shut up. He made it sound so bleak. But . . . how long *could* she do this? She had no idea if she could actually afford a place for herself and Murphy on her income. Maybe, if she worked more hours . . . and then what? Just leave Murph on his own more? She hadn't thought this through, he was right, and it scared the hell out of her.

"Listen." His tone was firm now, more confident than just seconds ago. "Take as much time as you need. Bond with your dad, get some sun. But then come back to me, Blue. We can work this out. Things will be different. You don't belong there."

He was right. Maybe nothing was as bad as it seemed. If it had truly been so awful, *she* would have left *him*, wouldn't she? It wouldn't have taken him leaving. He'd blindsided her when he'd served her with divorce papers. Now he was admitting he'd been wrong. She wiped her damp cheeks, not knowing what to say. This was what she'd wanted, for Brent to come to his senses. But as much as she wanted to tell him she'd come back, she couldn't ignore the churning, nauseous feeling in her stomach as she tried out the response in her head—*Yes. Okay.* She dug her fingernails into her palm, a distraction from the urge to throw up.

"Did you hear me?" he asked.

She nodded. Stupid, he couldn't see her. "Yes."

"Okay," Brent said, finality in his tone. "So . . . soon then. All right? Call me when you're ready, and I'll fly down and drive you home. Goodnight, Blue." The line went dead.

Blue shoved the bench back from the table and lurched to the kitchen sink. She splashed cold water over her face. It didn't calm the queasy feeling. She stuck her head under the faucet, the shock of the cold ridding her of the nausea. She stood up, gasping, and squeezed a kitchen towel around her wet hair. *No.* That's all she'd had to say.

★　★　★

Blue slept fitfully all night, her dreams filled with different versions of Brent—the young cop she'd met in her Tallahassee ER, proud Brent after the promotion wearing his dress uniform and cap; sweet, docile Brent on Sunday mornings in his pajama pants, drinking coffee; angry, red-faced Brent when she'd had to confess the fender bender she'd caused. There were more. She woke up drenched in sweat. It took a moment to get her bearings, to let her fear be replaced by the relief of the sun rising over the Intracoastal at home with her dad.

She showered, dressed, and shuffled into the kitchen in her scrubs, where she and her dad had fallen into a quiet routine. Mitch would hand her a cup of coffee, prepared with three creams the way she liked it. While she ate a bowl of cereal, he read the paper. After breakfast, he'd feed the cat while she made her lunch for her shift. This morning, her dad had a plate of his signature pancakes waiting for her.

"Oh wow. Thank you." She sat down and dug in. "Oh," she said, rolling her eyes toward the ceiling. "So good. You've still got it, huh?"

He shrugged. His newspaper lay untouched in front of him. "Figured you need more than that fluff to get you through to lunchtime," he said, jerking his head toward her box of wheat flakes on top of the refrigerator.

"True. I've been starving by ten AM lately. This was so nice of you." He must be in a good mood. Maybe now was the time for her idea. "Dad . . ."

"Hmm," he grunted in response. He stabbed his fork into a pancake, frowning while he chewed.

"I remember us picking out this wallpaper when I was around ten or so," she said, waving her fork around at the kitchen walls.

It had once been white with a green vine pattern. Dust or age or both had worn it down to a dull gray, with darker gray vines. "Murph and I would love to paint your kitchen for you."

"Why?"

She raised her eyebrows. "No reason. Maybe just to brighten things up a little? I painted every room in my house in Tallahassee. I swear I'll do a good job." She wanted to do so much more than spruce up the yard and paint the porch, especially if there was a chance she might end up leaving soon.

"It's a waste of good money," he grumbled.

"Oh—I'll buy the supplies with my first paycheck. It won't cost you anything."

He looked around at the walls. "Well. It's not necessary. It doesn't matter to me."

She had a feeling that was as close to a yes as she'd get. "All right then. We'll do it next week. It'll be fun." Mitch looked skeptical. Between the pancakes, the still folded paper on the table, and how easily he'd agreed to let her take charge of his kitchen, he was clearly preoccupied with something.

He cleared his throat. "About today. I'm thinking, maybe you want to see if Sierra will watch Murphy instead of him coming out with me?"

The day camp program Blue had arranged for Murphy covered her work days during the week, but she'd have to piece together other plans for him on the weekends she worked. He was supposed to go fishing with Mitch today. With his bushy eyebrows and overgrown beard, her dad was impossible to read. What if Sierra wasn't available last minute? "Do you not want him with you? I'm sure it'd be easier to get your haul if you're alone."

"That's not it. I think—maybe it's too soon, since you won't be with us today?"

She wasn't sure she was on the same page as he was, but she took the leap. "It's been ten years, Dad. Nothing that happened that night was your fault. I know you did everything you could to try and save Mum." She covered his hand with hers, his skin rough and weathered under her palm.

He met her eyes, deep lines etched between his brows. He nodded once, not speaking.

"I appreciate you letting us stay here," she said softly. The space between them was always so quiet, so pregnant with everything left unsaid. "When I left, I didn't have money or a plan. If Aunt Eva hadn't found me, I still don't know what I would've done. I think I always planned to come home when the trial was over and they let you go, but that didn't happen."

"Right. And you must've been a new mother by the time I got out," her dad said softly.

"I was so lost. This town was awful. The kids I'd thought were my friends just talked endless shit about you. Sierra was the only one who didn't. I was scared of having a baby, of being a mum myself, of never seeing you again. But I was more afraid of what you'd say if I came home with Murph."

Her dad's built-in frown deepened. "All I wanted was to know you were safe."

"I know that now." Lord, did she ever. She'd be out of her mind if Murphy ever disappeared on her.

He stood abruptly and went to the sink, bracing the heels of his hands on the counter with his back to her. He shook his head. "I need to say this. When you did call—you and your mother were both gone over a year by then. My whole world. The rage just—it ate me up." He turned and locked eyes with her.

When she'd finally called, Murphy was six months old, she'd just gotten her GED, and she missed home so much— her dad, her house, Sierra, Enzo, Bliss, even Hook. When he answered, she'd faltered at hearing his voice, overcome with emotion and stumbling over her words. He'd shut her down: *You may as well stay gone, Bluebelle. The daughter I had died with her mum.*

"I'm so goddamned sorry," he said. "I wasn't myself." He patted his chest pocket, checking for his cigarettes, a habitual, automatic motion. "I can't take back what I said. I hated myself for it, still do." He turned to head outside, the pack of smokes in one hand.

"Dad. It's okay. I never should've left." She stood, meaning to walk outside with him. "Since we're sort of clearing the air, can we talk about what happened at Enzo's house that night, a couple of years before we lost Mum? Being back here with Murph, knowing I'm going to have to tell Enzo about him, I can't help thinking of how this all might have been different. What happened? You got your gun the morning Enzo's parents came over here—what the hell happened? They were your friends."

Her dad put a cigarette between his lips and went through the screen door, standing with his back to her while he lit it. "I can't." Mitch exhaled smoke with the words, glancing at her from the corner of his eye.

"You carried her all the way home," she said. "I remember. I thought she was dying."

His head jerked as he stared at her. "Stop. I mean it. If there's ever a reason for you to know, I'll tell you." He turned and strode toward the boat garage, leaving her alone. She sighed, defeated again, and went back inside to collect her things and head out to work.

* * *

"You've got the recheck in Exam three," Blue's supervisor told her. She turned and called over her shoulder to the nurse on the other side of the nurse's station, "Go ahead and take your lunch now, Kathy, while it's quiet."

Blue cringed. She liked Char, the clinical supervisor working today. But for Pete's sake, anyone who'd ever worked in health care knew never to say the Q-word. It was like tempting fate. You could say it later, after you'd clocked out and gotten off the premises. But you never, ever declared an emergency room quiet. The moment you did, everything tended to go to shit. She met Kathy's gaze over Char's head. The seasoned nurse was shaking her head. She made the sign of the cross and Blue snickered.

"Good luck," Kathy murmured on her way to the break room.

Blue tapped the computer screen outside the curtain of Exam three, pulling up the patient's chart. Her heart lurched into her throat. Enzo Castellari was her recheck patient. And there was no way out of seeing him, with Kathy at lunch and Maggie the only other nurse on.

She'd suck it up and be professional. After all, it was a small town, and they were bound to cross paths. She moved to Exam three and tried to steel herself, imagining Enzo and his lovely fiancée on the other side of the curtain. She stepped inside. He was alone.

Enzo's face instantly broke into a wide grin. The little crinkles at the corners of his eyes, the way his full lips stretched into the smile she remembered so well, scrambled her thoughts. She swallowed hard, gripping the edge of the computer cart. He sat on the gurney, faded and worn denim stretched taut over muscled thighs, his black T-shirt with the Castellari and Sons logo leaving his deeply tanned arms bare. She focused her attention on the screen in front of her and took a slow, deep breath before looking back up, meeting his gaze.

"Blue," he said simply, killing her with her own damn name.

She moved to the sink and washed her hands. When she finally had to stand eye to eye with him, she knew she was doing an awful job of concealing her conflicted feelings—joy at being in his space; anger at the way he'd driven her away years ago; heartache at the distance between them now. She was a mess of painful longing and crushing loss in crisp blue scrubs and a poker face.

Enzo unclasped his hands and braced them on the edge of the gurney, leaning forward earnestly. "I'm sorry. Blue. I'm so sorry."

Her eyes widened. For what? For turning on her at the worst possible moment? For believing what the town said about her dad? Or for growing up and forgetting about her? She swallowed hard, frowning. "I never should have left." It was becoming her mantra.

"I should have gone with you. I should have come after you sooner. I could have pushed Sierra harder to tell me where you were."

Blue's heart beat triple time. "She wouldn't have."

"Then I should've sucked it up and gone to your dad. I can't believe you're back. Why are you back? Are you staying?"

"I think so—I'm not sure," she stammered.

"Oh." The single word was thick with disappointment. "But . . . you have a son? Was that your son?"

"What?" She stared at him. A sense of vertigo struck her, weightlessness, her world turned upside down. How did he know, before she'd even had a chance to tell him?

"I . . . uh. I saw you." Enzo took a deep breath, his broad chest heaving. He scrubbed a hand through thick, dark waves, and too many memories rushed Blue's mind at once. Her fingertips tingled, a tactile memory of the warmth of his skin under her hand, her fingers sliding across his neck and into his hair the night he first kissed her.

"When?" It was the dumbest thing she could've asked; why did it matter when he'd seen her with Murphy? She was stalling. She wasn't ready. It wasn't supposed to happen this way, the news flung out there to him in a curtained bay of her ER between an eye flush and his copay. She'd rehearsed how she'd tell Enzo about his son since the day she'd learned she was pregnant. Part of her never believed she'd actually get to do it.

"You were in the yard," he said. "Yesterday. I was driving by and saw you, the two of you. He's yours? Is he . . . how old is he? Did you, uh, are you married now?" Enzo's tone was strained at the end.

She stared at him, tongue tied.

"Ugh," he groaned, looking down. Blue's whole body swayed toward him of its own accord. He looked so lost. If she could only touch him, wrap her arms around him, she knew it'd help. It'd help them both. It was impossible. Her feet remained rooted.

"If he's . . . Blue, if that's our son I saw in your yard . . . that would be amazing. Is he mine? I wish—God—I've always wished things had been different. If you had our son, you have to let me help take care of him, I mean it, I'll do whatever you feel will be best for him. I have to support him. I—I really would love to meet him. Just me, obviously, with you there so he'd feel comfortable. Maybe we could do that? I know, ah . . . you met my fiancée the other day, but he wouldn't have to meet her yet. We haven't even talked about kids," he murmured, an afterthought.

"No," Blue said quickly. She didn't even know what she was saying no to—Jillian as Murph's new stepmom? Or everything.

His expression fell. She'd ripped hope away from him, after worrying all this time that he might be upset to learn he was a father. "What?"

"He's not yours," she said gently. Enzo was planning out Murphy's life with him—or with him and Jillian Josephson. What if she and Murphy went back to Tallahassee? What if Enzo fought her for custody? What if Jillian didn't want Murphy and got stuck with him anyway? She felt sick.

"Oh." He exhaled slowly, like a balloon deflating. "Okay. I . . . uh, I got carried away. That's embarrassing."

"It's understandable, you wondering." She was so going to hell. She'd just made everything worse.

He nodded once, silent for a moment. "Well. You have a son. I'm happy for you," he said, the words conflicting with his pained expression.

She started to correct her lie—she hated that she'd hurt him—when he spoke again.

"The two of you seemed happy. He looks like a sweet kid." He searched her eyes with his. "Are you happy, Blue?"

She took an involuntary step back, a rush of hot tears filling her eyes. It was like no time had passed at all. They were eleven and catching geckos in the sunbeams, fifteen and sharing their first kiss, seventeen and planning their future together. The last decade dissipated, a mirage, leaving nothing but the time before, when Enzo loved her. She shook her head, quickly, swallowing hard. "Oh," she whispered, one tear slipping down her cheek before she swiped it away. "Sorry. I'm—" She met his gaze and sucked in air.

Enzo stood up from the gurney, concern furrowing his brow. He put a hand out toward her but didn't touch her.

"I'm not. Happy," she said, trying to answer his question. "But it's okay. I'm working on it." She laughed softly and gave him a small, apologetic smile. "If that's not the saddest thing you've ever heard."

"I hate hearing that. I hate seeing you cry," he said, his voice low.

"It'll be okay. Really. You're happy," she said, forcing her own smile now. "I saw that the other day. I'm so glad you're happy, Enzo."

He leaned on the gurney, silent.

"When's the wedding?" she asked, her voice soft. It seemed like the thing to ask, but she didn't want to know. She didn't want to ever see his fiancée again, especially not in her head wearing a wedding dress. The woman was gorgeous and intelligent. She'd been a good advocate for him here last week. She was everything he deserved.

"In three months—September."

"Ah. Well, congratulations."

"Blue, I—"

Now she cut him off. She couldn't handle any more of this, standing here with her heart cut open and bleeding. "So your eye must be giving you trouble? Is that what brought you back in to be checked?" She pulled her gloves on and moved to the flex-light over the gurney.

"No," he said. "I came to see you."

Enzo missed Blue more than he had a right to. She was the same but different. When he'd thought of her all these years, he'd tried to imagine her as *grown-up* Blue. Not his best friend since they were two, not the girl he'd known so intimately and planned to spend his life with, but the adult version. Maybe grown-up Blue was different after running away from home, after losing her mom, after losing everyone—including him. Maybe she'd hardened and become cynical. Maybe she'd cut her hair. Maybe she hated him now. None of what he'd tried to imagine was true. She was still gentle and kind. Her hair was longer now than when they were kids. But she still wore her feelings inside out, in spite of her best efforts.

He'd come in today planning to say his eye was bothering him. Salvi had griped that Maggie had to work this weekend. Enzo filed it away, thinking if it also happened to be Blue's weekend to work, he might get her as his nurse again since Maggie couldn't treat him. But the moment he saw her, he forgot about his eye. He'd rapid-fired questions at her and made her cry and now she was retreating; he felt it.

"I came to see you." He squinted as she turned the light on to check his eye. "Can we just talk? Please? I promise I won't make you cry again," he said, looking from Blue's gloved hands up to her face, her pale pink skin, flushed cheeks, eyes bluer than any ocean.

"You can't promise that. I'll end up proving you wrong. Your eye is really fine?" She leaned forward, placing the gloved tip of one finger underneath his eye and peering at him. "Look up."

He did, moving his gaze in each direction as she commanded.

"No pain? No scratchiness anywhere?"

"Nope." He inhaled, trying not to be obvious. She was so close and she smelled so damn good. "Your dad must be glad you're back. Is he doing all right?"

"He's fine."

"He still comes to Captain Crab's for Friday fish fry once in a while, Salvi and I see him when we're setting up to play. He usually eats alone, or Rita from that shop in town joins him. I think sometimes I'll work up the nerve to go talk to him, but I never do. And he's gone before we play, before the bar crowd shows up."

Blue stared at him. "I don't want to go back through this with you. We'll have the same fight all over again." She stepped back and took off her gloves. "Your eye looks fine. I could check with the fluoroscope, but as long as there's no discomfort, I think you're all healed."

"I'm not. I have discomfort." He raised an eyebrow and grinned, trying to find a way through to her, to let her know he wasn't the enemy. He wasn't trying to flirt. It was like his body and brain were working against him. He shouldn't be flirting with anyone, especially not Blue. He wasn't sure he'd be able to find the off switch if it led somewhere.

Blue pressed her lips together. "I can't help you with your conscience."

"Damn." He shook his head. "It doesn't have to be like this. It's been ten years, Blue. It's in the past. Any animosity the town had for your dad is probably gone. I just wanted you to know we see him now and then."

"Right. And that he seems sober now."

"That's not what I was saying!"

"He doesn't drink anymore. He wasn't drinking the night my mum drowned. I don't know how yet, but I'm going to prove it. You want to know the last time I actually did see my dad drunk? It was at your house," she said, the words flung at him like an accusation. "I never saw him take a drink after that. Not even at dinner or with Mum. He still won't talk about what happened. But it changed them both."

"Okay. I don't want to fight with you. Let me work on it." He had to give; even if he didn't believe for a second that Mitch had been wrongly convicted, he wasn't going to convince Blue, he could see that. So he'd focus on the night at his house instead, the first time her dad had fucked up their future together. "My parents were a dead-end years ago, but maybe Marcello or someone saw something at the party that night that I didn't. I just keep thinking, if your dad hadn't cut us off from each other, everything would've been different two years later when your mother . . . well, when the accident happened. We wouldn't have had to sneak around. Maybe you would have been on the boat with them. Maybe we both would have been. Your mom might have survived."

"I do the same thing," she whispered. "The what-ifs, all the way through to the end, to you and M—" She cut herself off, eyes wide.

Enzo tipped his head. "To me and your mom," he said, filling in the blank. "I've gotta ask, after you left, and it took me a while to find out where you were—why wouldn't you see me? Was it really because you were still angry at me?"

She sighed heavily. "Oh, Enz." She opened her mouth to say something else, then seemed to think better of it.

"Hey. Don't do that. It's already weird between us. Don't make it worse. Say it," he told her. "Whatever you were about to say."

"I . . . um. There's just so much up in the air right now. And I want . . ." She twisted the hem of her scrub top between two fingers. "I don't want to be enemies. I was so mad at you for so long, Enzo. But I think I was mostly mad at myself."

Being face to face with Bluebelle Shea again, without Jillian as a chaperone, was like walking a tightrope. Trying to forge a new friendship, even starting with baby steps, might be a bad idea. He'd have to keep his feelings in check. "Well. I happen to have an opening for a friend right now." What the ever-loving fuck was wrong with him? Why had he said that?

She graced him with the bright smile he'd missed so much. There was his answer. "There's something I have to tell you," she said. "I—" The closed curtain on his exam cubicle rustled and a pair of nurse's clogs appeared below it. "Incoming trauma, three-car accident, ETA in five."

"Thanks," Blue called. "I have to run," she told Enzo, hurrying to clean the flex-light and wash her hands.

"Tomorrow," he blurted. "Breakfast tomorrow. Or lunch, whatever you want." He had to see her again, and she was about to disappear through the curtains. And it wasn't like he could just show up on the Shea porch and knock. Mitch would probably answer the door with a shotgun pointed at him just for being Gino's son.

"Okay."

"The Mariner at noon?"

"Yes," she said. "Sounds good." Commotion clattered outside the curtain, the sound of heavy equipment being moved and readied. She was gone before he could reply.

★ ★ ★

Enzo's trip to the ER didn't go unnoticed. He and Jillian met his brother and Maggie for drinks in the village and Maggie immediately exposed him.

"Let me see," she said, leaning over and peering at his eye. "I noticed your name on the board when I got back from lunch today. Is your eye okay? Your nurse didn't need to bandage it?"

"You went back?" Jillian asked, not giving him time to answer Maggie's question. Their server appeared and distributed the drink orders around the high-top table. They'd lucked into one of the spots along the railing, looking out over the Gulf.

"I figured I'd better. You'd have never let me hear the end of it if I blew it off and then it hurt later," he said, giving Jillian a wink. "I'm fine," he added.

Salvi shoved his wild curls off his forehead. "Takes more than a baby bird to knock my man out of the game."

"It wasn't—ah, forget it." Enzo took a swig of his cold beer. His brothers had been giving him crap about being assaulted by a baby bird since it'd happened.

"Did they have to do anything this time? More poking around in your eye, Babe?" Jillian's expression was filled with concern.

"No, it's all healed. No worries." He wanted to get off this topic; the connections were making him uncomfortable.

"Good. I meant to ask Blue if you were all right, but we had a trauma come in and the whole day flew by."

Salvi caught it. "Blue?"

"The new nurse. Weird name, huh? Who names their kid after a color?" Maggie chuckled.

"Well," Salvi said, staring at Enzo, "maybe they didn't. You never know. Could be short for something, like Bluebelle." He widened his eyes, questioning silently.

"Oh!" Maggie exclaimed. "Like the flower. I think you're right. I think Char actually called her that on her first day. Huh. Anyway, it's good to have more capable hands."

"I'm sure it is," Enzo said, studying his menu and avoiding looking at Jillian. There'd be no way for her to know his history with Blue. But he wished his brother would shut the hell up all the same.

"Let's have a toast," Jillian said, raising her wine glass. "To Enzo's two good eyes, to reserving Gulfscape Gardens as our venue, and to exactly three months and a day until the wedding!"

"Yay!" Maggie said. "And to bridesmaid gown shopping tomorrow!"

"Yes," Jillian said, grinning. "Wait'll you see the selection at Elegant Engagements."

"What colors are you thinking?"

Enzo relaxed in spite of Salvi's extreme stink-eye from across the table. Wedding stuff was a much safer topic than Maggie's new coworker with the weird name. He shot the dirty look right back at Salvatore. What did he want from him? Enzo had no control over the fact that Bluebelle Shea was back in Bliss and working with Maggie.

"I need another," his brother said, pushing his chair back. "We'll go grab the next round. Zo."

If he stayed put, Salvi would turn it into a whole thing. He followed his brother. When they reached the bar, Salvi set his half empty vodka tonic on the wooden railing and faced Enzo.

"Blue is back? When? Why? Were you even gonna say anything?"

He leaned on the railing. "I think she's only been back a little while. I didn't know until last week when I had to get my eye checked out and she was working in the ER with Maggie."

"Well, damn." Salvi frowned. "You all right?"

"I'm *fine*," he stressed. "It's been ten years. It's no big deal."

Salvi tipped his head back, looking at the sky. "No big deal. Right. It's not like we had you on suicide watch or anything after she was gone."

"Fuck off. Ma overreacted like always."

"Where the hell was she this whole time? Why is she back? Is she, like, okay?"

Enzo sighed. "I don't know. I don't know much of anything, except that she has a son now."

"Bro." Salvi punched Enzo in the arm. "Oh, man. You're screwed. How old?"

"He's not mine." Enzo tipped his beer all the way back, finishing it. It didn't help the burning, twisting feeling in his gut. She hadn't answered his question of whether or not she was married. Which led him to believe she was.

Salvi spoke to the bartender and ordered their drinks. He turned back to Enzo. "I'm sorry. Really. This has gotta be tough." He glanced over Enzo's shoulder toward their table. "Are you going to tell Jillian?"

"No!"

Salvi put his hands up. "Whoa, okay. I just wondered. She doesn't know anything about Blue?" He smiled. "She was a cool girl. The only girl I never minded having around, y'know? Not that she was allowed to come around."

"She still is. A cool girl," he clarified. "I fucking hated her dad. Not always, but after he stopped Blue from seeing me—or tried to, anyway. Hey, do you remember that one Fourth of July party when Uncle Ray drove the golf cart into the pool?"

He laughed. "How could I forget? Pops was so pissed. I was sure Dale Bryant was gonna arrest him after they got Ray out of the water."

"Nah," Enzo said. "They were all friends. Pops got over it."

"What made you think of that?"

"That was the party when Blue's dad made her leave early. He dragged her away from the bonfire while Mrs. Shea was crumpled up on the sand crying. It was weird—I thought that at the time, even before I talked to Blue later. He carried her mom the whole length of beach back home; what is it, like a quarter mile or something?"

"All right, yeah. I remember you telling me some of that."

"Do you remember anything else weird or off about that night? Besides Uncle Ray?" Enzo asked.

Salvi frowned, staring past Enzo to their teenage years. "I was, what, thirteen? Oh!" His eyes lit up. "That's why I don't remember anything about Blue's mom, I wasn't at the bonfire till it was almost out. I followed Marcello and his friends to the boat garage, they let me hit their joint a few times. Ma was gone, or I'd never have even tried it; she could smell that stuff on us a mile away."

"Ma was gone that night?"

"She was with Aunt Lorna." He shrugged. "They showed up after Uncle Ray killed our golf cart. I literally only remember that because I saw her car pull in and ran inside and soaked myself in cologne to cover up the weed smell. Ma would've killed me," he said, chuckling.

"What the fuck," Enzo breathed.

"What?"

"Ma said she'd seen Pops and Mr. Shea fighting when I asked her what happened that night. Like she was there."

"That's strange. Doesn't really make sense. But—I mean, it's all in the past, right? Blue's okay, from what you can tell?"

"She's kind of the same but different. I think she's had a rough time. She's sort of—I don't know, like—remember that cat we found in the boathouse last year? How she was so skinny and limping but she wouldn't let us close enough to help?"

"Yeah, it took days. She was so skittish." Salvi frowned at him.

He sighed. "Maybe I'm reading too much into the few minutes I've spent with Blue. She's so guarded. I don't remember her seeming fragile before," he said. He wasn't getting it right, the way he'd felt, watching her break down at the simple question of whether she was happy. "She's—it doesn't matter. Jillian doesn't know about her because there's nothing to know now."

"I get that. And it doesn't make sense to go through the whole story with Jillian. It's not like you're picking up where you left off."

He nodded, not commenting.

"Right?" Salvi said. He paid the bartender as their drinks were set out for them. "That'd be stupid. You're adults now. You're getting married, and Blue probably already is."

"I know! All right?" Enzo huffed his breath out in aggravation. "I fucking know. Nothing's going on. And nobody asked you to crawl up my ass. I got this." Salvi didn't know what he was talking about. There was no harm in having lunch with Blue.

"Listen," Salvi said. "All I'm saying is, don't be like Pops, playing both sides. Especially not over some broken girl from your past."

Enzo stared at him, incredulous. "What did you say?" He shoved his brother and Salvatore stumbled backwards into an older man sitting at the bar.

"I'm sorry, my bad," he apologized to the man, finding his balance. He darted in toward Enzo and grabbed his collar, their faces inches apart. "You'd better get a grip, man. You know I'm right."

"Get the fuck off me," Enzo growled.

Salvi let go of him abruptly and stepped back. He shook his head. "Whatever. Did you ever stop to think that if she cared about you, she wouldn't have let ten years go by without a word? I'm not watching you trash your life again, Zo."

"Salvi, man, nothing's going on. Nothing. Don't worry." His brother was only trying to protect him. Enzo handed him his new vodka tonic and Maggie's frozen daiquiri and then grabbed his own two drinks. "Come on. They've gotta be done with the wedding talk by now."

★ ★ ★

Hours later in his bed, Enzo stretched out on his side, propped up on an elbow. He ran a hand over Jillian's naked hip and she turned her face toward him, all long lashes and swollen lips, sated. She was still breathing hard, her perfect breasts rising and falling.

"I needed that," she said. She leaned up and kissed him. "Better than a workout, huh?"

She was beautiful. Jillian's body was sculpted and toned from hours spent each week in the gym. Her silky straight blonde hair fanned out around her, a few strands falling over one breast. He bent and kissed her again. "Way better."

She shifted, working to untangle her leg from his to get out of bed.

He slid his arm tighter around her and held her against him. "No. Stay." He nuzzled her neck, kissing her collarbone. They usually ended up back at his house because of Moon, but Jillian was never ready to snuggle in with him after sex. All he wanted was for her to stay like this, suspended in drowsy comfort. He was sleepy and hungry, in that order. Sleepy was going to win.

"Oh, Babe. I wish I could." She planted a kiss on his chin and snaked her way out of his grasp. She pulled her clothes on. "I've still got briefs to go over this weekend for court on Monday." She stopped buttoning her blouse and made a sad face at him. "Enzo."

He rolled onto his back. "It's all right. I know it's important."

Jillian knelt on the bed and kissed him, her tongue sliding over his bottom lip and mingling with his. He moved his hands up her ribcage, and she stopped him before he could unhook her bra again. "You're important. Nothing's more important than us. But I've got to go." She pushed off his chest and finished getting dressed. She stopped and turned back before leaving. "Oh, we have dinner at my dad's tomorrow, don't forget."

He'd forgotten. "Right. I'll pick up some wine."

"Oooh. Could you stop at The Mariner and grab a bottle of that cabernet? You know it's his favorite and no one else carries it. They'll sell it to you, won't they?"

Dennis, the proprietor, would probably sell it to him, but it went against The Mariner's policy. Enzo hated using Castellari and Sons to get favors. And how convenient that he would be there tomorrow to meet Blue for lunch. *Fuck.* He didn't want to admit Salvi was right. He looked up at Jillian, feeling like he was standing on too-thin ice and watching the cracks spider their way outward from him. "I'm sure I can convince him." He had to cancel with Blue. He didn't know how, they hadn't exchanged phone numbers, but he didn't want to be this guy.

"Love you!" Jillian blew him a kiss on her way out the door.

★   ★   ★

Enzo stood when he saw Blue come through the restaurant door on Sunday. He'd had to choose between involving Sierra and asking her to get a message to Blue, or just showing up. He still wasn't sure he'd made the right choice. He planned to keep this as short and impersonal as possible.

Blue smiled as she came toward him, stopping abruptly a couple feet away. "Hi."

"Hi." He reached past her, meaning to pull out her chair, but Blue misread his intention.

"Oh," she said, and hugged him.

He froze, his breath caught in his throat. He recovered quickly and folded her in his arms, his heart galloping at a dizzying clip. He closed his eyes and gingerly put his cheek against her soft hair and breathed in the scent of sweet pea flowers. He let go the moment she did, opening his eyes to find Dennis watching him.

✦ 9 ✦

Being in Enzo's arms was so instantly bittersweet that it hurt. Had he been this tall when they were teenagers? Or maybe it wasn't that he was taller. He was broader, wider, more . . . substantial. He smelled of oranges and soap, clean and masculine. She was eye level with his neck, the angular cut of his jaw tempting her to trace her fingers over it. She'd driven here fully intending to find a way back to her childhood friend, before they'd become more, but now she wasn't sure this was a good idea. She let go.

"This is nice. It was a Salty Dog when I used to live here," she said, trying small talk when they'd taken their seats. "You can't even tell now."

He nodded. "We got the seafood contract before they even opened." Enzo nodded over her shoulder and raised a hand in greeting to the man who'd met her at the door.

"Wow. You must know pretty much everyone in the village—in the county, probably." She didn't mean it as a dig, but it was clear he took it that way.

His brow furrowed. "We've expanded, but it's not like we've monopolized the market. There's plenty to go around. We're not trying to put smaller suppliers out of business."

"I didn't mean—of course not," she acknowledged. "I wouldn't think Shea Seafood is much of a threat to your

dad's—your family's—business." She shook her head, searching his expression. "This is hard. I didn't think this would be so
hard."

Enzo's shoulders visibly relaxed. "I'm glad you said it. It is,
isn't it?"

"I want to know about you," she said. "Tell me about your life."

He laughed. "That sounds a lot easier. Let me think. I run
the mechanical side of things at the company. I keep the boats
on the water, and I'm usually out fishing with Salvi a few days a
week. We all pitch in keeping up with the contracts, but Marcello and Luca are best at that. Matty is kind of half-in, especially
recently; he checks the boxes and tries to fly under our dad's
radar. Oh, Salvi and I are still playing. Captain Crab's gives us the
live band spot a few times a month. And I bought a little place
down the beach from my parents' house. This is my dog, Moon,"
he said, tapping his phone screen and turning a smiling black Lab
toward her.

"That face! Oh my goodness, what a sweetheart. He's a good
boy," she declared, looking from the phone to Enzo. She could
tell from the picture he was a happy dog.

"He is," Enzo said, smiling. "I guess that's it. Not as lengthy
a summary as I thought." He laughed.

"And your upcoming wedding," Blue prompted, determined
to find a way to toward normalcy—especially with what she had
to tell him today. It had to be today. She'd barely slept last night
after lying to him about Murphy.

"Right, of course. Jillian's an attorney for Suncoast Law. She's
the youngest partner they've ever had."

It sounded like a byline, not a description of his fiancée. Blue
already knew from Sierra that Jillian was impressive. And she
knew from seeing them together that she truly cared about Enzo.
"How did you meet?"

"Jillian's firm handles legal for us; we met when she was a
paralegal there. She was still in law school then."

Blue's eyes widened. "So you've been together a long time."

"Six and a half years."

"Wow."

"I'm not the biggest fan of marriage," he said, shrugging, as if he needed to explain.

She wasn't surprised at that. She knew Gino Castellari's reputation. Enzo had grown up seeing what a marriage *shouldn't* look like. Knowing he was loved now was a disorienting feeling, making her simultaneously heartsick but relieved. "I think that's awesome, Enz. I'm happy for you."

The server arrived to take their orders. Blue took Enzo's advice and ordered the crab cakes, certified caught fresh by Castellari and Sons. She felt like a traitor.

"I want to hear about you," Enzo said when the server was gone. "Tell me about Tallahassee . . . your life, your job. Your son. You never did say whether you're married."

"I'm in the middle of a divorce . . . a possible divorce, I guess," she said carefully, disliking the off-kilter feeling of her entire life being up in the air. "I have to tell you something. Please don't hate me. I . . . um." She frowned, staring down at the tablecloth.

"I could never hate you."

"My son . . . his name is Murphy. He's nine; he turned nine two months ago." She lifted her gaze to Enzo's. "Murphy is your son, Enzo. I'm sorry I didn't tell you yesterday."

He was silent. His dark eyes glistened, and he looked abruptly down at his folded hands on the table. His head moved as he swallowed hard, staying that way for a beat. And longer.

Blue's eyes burned with unshed tears. Was he happy? Angry at her? Sad? The only thing she knew for sure from yesterday was that he'd been excited, thinking Murphy could be his. When he finally raised his gaze, his tortured expression broke her heart in a hundred new places.

"How could you keep him from me?" Enzo choked out the words, so quiet she had to strain to hear.

"I'm so sorry—" She faltered for a moment and then rushed forward. "Learning I was pregnant at seventeen, no high school diploma, no parents, no—"

"That's all bullshit," he said. "Excuses. You had *me*. Always. Our whole lives, Blue, you've always had me."

"I lost you," Blue said, her voice cracking. She gritted her teeth, struggling to stay calm. "All I needed was you in my corner and everything would've been different. You weren't supposed to side with Bliss, to believe the town, our friends, everyone saying my dad was a drunk and a murderer."

"I didn't. I believed the police. I saw the news like everyone else, I knew your dad for years before that night, Blue. No one was even shocked that he was drunk."

"And you still don't get why I left," she said, hearing the bitterness in her own tone.

"Don't you see? I was always on your side." Enzo gripped the edge of the table, his voice rising, every vein in his neck standing out. "I never gave a shit about what your dad was doing. All I cared about was you. So you—" He halted abruptly, gaze darting around them, and dropped his volume. "So you got back at me by keeping my son from me all this time?"

"Oh my God, Enzo, no," she said, horrified. "No. I was so scared to see you that day, when you came to my aunt's. You would've known I was pregnant. I'd just found out from Sierra about you getting into the University of Miami, my dad was still in prison, our families were still torn apart—what was I supposed to do? Make you a dad before you even graduated? I would have ruined your future."

He leaned forward. "*You* were my future."

She sucked in a breath, struggling to make him understand. "I couldn't come home," she whispered. "I thought you'd moved on when your picture was in the paper with Melanie whatsher-name at homecoming, and getting into U of Miami, and the one time I called my dad after I had Murph, he told me I was dead to him. I couldn't come home."

"Fuck," Enzo breathed. "He said that? Son of a bitch." He sat back in his chair and raked a hand across the top of his head.

"I never, ever meant to hurt you. I'm so sorry. I'll do what-ever you want about Murphy. I can tell him soon, and introduce the two of you, or we can wait, maybe until after your wedding if you're worried about what Jillian will think. Just tell me what you want to do. He's your son, Enz. You should have a say. You should have long before now."

He'd started shaking his head before she finished. "Jillian will love him or she can find someone else. I'm not waiting three more months to meet my son. How soon can you tell him?"

"Soon. I know he's going to be excited to meet you. Within the week, okay? For sure before we head back home, but that's a few weeks away."

"You're leaving?"

"I think so. We might."

He slid the chair back and started to stand, and then stopped and sat back down, his posture rigid. "But—why would you tell me after all these years about Murphy and then take him away? How can you do this?" His eyes were huge.

"It's my husband," she said, the words laden with conflict. "He wants to work things out—"

Enzo leaned on the table, moving closer to her. "Don't do this. You came home for a reason. If you and our son were meant to be with this guy, you wouldn't be here right now. You wouldn't have moved back in with your dad, gotten a job, and finally told me about Murphy. The only thing I know about your husband is that he wanted a divorce, and that's enough. Why isn't that enough for you?"

"I don't know." She stood, her heart racing. "I thought I could do this, try to be friends, but I can't. I'll let you know as soon as I've told Murphy about you, I'll give you as much time as possible." She grabbed her purse and headed for the door as fast as she could without running.

Blue was on Live Oak Way, approaching her house, before she was able to calm down enough to think straight. She kept vacillating between feeling like her place was with Brent and feeling like Enzo was a hundred percent right. She still hadn't come to any conclusions when she parked in the driveway. A loud urgent knocking on her car window made her jump. Murphy's excited face peered in at her. "Mom, come on, I have to show you!"

He led her to the bench under the willow tree in the back yard. "Sit." He pointed.

She sat on the bench, and he sat beside her.

"What do you see?"

"Um. The fairy garden that's still a mess?"

"No! Mom, come on. What do you see that wasn't there before?"

She leaned forward, looking harder. "What is that?" Blue got up and moved to the trail through the fairy garden. In front of the first house was a dollhouse-sized wooden mailbox. The mailbox and house were both freshly painted in bright lavender and yellow. She knelt, careful to avoid the flowers and stay on the new wood chips she'd just started to spruce up the trail with. She looked up at her son. "I love this, Murph. Where did you get it?"

He sat beside her. "I didn't. And I know you didn't either. I mean, I don't think you would've had time. Hook and I were out here this morning looking for geckos. I went in for breakfast, and this was here when I came back out."

"It's so pretty!"

"Open it." He pointed at the little mailbox.

Blue leaned forward and grasped the tiny wooden knob on the door. It fell open, revealing a white square of paper inside. She turned and stared at Murphy.

"Read it. I put it back in for you to see. I swear this wasn't me. How would I even make something like that?"

Blue plucked the paper out and unfolded it, no bigger than a gum wrapper. "Oh my goodness, even the writing's tiny," she laughed. Someone was having fun with them. It seemed highly unlikely it was her dad, but she couldn't fathom who else would have been able to sneak into the yard and do this.

Murphy took it and read:

"Miss Bluebelle and young Sir Murphy –
Welcome home!
You are the entire ocean in a drop. —Rumi"

Blue leaned closer so she could see it better and read the words again. She sat back. "Hmm."

"What does it mean? Who is Rumi?" Murphy folded the paper and put it back, closing the little door on the mailbox.

"Rumi was a philosopher. Or more like a . . . kind of a poet, I think. A mystic?" She frowned. "I can't imagine Grandpa doing this. Murph . . . you're sure this wasn't you?"

He laughed. "I'm not that deep, Mom. You're the ocean in one drop? Weird."

"Well." She had no clue who had gone to the trouble to set this up and made it happen while no one was around. Should she be concerned that someone had crept into the yard to do it? It was such a kind message, there was clearly no malice or ill intent. "I hardly know anyone here anymore . . . we don't have neighbors, not really," she said, tilting her head to the right side of the yard. "The Oswald family are snowbirds, from what Grandpa says; they left in May. And the other side of us is condos. Maybe it was the fairies."

"I knew you were gonna say that," Murphy said, but he smiled. "Tell me how fairies would have built the mailbox. Or where they learned to write and how they write so small." He stood up and she did too, brushing the wood chips off her skirt.

"They go to school, just like you. And I'm sure they have tools to make a simple mailbox," she said, winking at him to say she knew he didn't believe. She took a few steps along the trail, into the thatch of trees. "The geckos like to hide in here? Where do you usually see them?"

Murph looked up. Long shards of sunlight streamed through the trees, bits of it filtering down and shining on the fairy village structures. "They're mostly here in the morning. I think the sun's too low now. They stretch out in sunspots on the roofs of your little houses," he said, pointing.

"That's awesome," Blue said. "I love knowing that. Hey, let's grab some lemonade and head down to the beach before we go to Sierra and Chloe's for dinner. Bring your fins." She rested a hand on his shoulder as they turned and walked back to the house. It was balmy, perfect weather to dip their toes into the Gulf.

She stopped outside her father's room, towel slung around her neck for the beach and bag packed with drinks and fruit. Maybe he'd want to come with them. She knocked but heard nothing. She hadn't seen him since getting back from her disastrous lunch. The door was cracked and she pushed it. It swung open on her dad sitting at the edge of his bed, rifling through a shoebox of pill bottles. He turned and looked at her.

"Dad—sorry. I knocked."

He motioned her in. "Didn't hear you. Everything all right?"

She nodded. "I, uh, I wanted to ask you something. The fairy garden out back—you haven't seen anything odd out there lately, have you?"

"Haven't been out there. Not since that night after you came home. Why?"

"No reason. Um . . ." Should she leave and give him his privacy? She started to and then hesitated. What if she didn't stay? What if she ended up having to leave him here on his own again? It'd be arrogant and presumptuous to think he couldn't take care of himself, he'd been doing it this whole time. But that box of pills was eye-opening. Her dad wasn't a young man anymore. He was almost sixty.

"Is that all?" Mitch Shea swiped the box off the bed and started to put it back in his dresser drawer.

"No. What is all that?" Blue perched on the edge of the bed and pointed at her dad's medication supply.

"Nothing. I'm fine."

"I'm sure you are. But can I see? Please?"

Her dad's natural scowl deepened. He set it on the bed between them and stood, moving toward the door. "You don't need to worry. I do what I'm supposed to."

A quick glance told Blue that Mitch was on a couple of heart medications, a cholesterol pill, and an arthritis med. Aside from the prescriptions, there were bottles and blister packs of cold medicine and antacids, a six-year-old bottle of baby aspirin, and random scattered pills in the bottom of the box. She picked up the bottle of Cardizem from the drugstore in town. "You take these twice a day?" The prescription was current, from a Dr. Harrison.

He nodded once. "Sure do. Listen. I know this is what you do, you're the expert and all, but my doc has it handled."

"Okay, good. I'm glad you have a good doctor. You see him regularly?"

"I was just there last year."

"Um. Maybe you're due soon? I could come with you if you want. Dr. Harrison probably likes to see you more than once a year?"

He shrugged. "I'm fine. I go when I have to."

She picked up the expired aspirin. "Are you supposed to be on aspirin?"

"Just the chewable. The heart guy put me on them."

How long ago? He seemed not to be taking them at all. "A heart guy? For what? How often do you see him?"

"I don't. I never had to go back."

She frowned. "What's his name?"

"Bluebelle. How am I supposed to remember that? I told you I'm fine!" He got up and strode from the room.

Blue stared into the shoebox, trying to quell the panicky feeling poking at her. Why was her dad on heart meds? Why had he had to see a cardiologist and start taking baby aspirin? Was it preventive or because of some cardiac event that he surely wasn't willing to talk about with her? And when was the last time he'd had his liver lab work checked, to make sure he was safe taking the cholesterol med? And where was his arthritis? Where did he hurt, for God's sake? He hadn't said a word about any pain in the nearly two weeks she'd been back.

She opened the dresser drawer he'd been reaching for and put the shoebox back in its place. The room looked untouched from a decade ago. Blue gave the closet door a light push and covered her mouth, her eyes instantly filling with tears. Good Lord. The right side of the closet still held all her mother's things. She stepped inside. Dresses and blouses and pants and skirts lined the wall, and a shoe rack full of dust-covered summer sandals and sneakers beneath them. She buried her face in an armful of her mum's clothes, breathing in. God. They smelled of her. Still. Under the dust and neglect, Ella was still there, the hint of lemons and her flowery perfume. Oh God. Blue knelt, fingers clutching fabric. Boxes labeled with her mum's handwriting were stacked in the corner, holding years of photos, Blue's school art projects, and every single card Ella had ever been given. Her dad hadn't gotten rid of a single thing. She rested her cheek against the pant leg in her hand and closed her eyes.

She found her dad in the kitchen, sorting through papers on the kitchen table. She started to ask about her mother's things, but the words wouldn't budge past the lump in her throat. She'd have to, someday soon. But she couldn't. Not now, not before she'd had her own chance to go back to that closet again and absorb as much as she possibly could of her mum before clearing it all out. "Dad. Let me just help a little with the medications, please?" She joined him at the table. "I know about the prescriptions you take. Can I ask you a couple of things?"

He looked at her and she was stunned to see he was genuinely angry. "I don't need your goddamn help. I didn't after you left and I don't now! Do I look sick to you?" Mitch's loud voice boomed in the small kitchen.

She sat back, flinching against her will. No one had yelled at her in almost three months. She'd almost forgotten how much it unnerved her. "No."

He looked taken aback. "Blue." His tone softened, quiet now. "I'm sorry. I didn't mean to yell."

She sucked in air, letting it out slowly. Her heart was racing. She took another deep breath. This was just her dad expressing frustration. What on earth was wrong with her? He'd made no move toward her, he'd said nothing at all threatening to her. Her pulse finally obeyed and began to slow. She met her father's eyes. "I'm sorry. It's okay, you're right. I'm sorry I overstepped."

"I—" The concern written in his features spoke volumes. "You did nothing wrong. I shouldn't have yelled. I, ah . . ." He rested his forearms on the table and stared at her, his gaze intense. "Bluebelle. Did your husband hit you? I need the truth this time. Is that why you came home?"

She shook her head, looking away. "No, it wasn't like that. I'm okay; I really don't want to talk about it right now. It just shocked me, you yelling, that's all."

She could see he didn't believe her. He pushed aside the stack of papers he was going through and moved on to the next pile. "I was trying to find my last doctor appointment printout. It's in here somewhere. I do go when I have to. I don't want you to worry."

"Okay. I'm glad you're on top of it." She started to stand; Murph would be outside waiting for her to go to the beach.

Mitch stopped her. He reached out and put a light hand on her arm. "I think you're right. It'd be good if you could make sure I'm doing things right. Come with me to my next appointment— we can schedule one. If you don't mind."

"Yes. Yes, please, I'd really like that. It'd make me feel better," she said, smiling. "Thank you."

"Bluebelle. You heard me yell about all kinds of bullshit growing up, and you've never reacted like that. No one should look so God awful frightened over a raised voice. I'm glad you came home. I hope you stay, for Murphy's sake if not for your own. A man doesn't have to use his fists to be a bully. And any man who hits a woman isn't worth the air he breathes. I'd hope—" He paused, chest rising and falling quickly with the rising color in his cheeks. "I'd hope you'd never let anyone hurt you or the boy, Bluebelle. I'll handle your husband if you need help."

She opened her mouth to counter her father's assumptions but didn't know what to say. It was more words strung together at once than she'd ever heard from him before. Her mind raced. She'd told him the truth, in a way. Brent had never hit her. He'd grabbed her, shoved her a couple of times, pinned her down. He'd dislocated her shoulder slamming her against their dining room wall the night they'd argued after she'd brought Murphy back from the ER—but the next day, he'd put the doors back up. When they fought, he always made her feel . . . stupid. Small. Incompetent. But the kind of abuse she saw in movies? The husband smacking the wife across the face, knocking her down? Brent had never treated her like that. She knew the things she'd put up with were wrong. The more time she spent here, the more she could see it. But he wasn't a monster. He was still her husband.

Her dad mistook her silence for agreement. His voice softened. "We'll get through it together. It's the right thing, you don't want Murphy to learn from the wrong kind of man."

"Brent's not what you think. He's—everybody fights, Dad. He was a good stepdad to Murphy." *Until he wasn't*, she thought. She cleared her throat. "We're okay. I have to go, Murphy's waiting; we're going to the beach."

She threw her bag over a shoulder and practically ran through the screen door. The last thing her father said stayed with her, repeating in her head, triggering a mental search of each argument her son had witnessed. When it all piled up and threatened to crush her, she used every bit of her resolve to put it away, just for now, just so she could breathe. She shed her sandals and chased Murphy into the blue water as he splashed at her, his laughter the reprieve she needed.

★   ★   ★

Later that night, Blue put her feet up and leaned back into the lounge chair beside Sierra and Chloe's pool, watching Murphy take turns on the diving board with Chloe's nephew. Sierra returned from inside the house and handed her a bubbly froufrou drink complete with a little pink umbrella spearing a maraschino cherry and a slice of lime.

"It's a cherry lime rickey. To die for, you'll see," Sierra said, sipping her own and taking the chair next to Blue.

She tried it. "Oh. My. God." She rolled her eyes heavenward. "Oh, that's amazing. It's sweet but not too sweet. What's in this?"

"You squeeze a lime into some cherry liquor with a few fresh cherries, shake, then add gin and ice. And then a splash of a lemon lime soda. We just use Sprite. And voilà!" Her friend's bracelets jingled on her wrist with her sweeping flourish.

"Mmm. I feel like I've escaped to some private tropical oasis when I'm here, you know that?" Blue lazily rolled her head on the lounge chair to smile at Sierra. "This is so good. Dinner was so good. Murph is so happy," she said, nodding to the boys in the pool. Chloe's nephew Jeremy was here for the week while Chloe's sister was on an anniversary cruise with her husband.

Jeremy was a year older than Murphy and the two had bonded instantly over video game talk. Chloe was off in Naples helping a laboring horse give birth.

Sierra reached across for Blue's hand and gave it a squeeze. "*I'm* so happy, Blue. You have no idea. You don't know how long I've wished we could do this—hang out, relax, laugh. I love that you're here."

"I do too," she said. She sipped her drink. "Hey, that mailbox in my fairy garden. You're sure you're telling me the truth? It wasn't you guys?" Murphy had already asked them when they'd barely walked in the door, and Sierra and Chloe had seemed truly baffled over what they were even talking about.

Sierra shook her head. "I'd tell you if it was me. I'm thinking it had to be your dad. Or . . ."

"What?"

"Or the only other person who knows you're back?"

"Enzo?" Blue scoffed. "I doubt he even remembers it's there."

"I'm sorry about what happened with him at The Mariner."

Blue sighed. She took another sip of her drink. "I don't want to think about it." She and Sierra had had plenty of time to chat this evening before dinner while the boys were playing. She'd already rehashed her encounter with Enzo at work yesterday followed by the awful meeting today. "Hey."

"Hmm?"

"Your wedding is only three weeks away. Are you super excited?"

Sierra turned to lie on her side, facing Blue and tucking one hand under her cheek. "I am," she said. Her tone matched her gaze, both with a happy, dreamy quality. "I mean, it's just a day. It's basically a formality. I don't need a piece of paper in order to know we'll be together. But it's going to be an amazing party. A celebration. And wait'll you see our gowns. Oh!" She tipped her head back. "They're gorgeous. I could show you a picture."

Blue smiled. She felt all warm and fuzzy inside at Sierra's joyful content. "No. I want to wait. I want to see it in person, on the day, both of you together."

Sierra raised her eyebrows. "So you'll be here?"

"Yes," she affirmed, committing at that moment. It meant she was delaying a decision about going back home to Brent until after the wedding. Three weeks from now. She'd have to deal with him at some point and tell him. But there was no way she could miss this. Sierra had been there for her through everything. "Sierra . . . How did you know? About Chloe. How did you know that she was the one?"

"What do you mean?"

Blue thought. "Was there a moment? Like, one thing, a defining moment when you just knew?"

"Hmm. There are many moments. It's not like bam, a sudden epiphany, a final decision that she's it for me forever. It's a lot of little things, random, unexpected, everyday things. Reasons you keep finding to fall in love and stay in love with each other."

"That's beautiful."

Sierra's brow furrowed, and Blue could feel her trying to see inside her head. "It is," her friend said. "But it's also messy. It's good days mixed with bad ones, wishes and feelings and hurt and healing. It's not perfect. But no matter how I'm feeling about Chloe, even if we're in an argument, I always want to lift her up. I'm happier when she's happy."

◆ 10 ◆

ENZO GRABBED THE PACKAGE of organic semolina flour for homemade pasta from the top shelf of the baking aisle at Gulfside Grocery. He deposited it in the cart and his mother kept moving, pushing the nearly full cart around the corner and stopping to peruse the cookies. Sweets were Sofia Castellari's weakness.

She chose a bag of Pepperidge Farm Milano cookies for herself. "What do you want, Vincenzo? Pick one." She smiled up at him, deeply etched lines at the corners of her eyes crinkling. Enzo's mother was child-sized next to him. At fifty-five, her shiny black hair showed no sign of gray, her floral outfit and red lipstick a constant whether she was out to lunch with Aunt Lorna and their friends or going grocery shopping. She was the face of Castellari and Sons as much as Gino when they were out, and she carried herself as such.

"I'm good, Ma, I don't need anything." But he knew better. She wouldn't let him leave the store without buying him something. He and Salvi took turns accompanying their mother grocery shopping on Wednesdays and Saturdays, and she pushed his brother to pick out something each time too.

"*Ciancia*," she said, followed by a string of Italian he couldn't follow. She frowned at his waistline and waved a hand at the rows of cookies. "I'm paying, don't argue. You need it."

He smiled at her. He at least had to try to protest. He couldn't eat the cookies in his kitchen fast enough to keep up with these shopping trips. He chose plain shortbread this time; they were best with his morning coffee. "Okay? What else?"

"I need a card for Christina. Your brother reminded me about her birthday tomorrow."

Enzo followed her to the card aisle. She'd started wanting them to take her shopping a couple of years ago. He understood. She wore several hats between the business, the house, and her work with the local preschool, and grocery shopping was probably much quicker and easier with her sons helping. Sofia also enjoyed knowing that the town noticed her sons doting on her; she wasn't subtle about that. He didn't mind.

"Did you see the necklace Luca bought Christina?" he asked, knowing he was stirring up drama. It had cost two weeks' salary, and it wasn't what Luca had wanted to get his girlfriend of two years. He'd initially showed Enzo a screenshot of an engagement ring he'd put money down on. Enzo had told him he was too young and it was too soon, and the moment Marcello and Salvi found out, they'd echoed the sentiment. Luca had given in pretty easily. Enzo suspected he'd wanted to make a grand gesture without the grand commitment.

"It's a lovely necklace," his mother said. "He has good taste, just like your father."

"Yeah." Ugh. He'd promised Salvi days ago that he'd talk to their dad, but it was already Wednesday and he still hadn't been able to catch him alone. He resolved to do it after dinner tonight, if he could get him away from the house. Everyone but Luca knew what Gino was up to. There was a sort of unspoken agreement among them to try and shield their baby brother from stuff like this. When the whole Nadine affair had blown up, they'd tried to keep Luca from learning the truth then too. Although now that Enzo was thinking about it, maybe they weren't doing Luca any favors. He was twenty-one, still in school, and wanted to propose to his girlfriend. Maybe it'd be good for him to get a reality check and see what marriage was really like.

His mother gasped, snapping Enzo back to the greeting card section. "Vincenzo," she whispered, hand closing on his forearm.

He followed her gaze and saw Blue and Murphy at the far end of the aisle in pet supplies. Would she even acknowledge him, after their explosive conversation at The Mariner? Her son—no, their son—was weighing his options between packages of cat toys as Blue stacked cans of cat food in the cart. That couldn't be for Hook. That cat couldn't still be around, could he?

"Is that Bluebelle Shea? She's *back*?" Sofia stared up at him. She gripped his arm tighter. "Did you know? Let's go the other way," she said, pulling on him and trying to turn the cart around.

Blue looked in their direction and met his gaze, then made eye contact with his mother. *Shit.* Enzo leaned down, speaking quietly to Sofia. "She just got home. It's all right, Ma. We've talked, everything's okay."

Blue said something to Murphy, and he glanced over at Enzo and his mother. Murphy waved at them, his hand tentatively up in the air.

"Well, now we have to say hello." Sofia's words came out in a hiss. He hadn't seen her so flustered since he didn't know when. The way he'd unraveled after losing Blue all those years ago had affected his mother almost as much as it had him. He knew that now that he was older. She'd been in full panic mode, afraid of what he might do.

It was going to be a major hurdle to get his mother to forgive Bluebelle Shea for breaking his heart. But it had to happen. He was determined to be in Murphy's life. How he and Blue were going to deal with each other was another story. He'd overstepped. He didn't care. The idea of her going back to a man who wanted to divorce her made him see red. He and Sofia met Blue and Murphy halfway up the aisle.

"Mrs. Castellari," Blue said, her voice soft. Her long blonde hair was pulled into a loose, messy bun and she wore khaki shorts with a plain pink T-shirt. "Enzo. Hello. It's so good to see you both."

Beside him, his mother activated her Castellari and Sons public persona. "Bluebelle Shea. You're just as pretty as the last time I saw you. And who's this handsome young man?"

Blue's smile reached all the way to her eyes as she looked at Murphy, and then back to Sofia. "This is Murphy, my son." Her gaze lit briefly on Enzo and then away. "Murphy, this is Mrs. Castellari and her son Enzo. They live just down the road from us. They run Castellari and Sons."

"The signs," Murphy exclaimed. "You have those billboards we always pass. Are those guys all really your sons?" he asked Sofia.

She laughed, a genuine reaction that gave Enzo some relief. "Yes, they are. Do you have any brothers or sisters?"

He shook his head. "Nope. Just me. I always wish I was in a big family, but we just have us and Hook."

Enzo swallowed hard, afraid to make eye contact with Blue.

Sofia spoke. "I don't really know if big families are better than small ones," she said kindly. "I think as long as you're in a good one, that's what matters. Right?"

Murphy shrugged. "I guess so."

"Well, our ice cream's going to melt," she said. "We'll let you get back to shopping."

"Sure," Blue said. "Have a nice afternoon. It was nice seeing you. Ready, Murph?" She put a hand on his shoulder.

"Oh. Nice to meet you." The boy turned to follow Blue, who was already heading back to her abandoned cart. "Wait, Mom. You should ask them," he said.

Blue looked back at him, her eyes wide. "What? Murph, come on," she jerked her head toward their items.

Murphy caught up with her, lowering his voice a little, but it still came through loud and clear where Enzo stood with his mother. "But you said they live right by us. Maybe they've seen something!"

Sofia called to him. "What happened—can we help?" His mother was a sucker for kids. Two minutes ago she'd been ready to bolt and pretend she hadn't seen Blue. Now she was dragging this whole thing out, trying to help this boy she didn't know was her grandson.

Murphy came back over to Sofia and Enzo. "We think someone's been sneaking into our yard. My mom has this fairy village and things keep happening to it, but we haven't seen who's doing it yet."

"My goodness," Sofia said, interest in her tone. "That's terrible! I hope you catch them!"

Murphy shook his head. "No. It isn't bad. Someone left us a note in a new mailbox that's like, fairy-sized. And then one of the houses got painted too, this really bright pink color."

"That is very strange. Someone is breaking into your yard and doing nice things," Sofia mused. "Who would do that?"

"We don't know," Blue said. She joined them. "It's definitely odd. Nothing funny has been going on at your place or anywhere else that you've heard about?"

"No, nothing like that," Sofia said. "I hope you solve the mystery. Blue . . . give my best to your father, please. I hope he's doing well."

She looked surprised. "I will. Thank you so much." She added, "And please give our regards to Mr. Castellari and the rest of your family."

They'd gone through checkout and were in the car on the way home before Sofia brought up Blue. "I don't want you seeing her, Vincenzo. She did enough damage before, I hope you remember that."

He stared at her. Was she kidding? He remembered better than anyone. But ten years had passed since then. He grew more and more angry the rest of the way home, as Sofia chattered about that night's dinner and her ideas for the new sauna she was having installed at the house. He carried in the groceries, held his tongue, and had one foot out the door to head back to the marina when his mother spoke again.

"I'm sorry."

He stopped. He didn't want to fight with his mother.

"I told you we should have avoided her," Sofia said. "I didn't know what to say to her."

"Really? It seemed almost calculated to me. I thought you were better than that." His mother making that last, insincere comment about saying hello to her dad had just felt mean.

"For your information, I was being polite," she said, setting her jaw. She stared back at him.

"Great. Nice that you're being polite to the Sheas *now*. We all know what Mitch Shea's been through. And you don't have any idea what Blue's had to deal with all these years."

"And you do?" Sofia challenged. "How long have you known she was back?"

"Why does it matter? What I don't get is why one minute you're trying to pretend you don't see Bluebelle Shea and the next you're acting like Mary goddamn Poppins, all sweet and smiley and wishing her dad well."

"Don't you swear in my kitchen, Vincenzo. Don't you dare take that tone with me!" His mother unpacked the produce, slamming each item onto the kitchen island as she went. Celery—thunk. "You need to stay away from that girl." Carrots—thunk. "Have you forgotten the way she skipped town without looking back, not even for you?" Onions—thunk. "I'm not happy that you've snuck around behind our backs seeing her again!" Green peppers—thunk. "Your father won't be either."

"I don't care," Enzo said. "And I'm not sneaking anywhere! God, Ma, I've got a fiancée in case you forgot."

"I'm glad you haven't forgotten," Sofia said.

"Why did you lie to me about the night your friendship with the Sheas ended?" *Fuck it.* She was already mad, but so was he.

He had nothing to lose. "Why did you say you saw Pop and Mitch Shea arguing when you weren't even there? What the hell really happened?"

Sofia stared up at him, hands stopped in mid-motion.

"You were out with Aunt Lorna—Salvi remembers. Why did you lie?"

"That was a long time ago, Vincenzo."

"So what? It matters."

Sofia sat down on a stool at the counter. "Because I should have been there. Maybe if I had been, I could've smoothed things over."

"Ma. Come on. You believe the whole falling out was over business?"

She frowned. "Of course. Nothing's more important to your father than family and business. Mr. Shea started the fight, he was always a drinker. You know that. He must've gotten out of hand. I didn't want anyone trying to create drama or make more of it than it was." Sofia folded her arms over her chest, her lips pressed together, her typical signal that the conversation was over.

It made sense, in a weird way, if he looked at it from his mother's point of view. "That's why you went over there the next morning? To try to talk to them? Blue told me what happened."

She nodded. "It didn't do any good—obviously. Please . . . don't let her hurt you again." Her brows furrowed with worry as she stared up at him. "Vincenzo, stop looking for trouble. Your father is a good man, he's built a wonderful life for us. My own father was never around. I've always been thankful, no matter what else, that I was able to give you boys such a great example of what it means to be a family man."

Enzo was in the driveway now, trying to decide if his mother was brainwashed or complicit, lying for and with Gino, when Luca found him. He was the last of them still living at home.

"Zo!" He'd sprinted around from the back of the enormous home. Luca was as tall as his brothers but thinner. They'd each gone through their skinny, lanky phase. Luca wasn't out of his yet. "What was all that? I heard you two from downstairs. Ma sounded super pissed."

"Yeah. It's a long story."

Luca jogged around and got in the passenger side of Enzo's truck, uninvited. Enzo laughed; his baby brother was always able to lighten the mood. "I got all kinds of time," Luca said. "I'm caught up on homework and Pops sent me home today and made Marcello go with Salvi out on the *Abigail* instead of me. I was only ten minutes late, but whatever."

"Typical. We'll take the *Minnow* out. We're under quota on king mackerel and we've got plenty of time till dinner."

Out on the Gulf, Enzo jotted initial course notes in the captain's log, an ingrained, almost automatic task their father had taught them, and then spoke into his end of the two-way radio they used to communicate on the *Minnow*. The commercial fishing boat was one of their largest at sixty-four feet. Like all commercial vessels, it was equipped with an on-board radio for communication with other boats or for distress calls. The Castellaris used the handheld radios to avoid having to shout—it was impossible to coordinate otherwise while Luca was at the helm and Enzo was setting the lines. Once things were running smoothly, Enzo joined Luca and grabbed them each a Coke from the ice box.

"I heard most of your fight with Ma," Luca confessed. "I remember when I was a kid that something happened, everyone was worrying about you. But I was like ten. All of that was over Bluebelle Shea? Was that when she ran away?"

Enzo took a swallow of his soda. "Yeah. We were just seventeen, but I really thought we'd end up together." He was dying to tell someone about Murphy, but Luca couldn't keep a secret to save his life. "But then Blue's mother drowned at the beginning of our senior year and her dad was arrested for it."

"But her dad's still working, he runs Shea Seafood. I've seen it listed as the supplier on the Captain Crab's menu," Luca said.

"Right. He served a manslaughter sentence, he was drunk on their boat the night it happened. You wouldn't remember Mitch Shea's wife, but everyone loved her. I loved her. She was the sweetest lady. People around here can't forgive him for her death."

"You guys don't tell me anything. I didn't know you were going through all of that because you lost Blue, Zo, I'm sorry. I remember her, she was always nice to me. You missed a bunch of school when that happened, right? Ma kept threatening to take you to a shrink. I thought for a long time that if I ever skipped school too many days in a row she'd make me see a psychiatrist too," Luca said. He gave Enzo a sheepish look and laughed. "But why were you yelling at Ma? I'd never get away with that."

"I didn't yell at her," Enzo said.

"Uh, yeah, you did."

He sighed. "She got all phony around Blue today in the market and then had to get a little dig in at Blue's dad—hoping he's doing well and blah blah blah, a bunch of bullshit. It surprised me. We basically control the seafood market on the Gulf Coast, but it wasn't always like that. After Mitch Shea's wife died and he was serving his time, Gino contacted Shea's contract holders and flipped almost all of them."

Luca stared at him, bug-eyed. Ooof. So much for shielding his baby brother from their father's ugly side. "Seriously? He did that?"

Enzo nodded. "Think about the timing. He built his ridiculous mansion the year I graduated high school. The house is money. Our marina and warehouse are even bigger money. We weren't in that kind of shape till Pops starting scooping up contracts."

Luca tipped his Coke all the way back, finishing it. His small gold eyebrow piercing twitched as he frowned at Enzo. "Motherfucking Gino. That's brutal."

★　★　★

Enzo found his opportunity to talk to Gino himself that night after dinner. They tried to get the whole family together on Wednesdays and Sundays for dinner, but the older they all got, the tougher it was. Luca bolted that night right after he'd finished Sofia's delicious risotto, and Marcello left shortly after, griping about reconciling billing statements and revenue. Matty hadn't shown up. Salvi and Gino were deep in conversation at one corner of the long dining table.

"—have a positive effect on profits. If you see an issue, talk to your brother. Marcello's already on board," Gino's voice rose.

Salvi leaned forward on his elbows, glancing at Enzo and then back at their father. "Papa," he said, calling Gino by the title he'd preferred since they were little, "I hear you, but the fleet is already substantial. And I'm not sure about the timing. I heard Marcello saying something the other day about unaccounted-for revenue; sounds like your books aren't up to date or something."

Their father grunted and moved to the refrigerator, taking out three bottled beers. He set them down and opened them, handing one each to his two sons. "That's your brother's department, don't worry about it. Enough business. Let's walk."

Enzo held an arm out for Sofia. "Come on, Ma, it's a beautiful night. Let's go see the sunset."

"You go. Thank you for thinking of me," she said, smiling. "I've got some prep work to do for my class tomorrow." His mother taught preschool three days a week in the village. Their father had pushed her to give it up, but she adored working with the children.

"What did you mean, unaccounted-for revenue?" Enzo spoke under his breath to Salvi as they lagged a few paces behind Gino outside on the wide, stone walkway that led through the rolling estate toward the water.

"Boys. That's enough business for today." Their dad had stopped and was waiting for them to catch up.

When they'd reached the end of their longest dock, their water frontage recessed slightly from their resort neighbors to the north, Enzo stood at the edge while his brother and Gino took a seat on the bench. "We want you to stop seeing the woman in Fort Myers," Enzo said with no preamble. He met his brother's surprised gaze briefly and then fixed his stare back on Gino.

"What?"

"I saw you. A couple of weeks ago. We all know what you're doing, and it's got to stop."

Gino's cheeks flushed a deep red, visible even in the oranges and pinks of the setting sun against the ocean. "You didn't see anything. Do you know how many clients I meet with every week? You saw a client, that's all." His brow was pulled low over his deep set eyes.

"You kiss our clients?" Salvi asked.

"Salvi's seen the photo," Enzo told his father. "Oh, didn't I mention I took a picture of you with her?" He pulled out his phone and began scrolling through his gallery. He didn't have shit, but it didn't matter.

"All right! Son of a bitch." Gino stood and began pacing the end of the dock. "Get rid of that," he said, pointing at Enzo's phone.

Enzo raised an eyebrow. "Uh, not happening. Ma believed you when you promised never again after Nadine. Break it off or we tell her."

Gino shook his head. "Ungrateful assholes. Everything you have comes from me. Your jobs, your homes, your lives, you owe it all to me. What do you know about marriage? Huh? This isn't your business."

"I can get another job," Salvi said. "I don't need you holding my fucking livelihood over my head."

"Y'know," Enzo said, looking at his brother. "That's a good point. There are a ton of jobs up and down the coast. Maybe Shea Seafood needs a good mechanical engineer."

"Son of a bitch!" Gino swung at him, throwing his full weight into it. Enzo moved to one side. Their father's momentum worked against him and he barreled forward and lost his balance, stumbling and then teetering on the edge of the dock. Salvi and Enzo exchanged a split-second glance and both took a step back, away from their father grasping at the air in front him. He disappeared into the water ten feet below.

They moved to the edge. Enzo finally exhaled, relieved, when Gino's head popped up in the roiling surf. He'd never have thrown his own father off the dock, but once it was happening, he couldn't bring himself to stop it.

"He's fine," Salvi muttered. "Maybe it'll wake him up."

A dripping, subdued Gino climbed the ladder a length down the dock and stood, glaring at them.

"We're sorry you fell in," Enzo said. "We're not sorry for wanting you to stop hurting Ma. Do you love that woman? Is she worth ending your marriage for?"

Gino laughed. "Christ, that's what you're worried about? Forget about it. It doesn't mean anything. Your mother doesn't know; no one's getting hurt. Give me your phone." He pointed at Enzo's hand.

"No. I'll delete the photo when you tell your *mistress* it's over. Do it now. Next time I see you with that woman I'm going to Ma with the photo."

"My children don't tell me how to live my life. I'm your father. You're bluffing." He ripped off his sopping wet jacket and threw it down on the planks of the dock. It made a loud, slapping sound.

Goddamn. Their dad was either more bull-headed than Enzo realized or in love with the woman in Fort Myers.

Salvi spoke up. "I'm done. I resign. You might want to get your books together, though, 'cause that's where I'm pointing Ma when she can't wrap her head around you cheating again. What's up with the surplus Marcello caught? Something's going on with the numbers and I'm thinking you're padding expense reports and funneling funds to your girlfriends. Or is it going somewhere else too?"

Enzo turned wide eyes on his brother—what the hell was happening with the books, and what was Marcello doing about it? Salvi spun, striding toward shore.

"Stop," Gino barked. Salvi faced him.

"I wonder how it'll look," Enzo mused. "Gino Castellari's sons going to work for the competition."

"Lemme use your phone," he growled at Salvi. "Your asshole brother won't give me his and mine's gone thanks to you two." He plucked at his wet trousers. Salvi handed over his phone without a word. Gino dialed. The sound of ringing came through the air, loud and clear, before he put it to his ear. "Cheryl? It's Gino, calling you from my son's phone. Hi there to you too, hon."

Enzo and Salvi stood and watched, their arms folded across their chests.

"Listen. We can't see each other anymore." A pause. "I can't. I'm sorry to do it like this." Another longer pause. "Yes. All right. I do too." He hung up and handed the phone to Salvi. "Now you." He nodded at Enzo's phone.

Enzo tapped the screen a few times, deleting the imaginary photo. "I'll be keeping an eye out. I saw what you were doing before, I will again."

"Nice." Gino's tone was hard and his face was still bright red. "I'll be keeping an eye out too. And boys. Vincenzo. That better be the first and last time you threaten me with going to work for Mitch Shea. If I find out you have anything to do with him, I'll make you wish you'd stayed out of this. Don't test me."

CAPTAIN CRAB'S WAS ONE of the oldest establishments in Bliss. With service from breakfast through to the after-bar crowd and a tiki-themed outdoor patio for live bands, the place was Blue's favorite in the village. Almost nothing had changed here in a decade. A girl in shorts and a Captain Crab's tee told her she'd find Dale Bryant in the back, at "his" table.

Being sent home from her shift this morning due to low census wasn't ideal for her paycheck, but her supervisor assured her it only happened a couple of times a year, so Blue had decided to make the most of her unexpected free day. She'd left a voice mail on Dale's cell phone and he returned her call minutes later, agreeing to meet her in town to talk.

"Got us coffees," he said as she sat.

"Thanks. I've been wanting to thank you for watching out for my dad. I know you kept him paid up on everything while he served his sentence. He'd have had nowhere to go if you hadn't done that—I abandoned him." She'd rehearsed what to say, but it still stung, hearing it out loud.

Dale shrugged. "He'd have done the same for me and Lynn."

"Well, even so, I don't know how you did it. Thank you. I . . . uh, I'm hoping to pick your brain a little about the night of the accident, if you don't mind?"

"Listen, I don't really know what I can tell you about your mom's accident that you don't already know. What are you thinking?"

"My dad still insists he wasn't drinking—he hadn't had a drink in two years when that happened."

Dale tipped his head. "Probably tough for him to admit the truth of things."

Blue squelched her kneejerk urge to defend her father. "Well, yeah, that could be. So, was it the Coast Guard that did the Breathalyzer? They got there first that night, right?"

"They arrived first, but I think it was our guys who did the Breathalyzer. It's our stamp on the report. I brought you a copy." He pushed a printout across the table to her from the folder on the table beside him.

She read through it. "The reporting officer was a Coast Guardsman, and then there's another signature." She pointed. "What does that mean?"

He leaned forward, reading upside down. "Looks like Guardsman Ken Franklin administered the Breathalyzer on scene, that's always the first name listed. Then one of us in the sheriff's office signs off on it."

"What about the blood alcohol test from that night?" She might as well play dumb and see what he said.

"No need for one. Breathalyzer results are admissible evidence."

"Oh. So they didn't draw any blood?"

"No. That would've been done at County General on direction of the Guardsman or the detective on scene. We don't have any report on our end of one being done. No results in his file either."

She frowned. "He says they took blood that night. He's never understood why that wasn't mentioned in court."

"He's told me that too. I'd think if there was any validity to it, his lawyer would've addressed it."

She tried to sort through possibilities in her mind. Even if her dad really had been drunk, and she didn't believe he was, how could he have imagined having his blood taken? "There's something else. He saw lights from a vessel nearby that night when he put out the distress call, but no one responded. No one came until the Coast Guard got there. I don't get that—don't boaters have to respond on the water?"

"They do. That's in here, he told that story on scene and again in his statement."

He was getting her hackles up. "You're his friend. You think it's just a story? Like, he made stuff up? Do you think he made up the blood draw too?"

The older man shook his head. "Didn't mean it to sound that way—you gotta understand, he was destroyed. Losing your mother like that. Blamed himself. Kept saying it was his fault, he should've been able to save her. Coast Guard documented no one else in the vicinity. Maybe it was easier for him to think it wasn't all in his control."

She scratched absently at a Sharpie drawing of a surfboard on the table surface, thinking. "Seems like those two things conflict. Either he blamed himself completely, or he blamed a non-responding boater, right? And why would he lie to me about having his blood taken?"

Dale Bryant sat back, silent. He stared at Blue like he was looking through her to ten years ago. He shook his head. "Can't figure a reason for that. I don't know." He finished his coffee.

She felt deflated. "You've spent a lot of time with him through the years, fishing together, helping each other out. Do you really think he was drinking the night my mum died? Do you think he never stopped, even though he said he did?"

Dale propped his elbows on the table. "Bluebelle, I got no way of knowing. He's had a rough run. Losing Ella, losing you, trying to keep his business afloat in this town; he's under constant stress. At least he has you back now. No point digging all this up." He placed a ten on the table and stood to leave.

Grumbling internally at the complete waste of a morning, she made up her mind to attack her dad's dismal kitchen wallpaper so she could at least get things spruced up there. She'd stop at the hardware store on the way home. She heard her name as she was on her way out of the bar.

"Blue! Bluebelle Shea."

She turned to find one of Enzo's brothers leaning on the bar, watching her. She wasn't sure which brother, but he was every bit a Castellari. She raised a hand in a tentative greeting. The man hopped off his stool and came over to her.

"I wondered when I was going to run into you," he said, grinning widely at her. Long, dark hair hung just past his shoulders. He wore a purple and white bowling-style shirt and clashing green shorts with a hibiscus flower pattern. The big dick energy he put off was tangible in spite of his mismatched clothes and neglected hair. She could feel at least three women here watching them. He wasn't one of the youngest brothers, Luca or Matteo, she decided. She took a guess, as he looked close to Enzo's age.

"Hey," she said, smiling tentatively. "Um, sorry. Marcello?"

"What?! God, no, kill me now. It's Matty!" He leaned in and hugged her before she knew it was coming. He stood back, nodding at her. "Goddamn. You look good, girl. It's about time you came back. Can I buy you a drink?"

"It's—" She stopped. She'd been about to say it was eleven in the morning. "No thanks. How are you? How are all of you doing?" Now she noted the grayish circles under his eyes. He looked fatigued and rough around the edges.

"All good. Fishing's fishing. You know." He tipped his drink back, finishing it. Blue had a feeling the clear liquid wasn't water. "Oh man. Enzo lost his shit when he found out you were back."

She raised her eyebrows. So he'd talked to his brothers about her. Did they know yet that Enzo was a dad? She'd loved each of them as if they were family, and she'd always had a soft spot for Matty. "He seems happy."

"He thinks he is," Matty scoffed. "He stays in his lane. He'll be the new Gino. Perfect wife, perfect life, white picket fence, and two point five kids. Running the family business. He's got it all figured out."

The sharp-edged tone behind the nice words lent them an ominous meaning. "That doesn't sound like it's perfect at all," she offered. She couldn't tell if Matty had an issue with Jillian, Enzo, his life, his job, or all of it. If she had to hear one more time about how awesome Enzo's fiancée was, she was going to scream.

Matty set his glass on the bar and picked up the new one the bartender had supplied. "Well, is it? Really? They want the same from me. I'm not doing it. I mean, okay," he said, cocking one thick eyebrow at her. "Don't give me that look. I'm doing it *now*, but not forever. Fishing's a cutthroat business the way our pop does it. I'm fucking out." He tipped the glass back and drained it. "We only get one life."

"You're right." He was, and it needled her. She'd made such a mess of her life. Matty was obviously struggling, lost. He'd been a cute, round-cheeked little kid the last time she'd seen him. Now he was sitting at Captain Crab's drinking at eleven in the morning, dissecting his own existential crisis. And Enzo's. The only other patron at the bar at this hour was the grandfatherly looking man a few stools down, three shot glasses of whiskey lined up in front of him. "Matty," she said, her tone soft. "Are you okay?"

He rested an elbow on the bar, meeting her gaze. "No. Not by a long shot. Are you?"

"No. Not yet. But maybe one day, right?"

He put his head down, locking eyes with her. "Fucking right, girl. We will be." She wanted to believe him. "Hey. How's your dad doing? I don't give a shit what my family thinks, I always liked him and your mom. It's not fair you lost her like that; I still wish—" He fell quiet abruptly, glancing down at the drink in his hand.

"What were you going to say?" She frowned, stepping closer to him. He'd been about to barrel forward but stopped himself—why? "Do you remember that night?"

He pulled his gaze from his drink to meet her eyes. "Everyone remembers that night, Blue. Most of all you, I'm sure." His expression was painted in sadness.

"Yeah."

"I'm so sorry. I never said it then, before you left. I was a stupid, cowardly kid. I'm sorry about your mom." He pressed a hand over his eyes briefly, head down.

Her own eyes stung, her throat thick. "Thank you." Seeing him like this, condolences offered by a man so obviously suffering his own demons, made Blue feel peeled wide open.

"Aw, no. Don't cry. I'm such an asshole for bringing it up." Matty put a hand out and rubbed her upper arm.

Blue shook her head. "It's okay," she said, shocked at her body's constant betrayal. Put her in the vicinity of a Castellari—any Castellari, apparently—and her crying switch flipped itself. She hadn't cried this easily in all the years she was with Brent. He'd left her a voice mail that morning about plans for when she went back to Tallahassee. Of course, her dad was happy she was home, but did she belong here? How was she supposed to know the right thing to do, the best thing to do, for her dad, Murphy, Enzo, Brent? She shouldn't be here, making Enzo's little brother worry about her when he clearly had his own stuff going on. She tried to smile. "You caught me on a bad day, I'm sorry."

He nodded, his expression serious. "Funny. You caught me on a great day. I always hang out drinking before noon in yesterday's clothes."

She laughed. At least he seemed to know this wasn't quite normal. "It's so good seeing you Matty. I've missed you. I've missed all of you. I'd better run."

"Take care of yourself, Blue. We have to. No one'll do it for us."

Blue hugged him impulsively. "Thank you. You do the same, please." She stepped back, looking up at him. "For real, okay? I know how much Enzo and your family love you."

★   ★   ★

She spent the rest of the day scraping wallpaper off the kitchen walls and scrubbing down as much as she could. She'd brought home paint sample cards from the hardware store for them to look through along with a few much-needed kitchen items to help with cleaning and organizing. She spotted the Yellowfin on its way in as she crossed in front of the picture window. It must have been a good day fishing; they were usually home before now. Murph hadn't gone back to Collier County day camp after last week, and she'd been lucky to get a refund for the full two months tuition. Andrea, the program administrator, remembered Blue from high school and had been uncomfortably accommodating when Blue explained that Murphy would be spending time getting to know his grandfather this summer and wouldn't need day camp. The woman's overly solicitous attitude reaffirmed for Blue exactly why she'd avoided trying to connect with any old friends since coming home. Her father's trial was still the biggest thing to ever happen in Bliss. She'd tried hard since she'd been back to avoid situations that would make her the target of anyone's suspicious, judging attitudes, and the pity heaped on her by Andrea made her feel fucked up and small.

She started dinner, the sizzle of the fat from the ground beef disappearing amid the white noise between her ears. She added the sloppy joe sauce, finished cooking the mixture, and set out hamburger buns. The screen door snapped shut. Murph headed to his room, calling behind him about the ibis stealing their bait again. Her dad moved past her to wash his hands at the kitchen sink and grabbed dishes to set the table with. Working with him in the kitchen, in easy, comfortable silence, she was glad she was here now, whether she stayed or not. Mitch was now scheduled for a long-overdue appointment with his doctor, and he had unexpired aspirin in his pill box. Over dinner, the back-and-forth volley between her dad and his grandson about the day on the boat and the sun sinking toward the horizon against a purple sky made her wish she could stay forever. Matty's words had been with her all day. *We only get one life.*

She left the dishes in the sink and went through the screen door to sit on her bench by the fairy garden. The mysteriously painted pink fairy house now had a mysteriously painted blue and green next-door neighbor that had been a dingy brown a couple of days ago. She had a notion to camp out here in a sleeping bag and try to catch the generous fairy-bandit red handed. Hook moseyed over, coming to weave his body around her ankles.

"Hey there, pal," she whispered, scratching around his ears.

She flipped on the switch that used to light the tiny fairy lights through the trees, but nothing happened. The whole thing probably needed to be restrung after all these years. She walked slowly along the trail, careful not to step on the bluebells. They were thriving here. The grove provided protection and shade, the soil cool and rich, even in the summer heat. In the couple of weeks she'd been home, the blooms had multiplied, becoming a beautiful violet border along both sides of the path.

At the last fairy house along the trail, new, bright yellow flowers had been painted on the base of the tree it sat in front of, and there was another brand-new minuscule mailbox, made of what looked like balsa wood. She crouched down. What in the world was going on here? Who would do this—sneak into someone's yard unseen to spruce up a make-believe world?

She carefully opened the mailbox and found another letter. Thrilled, she reached for it but then stopped. She had to wait for Murphy. It was what he'd done for her when he'd first discovered the oddities here. She closed the mailbox with the tip of her finger, leaving the tiny square of paper where it was.

She was on her way back inside when Murphy nearly collided with her, tearing into the kitchen. "He didn't leave yet, did he?"

"Not yet," Mitch said, coming in from the hallway. He held out Murphy's jacket. "It'll be cool on the water."

They were on their way out the door when she made a snap decision. "Wait. I'm coming too." She grabbed her boots and a windbreaker and followed them. Three people on his shrimp boat wouldn't boost his catch any higher than two, but something tugged at her. She needed to be with them.

Shrimping on Florida's southwest coast was starkly different than fishing on a longline vessel out on the open water of the sea. Shrimp were best caught at low tide in the shallow areas around small islands and outcroppings. Blue's dad followed the tide schedule, sometimes leaving the house at an ungodly early hour but more often coming out on the water late, like tonight. Shrimping on top of running the Yellowfin for kingfish and the like was a lot—too much, especially for a one-man show like her dad. Granted, he did have Kai, the fisherman he contracted to skipper the trawler two nights per week, but it wasn't much of a break. Blue figured he'd probably been running at this pace for years.

Mitch slowed the throttle to an idle in gear once they'd found the right spot, about twenty minutes from the house. Shrimping had changed since Blue was away. Her dad explained that regulations on trawling had gotten more stringent, the Florida government restricting specific areas and time frames when it could be done. Blue hung back and watched Murphy help his grandfather with the nets, connecting the bridles and straightening the mesh as much as possible before Mitch began to unspool the steel cable that ran through a winch powered by hydraulics. As the netting was pulled overboard to be suspended from the outriggers, Murph nudged Hook out of the way and Blue lurched forward, seeing the lines strewn over the deck much too close to her son's feet.

"Murph! Get—"

He stepped casually back, glancing at her with annoyance. "I *know.*"

She saw he'd had plenty of time to move. She still wished he'd take care of himself before worrying about the damn cat.

He sat beside her on the narrow bench against the wheelhouse, raising his eyebrows at her. "I bet you don't know who Ted is."

She frowned at him. "No. Another joke for the book? Who's Ted?"

Murphy laughed, making her smile. "Not who, what. Grandpa says all trawling nets have to have TEDs now—turtle expander devices. So sea turtles can't accidentally get caught."

"Really?" He'd learned a whole lot in such a short time.

"Excluder." Mitch set the winch and scooped up the excess lines, winding them into neat loops from his open hand around his elbow and back. "Turtle excluder device."

"Right. Excluder," Murph said. "Yeah, I guess that's different than a turtle getting *expanded*." He giggled.

"I had no idea," Blue said. "That's really cool."

"I'll show you when we bring the nets in," he told her.

Mitch returned to the wheelhouse and their speed picked up almost imperceptibly. It was full dark now. The shrimper was lit only by the red and green sidelights at port and starboard and the trawling lights that shone downward into the water ahead of the nets. Other lights dotted the ocean in the distance around them, no doubt other fishermen doing their thing. It was quiet, the only sounds the hum of the motor and the waves against the hull. Blue leaned back and let her body absorb the motion of the night tide, a gentle, rolling sway she'd never forgotten.

"Mom."

"Hmm?"

"Did you fish like this with Grandpa all the time when you were a kid? Did my grandma go too?"

"Yep. I did, and your Grandma Ella was out here with Grandpa as often as possible too. I think she enjoyed it as much as he does."

He fell quiet. Blue wished more than anything that her mum had gotten to meet her son. Hook ambled over on his seasoned sea legs and turned in a circle, curling himself into a ball between their feet. Blue tipped her head back. The night sky in Bliss held more stars than she'd ever seen anywhere else. "Your Grandma Ella would've loved you like crazy, Murph. For real." She turned and met his gaze; he was watching her. "You are the ocean in one drop."

"Huh?"

"I was thinking about that quote from the fairy garden. I forgot to tell you, we got another letter."

"No way! What did it say?"

"Well, I couldn't read it without you. We'll get it when we get back."

"It's gonna be like, past midnight. Can we really?" He looked so hopeful.

She put an arm loosely around his shoulders. "Absolutely we can. I make the rules now."

His face lit up. "Awesome." She didn't know if he meant awesome that they'd get to creep around the fairy garden in the middle of the night, or awesome that she was in charge for now, but he didn't pull away.

"Anyway. That quote. You are the entire ocean in a drop, or however it went. You are. So am I. It means . . ." She pursed her lips, biting the inside of one cheek. "We contain multitudes. We are more than one thing. How others see us is not necessarily how we have to see ourselves."

◆ 12 ◆

Enzo propped a hand on the cream-colored stucco siding of Matty's house and pounded again on the front door. He didn't have time for this today. Behind him, Jillian cleared her throat.

"Can we please just use the key? Our appointment's in less than an hour." She held the hide-a-key rock out to him.

He groaned. "I really don't want to. He wouldn't do that to me. It's only there for emergencies."

"What would you call this? It's important!"

"Look, it's my fault I forgot about today. Me trying to get my brother to wake up at the crack of dawn and cover for me is not an emergency."

She rolled her eyes. "You know this isn't the crack of dawn." She removed Matty's house key from the secret compartment and thrust it toward him.

Enzo took it, grabbed the rock from her other hand, and put it back in its compartment. He dropped it into the flower garden on his way down the front steps toward the car. "Forget it," he mumbled. He turned back to Jillian. "Come on. I'll call Gino and tell him I'll be in later."

"He'll be mad."

"And?"

Matteo opened the front door. Naked from the waist up, his boxers hung so low he was nearly naked below the waist too. His dark hair fell in tangled knots past his shoulders, and when he raised a hand to shield his eyes from the bright morning sun, gold and green paint was smudged over the tattoo on his forearm. "What?"

Enzo pushed past him. The stench of liquor bled from his pores. Matty's eyes were droopy and bloodshot. At twenty-three, he was second youngest after Luca, but today he could have passed for forty. "Fuck, man. You look like dogshit."

"I love you too. Oh hey, Jillian. 'Sup."

Enzo caught Jillian's look. No wonder she never lost in court. If opposing counsel had to recover from the glare she'd just leveled at his brother, he was sure they'd probably hand the case to her and quit on the spot. "I need you to cover me this morning. Like I've done for you almost every day this week. What's going on with you?"

His brother shrugged. "Nothing. Coffee." He spun and moved toward the hallway and fell into the wall on his right. "Who put that there?" He pushed off and disappeared through the archway into the kitchen.

Enzo joined Jillian back on the porch, pulling the door almost closed behind him. "I can't leave him like this. He's blown off work so much lately it's not funny, and now—you saw him. He's not okay. Something's wrong."

"Oh my God," Jillian said, the words hissed through her teeth. "Something's always wrong. If it's not Matteo it's Luca. Or your mother. Or—" She stopped, locking eyes with him.

"Don't say something you can't take back," Enzo cautioned her. "You want to keep going?"

Jillian's brows rose in surprise. "You know I'm right. Why is it your job to fix everything? Why does everyone in your family always come before me?"

"Hell, Jillian. That's not true." It stung. It was a little bit true. He slid an arm around her waist and pulled her to him. "You come first. You know I always make sure of that," he said, lowering his voice. He kissed the side of her neck.

She sighed, one hand pushing on his chest, but he felt her melt into him. "Stop it. Fight fair."

"Go ahead to the church. I'll be right behind you," he said, loosening his hold. "I swear. I just want to make sure he's all right. I'll take his car and meet you there." He felt a little guilty at how easily he'd just defused her anger. But family was family. Jillian was an only child. She'd never understood his tie to his brothers.

He found Matty sitting on the gray ceramic tile of the kitchen floor with Ghost, his fluffy white cat. He was feeding her one treat at a time from the palm of his hand while she purred up a storm. Enzo pulled items from Matty's nearly empty fridge, thinking on his feet to come up with something. Ten minutes later, he helped his brother to the table and placed coffee and a steaming vegetable and cheese omelet in front of him. He poured himself a coffee and joined him.

Matteo dug in. "Not bad. Thanks."

"You want to tell me why you're drunk on a Friday morning?"

"Technically," his brother pointed a fork at him, talking around a mouthful of omelet, "I'm not. I haven't had anything to drink in hours. This is hungover, not drunk," he said, making a sweeping motion from head to toe with his other hand.

"Why?"

"Why not?" He continued shoveling eggs into his mouth, ignoring Enzo's gaze.

"Okay, you get that every time you blow off work, one of us has to cover for you, right? The old man's starting to notice. You missed the meeting last week too."

"Oh no, do you think he might fire me? If I'm really fucking lucky?"

Enzo stood. "You need to talk to him. Make sure he gets it this time. Tell him you're just not into it." He knew Matty had already tried that.

"Sure. That'll solve everything. Because Gino's not a toxic piece of shit. And he's *all* about individuality and self-expression. You think he's ever even seen any of my stuff?" He pushed long strands of hair off his face, scowling at Enzo. "I'm a goddamned five-year-old finger painting to him. I tried to show him that print I sold to *Vogue*. Know what he said? *'Grow up, anyone can take pretty pictures.'*"

Matty's home reflected his tastes—situated in Naples, a few miles north of Bliss and inland from the coastline, the interior was ultramodern and mostly decorated with his own photos, paintings, and sculpture. Enzo didn't know much about art, but he liked the way Matty's work and home made him feel.

Enzo stood. "What he thinks doesn't matter. You can't keep going like this—avoiding all of us and getting wasted every day."

"Fuck off. It's not every day."

"In the last couple weeks it is. What are you doing? Is it more than just booze? Do we need to worry?"

Matty sat back, glowering at him. "You can get the fuck out, Zo," he said, his voice level. "I don't need this shit. I don't need any of you. Go." He jerked his head toward the doorway.

Enzo leaned in. "Make me. You're off the rails, idiot. I could barely understand you last night. Salvi said you were taking tequila shots with some girl Monday afternoon at Captain Crab's and a different girl Tuesday. That was after you and Luca went on that booze cruise last weekend, remember? *Do* you remember?"

Matty speared the last bite of egg and shoved his chair back, wobbling on his feet at first. "I remember everyfuckingthing, Saint Vincenzo. Everything," he spat the word, his mouth turned down in distaste. He shook his head. "You don't get it. You can go now, you did your good deed." His dish clattered into the sink. He grabbed a beer from the fridge and cracked it open while he shuffled down the hall toward his bedroom.

Enzo watched him, silent. The sun had just come up, and his brother was going to have a drink, take a nap, and wake up this evening and get falling down drunk again. The difference between Matty and Luca was that Luca knew when to stop. And still showed up for school and work the next day. Enzo yanked his phone from his pocket and tapped it to stop the constant buzzing: it was the third text from Jillian.

I'm here, when will you be here?
Just saw the pastor arrive, are you on the way?
Ten minutes Enzo.

Ugh! He went after his brother. Matty was sprawled face down on rumpled sheets, his arm flung across a naked, snoring redhead. No doubt a different girl than the one from Tuesday. He had to deal with this or his brother was going to end up sick or hurt or worse. But he had to get to the church first. He sprinted up the hall, set out fresh food and water for Ghost, who was weaving her way around his ankles purring, and grabbed the keys to Matty's Mustang on his way out.

Enzo sped into the driveway at Jillian's church, his tires squealing. He was three minutes late. He couldn't miss this appointment again. He'd already made Jillian reschedule it twice because of extra shifts he'd had to cover—for Matteo.

He burst into the unfamiliar church vestibule and checked his phone again for her directions. Left and then another left at the end of the hall finally delivered him to the pastor's office. Jillian turned in her chair and smiled at him. She was not pleased. "Hi, sweetheart," he said, leaning in for a quick kiss before focusing on the pastor. "Pastor Steve, I'm sorry I was held up. Vincenzo Castellari."

The pastor stood and offered Enzo his hand across the desk. Between the firm handshake and the man's warm smile, Enzo liked him instantly, though he'd been prepared not to. Premarital counseling sounded like prayer-laced torture, but it was a requirement if they wanted to be married in the Josephson family's church. He knew how important this was to Jillian.

Over the next hour, the pastor outlined what they could expect from the requisite sessions. Four to twelve hours of counseling, at the pastor's discretion, would involve assignments, prayer, and open dialogue to prepare Enzo and Jillian for the *trials and joys of married life*—Pastor Steve's catchphrase. He'd already used it three times in the first twenty minutes. As congenial as the man was, Enzo's eyes glazed over, and he missed a chunk of the conversation until Jillian's words jarred him.

". . . for Vincenzo and me as we start our lives together. What do you think, honey?" She curled her fingers around his forearm, peering into his eyes.

He was lost. "I think you're right. I can't really say it any better."

"Excellent!" Pastor Steve folded his hands under his chin, looking from Enzo to Jillian. "You two are already on the right track. We're starting from a good point. Keep in mind, though, we'll hit some obstacles along the way, which is to be expected in this type of counseling, just as in marriage. The key is to work through them together, right, folks?" He stood, signaling the first meeting was at an end.

"You got it, Pastor," Enzo said, shaking his hand. "Good advice."

"We'll see you next week!" Jillian had an armful of papers and two workbooks. Enzo held the door for her and she turned back as they exited. "Oh! I guess we'll see you before then, won't we?" She looked from the pastor to Enzo.

"Uh."

"For church this Sunday," Jillian prompted.

Church on Sundays on top of marriage counseling each week? "Right! See you Sunday, Pastor Steve." Enzo doubted his own words as he spoke them. His idea of church on Sunday mornings was solo fishing out on the *Mona Lisa*. He always felt renewed when he came back. Was he going to have to give that up now?

"I know it's a lot," Jillian said when they'd reached their separate cars. "But it's short term, and it'll be worth it." She slid her arms around his waist and kissed him.

He nodded. Church every Sunday was short term or counseling was short term? He started to ask but thought better of it. An
hour ago she'd accused him of never putting her needs first. Now
was his chance. He held her to him and kissed her back. "It's all
good. I don't mind." He felt her smile under his lips.

"That's exactly what I wanted to hear. You're perfect. All
right, I've got court at noon. Gotta run. Are we still meeting for
dinner tonight?" She stepped back, smoothing her black pencil
skirt and straightening the seams.

"Yeah, we've got reservations. Should I pick you up?"

"Maybe. In that?" Jillian raised an eyebrow at Matty's red
Mustang.

He laughed. He already missed his truck. Jillian had picked
him up that morning. "I doubt it. He'll be looking for it when
he sobers up."

She made a pouty face. "Maybe he won't notice." She got
into her Lexus. "I'll just meet you at the restaurant. See you
tonight. Love you, Babe!" She blew him a kiss as she pulled
away.

★   ★   ★

Enzo spied Salvi heading into the warehouse as he arrived on the
Castellari marina lot. He ducked in after him rather than walking
through the office where their father was probably going over
sales with Marcello. "Hey!"

"Oh, man." Salvi looked him up and down. "What are you
wearing? Where were you? Pop's head's about to explode, we
were supposed to be on the water hours ago."

He looked down at his gray dress pants. Shit. "I know, I'm
sorry. I had a thing with Jillian I forgot about. I tried to get
Matty—ah, never mind. I'll tell you later. Let's go, before he sees
the car." He stopped at his locker and traded his nice clothes for
cargo shorts and a T-shirt and the cap he'd started wearing since
Jillian told him about the incidence of skin cancer in fishermen.

He and Salvi were in the channel on the longliner less than ten minutes later.

They caught their kingfish quota in the first three hours out. Some days were like that, and others they'd hit all the hotspots and come back with a bunch of grouper and not much else. Salvi handled the lines on deck while Enzo set their course home in the wheelhouse and jotted today's course coordinates in the captain's log. The radio overhead to his left crackled and he turned the knob, lowering the volume. The radio stayed on all the time; it was a safety thing. But the static got annoying.

Salvi spoke up behind him. "So why do you have Matty's car? What's up with him?"

Enzo groaned, casting a glance over his shoulder at Salvi. "I tried to get him to cover for me this morning. Y'know, like the dozens of times we've done it for him lately. He's got a problem. I mean, I guess I already knew that. I haven't seen him sober in days."

"I didn't want to be the one to say it. I know he's worse lately for some reason. You really think he's in trouble?"

"He was an asshole this morning. Hey. Who was he drinking tequila shots with when you saw him at Captain Crab's on Monday?"

"Kelsey, from the post office. They were both pretty far gone," Salvi said.

Enzo faced him. "Luca said last weekend that Matty went home from that party boat bash with—" He snapped his fingers, trying to remember. "Whatshername, his ex before Robyn. Um. Short blond hair, the bank teller from Bonita Springs."

"Teri, I think?"

"Oh, right, Teri. And the naked redhead in his bed this morning wasn't Teri or Kelsey."

Salvi laughed. "I get your point, but shit. Who doesn't wanna live like Matty?"

Enzo shook his head. "It's getting old. He's not right."

"I know. Maybe we all need to go talk to him. Before Pop rips him a new one for slacking. Before he pisses off the wrong ex or crashes his car or—"

"Wait." Enzo turned the knob on the radio. "I thought I heard something."

"What?"

"Just—" He frowned at the radio. Now there was nothing but static.

"I hear junk all day long. This channel's not coming in, go to a different one." Salvi reached over but Enzo stopped him.

"Hold on." He adjusted the squelch, quieting the sporadic fuzz sounds. "I swear I heard the word shamrock."

"*Shamrock*," Salvi repeated. "Isn't that Mitch Shea's boat?"

The radio crackled to life and they both heard it clearly now. "*Need help, we're on Shea's Shamrock, SOS, somebody help, over.*"

Enzo grabbed the handheld microphone. "We read you, we can help." He let go of the talk button. "That's not Mitch. Or Blue." He spoke again into the mic. "Murphy Shea. Is that you?"

"Yes! My—" The radio cut out and then crackled with more static. "—the deck. He's not moving."

Enzo stared at Salvi. "Oh fuck." He pressed to talk. "All right, we're on the way. Your mom's not with you? You're alone?"

"My grandpa's here, but he can't—" The radio cut out, but this time there was no static.

"It's okay. Before anything else, I'm going to tell you how to send up a distress flare. Did your grandpa ever show you where he keeps the flares?"

"I did that," the boy's response came through. "There's a bunch of orange smoke above us now."

"Smart boy," Enzo praised. "That was quick thinking. Now I need you to look at the screen that's somewhere near the radio you're using. You see the digital readings? They're probably in green or yellow." What were the odds he'd be able to get the location? Had anyone else heard the call? What about the U.S. Coast Guard? He hoped someone would spot the distress signal.

The radio was silent. Enzo's pulse thumped hard in his throat. Finally, the boy's voice came through again. "—flashing. There's all kinds of lines and numbers and stuff."

"All right. You're going to look for coordinates. They'll be along one side or else across the top somewhere. Look for two sets of numbers that have two letters in front of them. Like NW or SE and then some numbers. Do you see that anywhere?"

"No. Where again? I don't see it!"

"No worries. Listen, Murphy, are there buttons or dials or anything near the screen?"

"No, there's nothing like that! It's just the water and the bottom depths like he showed me—" The boy's voice was finally coming through clearly thanks to Salvi tweaking the radio's squelch and amplifier. "Wait! Maybe this is it?"

"I'll bet it is. Read them to me." His son read the coordinates for his location and Enzo repeated them as Salvi entered the destination into the *Minnow*'s Nav system and began the turnabout. "You did great. We're on the way. Tell me again what's going on with your grandpa."

"He was getting a kingfish off the hook and he bent over but then he couldn't stand up again. He—"

Enzo had a feeling the silence was Murphy trying to collect himself. His son's voice kept breaking, gripping Enzo's heart in the process. "Murphy, it'll be okay. You're doing everything right, I promise." He swayed as the *Minnow* completed its turn.

"Hang on," Salvi said. He gripped the bar overhead and Enzo hooked an arm through the railing on the left wall of the wheelhouse as the brothers were pulled backward with the vessel's acceleration toward full throttle.

"Murphy?" He raised his voice over the engine. "Are you with me?"

"I need my mom." His voice was almost too quiet to hear.

"I know you do," Enzo spoke into the mic. "It'll be all right. We'll get ahold of her. Where is your grandpa right now?"

"He's on the deck right here by me. He passed out, I think. I—I think he's breathing, but I don't know," Murphy said, his voice hitching. "He might be dead. I don't know what I can . . ." The words were muffled at the end. He'd left the mic button pressed; they heard his frightened sobs.

He looked at Salvi helplessly. The boy's distress was twisting a knot in Enzo's stomach; he was just a little kid. "What can we do?"

"We could put out our own distress call, but I'm worried we'll lose him if we do," Salvi said. "We aren't far. Keep talking to him. It helps."

Enzo waited until the speaker fell quiet. "Hey, Murph," he said, keeping his tone calm. "Listen. I'll bet you can see your grandpa's chest moving if you watch."

"What are you doing?" Salvi asked him when the mic was off. "You're gonna really freak him out if Shea's dead!"

Enzo shook his head. "He's already freaked out. If it's the old man's heart and he's not dead yet, he will be by the time we get there. I've got to get Murphy to try and help him." All he could think of was Blue. Not Mitch Shea, and not even his poor, distraught son. Blue finding out her dad was dead filled Enzo's head and he squeezed his eyes shut. It'd tear her apart. "Murphy? You there?"

"He's breathing! I think he's breathing, it looks like his chest is going up and down. Hook is sitting on him." He'd stopped crying.

"The cat? Is sitting *on* your grandpa?"

"He's on his legs. I think he's worried about him."

"I'm sure he is." Enzo smiled in spite of himself at the visual. "Hey, Murphy, can you put the mic down for a minute and go find a life jacket or cushion? You're going to put it under your grandpa's feet to get his legs elevated a little. Hook will probably have to move."

"What the hell do you think happened?" Salvi wondered while they waited for Murphy. "Does he have a heart problem?"

"I know as much as you do," Enzo said. He was not going to get into another argument now about whether he'd been talking with Blue. He hadn't, unfortunately. But he couldn't keep the biggest secret he'd ever had any longer. "Except—" He double-checked to make sure his thumb was off the mic button. "Salvi, you were right. Murphy is my son."

"What!" Salvi's eyes grew huge and he hit him in the chest, catching him off guard.

"I've only known for a few days." He couldn't keep the smile off his face, as wrong as it felt at the moment. "Murph doesn't know yet, Blue's going to tell him."

"Holy shit. You're a dad." He grabbed Enzo's hand and yanked him in for a hug. "Congratulations, man! I totally called it." Salvi smiled smugly.

The radio crackled to life again with Murphy's voice.

"I got two cushions and propped up his feet and legs with them. I put my hand on his chest and he's breathing. And I checked his pockets to see if he has any medicine he's supposed to take, but there isn't any."

"Well, damn. Nice work, Murph," Enzo said. "Listen, we see you. We're a ways out but I see the Yellowfin. Hang in there. I need you to do one more thing, all right?"

"Yes."

"I want you to put the mic down and just go sit on deck with your grandpa. Talk to him."

"I—he's not gonna—"

"He'll hear you. Your mom would tell you the same thing. He needs to hear your voice, Murphy. Just talk to him. About school, your friends, your mom, the cat. Anything you want."

"Okay," he said.

When the radio went quiet again, Enzo dropped his mic and sprinted all the way back to the stern. He yanked open the compartment that held the defibrillator and grabbed the heavy case, collecting rope and flares on his way back to the wheelhouse. He stared at Salvi. "Anything?"

"All quiet. He must be doing what you told him." Salvi was looking at him as if he'd never seen him before. "How'd you know what to say to him? I would've fucked that all up. You got like instant dad genes or something?"

"Nah. I just tried to remember what Aunt Lorna did when Uncle Ray had his heart attack. I can't really think of what else could be wrong, can you?"

Salvi frowned. "No." He slowed the vessel as they approached Blue's father's boat. "But . . . well shit, Zo. You know how fast the ambulance came for Uncle Ray and it didn't matter. We don't even know how long the kid was calling for help before we heard him. If it's Mitch Shea's heart, this is really bad."

"I know. Get me as close as you can. I'm jumping."

As they maneuvered and aligned as well as possible with the smaller boat, the scene on the starboard deck came into view: Murphy sat beside his grandfather, holding his hand and talking to him. Mitch Shea lay sprawled on his back, lifeless.

♦ 13 ♦

Enzo leaped. He was aboard Shea's *Shamrock* before he could stop to worry about getting there. From the *Minnow*, Salvi shouted at him about all the fishermen who'd been crushed to death in the process of changing boats on the water, whether using a rope ladder or a gangway or simply leaping off the bottom rung of the boarding ladder as Enzo had.

"Throw it!" he yelled back, pointing to the defibrillator. Salvi shut up and heaved it, the weight of the thing nearly knocking Enzo off his feet. He moved to where his son was huddled over Mitch Shea.

The boy met his gaze with wide, panicked eyes. He opened his mouth to speak but nothing came out. Enzo placed a hand gently on his shoulder. "Murphy. You did great. I'm Enzo." He bent and put his ear near Mitch Shea's face, praying he'd feel him breathing.

"Mom's friend Enzo," Murphy said.

Enzo glanced sharply at him, an odd pang hitting him in the gut. *No. Your dad, who never even knew you existed until last week. Your dad who's missed out on every moment of your nine years and doesn't want to miss another second. That's who I am.*

He shook it off, shoving his hurt to the back of his mind to be dealt with later. "Yes, your mom's friend Enzo." He turned his head, finally feeling the man's breath on his cheek, thank God.

"Can you help him?"

He nodded. "Yep. Okay," he muttered, grabbing for the quick reference card in the defibrillator box. He scanned the instructions. "For no breathing . . . for no pulse . . . um." He was in way over his head here. How to find the pulse. Looking at the diagram, he slid two fingers down from the man's jawline onto his neck through his beard. Nothing. He went through the same motion again, still not feeling a pulse. "Fuck. Sorry," he said to Murphy. "Fuck. What do I—"

"This part," Murphy leaned over him and pointed at the series of images on the reference card. "I think we put those sticky things on him like it shows."

Enzo read from the card, struggling to stop his hands from shaking. He had to get this right. "To analyze heart rhythm, place pads as shown over bare skin, do not touch recipient, and press red analyze button on defibrillator." Goddamn. His kid was cooler under pressure than he was. He struggled to get Mitch Shea's shirt open and placed the pads at his chest and ribcage. He was the last person who should be doing this. If Shea came to right now he'd be pissed or embarrassed or both to find Enzo trying to help him. "Okay, you have to let go of him for a sec," he told Murphy. He grabbed Hook and swept the hissing cat away from the man's side. He pressed the red button.

The machine whined and then blipped steadily as a computerized voice announced *Normal sinus rhythm detected. Do not shock.*

Relief washed over him. Enzo covered his face with one shaking hand. He gulped air, raking his fingers back through his hair. All right. "All right, Murphy," he said, looking at him. "That's good. I think that's probably really good. Let's get him to the hospital. My brother's going to follow and keep working on getting us help on the way."

Murphy nodded. "Okay." He reached for his grandfather's hand but stopped. "Can I touch him?"

Enzo removed the leads, closed the case, and hastily pulled Mitch Shea's shirt closed. "Give his hand a good squeeze. You keep talking to him."

In less than ten minutes, the Coast Guard bore down on them like knights on white horses. Enzo had never been so happy to see anyone in his life. The bullhorn came out and one of the Guardsmen issued instructions to them, and then two medics boarded Shea's *Shamrock* and took over. Enzo stood out of the way at the helm, gently guiding Murphy to stand by him. When the first medic set his kit down and knelt on deck, Hook stood up from where he'd maintained his vigil at Mitch Shea's hip, his back arched and hackles raised as he hissed and growled. The medic attempted to shoulder the big cat out of the way as he leaned over Blue's father, and the animal launched itself at his arm, claws digging into the man's uniform shirt. Bright red dots of blood appeared on the white sleeve and he reflexively jerked his arm, sending Hook skittering across the deck. The cat regained his footing and started back toward the medic, undeterred.

"No!" Murphy darted over and grabbed the cat, scooping him up and squeezing him tightly against his chest.

Enzo pulled Murphy and Hook back toward the helm and grabbed a towel, wrapping it securely around the cat in the boy's arms. "Hold him tight. Damn." Enzo raised his eyebrows at the boy. "Better than an attack dog, huh? But he likes you, doesn't he?"

Murphy nodded. "Yeah, he loves me." He sat and rested his chin against the seat back, watching the scene on the deck.

"Did you have any pets where you came from?" He had to get his son—*his son*—talking. Distracted. Mitch Shea's skin was a sickly shade of gray. Enzo didn't want what was going on twenty feet from them to be Murphy's last memory of his grandfather—needles poking into the old man's neck, IV lines, a respirator mask covering his face, scary words like *cyanotic* and *thready pulse* spoken in low tones among the medics.

"I wasn't allowed to have a pet."

Enzo guessed that was due to his dick of a stepfather and not his mom. Granted, he knew nothing about Blue's husband, but he was certain the man was a douche. Anyone who'd let Blue go was an idiot. Including himself.

"I wasn't allowed to have a pet either," he told his son. "But the minute I got my own place, I went to the shelter up in Bonita Springs and adopted a dog."

It worked. The boy tore his gaze away from the medics bent over his grandfather's body and looked at Enzo. "A puppy?"

"Nah. Puppies are cute and everything, but this guy," Enzo said, pulling his phone from his pocket and turning it to show Murphy, "picked me right away. He was almost a year old then. He wouldn't stop whining and pawing at his cage door until I came over and scratched his ears. His name's Moon."

"You're so lucky! Mom still says we don't have time for a dog." He pointed at the picture. "Why's he eating your shoe?"

Enzo swiped through the plethora of photos of his dog. "'Cause he got mad that I wouldn't give him more treats. He's smart. And bad sometimes." He showed him a few more. "Moon's my favorite camera subject. I've got a few of him like five feet off the ground catching a frisbee. Oh, here's one."

Minutes later, Shea's *Shamrock* approached the large Collier County harbor flanked by the Coast Guard boat and the behemoth Castellari fishing vessel. Mitch Shea was quickly moved off the boat and transferred from a spinal board onto a rolling stretcher and loaded into the back of an ambulance. Murphy let Hook go and took off, running to try and climb into the back of the vehicle with his grandfather. "Murph!" Enzo shouted. He grabbed the unhappy, fighting cat and went after him.

The paramedic inside shut the ambulance doors firmly before Murphy made it. The Coast Guardsman who'd been scratched by Hook shook his head sympathetically at Murphy. "I'm sorry, son. You can't ride with him. But you'll be right behind him. The harbormaster's going to give you two a ride to the hospital."

Enzo got Blue's number from Murphy and tried to call her on the way, but it went straight to voice mail. He didn't know what to say so he hung up, texting her instead with *This is Enzo. Please call me.* And then *Call me right away it's urgent.* He kept his phone in hand until the harbormaster pulled into the circle drive in front of Collier County Hospital. She probably didn't keep her phone on her at work. He ushered a shellshocked-looking Murphy with the cat in his arms through the emergency entrance where Blue's father had just been taken. Fucking hell. Was there any chance at all she might already have clocked out and left? He turned to ask Murphy what time his mom's shift ended, and then he saw her.

Blue stood, stock still, staring down the hall to the treatment rooms. Purple gloves covered her hands, which she held in midair in front of her. Another scrub-clad woman raced past her pushing a red crash cart.

"Mom!"

Blue looked slowly toward them, as if underwater. Murphy shoved the big cat back into Enzo's arms and threw himself at Blue, nearly knocking her down. Enzo wrestled with the growling cat, wrangling the blanket someone had given them more snugly around Hook to calm him. Blue wrapped her son in a tight hug and pressed her cheek against the top of his head.

Enzo ached. Every part him ached to pull the two of them into his arms and comfort them, his son, his family, what it could have—should have—always been. Blue and Murphy and him. She met his gaze, her wide, glistening eyes bright blue against ghost-white skin. She looked as if the only thing keeping her on her feet was Murphy. "I'm so sorry," he said. It was so inadequate. Was her father dead?

✦ 14 ✦

"H E'S IN V-FIB." BLUE stared unblinking at Enzo. He frowned, looking confused, so she said it again. "He's in V-fib. I don't—" She fell quiet as Dr. Jackson came around the corner and sprinted past them, going through the same door the crash cart had disappeared through. She started after him and then stopped, looking down at her gloved hands. She'd jumped into CPR as they rolled him in, replacing the paramedic, and then Char had pulled her away. She stared at her hands, still seeing their purple outline on her father's unmoving chest.

She became aware of Enzo's hand on her elbow, gently moving her to one side in the hallway. "Blue, maybe there's somewhere we could wait?"

She kept an arm around Murphy and led them into a small room across the hall. She shut the door and took Hook from Enzo, setting him on the floor. The cat darted underneath the green vinyl couch Blue perched on. Five minutes ago, she'd been sitting at the nurses' station with her supervisor Char, sipping coffee. Next shift was coming on and things had been slow except for the incoming Coast Guard patient. She looked up at Enzo. "They won't let me in there."

He took a seat and leaned toward her, elbows on knees. "That's okay. You trust them, right? I'm sure they're doing everything they can."

She scowled at him. "Don't. I hate that. That's what we always say. It doesn't—" She cut herself off, feeling Murphy watching her.

"Is he gonna die?" he demanded. "He was fine! He was fishing and he got a big one and he was laughing at my joke! He was okay. I don't get it!"

"Murph." She tried to pull him closer but he jerked away. Blue folded her hands in her lap. "They'll help him, Murph. They will. That's my team. They're good. They'll save him." Oh God, what if she was lying? She'd seen the EKG readout, his blue lips, his purple nailbeds. She'd heard the paramedics. Her dad had failed to respond to everything so far—epi, atropine, amiodarone. Through the window of the family lounge, she saw the cardiothoracic surgeon on call go into her dad's room. It was killing her not to be in there. Char had told her they'd come get her as soon as they could.

Murphy slid off the couch to the floor, putting a hand out to the cat. He drew his knees up to his chest, which made him look even smaller than he was.

"Why are you here?" Blue asked Enzo. It had just occurred to her. How had he even gotten involved in all this? How had Enzo ended up with their son?

He stood. "Oh. I'm sorry. I'll go."

"No," Blue said, suddenly gripped with panic. Which was at least better than the thick dread pressing down on her. He couldn't leave, she needed him here. "No, please, Enzo. Don't go. I meant, how—how did you end up with Murphy? Nobody has told me what happened."

"Salvi and I were on the water and heard Murphy's distress call. He's smart. He kept his cool and got help when your dad collapsed . . ." Enzo's gaze rested on the boy, who'd now curled up on his side under the couch by the cat. "You know, I'm thirsty. I bet we all are. Maybe we can find a vending machine? I could use a soda." He opened his wallet and pulled out a few singles.

Murphy scooted out. "Me too. I can go." He eyed the money.

"Juice or water," Blue told him, a reflex. "You remember where it is, right down the hall. Come right back."

"Okay." He pushed through the door.

"Blue, is there someone you want to call? Maybe, I don't know, should Murphy not be here for all of this? I can take him home and stay with him or whatever you want. I didn't say a word to him, don't worry. I've been waiting for you to."

She knew instantly what he meant. "I was planning to this weekend, Enz, I'm sorry. You're right, he shouldn't be here." She bent at the waist, looking at the traumatized cat, puffed up in the corner. "They both need to go home. Let me call Sierra to wait with me."

"Good idea."

Sierra arrived just as the surgeon exited the treatment room with Maggie and Char. The small family lounge was suddenly very crowded.

"We got his rhythm stabilized." Char spoke first, giving Blue's arm a squeeze. Blue was flooded with momentary relief.

Dr. Nakamura consulted the tablet in his hand and then focused on Blue. He was a slight, soft-spoken man who somehow brought calm to the few frenetic emergency room situations she'd worked with him in. "He's had a STEMI—a heart attack," he said, glancing briefly at Sierra and Enzo. "The echo shows multiple occlusions, he may need four or five grafts. I'll know more once I'm in. He's stable for the moment. I'll have my anesthesiologist go over consent with you, but we need to get started quickly. Blue?" He paused.

Her mind was reeling. Her dad needed heart bypass surgery? "He's got a cardiology appointment next week. His aspirin was expired."

Dr. Nakamura blinked at her. "That wouldn't have mattered," he said. "This was major. It's probably been coming for a while."

"He smokes a lot," Murphy spoke up from the floor in the corner beside the cat. Blue whipped her head around, staring at him. Jesus. She'd forgotten he was in the room, listening to all of this. "All that stuff means it's his heart, right? Is he gonna die?"

"He's going to be okay," Blue told him, her quaking voice betraying her. She moved toward him and he stood up.

"Can we see him?" he asked. "I want to talk to him."

After a brief private chat outside the door with Dr. Nakamura, Blue took Murphy across the hall. Maggie stopped them before opening the door. "Hey, Murphy. Your grandpa has a lot of tubes and wires on him. They might seem scary but they're all to help him. He won't be able to talk to you, he's asleep; but he can hear you. I promise. Okay?"

The boy nodded silently.

Even with Maggie's preparations, even with Blue's years of experience as a nurse, she wasn't prepared to see her father this way. He looked like a bad imitation of himself, the ruddiness gone from his cheeks, his normally robust form somehow slighter now beneath the starched white sheet. She put a firm hand on Murphy's shoulder and he let her keep it there. She slipped her other hand underneath her dad's and wrapped her fingers around his. "Dad, Murphy and I are here."

Murphy looked up at her, and she nodded encouragingly. He stepped closer. "Grandpa, please get better. You—" He swallowed hard and tears rolled down his cheeks. "I never had a grandpa before. I need you. Mom missed you a lot, and Hook is really old, he might die without you. Please get better. And"—he put a hand on Mitch Shea's arm—"I'm sorry I said you were crabby when we first got here. Sometimes I get crabby too. I love you, Grandpa."

Blue hugged her son and kissed the top of his head. "He hears you."

Murph sniffled. "I'm done, it can be your turn."

"Dad, we love you. I just got you back," she whispered. "You can't leave us now." She leaned in and kissed his cheek.

The anesthesiologist poked his head in the door. "Sorry, these are ready for you to sign."

When they'd taken Mitch upstairs, Blue collapsed onto the vinyl couch. Sierra pulled her into a hug. "I'm so sorry, honey. What can I do? Are you starving? What about you, mister?" She turned her stare on Murphy.

"He needs to go home. It's going to be a long night," Blue said. She was already exhausted, and she knew this surgery would take at least five hours or more.

Enzo cleared his throat from where he was leaning by the door. He had already texted Luca and asked him to pick up Moon from his house. He didn't know how long he'd be needed, and his dog would be watching out the window for him by now. "I can take them," he told Blue. "We can grab burgers on the way. I think that guy's had enough of this place too," he said, pointing at the cat, who was now curled into a ball with his face tucked under the boy's knee.

"Where am I going?" Murph asked. "Grandpa's? I don't want to be there without you," he told his mom. "Can't I go to Sierra and Chloe's? Please?" He swiped at his eyes, fresh tears starting.

"Of course!" Sierra moved to the corner and knelt down in front of him in a swoosh of fluttery orange and yellow fabric. "You poor thing. Come on." She held a hand out, and Murphy gathered up Hook and the blanket and stood.

"Thank you," Blue hugged Sierra tightly, and then Murphy and Hook together. The cat squirmed but didn't even bother to growl. "I'll let you know as soon as he's out of surgery. Even if it's late, okay?"

He nodded. His expression, the circles under his damp eyes, took Blue instantly back to the first time Brent had shoved her in front of him. He'd been six. He looked just as young and afraid now. She'd do anything to never see this look on his face again. Blue cupped his cheeks in her hands, locking eyes with him. "Listen to me. Your grandpa is one tough guy. You don't single-handedly run a fishing business and reel in eighty-pound kingfish if you aren't a badass. Right?"

Her son's eyes widened at the curse word. "Yeah."

"He will be okay. I really believe that. You have to too, Murph. He's not going anywhere."

The family lounge, full a few minutes ago, now felt stifling even though everyone was gone except Enzo. He hadn't moved from his position holding up the wall. He looked tired, rough around the edges; she had a pang of guilt for hoping he wouldn't leave.

Blue pulled the door open. "I can't stay in here. I need to do something and there's nothing I can do." She started down the hall, just needing to get out of that little room.

Enzo walked with her down the long hallway to another hallway and another, matching her pace, quiet. After a while, near the outpatient rehab wing, he stopped. "Um. Blue?"

She stopped and looked up at him. "Enzo. I'm so sorry. You probably need to go. I'm—"

"No, I don't. I've got nowhere to be. Unless you want to be alone? I can leave. It's up to you."

"I want you to stay. Please," she said. "I know you've already done so much. You saved his life."

"I just helped. Murphy kept it together and got us there," he said. "You're raising a seriously great kid."

His kid. His son, who had no clue this man was his father despite Enzo coming to his rescue, saving the two most important people in her life. She covered her face with shaking hands. "I'm screwing it all up."

Enzo closed the space between them and pulled her into him. He wrapped his arms around her, cradling her against his chest.

"You're not. You're doing amazing," he said, his voice quiet and deep. He held her, and she gradually relaxed, breathing easier, leaning into him.

She turned her face into his neck, closing her eyes, and hugged him back. Her hand brushed over the hot, smooth skin at the back of his neck, and she slid her fingers into his hair. Like she'd waited forever to do when she was fifteen, like she'd done so many times after that. His breathing quickened with hers. His strong arms around her tightened as she felt his arousal against her and she pressed her lips to his neck without any conscious thought. He tasted of sweat and citrus.

Voices carried from around the corner and Enzo let go, stepping back. Blue covered her lips with her fingertips, her eyes wide. What had she done? What was wrong with her? "Oh God. I'm sorry," she whispered.

★   ★   ★

Enzo's heartbeat thrummed in his throat, the air between them charged. He'd pulled back, but he couldn't break the spell, couldn't look away. The hair at her temples was pulling loose from her ponytail, tiny ringlets and wispy strands giving her a disheveled look. Smudges of dark mascara marked the skin around her eyes. The shoulder of her scrub top was damp with their son's tears from when she'd hugged him. Something stirred deep inside him, making his pulse quicken and his mouth dry. He had the oddest sensation, looking into her eyes, of time unspooling, his world tilting. He couldn't stop it.

Enzo turned away, head down, head down, as a pair of doctors passed them in the hall. When they'd gone, he met Blue's gaze. "Can we go outside? Where—I need some air." He had to get out of here.

"Yes. Right up here." She led him through a set of double doors to a large, flower-filled courtyard that opened out to the parking lot.

He sat on the opposite end of the bench from her. She turned to face him, leaving the three-foot void between them. "If you want to leave now, I don't blame you. Maybe you should."

Their fight at The Mariner seemed insignificant now, but there was so much unsaid between them. "I don't want to leave. I think . . ." He leaned back, running a hand across the top of his head. "This is a really confusing time. For both of us."

She nodded. "That's true."

"I don't know what the hell I'm doing," he admitted, his voice quiet. "When you left, it was like there was this crater. A hollowed-out space in me." He pressed his open palm flat against his chest. "You were my person."

"You were my person too, Enz."

"I don't think that ever really healed. Or closed. Or went away." He looked up at the blue sky, dropping his hand. "I thought I was okay until I saw you in the ER that day."

"Me too. I should have come home. I should have known my dad didn't mean what he said. And I shouldn't have decided for you that you'd be better off not knowing about Murphy. You deserved to know about him, right from the beginning."

He shook his head. "Those don't get you anywhere, you know. The should haves."

"You sound like Sierra."

"Maybe we have more in common than you think."

"I know you do," Blue said. "You're both still here for me even when I don't deserve it."

"Don't say that." He ached to touch her. Her hand was hooked over the back of the bench just inches away from his own. He couldn't do it, couldn't take the chance of fueling what was still between them. He jumped as his phone rang. "Nobody calls me but my mother." He fumbled it out of his pocket, swiping to answer before checking the screen. "Hello?"

Jillian's voice came through the phone. "Tell me you caught the biggest fish in the Gulf and you're running late and you'll see me in a minute." Her words were clipped, her tone angry.

"Um." He stood, moving away from Blue. Shit! They'd had plans tonight. With everything that'd happened, it was the last thing on his mind. He pulled the phone away from his ear, checking the time. It was 8:25, way past when he was supposed to meet Jillian for dinner at The Mariner. He tapped the screen. She'd texted him six times.

"—believe you think it's okay to just stand me up! I've been sitting here since seven thirty, Enzo," Jillian hissed the words in a stage whisper. "Friday night, prime time slot, surrounded by couples. What the actual fuck?"

"I'm sorry."

"So you're almost here? What was it, Matteo again?"

"It's—ah—I'm at the hospital. Not for me," he added quickly. "Salvi and I answered a distress call on a fishing boat a few hours ago and I had to go—I'm sorry. I'm leaving soon, I can meet you." He knew as he said it that it was a lie. He'd be here as long as Blue needed him.

"Forget it. I'm going home. You could have let me know." Her tone was calmer now. "I've been trying to reach you. You haven't been home at all? What about Moon, should I go let him out?"

Enzo smacked a hand to his forehead, closing his eyes. Nice. He'd been on top of things enough to get Luca to take care of his dog but had completely forgotten about plans with his girlfriend. This was so messed up. "It's okay. He'll be fine, I'll be home soon. Jillian, I'm really sorry. Time got away from me."

"Is the fisherman okay?"

"What?"

"The distress call. Is the guy okay? You're still there, they probably had you make a report about the accident or something?"

"Yeah. I think he'll be okay."

"Well, it's a good thing you were there. I'm going to pay for my drinks and get out of here," Jillian said.

"I'll see you tomorrow," he said. They were going with his family to an orchestra concert his aunt was playing in.

"I'll pick up some flowers for Aunt Lorna. 'Night, Enzo."

"Hey." He lowered his voice, painfully aware Blue could hear everything. "I really am sorry. Love you." He felt like utter shit. He was not this guy.

"Love you too, Babe. Get home soon, get some rest. It sounds like you've had a rough day playing Good Samaritan."

He cringed as the call ended. If only that was all he'd done— helped a fisherman in trouble. When he turned back to face Blue she was gone.

Enzo went to the edge of the courtyard and scanned the parking lot, but he knew better. She would've gone back inside; she wouldn't have taken a chance on the team being unable to find her with updates about Mitch. He wandered through the hospital hallways, taking a few wrong turns before finding his way back to the emergency room, but never located her. Her phone went straight to voice mail. He finally gave up and got an Uber.

He stopped at his parents' house to grab Moon from Luca. His mother handed him a heaping plate of gnocchi while he filled in the holes Salvi had left in the tale of their heroic rescue, making Blue's dad a random tourist who'd had a heart attack while out fishing with his grandson. He just hoped nothing would get back to his father from any of the Coast Guard guys. Though he'd like to think that even Gino would've stepped up and helped Mitch Shea under life-or-death circumstances.

Enzo was back home in bed, nearly asleep, when Blue texted him. He fumbled his phone on the nightstand and dropped it, waking up Moon. "Sorry, bud," he whispered. He grabbed the phone and turned onto his back, kicking one leg outside the bedclothes, hot.

Thank you for saving my dad's life, and probably Murphy's too. Dad is out of surgery and critical but stable. I'm sorry Enzo. For what I did, for all of it.

He typed his reply and hit send before he could second guess himself: *I'm glad to hear about your dad. Don't be sorry. I'm always here for you.*

He waited, but she didn't answer. He remembered their first day of kindergarten together, when Blue had lost her first tooth. Mrs. Jenner had put it in a little pink plastic treasure chest and Blue made him carry it home for her in his pocket so she wouldn't lose it. He remembered their mothers taking them trick or treating when they were six, then going back to his house where their dads were shouting and laughing at the kitchen table over a deck of cards and a few beers. Luca wasn't even born yet. Marcello was crying because he was sick and couldn't go out for candy, and he and Blue had dumped theirs onto the couch next to him and let him pick as many as he wanted. He remembered their first time together, on a blanket in the loft of the boathouse, moonlight streaming in around them, Blue gingerly touching his chest, wrapping her arms loosely around him, and then more tightly, urgently, his lips pressed against her neck. He remembered their last time together, when she'd told him she loved him, and he'd made her promise they'd be together forever. *Always*, she'd whispered. How was he supposed to just put all of that away, all those shared memories, every promise they'd made? He couldn't remember a time when he hadn't loved her. That mattered now that they had a son. He and Blue couldn't be together, but he was determined to be a good father to Murphy. He was an adult now. He could handle his fucked up, confusing emotions if it meant Murphy and Blue stayed in his life.

BLUE TYPED AND DELETED so many text messages back to Enzo she lost count. There was really nothing else to say. She had no excuse. She'd been so upset, and then melting into his arms, his scent and warmth mingled with memories, and she'd forgotten herself. For only a moment, but long enough to cross a line. He'd been right; things were confusing. He was engaged to a gorgeous, intelligent woman who obviously loved him. Blue was still married. And yet every part of her ached to be near him, like a million magnets drawn toward the stars. But it was impossible. There might as well be galaxies between them.

Before she went to bed, she shuffled through the papers from the hospital, setting them on the kitchen counter after she'd reread what the plan was following surgery. Her mind raced with all the scary possible outcomes of her dad's heart attack. Complete recovery? A post-op lung clot? An undetected stroke during his bypass surgery? Another heart attack, or worse?

When she finally drifted off, she dreamed of Enzo. She was in the hospital hallway with him but then she wasn't; they were on the Castellari docks together. She opened her mouth against his neck, her tongue tasting his warm skin, and his hands slid down and picked her up, her legs wrapping tightly around him. His chest was firm against her breasts, and when he bent and kissed her collarbone, she gasped aloud, waking herself up. She turned her face into her pillow, breathing hard. Jesus. Blue stretched out, flinging one leg outside the covers, hot. She willed herself back to sleep, back into the dream.

When she woke again she was crying. Sunlight streamed through the curtains and she turned her back to the window, curling herself around her hurt. She'd been at Enzo and Jillian's wedding. She and Brent were there together, holding hands, surrounded by Enzo's family. Jillian's white silk gown billowed out behind her in the beach breeze. Enzo stared at his bride with the same barely controlled passion in his gaze that he'd fixed Blue with just hours before in the hospital hallway. Tears rolled down her cheeks and Enzo's mother and Aunt Lorna glared at her but she couldn't stop. Blue tried to pull her hand from Brent's grip, but he held on tighter. She'd shouted at him. *Let me go!* She yanked her hand away and her knuckles rapped the wooden headboard, jolting her awake.

Four hours' sleep would have to be enough. Blue carried her steaming coffee out to her father's boathouse where his office was. The building consisted of one large room with a high ceiling and a large boat cradle sitting empty, waiting for the next time one of Mitch Shea's two fishing vessels needed some work. At the end closest to the house was her father's extremely cluttered desk. Three bulletin boards took up the wall above the desk. Blue sat in his chair and stared up, trying to make sense of it. There were pieces of notebook paper with scrawled handwritten notes right alongside official-looking spreadsheets, records of business phone and fax numbers, a listing of restaurants and bars throughout Collier County, some crossed off, some highlighted in yellow or pink. Scattered throughout were random pictures that had nothing to do with fishing.

She smiled at the largest photo, front and center: her and her dad posed with the ninety-seven-pound king mackerel between them that she'd caught the summer she'd turned sixteen. There were so many others . . . her mother holding her as a toddler, Blue's little face covered in chocolate and Ella's head tipped back laughing; Blue at age seven or eight, dressed as a bumblebee for a school play; Ella and Mitch standing in front of the Yellowfin the day they'd bought it; Ella as a girl in the yard at the Killarney house, flanked by the sisters she'd left in Ireland when she and Mitch moved to the states. She'd seen a similar one in the photo album in the house. Blue peered at the photo next to it—Sofia Castellari and Ella in the cockpit of what must be one of Enzo's family's boats, as she didn't recognize it. The camera had caught the women laughing, heads close together, sharing some long-ago moment. A heavy sadness landed on Blue's chest. Her mum and Enzo's mother looked to be best friends, something Ella had probably sorely needed, being away from her sisters. Enzo had filled her in on his mother's version of events that night, an argument over fishing contracts, punches thrown. It didn't explain her mum's limp body in her dad's arms, the hushed tones in their bedroom that night when she'd been put to bed, or her father's extreme reaction, pulling his shotgun on his friends. Was it simply a result of their competition?

Blue untacked the spreadsheet from the bulletin board and grabbed a fresh sheet of paper to use for notes. She opened her father's laptop but had no idea what his password was. She began jotting down names of businesses that seemed to have active contracts with Shea Seafood, glancing now and then back up at the photos. By nine in the morning, she'd come up with a game plan for keeping her father's clients happy. She used the old rotary phone on the desk and dialed her dad's subcontracted fisherman who helped him periodically on the shrimper. Kai picked up on the first ring.

"Hey, Mitch, good morning! What the heck—you're not on the water yet?"

Blue smiled to herself. Her dad was always out on the Gulf by seven or seven thirty, like clockwork. "It's Mitch's daughter, Blue. Good morning Kai, how are you?"

"Oh. Uh, is he okay?"

"My dad had a heart attack yesterday out on the water," Blue said, the words strange on her tongue. "He had to have bypass surgery. He was still in ICU but stable when I left last night. I think he's going to be out of commission for a while. I wondered what your availability is like?" So her plan wasn't the greatest. It'd have to do. She needed a whole lot of help from Kai but could only schedule a little or she'd cut into her dad's profits.

"My day job goes from nine until around four," the young man said. "But I can clear my evenings for a while and handle most of the shrimp runs. Would that help?"

She blew out a long breath, tapping her pencil on the desk. She'd hoped not to have to man the Yellowfin on her own, but it'd have to work. "That would be really great. Thank you."

"Give him my best," Kai said. "Your dad's a good guy. I hope he'll be all right."

"I'm going to see him in a bit. Thanks so much for that," Blue said.

Rita of Rita's Roses was waiting on the porch when Blue emerged from the boat garage. She met Blue halfway across the yard and pulled her into a hug without a word.

"How did you—"

The older woman let go and made a pfft sound, pushing air through her teeth. "There are still a few people around here who care about your father. Your dad's friend Dale called me. How is he?"

Blue repeated what she'd told Kai, adding, "I still can hardly believe this happened." She was warmed, knowing that her dad had a small support system, at least—Kai, Rita, and Dale in his corner. Her hackles being up during coffee with Dale the other day at Captain Crab's had more to do with her aggravation with Bliss as a whole than it did with anything he'd said. "How did Dale find out?"

"That's a tight circle—cops, Coast Guardsmen, medics. One of them must know Dale and your dad are friends and let him know."

"Makes sense. Hey, is his daughter okay? Missy was a couple of years older than me in school. Dale seemed kind of off when she came up in conversation the other day."

Rita pressed her lips together. "I don't know much, other than he and Lynn are raising Missy's son. She's still in and out of rehab. Really, I don't know how I'd look at myself in the mirror if I'd been through what that girl has."

"Oh no. I didn't know any of that. Poor Dale," Blue said. "Poor Missy and her son too. Wow."

Rita stopped as they reached the porch steps, turning to face Blue. "You're right. Living here, it's easy to forget Missy's caught up in the disease. It is a disease," Rita said firmly as they reached the porch. "Maybe folks around here don't see it like that, but she's as much a victim as Jim Arden in some ways, I suppose." She climbed the porch steps and picked up two heavy-looking, stacked casserole dishes she'd left there. "This should take care of dinner the next few nights. I'll bring over more on the weekend, if that's okay with you? I don't mean to overstep."

"Oh my goodness," Blue laughed. "Please, overstep all you want. You're a lifesaver, Rita, thank you." She started to ask who Jim Arden was, but Rita was rattling off reheating directions and finding room in the refrigerator. She filed the name away in her brain to look up or ask Sierra about later. It didn't sound familiar.

Blue moved things around in the refrigerator and got the dishes put away. She offered Rita a cup of coffee, which the woman politely declined, saying she had to hurry and go open the shop. "Oh," she said, stopping in the driveway near her car and digging around in her shoulder bag. "I almost forgot; this is for you."

Blue took the small, tissue paper–wrapped package, touched. "Rita, this isn't necessary. You've already helped out so much. All that food, plus just being there for my dad."

The woman shook her head, smoothing a strand of red hair off her face. "He doesn't need me. Mitch is an island. I'm not in his life out of charity—he's the best guy I know. He's talked about you so much through the years, I'm just glad to finally know you. This," she nodded to the package, "is something we found while cleaning the boat a couple of years ago."

Blue unwrapped the paper to reveal a delicate gold necklace with a small, heart-shaped aquamarine charm she hadn't seen in years. The jewelry instantly blurred and she met Rita's gaze through tear-filled eyes.

"Mitch thought it must've come out of your mother's earring. He said she had a set like that. He didn't know what to do with it, so I saved it. I don't know why. I guess it didn't seem right not to. Anyway, I think that chain is perfect for it, but we can swap it for a different one at my shop if you—"

She grabbed Rita and hugged her tightly, choking back a sob. She'd saved her allowance for weeks for her mum's birthday gift, birthstone earrings in the shape of hearts. She'd been short—a lot—and her dad had covered the rest. The idea that one had now come back to her . . . she finally let go, stepping back and blinking at Rita.

The older woman's face crumpled into a worried smile. "I didn't mean to upset you."

"You didn't. Rita, thank you. I bought those earrings for her when I was nine or ten. This is just—" She swallowed around the lump in her throat, smiling.

"You're very welcome." She opened her car door, climbing in. "Blue, will you tell your father I'll be there after work today? And tell him I . . . uh . . . just tell him I'll be there."

"I will. I promise."

★ ★ ★

She was almost to the hospital when Murphy called. She was wearing her navy blue skirt and jacket she'd pulled from the bottom of her yet to be unpacked suitcase. She'd located the decades-old clothes iron in her dad's laundry room and gotten most of the wrinkles out; she wanted to look professional for the task after this. She hoped to find her dad awake and maybe even transferred to a step-down unit. Last night he'd gone straight from post-op to ICU.

"Hey, Murph," she answered, making the right turn into the parking lot.

"How's Grandpa?"

"I'm pulling in now and I'll text you with an update once I'm with him. I'm coming to pick you up in an hour or two." She had to tell him about Enzo. Today. She'd let too much time slip by already.

"Actually . . . could you just get me later? Or tomorrow? Sierra and Chloe are taking Jeremy to the drum circle tonight and I really want to go."

"*I* want to go!" She hadn't been yet since coming home, but she'd been promising Murphy they'd get to one soon. Bliss Beach drum circle had been going on every Saturday night since forever; other beaches and communities held them too, but the one here was the best. It was an informal gathering at dusk that started with a handful of folks with their own drums in a wide circle, and always turned into a large-scale event with the sounds of dozens of synchronous drumbeats providing their unique music for a constantly rotating crowd of locals and tourists in the center of the circle, dancing, juggling fire, hula-hooping, celebrating the sea air and the night.

Blue promised Murph she'd find him there and warned that he'd better stay close to Sierra and Chloe. She cut through the emergency room to say hello to the coworkers she'd grown to like in just a few short weeks. She didn't see Maggie, but her boss Char stopped to tell her she hoped Mitch would have a smooth recovery. Up on the third floor, she found him in the cardiac stepdown unit.

She took his hand and his eyes drifted open. He stared at her groggily, and her nurse brain ticked off every drug that was likely coursing through his veins. Not to mention the after-effects of anesthesia from his five-hour bypass surgery, which would take another forty-eight hours or so to fully clear his system. He blinked and his eyes stayed closed. "Hi, Dad," Blue said softly.

His eyebrows went up and he opened his eyes again, meeting hers. He was silent, and for a moment the post-op possibilities she'd worried about last night stopped her own heart. But then he squeezed her hand, his skin weathered and rough on hers. "Bluebelle."

"How are you feeling?"

"Bit rough. I've been worse." Her father's Irish accent was thicker than usual, his words drawn out and his voice hoarse.

She sat on the edge of the hospital bed and placed a small photo in his free hand. Brent had snapped it last year of her and Murphy at his company picnic. She'd been happy that day. It was fleeting, but she liked to think of herself as the woman in the photo. She'd like her dad to as well. "I thought you might want to keep this while you're here."

Her dad studied it. "Cripes. Bluebelle Bryna Shea. You look so much like your mum here. Did y'know she let me choose your middle name?"

"I didn't know that."

"I knew you'd be," he murmured, not making sense. His gaze slid to the rolling table near the bed and his untouched breakfast tray. "Is there Jell-O?"

"Hmm." She lifted the cover. "Ah ha. Jell-O, broth, apple juice. Yum." She opened the little plastic cup of lime Jell-O and stuck a spoon in it. "Should I sit you up a little?"

When Mitch was in a comfortable position, he took it from her. He closed his eyes with the first bite, cringing as he swallowed. He put a hand at his throat and set the Jell-O down.

"It's because of the tube they had to put in to breathe for you," Blue said, grimacing in empathy. "It'll get better. Look, see this little red button? All you have to do is push it and you get a dose of morphine." She held up the patient-controlled analgesia button connected by a cord to the pain pump.

"Really?" He picked it up and pressed it. "I think our Murphy saved my life."

She nodded. "I think so too. With some help from Enzo Castellari and his brother."

"I like this," Mitch mumbled, pressing the red button again.

She smiled. "It only releases a dose every so often." She'd worried about how to tell him who had rescued him, but she shouldn't have. She doubted he'd remember much at all of this conversation.

"The Castellaris?" He frowned at her. His processing was slow; he kept falling behind and catching up.

"Murph put out a distress call, and they were the closest. I still can't believe he knew what to do to get help. I'm so glad you're okay."

His eyelids drooped as the morphine hit him. "Did you tell them?"

She knew instantly what he was referring to. "I told Enzo. I'm going to tell Murph tonight or tomorrow. Is the pain better now?"

"Bluebelle Bryna Shea," he said her full name again. "I feel no pain. But I'll bet it's comin', ain't it?" He looked down at the long vertical bandage over his breastbone.

"Not for a while," she assured him. "Dad, Rita says she'll come up later today, and she sends her love. Look what she gave me." She leaned in, touching her mum's birthstone heart on the chain around her neck.

"God love her. We found it on the Yellowfin." His eyes closed. "Tired."

"Rest. That's your only job right now. I'll take care of everything else."

Her dad's eyes opened in slow motion, finding hers. "It ain't yours to carry. Might be time to let it go."

She shook her head. He meant his fishing business, and that scared her. It was his life. "Not a chance. I talked to Kai, I've got a plan. Your boats will be ready for you whenever you are. Rest, Dad. Heal." The curtain behind her was drawn open, and a woman in green cardiac unit scrubs smiled at them. "And listen to your nurse," Blue ordered.

Her father's eyes stayed closed with his last blink. Blue leaned in and kissed his cheek. His words stopped her at the curtain as she was leaving. "It was the right choice. I told her it would be."

She came back over the hospital bed. "Dad? What do you mean?"

"Your mum named you for the fairy flowers, but I knew you'd need something more. It fits you."

She pulled her phone out and searched her middle name. *Bryna—Strong One, Irish Celtic origin.* She'd never known there was any meaning attached to it. "It's perfect." It wasn't at all, but her father had bestowed the name upon her like a gift. Why was he telling her this now? She put a hand gingerly on his shoulder, needing to feel the life in him still, his eyes already closed again. "Dad."

"Hmmm."

The nurse turned from the new IV bag she was hanging on his pole. "He's in and out, no worries. I'll call you if anything changes."

"Thank you," she said, her voice lowered to a whisper. "I'll let him sleep."

Captain Crab's was Blue's first stop after leaving the hospital. She planned to check in with each place her father supplied and let them know he'd be out of commission for a while. She already knew she couldn't keep up with the direct marketing arrangements Mitch had with his contract holders. She knew what she'd be taking on simply trying to duplicate his catch each day. There was no way she could handle getting it all sorted and out to seven different places. She'd have to go through one of the wholesalers for processing and distribution. Mitch might be a one man show, but Blue was rusty and expected to be slow, at least at first. All she could do was explain about her dad and beg each place to use Mitch again as soon as he was back. He didn't need to know she'd be using a wholesaler; it'd only stress him and slow down his recovery.

She knew that would take several weeks—six to twelve if all went smoothly. She could have told Char today on the spot that she'd need to take a leave while she took a stab at keeping her father's business from going under, but she needed to summon her courage for that. Even though she'd been in the same hospital system for years, she was still new to Collier County ER. She had no idea whether they'd really have to hold her job or how she and Murph, and now Mitch, would get by without her paycheck.

After Captain Crab's, she successfully connected with the other six contract holders her dad supplied: three more restaurants, two markets, and Gary, the guy who ran the food truck on Gulfview Avenue. Everyone was overwhelmingly nice. Now she just hoped she could keep her dad's business going until he made it back to work.

Blue dropped her minivan off at home, changed into a pink sundress, and grabbed a couple of beers from the fridge, dropping them into a tote bag with a beach towel. Her phone buzzed as she was leaving the house and she grabbed it, about to answer, thinking it was the hospital. She froze, seeing it was Brent. He'd texted her several times that day and she'd been trying to ignore them. Each one was patient and kind . . . just checking on her, how she was feeling, when she thought she'd be coming home. And now he was calling her. She silenced her phone and stowed it in a pocket of the tote bag.

The trolley that ran up and down their little peninsula picked her up in front of the resort next door and dropped her at Bliss Beach in the village two miles away. She heard the drums before she even got off the trolley. She followed the sounds along the concrete path and around the sprawling brick concession building onto the beach, where a hundred or so people were gathered. The whole circle was lit from the orange and red glow of the recently departed sun and scattered tiki torches in the sand.

Blue made her way around the outer perimeter and then wove her way between the clusters of people dancing and laughing, letting the music of the drums seep into her, breaking apart the tension in her limbs, her mind, her very core. She stood at the edge of the inner circle. Across from her, a dozen or more people with various sized drums created the beat, each adding their own unique nuances. A guy with dreadlocks juggled small flaming torches that threw a glow over the crowd with each arc into the air; two belly dancers in multicolored hip scarves jingling with gold coins danced around a woman with several hula hoops spinning about her waist and arms; brightly colored glow sticks were scattered among the crowd, and a handful of little children danced on the sand with the women. The drum circle was a living, moving thing.

She tipped her head back. It was dark enough now to see the first few stars. Small pink and purple glowing fairies spiraled through the air above, toys operated by a group of kids on the outer perimeter, reminding her of the note she and Murph had pulled from the second mysterious fairy mailbox. They'd crept out to the grove of trees in the backyard as soon as they'd finished on the shrimp boat that night, as Blue had promised. It had been another quote from Rumi: *Raise your words, not voice. It is rain that grows flowers, not thunder.*

She'd barely finished reading it before Murphy had decided it was about his stepfather. Blue was surprised. Brent had been skilled at cutting Murph down while making him feel like he brought his dad's temper on himself. He'd done that to both of them; she was only now starting to see it. Her son beginning to view his stepfather's behavior through a clearer lens gave her hope for herself.

She closed her eyes and inhaled, breathing in the salt air, tiny flecks of sand drifting across her feet and ankles. She was jostled abruptly and then a laughing Sierra grabbed her and slid her arms around her. "Blue! You're here!"

"Where'd you come from? I love the look!" Sierra wore a headband and bracelets made of glow sticks.

"Why, thank you! Compliments of your son," she said, inclining her head toward the other side of the circle near the drummers.

Chloe waved at them from where she stood behind Murphy and Jeremy. The boys had assembled dozens of glow sticks into necklaces and were handing them out to the crowd. As Blue approached, Murph met her halfway across the circle and placed one on her head, a rainbow-colored crown.

She pulled him into a brief hug and he let her.

"Is Grandpa all right?" he asked.

"He's doing better. They're transferring him to a regular unit, that's a good sign," she said. "We'll go see him tomorrow." She was nearly shouting to be heard this close to the drums.

"Good. Mom, I love it here!" He bounced up and down, a goofy grin plastered to his face. "Sierra says I can play next time if we bring a drum."

"Awesome." She took his hand and stepped away from him, spinning him in a circle. Murph laughed and did the same to her, holding his arm up high for her to duck under. As she did, she caught her son's glowing expression, nearly unrecognizable in his carefree joy.

♦ 16 ♦

Enzo firmly decided after Friday night with Blue that he was going to mind his business and let Blue mind hers. Though not knowing if she had a plan or what it was made him a little crazy. Would she try to hire help to meet her dad's seafood contracts? Would she know she couldn't just not fulfill them without at least bringing Mitch Shea's clients up to speed? How long did it take to recover from heart surgery? Would it even be possible for Blue's dad to go back to work on his boats? She had to be freaking out.

Sunday morning on water like glass under a clear blue sky, Enzo couldn't stop running through the possibilities when he should have been enjoying the solitude.

She must have someone. Maybe some worker Mitch contracted with, or a cousin or friend, or . . . Enzo's fabricated image of Blue's husband popped into his mind, the fucker. No way. She hadn't said more than two words about the guy, and he was hours away. He didn't seem like the type to come to her rescue.

"Ugh!" Enzo growled aloud with aggravation. He scrubbed his fingers roughly through his hair, scowling up at the sky. When he returned his attention to the horizon, he saw what looked like Shea's *Shamrock* powering out of the canal onto the Gulf. He grabbed the binoculars behind the wheel and peered through them.

Blue was at the helm of the Yellowfin with Murphy behind her in the cockpit. Holy shit. They were doing it. In a pink windbreaker and cap with her hair pulled back into a braid and Murphy on the bench seat laboring over what looked like a tangled reel or maybe some lures, they were really doing it. His hypothetical musings hadn't involved her trying to keep her dad's business running. Even if Mitch only supplied Captain Crab's and the few other places Enzo was aware of, he didn't know how Blue thought she'd make this work. Though he didn't know anything about her life up in Tallahassee, he was pretty sure she'd been off boats for a decade. Watching them from a distance, his gut twisted with regret, an angst-filled longing to be near them, to know his son. He was finished watching from a distance; the first chance he got to talk with Blue, he'd press her to tell Murphy about him. Nine years were gone that he'd never get back with his son. He couldn't waste any more time.

Enzo realized suddenly that he was several degrees off course. He picked up the captain's log to make a note and was struck suddenly with an epiphany; how had it taken him this long to see it?

Each of Castellari and Sons' boats had a log, and each one was packed full of notes on daily courses and coordinates and any other pertinent information, organized by date. The night of Ella Shea's drowning, Blue had left so that she could put a casserole in the oven and have it ready when her parents got home. She'd timed it, knowing when her parents were expected. Around forty-five minutes later, Enzo had watched his father's fishing vessel approach from out on the Gulf, speeding into the canal. When he'd learned about Mrs. Shea, he'd asked Gino about his course. Had he been anywhere near the *Shamrock*? Had he heard anything at all on the radio? Gino had given him a curt *No* to every question, insisting to Enzo that he was trawling near the shoreline, not typical for that boat at night. Blue's dad had always maintained there was a boat in his vicinity that night, but there were always a handful on the water at any given time; Enzo had followed the court case like it was his own life on the line. In a way, it was.

Mitch Shea had been discredited as a drunk, so the court hadn't given credence to what he thought he remembered of that night. But Enzo had always wondered. Maybe the answers he needed had been in the captain's log this whole time. The archived logs were kept in the filing cabinet in Marcello's office.

Enzo noticed he was heading straight for the Yellowfin. He corrected, keeping Blue's boat to his left. He made sure to keep them in his sights while trying to aim toward yesterday's hotspot for mackerel. He maintained his distance but checked on them with the binoculars every so often over the next few hours, catching her and Murphy in various stages of setting up and fishing. She was stronger than she looked.

Enzo lost Mitch Shea's boat around noon. He panicked at first, making wide arcs in different directions and completely ruining his take for the day, but he couldn't spot them. Would she know how to use the GPS system on the vessel? Had her dad taught Murphy at all? The boy knew emergency protocol but was clueless in front of the Nav screen. What if they were lost? On a whim, he turned the volume up on his marine radio and switched it to the channel Murphy had used Friday. With luck, the *Shamrock*'s radio was still set the same. If they were in trouble, Murphy knew how to call for help.

Enzo stayed on the water another hour or so. He was tossing around the idea of grabbing Marcello—who was undoubtedly in the marina office going over the books on this beautiful day—and commencing a wider search area to find Blue and Murphy, when the VHF marine radio squawked with the boy's voice coming through along with ear-piercing static. He adjusted the squelch and grabbed his handset. "Say again. This is the *Mona Lisa*, could you repeat that?" Hell! Twice in three days—what had happened now? Enzo's heart was in his throat. What if something was wrong with Blue?

"Yessir." His son's voice came through much more clearly now. "Why do fish swim in schools?"

He frowned, thinking before he pressed the button to reply. Weird question. "Um. I think it's a way to stay safe from predators. And get better momentum."

"Nope. It's because they can't walk!" Murphy's voice rose in pitch as he laughed at his own joke. Enzo caught Blue in the background, saying something about the radio. Probably telling him to keep the marine channels open for real issues.

He smiled and shook his head, leaning on the wheel.

The radio crackled again. "Get it?"

He laughed aloud. "I get it." He let go of the button, thinking fast. "What does the Pope eat during Lent?" Shit, would he know what Lent was?

The radio was silent. Enzo waited. It finally crackled to life. "Holy mackerel."

Enzo stared at the radio. What the heck? He was clearly dealing with a pro. "Wow. Nice one—" He stopped himself abruptly—he'd been about to use his son's name. He didn't need Blue to know he was keeping tabs on her.

"Why is—oh. I gotta go, sorry," Murph said, cutting out abruptly. The radio returned to silence. He was willing to bet Blue had made Murphy knock it off. He'd done the same thing as a kid, messed with fellow boaters on the radio, but he'd always gotten in trouble when his dad caught him.

His connection to Blue broken, and knowing she and his son were fine, Enzo guided the *Mona Lisa* toward the Castellari marina. He was even more impressed with the two of them now. Murphy was only nine, had spent a handful of days with his grandpa on the Yellowfin out there, and, from a distance at least, appeared to know his shit. Blue hadn't hovered over him either. They had both been busy with the outriggers the entire time he'd spied on them.

Enzo pulled into the slip and made sure all of the *Mona Lisa*'s lines were securely tied. He found Jillian waiting for him as he crossed the parking area toward the marina warehouse. He'd screwed up—again.

"Good day fishing?" Her tone and expression did not match her casual question.

"No. I'm so sorry." He moved close but didn't touch her. He had to tread lightly. He'd only seen her this pissed a few times, and never at him.

"Are you not into this? Because I'm not sure what I'm doing here. I'm not going to ignore your red flags, Enzo."

"You know I'm into this. You. I lost track of time. No red flags here." He nearly shivered from the ice-cold attitude emanating from her. "Babe." He used her pet word for him, cringing inwardly. But he had nothing. No excuse. What could he say?

"If you didn't intend to come to church with me, you shouldn't have lied to Pastor Steve. How do you think it makes me and my parents look? My dad was furious."

He sighed. He knew he should care about angering his future father-in-law, who was also lead attorney for Castellari and Sons' legal team. He'd known the moment he started dating Jillian what the stakes were; he'd never made waves like this until lately. "I planned on coming today. I'll be there next Sunday. I'll set an alarm. I promise."

She softened, he could feel her posture relax. She tugged at his T-shirt, wrinkling her nose. "You smell like fish."

He laughed. "Big surprise. I'll go shower. Hey." Enzo hesitated, not sure he was really up for what he was about to say. But he kept letting her down. Maybe this would fix some of it. "What are you doing later? Let's check out that sunset cruise out of Naples. The one you told me about?"

Her face lit up. "Really? Tonight? Oh, that'd be so great. What time is it?" She checked her phone before he could answer. "It's only three. I think it's a seven o'clock departure, let me check."

Enzo unlocked his car beside hers and tossed his duffel in. "So we'll leave at six?"

"Let's say five thirty." She turned and slid her arms around his waist, hugging him. "I can come help wash the fish smell off of you," she murmured against his neck.

"I'm not quite done here. Marcello needed some help," he lied. "But then I'll run home and shower and I'll pick you up at five thirty. Sound good?"

"Okay!" Jillian's chilly ire was completely evaporated. She kissed him before climbing back into her car. "Wear that new shirt I bought you," she called, waving on her way out of the parking lot.

Enzo went inside, the heavy door banging closed behind him. Marcello's office door stood open, his desk vacant. Had he left for the day? An electric drill whirred from one of the bays on the opposite end of the cavernous warehouse, a mechanic working on the small vessel they'd pulled off the water for repairs.

The filing cabinet against the wall behind Marcello's desk was a relic. Castellari and Sons was fully digital now but still had paper records going all the way back to when Gino had started the company thirty years ago. Enzo'd just pulled the top drawer open when Marcello came through from the conference room, startling him. "Hey, Zo. I thought you left."

"Fuck!" He shoved the drawer closed and turned toward his brother. "I thought *you* left. Don't sneak up on me like that."

"I don't sneak. You're jumpy. What're you looking for?"

"I need the captain's log for *Dollar and a Dream* for the night Mrs. Shea drowned."

"Really? Here, it wouldn't be in that one. Let me take a look. What're you hoping to find?" Marcello moved to the file cabinet and began quickly rifling through records.

"I want to see what his route coordinates were. Should be easy enough to check, just to put something to rest."

Marcello's hands stilled. He stared at Enzo. "Blue's getting in your head, isn't she?"

"No. This has nothing to do with her." He frowned.

Marcello pushed the second drawer closed and opened the one beneath it, browsing. "It's not here. I don't see it."

"What? No," Enzo groaned.

"It's been ten years. I'll let you know if it turns up."

"Gino would know. He's here, right?"

Marcello raised his eyebrows. "Uh. Yeah, now might not be the best time to ask him anything." He inclined his head toward the conference room. Through the frosted glass, Enzo made out his father's back and another figure.

Enzo lowered his volume. "Who's he meeting with on a Sunday?"

"Hamish Josephson. We just got started. Going over some accounting issues." He frowned at him. "What's up with you, man?"

Enzo pulled up the chair across from him and grabbed the plastic model of the *Minnow* on Marcello's desk. It was a close replica of theirs, with moving gears and detachable rigging. He leaned forward, elbows on knees, and flipped the top mounted pole back and forth, thoughts spinning. "Jillian just offered to scrub the fish smell off me, and I turned her down." He kept his volume low, not wanting his fiancée's father to overhear.

Marcello matched his tone. "Bro. When your girl offers to shower with you, you say yes. Jillian's the dream."

"Yeah. So why does she irritate the crap out of me lately?"

Marcello rose and grabbed two Cokes from the refrigerator, handing him one. "Is this about Blue?"

"What? No." He slammed the model boat down on the desk. The tiller flew out and hit the floor. He grabbed it and worked to get it back into place. "Blue's married, I'm engaged. It has nothing to do with her."

"Uh huh."

"Hey! It doesn't. Jillian's pissed at me because I missed church this morning. It's a whole thing we have to do to get ready for the wedding."

"Why'd you miss church?"

"I was fishing."

Marcello cocked an eyebrow at him.

"I. Was. Fishing."

"Okay."

"Oh, fuck off." Enzo stood. "This is broken," he said, putting the *Minnow* back on the desk. "I think it's just stupid cold feet. It doesn't mean anything." He felt instantly better realizing it. That's all it was. "We had this intense meeting with her pastor, and everything lately is about the wedding. I think it's getting to me."

Marcello walked toward the door with him. "Hate to tell you, but your girl could have anyone she wants. Maybe you're second guessing because—"

Enzo cut him off. "I'm not second guessing."

"Okay. Maybe it's cold feet because you've built up what you and Blue had as teenagers into this wild, unrealistic fantasy. You don't even know her anymore. Have you even spent any time with her since she's been back?"

Enzo stared at him. "What the—have you talked to Salvi lately?" How was his brother totally unaware of all he and Salvi had been through the other night? Salvi didn't know what had happened at the hospital, but they'd been talking about his run-ins with Bluebelle Shea for two weeks now. It hit him as strange that Salvi hadn't mentioned a word of it to Marcello.

"You are all over the place, man," Marcello said. "I haven't talked to Salvi. Why?"

Enzo stopped at his truck and faced his brother. "Blue and I have talked. Her nine-year-old son Murphy is mine. I'm his dad."

Marcello stepped back, stunned. "Well, holy shit. And you believe her? You're gonna get a DNA test, right?"

"Why would I? He turned nine in April, and with it being June now, that'd mean Blue must've been pregnant when she ran away that August. I mean, not by much, but Murphy was born nine months later."

His brother shrugged. "Look, I'm only thinking like Pop. Think about it. You don't know you were the only guy she was with. You don't know the kid was born at full term, do you?"

Enzo scowled at Marcello. "What is wrong with you? This isn't about Pops. It won't affect him. It's about my son. It's about Blue and my son and me."

"Right. So what does she want? Has she said yet?"

Enzo's ire spiked. "Y'know, out of everyone, I thought you'd have the most level-headed response to this. Blue had my child and took care of him without me for over nine years. I loved that girl my whole life. Maybe shut your goddamn mouth if all you have to say is she came home to bleed me dry." He yanked the door to his truck open and got in.

Marcello had the balls to look surprised. "Wait, Zo, I'm sorry. Don't listen to me, work is stressing me out lately. What did Jillian say about all of this?"

"She doesn't know yet. I'm going to tell her eventually," he said defensively. "Blue has a husband, this doesn't change anything as far as me marrying Jillian."

Marcello chuckled and shook his head. "I'd recommend you say it differently when you talk with her. That made it sound like the only reason you're still marrying her is because Blue's not available."

"Yeah. Well," Enzo said, "Murphy being my son kind of changes everything and nothing. I know I'm lucky to have Jillian."

"Now that's true," Marcello said. "You two just make sense."

★   ★   ★

After a shower and then rummaging around in his closet for the short-sleeved dress shirt Jillian had bought him, he threw the front door open so Moon could rush past him out toward the beach. He'd made sure to leave enough time for a walk.

He was a few minutes late to pick up Jillian. "You look gorgeous," he said, meaning it. She always did, whether she was angrily facing off with him in the marina parking lot or sliding the skirt of her sleek black and white halter dress up one tan, toned thigh to climb into his truck.

Jillian used the drive up to Naples to go over the Gulfscape Gardens catering menu for their wedding reception dinner. By the time Enzo found the departure dock for Jack Kelly Cruises, they'd settled on the seven-course dinner option for the reception venue in September and chosen the china they wanted the food served on. Jillian submitted it from her phone. "All set! That was easy. I can hardly believe it's ten weeks from now," she said, smiling at him. "The last thing left to plan is our honeymoon."

Ten weeks sounded a lot closer than three months to him. His wedding was approaching at an alarming rate. He parked and came around to open the door for Jillian.

She slipped her arm through his. "I know it's a tough choice, but we're going to miss out on the best packages if we don't decide soon. What did you think of the Barbados resort I sent you?"

"When? In the mail?"

She laughed. "You really never check your email, do you? I narrowed it down to those three places we talked about—just check later when you're home. We should sit down one day this week and get our flights booked."

"I'll check. In here?" He stopped outside a tan brick building.

"No, we get to board before the crowd because I know the owner," Jillian said. She flashed a grin at him.

He narrowed his eyes. "Should I be jealous?"

She lifted one perfect eyebrow. "Always."

Once they were aboard, a deeply tanned, ruggedly handsome older man with a trace of silver at his temples approached them, throwing his arms wide for Jillian. They embraced briefly and kissed cheeks, and then she tucked her hand under Enzo's elbow, drawing him into their little circle. "Enzo, meet Captain Jack Kelly. Jack, this is my fiancé, Vincenzo Castellari. You two have a lot in common."

"Vincenzo—" Jack said in greeting, extending his hand.

Enzo shook it firmly. "Just Enzo. It's nice to finally meet you, Jack. Jillian thinks the world of you."

Jillian giggled. "You're not supposed to tell my secrets," she said. "I am fascinated, though, with how you came to do this. All of this," she said, tipping her head back and taking in the upper deck seating.

Jack shrugged. "I started out working for my uncle, years ago. You know, fishing, shrimping, that kind of thing. Worked my way up, got lucky with some investment gambles, and eventually bought a boat. Come on, I'll give you a tour."

"Wow," Jillian said. "You're not kidding those were lucky gambles."

The man laughed, a deep, friendly sound. Enzo couldn't really tell yet whether this man was a boasting blowhard or simply a fisherman who'd changed captain hats, but he liked him. Jack held a hand out to usher them up the stairway. "This boat is not the result of that first step; now that'd really be something. No," he shook his head. "The *Anna Marie* is my—" He paused, silently ticking off boats with the fingers of one hand. "She's my fifth and biggest. I've been able to upgrade every few years."

Enzo followed Jillian out onto the deck. She moved to the railing and peered down at the cruise patrons beginning to gather below behind the ropes. "It must be a lot of fun. Meeting new people every night, narrating the sights, hosting your live band. Much different than fishing."

A prickly feeling crept up Enzo's neck. His gaze moved from Jillian to Jack Kelly. Was he crazy, or was she having her friend— her client—whatever—run through all the reasons why captaining a sunset cruise was so much better than fishing?

"I can't complain," Jack replied to Jillian. "It's definitely got a nicer dress code." He chuckled.

"Better hours too. I've never heard of a crack-of-dawn cruise, right?"

"That's a perk for sure. I'm just happy I found a way to stay on the water in some manner. You know what I mean," he said, turning toward Enzo. "You're a Castellari. You've been on boats your whole life, the same as me."

He nodded. "Yeah."

"It's not for the weak, is it?" Jack mused. "Takes something special to hit the waves for hours or days on end. Never knowing if you'll come back with junk or hit the jackpot and catch enough to cover all your contracts at once."

"Enzo works his butt off," Jillian spoke up. "It's a tough, physical job. You've said it yourself, Jack, when you'd talk about fishing for your uncle. At least with the cruises, you don't get your hands dirty. Plus I'd think the income's steadier."

Jack didn't answer right away. He and Jillian stared at each other, and he finally adjusted the visor on his captain's hat, turning his attention back to Enzo. "Fishing's the easiest, truest work in the world if you love it. I did. I just didn't know it then." He cleared his throat and clasped his hands together, taking a step back. "I've got to get down to the gangway for greetings. The bar is open, you folks should grab a cocktail and settle in for a great evening." He touched the brim of his cap and trotted down the steps.

Jillian headed toward the upper deck bar and Enzo followed, fuming. The whole thing had been a setup. She was smooth, but he saw right through her. It probably would've gone better if she'd clued in poor Captain Jack ahead of time.

Jillian rested a hand on the bar and turned back to Enzo. "Try a fun cocktail, Babe. How about a mango margarita, like mine?"

He addressed the bartender, speaking over Jillian's head. "Beer. Whatever's on draft." He felt her staring at him. He clenched his teeth and watched the bartender pour his beer. If she had a problem with his career, she could have spoken up at any point at all in the last six and a half years. He took his beer from the bartender and put two twenties down to cover their drinks.

Jillian followed him, struggling to keep up with his long-legged stride toward the stairway. "Enzo. Hey. Vincenzo!" She stomped her feet and stopped moving.

He turned and glared at her. "You could have orchestrated that so much better." Below them came the sounds of patrons boarding, Captain Jack greeting them heartily.

"I don't know what you mean," she said, stepping closer to him.

"Yes, you do. You know, when I hear people say *that lawyer Jillian Josephson's a shark*, I've never heard it as *oh hey, that lady's a great person*. Do you know what it means when someone says you're a shark?"

She shook her head, her eyes filling with tears.

"It means you're a predator. You prey on the weak. But I'm not weak. And if what I do for a living isn't good enough for you, maybe that's a red flag I shouldn't ignore, *Babe*." He was done. He wasn't going to be stuck on this boat with her for the next three hours while she tried to convince him he'd overreacted. She could find her own way home. Enzo turned and took the steps two at a time. He froze halfway down.

His father stood on the bottom step, staring up at him. With him was an attractive young woman, her arm linked through his as she laughed at something he'd just said. Gino's expression reflected shock. Or fear. Possibly both. He began to speak, and Enzo vehemently shook his head, every muscle in his body tensed.

"Don't." He spit the word at his father as he reached the bottom of the stairway. "Don't say a goddamned word." He looked his father's mistress in the eye, prepared to hate her. She couldn't be more than twenty-five, younger than Enzo for sure. Half Gino's age and then some. All he felt was pity. "Ask him about his wife. Her name's Sofia."

Enzo was off the boat and halfway to the parking lot when he felt a hand on his arm. Fucking Gino! He spun around, ready to fight, and saw it was Jillian. He put his palms up. "I just want to go home."

"Okay," she said, nodding. As Enzo dug in his pocket for his keys, his father approached behind Jillian. He'd left his date on the boat.

"Son," Gino said. "I can explain."

"There's nothing to explain." All Enzo could think of was his mother. She was probably so used to Gino's lies she couldn't tell them from truth anymore.

Gino addressed Jillian. "Would you mind giving us a minute?"

Enzo scoffed. "Why should she? You think she doesn't already know all about you, Pops? She's practically family now. Whatever you have to say can be said in front of my fiancée."

"Look, Kendra is a client. That's all. Sometimes it takes a little extra time, getting new contracts. She just wants to know about our business."

He shook his head, incredulous. The woman he and Marcello had forced Gino to call was named Cheryl. How many were there? "You're serious right now? What, do I look like I'm still twelve and buying your bullshit? Where does Ma think you are this time? You know what? It doesn't matter. I'll fill her in."

"I'd think twice about that," Gino said, his tone menacing. "I played golf with Harry Patterson yesterday. You know, the county harbormaster. He told me this crazy story about a kid and his grandpa being rescued Friday night."

Enzo's fingers twitched. He'd never wanted to strangle someone so badly before. Gino's jaw was thrust stubbornly forward and that arrogant expression he wore was maddening. "You're a piece of work." So, unless Enzo made it clear he wasn't going to say anything to his mother, Gino would spill the news in front of Jillian that Blue was back in town. His pulse pounded in his ears. He hated his father.

The cruise ship's horn sounded, signaling that departure was imminent. Gino raised his eyebrows at Enzo. "I'd better go, don't want to miss it. We're good then? Your mother knows I'm with a client, Enzo. That's all she wants to know. Leave it at that."

Enzo glanced at Jillian. If she learned Bluebelle Shea was home before he was ready to tell her about Murphy, he'd have a lot of explaining to do.

"Enzo?" Jillian's face was painted with concern. "Whatever you want to do, I'm with you," she said quietly.

He'd made her cry not five minutes ago. Goddammit. She made it hard to stay angry at her when she so wholeheartedly supported him. "Let's go," he said, starting to turn away from Gino. "I want to talk to my mother in person. She's going to have some thinking to do."

"Jillian," Gino spoke, completely bypassing Enzo. "Did my son ever tell you about his first love?"

Behind them, the crew tossed the lines onto the deck, freeing the cruise ship from its mooring rope by rope. The horn sounded twice, last warning. "Mr. Castellari, sir." One of the crewmen called out to Gino. He was obviously known here.

He didn't turn away from Jillian and Enzo. "I'll be right there."

"Go ahead, Pops. You don't have anything on me because there isn't anything. I'm *nothing* like you." Enzo's voice shook and that only infuriated him more.

"She ran away years ago and it almost killed him. I didn't know she was back until the harbormaster told me he dropped Enzo off at the hospital Friday with Bluebelle Shea's son after he'd rescued the boy and her father. Interesting he kept that from you." His shot fired, he turned and began to walk back to the gangplank where two crewmen stood. He turned back momentarily. "Your mother is the only one who will be hurt if you run and tattle. It won't affect me. She'll forgive me; she has before."

Neither Enzo nor Jillian spoke in his truck until they'd been on the expressway a good ten minutes. His mind was racing. He wanted nothing more than to bust Gino and go talk to his mother. But he had a sick feeling his father was right. And the callous way in which his father had tried to blackmail him into silence blew his mind.

He looked over at Jillian. "Mitch Shea was the fisherman I helped on Friday. You know, Shea Seafood, you've probably seen his truck around. He'd had a heart attack. Salvi and I heard his grandson's distress call and we got the Coast Guard out to help him. After they took him in, I just got the boy to his mom." *My son*, his mind shouted back at him. A lie of omission is still a lie; and if he hadn't already known that, years of listening to Jillian practice closing arguments in front of the mirror certainly would have enlightened him. He didn't have a clue how to untangle all of this.

Jillian stared out the windshield, lips pursed.

"My father is just trying to hurt me—us," he said.

"Don't put this all on Gino. He wouldn't have used it against you if it wasn't incriminating. Be honest with me, Enzo. How long have you known she was back in town?"

He narrowed his eyes at the road in front of them, thinking. Not about her question, but the uncharted territory it sat in the center of. Almost a month. Ever since the ER. *I've known Blue was back since she held my head in her hands and stared into my eyes looking for damage.* The words ricocheted around in his head, unspoken. How much honesty was too much?

"How long?" Jillian's voice was quiet.

"I found out a few weeks ago. It doesn't matter. I told you, my dad's goal was to hurt me and it worked. He's made you doubt *us*." He reached for her but she pulled away.

She shook her head. "You did that." She was as far away from him as she could get, pressed against the door on her side of the truck.

Enzo slammed on the brakes. His tires squealed, and the red sports car in his rearview mirror raced toward them too fast before finally stopping. He made a hard right onto the side street he'd been about to pass. The man in the sports car veered around him, laying on his horn. Enzo put the truck in park and faced her. "Don't make this bigger than it is. Jillian, look at me."

She wouldn't.

Goddamned Gino. He ruined everything. This was exactly what he'd wanted. Enzo threw his door open and left it that way, cursing his father under his breath as he walked around to Jillian's side.

Another car honked at them as it passed. He'd turned but hadn't gone more than twenty feet before stopping; the rear of his truck was blocking side street traffic. Jillian's gaze went from the rearview mirror to the window behind her as he pulled open her door. "Enzo, stop! What are you—"

"Look at me, Jillian, please." He waited.

She huffed out a breath, unbuckled, and turned sideways toward him. "If Blue being back is no big deal, then why didn't you tell me? Why leave out the important details and tell me you rescued some fisherman?"

"I should have told you the whole story. It . . . I don't know. Maybe I didn't want to put more importance on it than it warranted." Fuck. He was trying to say this right. "The ambulance took Mitch Shea and left me with Murphy. When the harbormaster took us to the hospital it was so I could drop him off with her and go. But she had to talk to the doctors, it sounded like her dad had to be resuscitated, and then he needed surgery, and Murphy was upset, plus he had their cat with him, and—I just felt like a jerk every time I thought about leaving. That's the truth." Some of the truth; how the hell was he supposed to tell her that Murphy Shea was his son?

"We should move." Jillian glanced toward the road. Her expression had softened.

"I'm not my father."

"I know you aren't." She nodded. "I know that."

"Good."

"You swear that's all of it? Tell me, Enzo. If there's more, if you're not sure of your feelings, tell me now."

His gut twisted. There was so much more. "That's all. I'm sure. I love you." That much was true—he loved Jillian. But did he love her enough?

"Okay," she said. She wrapped her arms around him and he hugged her. Another horn sounded, startling them, and Enzo put a hand up and jogged around to his side, getting the truck moving again.

Jillian slipped her hand into his on his thigh. "I'm sorry we fought about Jack Kelly," she said. She squeezed his hand.

He groaned inwardly. How had their evening turned into such a shitshow so fast? "I like the guy. But the direction you steered things in caught me off guard," he admitted. "I never knew you had a problem with my job."

"I don't," she said emphatically. "I overheard you and Salvi a while ago, complaining about your calluses and working late, and—I thought this might be helpful."

"Oh." He was the asshole, not Jillian. Big surprise; it was his theme for today. "I'm sorry. I—I'm sorry for what I said."

She nodded. "Yeah."

Shit. "I didn't mean it. Any of it. I was hurt. I . . . uh, I obviously blew that way out of proportion." He brought her hand to his lips and kissed it. "I'm so sorry."

They rode the rest of the way to Jillian's house in relative silence. He walked her up to her porch but she didn't invite him in. His churning thoughts battled with his queasy gut on his drive home. Enzo turned onto Live Oak Way and his glance fell on Blue's cottage as always.

He'd been haunted by her all these years, at first certain she'd come back, and later, barely daring to hope, the mere idea almost too bittersweet to entertain. Seeing Blue again had become a dream, an impossible someday he'd kept secreted away in the furthest corner of his mind, knowing it'd never happen but hoping somehow it might.

Blue was home. With his son. And already married, and the whole thing was a mess. And he'd been wrestling with the what-ifs since that day in the ER. How could he even consider abandoning Jillian, after nearly seven years planning a future together, their wedding just weeks away? But how could he pretend it didn't matter that the only future he'd ever been able to imagine was with Blue?

BLUE WAS EXHAUSTED. SHE'D stopped for a moment on her way across the yard from the boathouse to admire all the work she'd done so far on the yard since coming home, but sitting down was a mistake. The newly painted aqua bench was smooth under her legs and she slumped down, letting her head tip forward. She'd just rest her eyes for a minute.

"Mom!" Murphy startled her awake. "You can't fall asleep, you promised we could go to the movies tonight!"

She raised her eyebrows and nodded. "I know. What time is it? That might have to wait, buddy."

"I knew that was gonna happen," he grumbled. "When is Grandpa coming home?"

"Um." She'd only been doing her dad's job for three days, and she was wiped out. Nine o'clock on a Tuesday felt like midnight at the end of a work week. They were up before the sun, out on the water all day long, then getting their haul to the wholesaler and cleaning up the Yellowfin before tucking her in for the night so she'd be ready to go the next day. Dinner was now way after dinnertime each evening, and she hadn't stocked groceries or touched laundry or done any cleaning in days.

"*Is* he ever coming home? Mom, are you even listening to me?"

Blue patted the seat beside her. "I always listen to you. They're transferring Grandpa to a cardiac rehab unit. I have to meet Sierra in the morning for something, but then I'll pick you up and we'll go see where he'll be working on getting better. He is coming home, Murph, but it's going to be a while. Hey." She had to tell him. She'd tried the other night after they'd left the drum circle, but she'd lost her nerve again.

"Yeah?" He sat down.

"I have to talk to you about something kind of heavy."

"Uh. What? I didn't do anything. I swear!"

"I know. You're not in trouble." She sighed and leaned forward, elbows resting on knees. She'd played versions of this over and over in her head. She turned and looked at him. "You know Dad isn't your real father."

He nodded. "Yeah. I know that, Mom."

She took a deep breath. "I've never told you about your biological father because it was too painful for me, and that was selfish. I'm sorry. I was never sure how to handle it. Just because you become a parent doesn't mean you instantly have all the answers." Her son's wide-eyed stare made her heart hurt. "You've already met your real dad, Murph. The man who was at the hospital with us—who helped you with Grandpa—Enzo is your father."

Murphy sat stock still, looking back at her. When he didn't speak, Blue pushed forward. "I met him when I was little, way younger than you, and we were friends our whole lives. We were best friends. We started seeing each other differently, I guess, as we grew up. We fell in love. I . . ." She faltered. "This is hard. I'm going to try to say this right, Murph. I really thought your dad and I would be together forever. We had plans. I didn't know until after I was already in Tallahassee with Aunt Eva that I was pregnant with you."

"So why didn't you go home? To my real dad—to Enzo? What about Dad—my stepdad?" He frowned, shaking his head, and she read his thoughts.

She took Murphy's hand, surprised when he didn't pull it away. "When I learned I was going to have you, I was so happy; but I couldn't come home, for reasons I can't really explain to you yet. We're using these titles, Dad, Father, Stepdad, Real Dad. There is so much wrong with the way your—" She broke off with a huff, frustrated over the same issue she could feel in her son, the dissonance of comparing the two men in their lives with the same official title. "There is so much wrong with how your stepdad treats us. I'm not sure he knows how to be a good father and husband. Dammit." She sucked in air, squeezing her eyes shut, her stomach clenching with the gravity of speaking those words aloud.

"Mom?" Murphy's voice was small.

Blue tipped her head back, looking up at the night sky and blinking rapidly. "I'm sorry. I'm still figuring things out myself. Maybe that makes me a bad mom. I just—" She focused on her son's sweet face. "I just don't want you to feel like you're being disloyal to your stepdad, Murph, as we talk about Enzo. I don't know what I'm going to do about . . . Tallahassee. The only thing I know for sure is that your life is better with Enzo in it. He didn't know you existed until a little while ago, but he would have been such a good dad to you." Her tears overflowed and she smiled through them. "It's not too late for him to start. He wants so badly to know you."

Murphy's face crumpled. He threw himself at her, scooting over on the bench so he was almost in her lap, arms wrapped around her. "It's okay, Mom," he said, his voice hitching with tearful breaths. "It's okay. Don't be sad. I like Enzo."

She laughed softly and stroked his hair, his sweaty, sea air scented head on her collarbone. "I love you so much."

"I know. You aren't a bad mom. I love you too." His mumbled words drifted to her, pinching with a bittersweet sting in the back corners of her jaw. She kept her arms around him, not too tight, letting his calmer breathing now soothe her. When he finally let go, sitting up, Blue moved a strand of hair out of his eyes. "What happens now?"

She raised her eyebrows. "Um. What do you want to happen?"

"I wanna meet him. Like, again. Y'know? He's my dad. But—" He bit his lip, thinking. "I guess he's not a stranger 'cause he helped me save Grandpa, but I don't really know him. Can we see him, but can you stay too?"

"I can stay. Don't worry. We'll set something up, okay?" Her life had never seemed so screwed up yet so hopeful all at once. A ten-thousand-pound weight was finally lifted, the absence of it unbelievably freeing.

"Hook didn't bite him, at least. And Hook tries to bite everyone," Murphy said, reaching down and running a hand along the cat's back. Hook made figure eights around their ankles. "So we're not fishing tomorrow?"

She rested her arm along the back of the bench. "Well, I'll probably still go out for a while when we get back. We can't afford to miss a whole day. But . . . you don't always have to go. I know it's a lot of work."

"I want to," he said. "My livestream got five new viewers today right after I posted the video of us pulling in that big kingfish. Cooper said he's gonna show his archery group tomorrow, and there's like, ten guys in that! I can keep posting cool stuff until we get too far out from shore. Maybe you can steer us toward some sharks tomorrow."

She laughed. "I'm glad you came up with a way to make it fun." She stood and moved to the fairy village trail entrance. "All right, let's see if there are any new developments."

Murphy scrutinized her. "I think it's you doing it. You sound like you already know something else has happened."

"It's not me. And I don't know anything, I swear." She let him go ahead.

He took her phone and shined the flashlight along the trail. "Oh wow! Check it out!" Three houses in a row were now freshly spruced up with glossy yellow, pink, and aqua paint. "Someone painted more houses. What—Mom, look!" He darted over to the opposite side of the path. Blue caught the way he glanced at his feet, making sure not to step on the bluebell flowers. He crouched down. "The camper looks so cool now!"

Blue peered over his shoulder. The once dingy looking Airstream-style camper was now a shiny silver chrome with a bright teal stripe down each side. She knelt next to him. "I can't believe this. Who's doing this?" She touched one of the two new small orange and white lawn chairs set up on a square of green outdoor carpeting under the camper's awning. "These fairies are living it up," she said, smiling, more to herself than to Murphy. She knew he was too old for this stuff.

"Seriously." He laughed. "Mom, it's really not you? Who is it then?" Murphy straightened up, continuing on the path through the grove of trees.

She shrugged. "I honestly don't know. I've even tried to peek out here at random times, but I've never seen anyone."

"Huh. Look! There's another mailbox!"

Murphy had found a new naked balsawood mailbox at the fairy house next door. He gingerly moved a cluster of flowers and knelt on the cedar chips. He looked up at her, waiting.

She joined him on the soft ground. "Look at that, they painted clouds," she said, moving the light in his hand. White, fluffy looking clouds decorated the bark of several trees. A bright orange sun now adorned the tree in front of them, smudged yellow and white painted rays extending outward. Someone was putting serious time into their fairy garden.

"Dang," Murph said. "I know it's all fake and there's no such thing, but whoever's doing this is, like, trying to make it extra nice for the fairies to live here. Don't you think?"

"I do. That's sure how it seems." She looked down at the mailbox. "Is there another letter?"

He extracted a tiny square of paper and read it by the light of Blue's phone.

"*Miss Bluebelle and young Sir Murphy—Take heart. Where there is ruin, there is hope for a treasure. —Rumi*"

"Oh," Blue said, her voice quiet. "I love that."

"What does it mean?"

"What does it mean to you, Murph?"

He rolled his eyes and leaned back on his hands. "Brain. Does not. Compute. Summer break. No school. Allowed."

She laughed. "Oh no, I'm so sorry, Young Sir Murphy." She took the paper from him and read it to herself. "Hmm. Where there is ruin . . . where something is wrong or broken or messed up. There's hope for treasure. Hope for treasure," she repeated. "If I think like my high school English teacher," she began, nudging Murph.

"Stop! No use of school-related words either. I'm sorry, but it's the rule," he said sternly.

Blue nodded. "My bad, I forgot. All right. I'd say this quote is about hope or resilience. It means, even when things seem to be at their darkest, we can find the glimmer of possibility and turn it into something amazing. It's about finding the good within the bad, I guess."

Her son was poking at the dirt with a stick. "Huh."

She understood. It was hard to believe right now, with Mitch in the hospital and her and Murph working their asses off and Brent calling her constantly. But it was a beautiful sentiment.

"What's the deal with the bluebell flowers? You started to tell me about it before." He looked sideways at her. "I mean, I don't care. But if you really wanna tell me, you could."

She gave him a small smile. Nine-year-old enthusiasm not-withstanding, she was happy he'd finally asked. "Your Grandma Ella believed in fairies. She shared so many Irish folklore stories with me when I was growing up. In her village in Killarney, she and her friends knew they had to be careful around the bluebell flowers. Fairies use the flowers for lots of things. See how they look like little bells?" She touched one, showing Murphy.

"Well, yeah, I already knew that's why they're called blue-bells," he said.

"Right, of course," Blue said. "Fairies would ring the blue-bells when it was time for a gathering or meeting. I'm sure we can't hear it, but the sound would travel to their kin—their family—and let them know to come. And maybe even more importantly, it's believed that fairies hang their magic spells on bluebells. That's why they're such precious things. Picking one isn't good, but trampling a bluebell is much worse. Wild magic or fairy wrath will be unleashed on anyone who willfully crushes the bluebells."

Murphy sat back. He leaned on his hands and turned his head, looking from the entrance of their grove of trees to the path out, beyond where they were. "Did Grandma Ella plant them here? To go with the fairy garden?"

She raised her eyebrows. "Oh." She tipped her head at him, thinking. "I'm not sure. That'd make sense, right? The flowers have been here since I can remember, even when there were only a couple of little fairy houses. I've always assumed they grow wild here. I wonder if your grandma got them started years ago, after I was born . . . or if they were already here and reminded her of her childhood." Blue lightly ran the backs of her fingertips along the cluster closest to her, barely moving them. What a thought, if the bluebells were ringing now.

"Grandma really must have believed," Murphy mused, "to have named you Bluebelle."

She nodded. "I think she really did," she said softly. "I wish you could have met her, Murph. She was lovely. She was so sweet and fun and kind. Though she could be fierce when she had to." Lord, how she missed her mum.

Murphy bumped his shoulder lightly against hers and then swayed away. "Mom. I think you're just like her."

Blue's breath caught in her throat. She stared at him and smiled. "That's—thanks, Murph. I'd love that to be true."

★ ★ ★

Wednesday morning's shopping trip with Sierra to the women's boutique in Bliss was a bust. Blue had hoped to find something to wear to the wedding, but the racks were filled with sundresses and sarongs. "I'll just order something online," she said as they crossed the street, heading back to the village park and pay.

"Are you sure? We were probably crazy to think we'd find your dress without leaving town. Let's go to Naples this weekend."

"Maybe that's a better idea." She was fishing in her purse for her keys when Sierra gripped her arm, pulling them to a stop. "What?"

Sierra tipped her head toward the store front. "Look."

Through the red and gold **Rita's Roses** lettering on the display window was a gorgeous turquoise gown. Rita's shop was aimed at the tourist crowd, an eclectic collection of expensive event wear, jewelry, and locally crafted trinkets. It was one shop Blue rarely ventured into when she was younger; nothing was in her price range.

"You have to try that on." Sierra steered her inside. "It's calling to us. That's your maid of honor dress."

Rita greeted them from behind the counter. "Hello, ladies, good morning!"

Blue spoke. "Rita, have you met Sierra Jones—"

Sierra pointed to a rack of her own custom-designed jewelry on the checkout counter. "Rita and I go way back. Our friend here wants to try on that gown, please," she told Rita.

Blue spied the price tag. It was nearly half a week's paycheck. "Ah, no, actually, I think it's the wrong size." She could feel Sierra frowning at her.

"I'm paying," Sierra blurted.

"No you're not!"

She shook her head. "Don't even try to argue with me. It's my wedding. You have to do what I say. This is your dress, Blue-belle Shea."

"Actually, this one is on sale right now," Rita said, poker faced. "I just haven't had time to change the price tag. Let's have you try it on." She plucked the hanger from the display rack and draped the full skirt over her arm. She was pretty and put together as always, but Blue recognized the grayish circles under her eyes.

"Dad's transferring to the cardiac rehab wing today. He's feeling pretty good," Blue offered, gratified when the older woman sighed in relief.

"I'm so glad. I worry about him all the time," Rita said. She unlocked the fitting room door. "Here you go, just let me know if you need any help."

While Blue slid the divine gown over her shoulders, she called over the fitting room cubby. The shop was empty; it was still early. "Rita, what was the name you said the other day, when we were talking about Dale Bryant's daughter?" She'd made a mental note to look up what Rita had been talking about but her mind blanked on the name—it couldn't have been a local unless he was new.

"Oh, Missy? I'm not sure."

"You said—hold on." She wiggled, trying to get the zipper up in the back. There were no mirrors in Rita's fitting rooms. She opened the door and turned her back on Sierra. "Can you try to zip it?"

Sierra got the zipper up easily. She turned around to see both women beaming at her. Rita pushed the fitting room door closed so she could see herself in the full-length mirror on the outside of it.

She barely recognized herself. The halter-style turquoise gown perfectly complemented her newly tanned skin and sun-kissed hair. The delicious fabric skimmed over her curves, baring her shoulders and upper back, with a beautifully draped, airy chiffon skirt.

"We'll take it," Sierra said.

"Gorgeous," Rita agreed. "Oh, and the other day I think we were just talking about poor Missy and all she's been through, weren't we?"

"Right," Blue said, turning to be unzipped. "What was the name you said? I was just curious, you said someone was a victim or something like that."

"Oh." Rita drew air in through her teeth and shook her head. "That. Well, you know about Jim Arden, the whole town did."

Blue shook her head. "No, the name doesn't sound familiar."

"Arden," Sierra said. "That's the guy who was hit and killed on 41, right across from the drum circle, right?"

"What? When? What happened?" Blue asked.

The bell over the shop door jingled and two women with a little girl burst in, fanning themselves. "Oh, it feels good in here," the older woman gushed. "My goodness, how cute is this place!"

"Go change and I'll fill you in," Rita told Blue. She followed them out into the heat on their way out with the red Rita's Roses garment bag. "Dale's daughter was driving the car that hit Jim Arden. It happened a long time ago, you two had to have been just kids."

"But—Missy was only a little older than us," Blue said. "She really killed someone?"

"We'd remember that," Sierra said. "I don't get it."

"The details were kept out of the paper," Rita said, peering into her shop to check on the patrons. "Maybe because Missy was a minor, I'm not sure. Mr. Arden and his wife ran the bait shop next to the marina back then, you might've crossed paths with him there."

"I think—he had that little fluffy dog that was always hanging out under the counter, right?" Blue asked. "Oh my God, I remember him. Missy hit and killed him? So she went to jail?"

"I thought she just dropped out of school," Sierra said.

"Well, she did, but it was because she had her baby, right?" Blue added.

A crash came from inside the shop, drawing Rita's attention. "For Pete's sake," Rita groaned, pulling the door open and starting back inside. "Got to run!"

"What was that about?" Sierra asked in the parking lot.

"I talked to Dale Bryant last week at Captain Crab's. He kept my dad afloat while he served his sentence. I asked him about the night my mum died; how my dad swears he wasn't drinking but the evidence showed otherwise. I mentioned Dale to Rita the other day and she brought up the guy at the bait shop."

"I don't remember him, but I wasn't born with a fishing pole in my hand," Sierra said. "I don't remember much about Missy back then either, but I can tell you, since you've been gone, that girl hasn't spent more than a few days in a row clean and sober. It's heartbreaking. I'm sure you've seen her around since you've been back."

"I don't think so."

Sierra shrugged. "She was at the drum circle this weekend, hanging on the fringes, probably looking to get high. When you leave the village and turn onto Live Oak Way, check out the parking lot of the Gas and Go. She's usually there."

"Oh wow. That's awful. Maybe I should try and talk to her?"

Sierra's eyes widened. "I don't see the connection."

"I don't either, but how the hell did Dale pay all my dad's bills for six months on a deputy's salary? Think about it. That money came from somewhere. Something doesn't add up."

Sierra pursed her lips. "Who does Dale know that'd have that kind of money?"

"There's only one person I can think of," Blue said. "And there's no way Gino Castellari would lift a finger to help my dad. But . . . I always thought it was weird that Dale could be friends with Enzo's dad and also with mine, even after their falling out."

Sierra's eyebrows went up. "Dale's daughter killed a guy when we were kids, and this is the first we're hearing of it. In *this* town. Maybe being friends with a Castellari has its perks," she said.

Blue's mind was spinning. Her phone dinged. "Crap. I've gotta grab Murphy and get to my dad, I promised we'd be there before noon."

Sierra pulled a business card from her purse and pressed it into Blue's hand. "I want you to do something for me."

Blue read the card and frowned at her.

"I've been wanting to bring this up. This is a therapist I've seen off and on for years. She's wonderful. I think it'd be good for both you and Murphy to get some counseling. It doesn't have to be with Shannon, this is just a suggestion."

She pressed her lips together and looked again at the card: *Dr. Shannon Harbrough, PhD, Licensed Family Therapist*. Phone, fax, and address were listed in Bonita Springs. Blue met Sierra's eyes. "I think we're doing okay. I mean, mostly."

"I think you're both doing amazing. I'm not kidding. It's just—you've been through a lot. I'm not sure you even realize that. Same with Murph. It couldn't hurt, right? Meet her, talk to her. If it's not for you, then try someone else."

"Maybe," she agreed. "I promise I'll think about it."

"Think hard. This is important, Blue. For both of you. I believe that in my soul."

Brent called again when she was almost home to pick up Murphy. She bit the inside of her cheek and groaned. If she didn't answer, he'd just keep calling. "Hi, Brent."

"Blue? Well, goddamn. I was getting ready to leave another voice mail."

"I'm sorry," she said. "It's been a little crazy here."

"Sounds like it's time to come home. I've been plenty patient."

"I'm not sure whether—"

"Whether what? This has gone on long enough. You said you needed time to think, and you've had that."

"Brent, this was your idea," she said, mustering the strength Sierra kept saying she had.. "You wanted a divorce. I'm trying to find a way forward for Murphy and me. I've been meaning to call you."

"Right." His sarcasm came through in a growl. "I told you I changed my mind. You think it's your place to punish me? I'm not going to beg. All this bullshit is over. I bought my plane ticket to come down there and we'll drive your van back home."

"What? Why would you do that? I can't leave now. A lot's happened . . . my dad needs me here. You don't know—"

He cut her off. "And I don't need you? You're my wife. Your obligation is to me. Think about that for a second. Think about where you'd be without me. Your dad managed for ten years on his own; he'll be fine when you're gone."

"He had a heart attack," she said quickly, before he could barrel over her words again. "He had bypass surgery Friday night. That's what—"

"Jesus Christ!" He interrupted again, shouting. She pulled the phone away from her ear. "Sure he did. That's just perfect. So now you can't leave. That's it, I'm done with this."

Blue's heart leapt at his words. *This*—did that mean *her*? Four weeks ago the thought would've crushed her. She'd been struggling with what she'd say to him when she finally called him back, but maybe this was why she hadn't. She was afraid to tell him how firmly she believed she and Murph belonged here.

"Figure it out," Brent said. "Get your father to hire some help. I don't care how you make it work, Blue. I'll be there next week to bring you two home." He hung up.

Blue carried her Rita's Roses package into the house, moving as if she was underwater, in a daze. She was numb. It couldn't happen. She couldn't let him come, but how could she stop him? Sierra and Chloe's wedding was ten days from now. And it was still several weeks before her dad could step back into his fishing boots. Next week was too soon. *Never* was what she wanted. She wanted never to see Brent's face again. She stumbled to the bathroom and splashed cold water on her face, heart racing. She sucked in air, trying to calm down. She imagined Brent climbing out of a cab in her dad's driveway, marching up to the front door; she scooped water into her mouth, splashing more on her neck, and the bathroom lights flickered, growing dim. Shit. She slid down the bathroom wall and dropped her head below her knees, hands clasped on the back of her head. She felt as if she might pass out.

"Mom!" The screen door banged as Murphy came in from the yard. "Are you ready to go?"

She forced breaths in and out, trying to keep them measured and equal. "I need a few minutes," she croaked.

His footsteps retreated toward the kitchen.

She forced herself up. The Blue in the mirror looked haunted and pale. She drifted to her parents' walk-in closet, allowing her mum's clothing to brush against her face and inhaling deeply. She sat down and pulled the lid off the box of photos she'd spied here the day she'd stumbled upon her dad sorting his heart medications. Blue flipped through the photos quickly; she'd promised her dad she'd be there for his transfer. She and Murph had decorated a piece of foam board with photos they'd chosen from the ones she'd carted here from Tallahassee. She had several of Murphy as a baby and toddler, Murph and her together, one of herself in her white nurse's uniform and cap on graduation day, and the picture of the Yellowfin from her dad's office. She'd left space to add whatever she found here. Maybe seeing all of these pictures would give him extra incentive to work hard and regain his strength.

She turned the box upside down and spread them out, her gaze roving over them. She plucked one of her mum on the beach, a hibiscus flower tucked behind one ear; one of herself on her dad's shoulders, her face painted with a pink butterfly pattern from the Sarasota Circus; a great one of the three of them out on the docks before heading out for an overnighter, Blue between her parents with Hook at their feet. Then one more of her parents on the bench out front, where he and Ella would sit every Sunday evening watching the sunset over the ocean. She began gathering the rest back into the box and paused. Near her knee was a foursome: Mitch and Ella with Enzo's parents. It looked like the same setting as the one over her dad's desk, probably out on one of the Castellari yachts. But it wasn't the setting or even the couples together that caught her eye. Blue stood and carried the photo out into the bedroom where the lighting was better, frowning down at it. She wanted to make sure she wasn't imagining things.

The two men sat beside each other, and Ella and Sofia were next to them. Nobody seemed aware of a camera capturing the moment. It must have been snapped by a crewman. Her mother and Sofia were mid-laugh, mouths open and smiling at each other. On the end, Mitch stared off toward some unseen horizon, appearing lost in thought. Between Mitch and Ella was Enzo's father. Gino was turned toward Blue's mum, one arm resting along the railing behind her shoulders. His expression—the intense way he was gazing at Ella—made Blue shudder. She dropped the photo onto her father's dresser and switched on the lamp, illuminating the old photo.

He looked like a man in love. Or lust. He wasn't laughing or smiling with the women. He didn't seem to be part of their conversation. He was simply staring at her mum, rapt. Absorbed. Predatory. His posture arched toward her, his legs splayed open and angled toward her.

She left the photo on the dresser and darted back into the closet. If there was one, there had to be more. She shuffled them around on the floor, trying to see all of them. Murphy startled her and she let out a little shriek.

He laughed. "Sorry. When are we leaving? Because Cooper and Josh are gonna be watching for my livestream at one, but I can tell them it'll be later if you think I should."

"I'm ready. I still want to be on the water by one. Grandpa will be in a physical therapy session by then anyway." She got to her feet. Her dad was probably wondering where they were. She'd have to come back to this later. She scooped up the few photos she wanted to add to their foam board and started toward the bedroom door.

"This one too?" Murphy held up the photo of Gino being . . . Gino.

"Not that one. Leave it there."

★   ★   ★

By two o'clock, Blue was ready to sink the damned Yellowfin vessel and never look at another fish again. They'd spent an hour with Mitch, helping him get settled in and updating him on how the business end of things was going. She kept the details sparse, not wanting to upset him with the fact that she'd switched to a wholesaler for the time being. They were at the docks ready to head out by one. "See, right on time for your fans," she'd joked to Murphy.

Now it was an hour later and they were still in the boat slip, unmoving. Blue had tried everything she could think of to get the stupid engine going, to no avail. It had been fine yesterday. Murphy came back to the cockpit from his position on the bow; he'd been about to throw the lines off and free them, but nothing was happening.

"Did you check the fuel-water filter?" Murphy turned Blue's phone toward her, showing her a paused YouTube video. "That's usually one of the most common problems."

Blue took the phone. "I don't even know what that is." She swiped a forearm across her brow, her liberal application of SPF 50 mingling with sweat to make her even hotter, and pressed play. When she'd put the phone down and duplicated every step of what the video advised, the engine sputtered but still wouldn't start. She'd been through the troubleshooting pages in the Yellowfin's ancient owner's manual and had watched six videos on starting stalled motors. She was acutely aware of time getting away from her; she couldn't afford to lose an entire day's profits.

"Mom. Call my dad—call Enzo."

"We aren't doing that."

"Why not? He'll help, call him."

"Murph. He has his own job to do. I'm sure he's busy." She was not calling Enzo to come save his competitor.

"I bet he'd come."

She sat down and scrolled through her phone. She put a call in to Kai even though she knew he was at work. She left him a voice mail; but by the time he got it it'd probably be too late for them to go out.

"Crap," she murmured. Who else? The few connections she had left here weren't fishing folks; they couldn't help her. She gritted her teeth and dialed her dad. Mitch Shea answered right away.

"Did you prime it first?"

"Yes."

"You have gas?"

"Dad. Yes."

"You're in neutral?"

"Yes. We primed the motors, tried the manual choke, made sure there's no kinks in the lines. I don't know what else to do."

"Okay, listen, you won't get Kai this time of day, but let me give you Dale's number. He'll help."

She took the number as if it wasn't already in her phone—she really didn't want to call him, not with so many unanswered questions involving him; she still didn't know why he'd been evasive about the night her mum had died. She hung up with her dad and dropped her head into her hands. She was going to have to sacrifice a whole day's profits. And then what? Just hope the stupid motor fixed itself by tomorrow?

"Mom. Call my real dad. He told me his job is fishing and fixing boats. Just stop being stubborn and call him."

She frowned. "I'm sure he's already working."

He took her phone and scrolled through her contacts. "So just text him."

"Give me my phone; it's not a good idea."

He handed it to her. "'Kay, here. I texted him."

"You *what*??" The phone rang in her hand. She gasped, nearly flinging it off the boat.

"Answer it," Murph reached to take it from her.

"I've got it," she grumbled at her son. "Hello?"

Enzo's deep, warm voice came through the phone. "Is another rescue in order?"

She laughed. "Oh no. We're still at the docks. I am so sorry to bother you. I'm having trouble getting the engine started. We may not be fishing today."

"I'll be right there, I just brought Ma back from the grocery store. Hang tight."

Blue's gaze went from the phone in her hand to Murphy. "He's coming over to help."

◆ 18 ◆

Enzo was boarding the Yellowfin in less than ten minutes. Before he could even say hello, Blue summoned nerve she'd been building for a decade and jumped in with both feet. "Murphy knows. We talked last night. Murph, this is your father, Vincenzo Castellari. Enz, this is your son, Murphy Shea."

Enzo set down the large canvas case he carried and straightened up. "Hey there, Murphy." His tone was subdued, his face painted with something resembling fear.

"Hi." Her son's tone matched his father's. He stared up at him, and Blue saw Enzo through her son's eyes—this tall, broad-shouldered, superhero of a fisherman who could just as easily fix a boat engine as save a life.

Enzo took a seat, putting him closer to eye level with the boy. "Listen, I just want to say, when your mom told me that I'm your dad, that I have a son and it's *you*, Murphy, I've never been so happy. I'm sure this is probably upsetting and a little scary for you. And I know you already have a dad. But I'm so glad to officially meet you."

"It's not scary. My friend Josh has two dads. And Jeremy has two houses, with a mom, dad, and stepmom."

Blue smiled. "I didn't even think of that, Murph."

"What do I call you? 'Cause if I call you Dad then I don't know if my other Dad will get mad."

Blue closed her eyes. She wanted to dismiss that fear for him, but chances were, Brent was going to lose his mind when he found out she'd introduced Murphy to his real father.

"You can call me Enzo or anything you want. Whatever feels right."

"Okay," he said. "I'll think about it."

"You want to help me get this beast out on the water? I could use an extra set of hands." He dug into the tools he'd brought. "Let's see what's going on." He moved to the four large outboard motors at the stern, Murphy shadowing him.

"What's that for?" Murph pointed at something under Enzo's hands. It was the first of many, many questions, each of which Enzo answered patiently.

"That's the top of the cylinder, where the fuel burns."

"What's that thing down there?"

"One of the fuel filters, we're going to check each of them."

"What are you taking out, what does that do?"

"This," Enzo said, his Sharky's T-shirt pulling taut as he leaned lower momentarily, "is a bad spark plug." He held it up, scrutinizing it. "Could you go into the left zippered pocket on my bag and grab the clear plastic case for me?"

Murphy squared his shoulders and nodded. "Sure." He moved to the bag and did as Enzo asked, returning with the item.

"Thanks." Enzo set it down and opened it, revealing several different sizes of spark plugs. He chose one and began to lean over the first motor but paused. "You know what, I need my other wrench, Murph. If you don't mind."

"I can find it! What does it look like?" The boy was standing at attention by Enzo's bag, waiting for instruction. Blue watched the exchange, silent.

"All right, this might be tricky. It's a socket wrench, it'll be in the main compartment. Look for one with a long handle and little round head, with a square in the center of it."

Murphy crouched down, concentrating. After a minute he held it up, triumphant. "This one?"

"Yep, you got it. Now we need the 3/8-inch socket. Those are all in a black case near where you found the wrench."

Murph followed the instructions and began to carry the wrench and case over to Enzo.

"Oh, could you just grab it out of there for me?" He turned toward the second motor and fiddled with something. "My hands are kind of full."

"Sure," Murphy said. He pored over the dozens of silver socket attachments in the case, brow furrowed in concentration. Blue expected him to become frustrated and demand she help, or else just give up and take the case to Enzo, but he didn't. He chose a few, checking their size, and finally selected what Blue painfully hoped was the right one. This was all new territory for him. Enzo involving Murphy reminded her of her dad teaching her how to do whatever he happened to be working on at the moment—from replacing a doorknob to changing the oil on his car to manning an outrigger. He'd never seemed to mind having her underfoot, always involving her in the work, the same as Enzo was doing now. Murphy handed him the chosen socket and wrench.

"Perfect! That's exactly the one I needed," he said, smiling at Murphy. The boy stood straighter, glowing with pride while the new spark plug was installed. "All right now," Enzo said, standing. He moved aside and passed the motor cover to Blue's son. "Go ahead and put that back on. You'll feel and hear the clicks that'll tell you it's in place. You can get the other ones too."

She watched as her son turned the cover this way and that, and then successfully get it snapped on. He did the same with the other three. Blue glanced up at Enzo. He winked at her.

"Can you make sure I did it right?" Murphy asked. "I don't want to blow the engine up or anything."

Enzo laughed. "No worries." He reached over and checked and gave Murphy a thumbs up. "All good. Nice work, man. Ready to try it?"

Murphy looked at Blue and then back at Enzo. "Um. Me?"

"Go for it, key's still in the ignition." He gave Blue a sideways glance, lowering his voice a bit. "As long as that's all right with you, Mama?"

Blue's heart somersaulted. She nodded. "Yes. Sure, go ahead, Murph." Damn. She was suddenly clammy and jittery in the most oddly pleasant way. She tried to focus on the boat starting.

The Yellowfin's engine rumbled to life on the first turn of the key. She clapped and let out a little whoop. "I can't believe it! Thank you so much, Enzo!" She'd have hugged him if he was anyone else. "And Murphy! You make a great assistant."

"You're going to be an expert at all this by the time your Grandpa's back. Go ahead and turn her off for a minute, we'll wait and then do a recheck just to make sure she's good to go." Murph complied, killing the engine. "How's your dad doing?" he asked Blue.

"Not bad, considering. He's tough. Probably due to this life," she said, glancing at the boat. "They want him to do a couple weeks of cardiac rehab, but he's already threatening to leave early. It's only been five days since surgery. He needs to give himself time to heal."

"I remember your dad. No one's going to get him to do something he doesn't want to do."

She smiled. "Very true. Hey, listen, thank you so much for helping us. I wouldn't have bothered you. Murphy got ahold of my phone and texted you before I knew what he was doing."

★   ★   ★

Her words hit Enzo like a dart to a balloon. He'd just carried in the last bag of groceries for his mother when that text had come through. He'd been happily surprised that Blue felt comfortable enough to reach out. But she hadn't—their son had. He turned to Murphy and told him to start the engine again. It fired right up with no trouble.

"You're a lifesaver," Blue said. "Literally. I'm sorry we've held you up, I'm sure you've got your own fish to catch."

"No!" Murphy said, turning toward them from the helm. "Do you really have to go?"

Enzo already loved this kid. "Well . . . I don't want to be a third wheel. You and your mom have your own little rhythm going each day out on the water."

Blue stared at him, expression painted with curiosity. "We do? I guess I hadn't realized."

Shit! "I only meant, you must by now. Do you feel like it's all coming back to you?" He hoped he was covering any hint of his slightly stalkerish behavior.

"I think so. I haven't forgotten much, and what I did is coming back. Murph is picking up this stuff lightning fast. I'm positive I couldn't do it on my own," she said.

"You could come with us and keep the fish you catch, since you have to work too," Murphy suggested.

Blue raised an eyebrow at him. "Murph, he's got his own boat. People are probably waiting for him."

"Just Salvi, and he can get Luca or someone else to go with him. I don't mind coming out on the *Shamrock* for the day, maybe an extra person will give you some extra profit." If Gino found out he'd spent the afternoon on Mitch Shea's boat, he'd disown him. But how would he find out?

Blue was nodding. "If you really don't mind, that'd be so great. Even with the two of us we're not bringing in the weight my dad usually does."

"I don't mind at all." He texted Salvi that he'd gotten tied up and to take Luca instead. It was too much to hope that Matty would be upright and sober. He'd hoped to catch him tonight at dinner, but now he wasn't sure he'd be back in time. Which was fine. He hadn't missed a family dinner in months, and he doubted his brother would show up anyway.

Once they were out of the channel, Blue steered them into the wind, heading southwest. They'd been out on the water for a couple of hours when one of the outriggers Blue was minding released its clip and began unspooling—she had a bite and it was substantial. She grabbed hold of the rod as the end of it arced heavily down toward the water and began battling to bring in what looked like a sizable fish on the line. As she worked, Murphy darted over to watch and give her pointers—God love him, giving tips to someone as seasoned as his mother. Enzo kept an eye on the other poles while making sure she didn't need any help. He'd meant it when he said he didn't want to intrude on their fishing rhythm.

As Blue and Murphy brought a hefty red snapper aboard, the clip on the line behind Enzo released. The rest of the afternoon flew by with that same fast-paced cadence—they'd reel one in, a bite would hit another line, and they'd work on that one while the first fish was stowed in the freezer, and by the time the next line was set with bait and in the water again, another clip would release. Murphy had rigged holders for the cell phone on each side of the center console, letting him capture hands-free footage of their catches. He landed a large king mackerel right after Blue had officially called it a day.

She stood, staring at the fish and then at her son, hands on her hips. "It's been years since I've seen one that size, Murph. Wow!"

He was grinning from ear to ear. "Think he'll fit in the cooler with the others?"

"Let me help," Enzo said, coming over to them. "How'd you land this guy? He's huge, must be at least thirty pounds."

Murphy held the door open on the deck floor while Enzo fit the fish into a very full freezer. "I gave him some drag, instead of setting the line right away, like you said. It worked great!"

Blue moved to the side near the stern and leaned toward the water, dipping her hands in to rinse them. She lost her balance for a second, pink fishing boots scrambling for purchase as she straightened up, and Enzo lunged toward her but then stopped. She was fine. She scrubbed at her hands with the towel she kept tucked into the back pocket of her shorts. "Ugh." She wrinkled her nose. "It's the one thing I didn't miss. I've been using lemons at home, and my dad's orange soap works pretty well for both cleaning and the smell. But there's not much point to worrying about it out here," she said, chuckling.

"I don't think it smells bad," Murphy said. "It smells like a hundred fifty followers on my YouTube channel."

Enzo raised his eyebrows. "Dude. A hundred fifty followers? That's more than my brother Luca's got on his gaming channel and he's been posting since last year. You're killing it."

Blue slipped past Enzo to get to the helm so they could start heading in. They rode the waves in silence for a while. The sky to the west was just beginning to fill with strokes of pink and purple, about an hour until sunset. "Enzo." Blue spoke again when they were a few minutes out from the channel. "Did you ever learn anything else about what happened that night, at the party at your house? When my dad came and got me from the bonfire?"

"Ma lied about that night. She always acted like she was there; she said our dads were fighting about contracts. But she wasn't even home until after you'd left. She was out with my aunt. Salvi remembered. When I called her out on it, she played it off like it was no big deal."

"Why would she lie?"

"I don't know," he said, shaking his head.

Blue rolled the cotton edge of her shirt between her fingertips, biting her bottom lip. "I found something in my dad's

things. I think it's . . . I don't know. It struck me as kind of—"
She stopped again.

"What?" He leaned forward. "What is it?" Her troubled
thoughts were telegraphed in her hesitance, her tense, stiff posture, as she continued to twist her shirt.

"I think I should just show you, if you have a couple minutes
when we're back. It's easier than explaining."

"Sure, that's fine." Enzo ached to touch her. Being this close
and unable to do a thing about it was torture.

It was almost dark when they made it back to the Shea cottage. Enzo examined the photo under the porch light. It was
their parents out on the water, a sunset sky in the background.
But that wasn't what Blue was showing him. He narrowed his
eyes and brought the photo closer. His father . . . the way he
was staring at Ella Shea. Ella and his mom were totally unaware,
laughing at something, and Mitch Shea on the opposite side was
off in his own world. And Gino looked at Ella like he might take
a bite out of her.

19

ENZO STOOD IN HIS parents' driveway clenching and unclench-
ing his fists. At only nine thirty, the house was dark. He
punched the keycode and opened the garage door. His mom's SUV
was there along with the Castellari and Sons van. Gino's sedan was
gone. He closed the door and headed around the outside of the
house to the back, where Luca's entrance was. A couple of years ago
Luca had moved from his upstairs bedroom to the guest wing, the
pretentious-sounding east end of the estate that Gino had insisted
on when he had the place built. Luca's car was parked in the drive.

Christina opened the door for him and the aroma of buttered
popcorn wafted out. "Hey, Enzo! Come on in. We're watching
Avengers; I've never seen it." His brother's girlfriend had the sun-
niest disposition of anyone he'd ever met. She bounced back onto
the couch beside Luca and he fanned the blanket up for her to
slide under, pulling her against his side.

He raised the remote and paused the Marvel movie. "What's
up, Zo? Want some popcorn?"

"No. Do you know where Pops is? When he'll be back?"

"He's not home? Are you sure?"

"Yeah," Enzo said. He wished he'd just texted Luca instead
of coming in. The scene was bumming him out, the two of them
all cozy and happy, Luca clueless about what a shit their father

was. He needed to get out of here before his mood boiled over. He put a hand on the door.

Luca jumped up and came over to him. "What's going on? Did you try calling him?"

"No. It's all right. I'll catch him tomorrow. I'm sorry I interrupted. It's a great movie," he told Christina.

Luca followed him out onto the drive. "Hey. Seriously, what's going on? Did something happen?" His brow furrowed with worry. "You look like you're about to go off."

Enzo looked up at the sky, exhaling forcefully. "I'm okay. It's just something I need to see him about." His youngest brother had made it this long without knowing about Gino's affairs, and Enzo wasn't going to undo that now. Not for their father's sake, but for Luca's. Years ago when Enzo'd learned about Nadine, it had been a total mind fuck.

"Is it about where he's at right now?"

Enzo frowned at him. "What do you mean?"

Luca looked down at his feet. "I don't know. What do *you* mean?"

He shook his head. "You're not making any sense."

"Just . . . why don't you call him? That way you'll know when he'll be back and if you should wait for him or see him tomorrow."

"Yeah. I can do that." He started to back away toward his car. Luca was acting weird, even for Luca.

"Do you—I mean—why do we protect him? Do you know?" Luca demanded, taking a step toward him.

"Shit," Enzo muttered. "So you know."

"About Kendra? Yeah. You guys all know? Why the hell aren't we doing anything about it? What about Ma?"

"How do you know her name?"

"I heard him on the phone and confronted him."

Enzo raised his eyebrows. "Really. Did it . . . have any kind of impact? Fuck that; never mind. The one before her was named Cheryl. He's never gonna stop."

Luca shook his head. "Whoa. There've been others? But if you know too, then shouldn't we do something?"

"I'm working on it," he said. "Marcello and I thought we took care of it, but I guess it's just a constant fucking thing with him. I'm sorry, man. We really didn't want you to find out."

"And I hate that, for real. Knock it off. I'm not five anymore."

Enzo could count on one hand the number of times he'd seen his brother mad. "I'm sorry. You're right." He put a hand on his back pocket, where Blue's photo was, considering. He pulled it out and handed it to him.

Luca waved a hand over his head so the motion sensor light would come back on. He took in the photo, looking closer and then handing it quickly back to Enzo. "Who is that? Who's the lady next to him? He sure as hell isn't looking at Ma."

"It's Ella Shea."

"Oh. *Oh.*" He looked again. "And that's Mitch Shea right there? When was this?"

"The date stamp says twelve years ago, June. That was the summer our families split apart—Blue's dad cut us off, wouldn't let her have anything to do with me or any of us. You would have been around nine; I don't know if you'd remember, but she used to be here all the time. Then something happened. It was the night Uncle Ray drove the golf cart into the pool, remember?"

"I remember that party. Shit." Luca took a step back, cupping the top of his head with one hand and staring wide-eyed past Enzo, into the darkness. "You think . . . what do you mean, something happened? 'Cause I remember that party, Zo. Mrs. Shea was bleeding."

"What?" Enzo's heart pounded in his ears. "What did you say?"

"I—he was carrying her, and her lip was bleeding." Luca touched his own bottom lip. "Me and Matty were racing in the upstairs hallway when we heard Pop and Blue's dad shouting about something. Then Blue's dad bumped into me. I thought he was

gonna drop Mrs. Shea. I thought—Mitch Shea's a drunk, everyone knows that. I don't know what I thought. Maybe that he'd
already dropped her and she got hurt, I don't know. I was a kid!"

"Hey. It's all right. You were a little kid. Her lip was bleeding? Why was he carrying her?"

Luca shrugged helplessly. "I don't know. It didn't seem weird
at the time, or maybe it all seemed weird. She was crying and
bleeding, I guess nine-year-old me thought it made sense he had
to carry her."

"In the upstairs hallway. Where?"

"What—um. The end of the hall, by their bedroom." Luca
grabbed the photo and peered at it, raising his gaze to Enzo.

"Yeah." Enzo clenched his teeth, the events of that night taking shape in his mind.

"But what if Pop—"

"Yeah," Enzo repeated again. "There's gotta be a different
explanation. I don't even wanna say this out loud."

Luca saved him the trouble. "Either Blue's dad walked in on
Pop and Mrs. Shea, or else Gino—" he stopped talking, unable
to finish.

"I know. I know, man, but—" God. He couldn't bring himself to consider it, but what were they supposed to think, in light
of everything? "I have to talk to Blue."

"Can she handle this? Salvi said—"

"Oh, fuck Salvi," Enzo growled. "And Marcello too. I know
she's been gone, but she grew up with us! She loved us. She'd
have done anything for any of us, and you all should know that."

Luca's eyes were huge. He nodded. "You're right. I'm sorry.
When I heard she was back, you know the first thing I thought of?"

Enzo shook his head.

"The time Xander Petosky kicked my ass after school and
she stopped him. I don't even know how, I mean, she was older,
but he was a frickin' moose. She made him *cry*—I still remember
that."

"What? How? Did she hit him? You never told me this."

Luca grinned. "She didn't touch him. She bitched him out so bad for picking on scrawny little me, for being a bully and letting her down after she used to babysit him, that he started bawling and took off. Blue gave me her Kleenex from her purse for my bloody nose and walked me home. That's what I thought of."

He smiled, picturing it. This ache each time she entered his thoughts was getting harder to ignore every day.

"Oh, man," Luca said, grinning along with him. "You should see your face."

"What? Shut up." Enzo scrubbed both hands through his hair. "When does Gino usually get home?"

"No clue. Could be any minute or not till four AM," Luca said. "You wanna come hang out? Or maybe go get some sleep and we'll catch him in the morning."

"Yeah. I guess I'll go." Enzo wasn't used to taking advice from his younger brother, but there was nothing he could do right now. He was turning to go when Luca stopped him.

"Hey, Zo. I never see you look like that over Jillian."

"That's different—"

Luca shrugged. "Whatever. Just saying." He went back inside, leaving Enzo staring after him, feeling like he had just been called out—by his little brother. What the fuck.

He was coming around the corner of the house toward his truck when headlights moved across the driveway. Gino pulled in and sat in his car talking on the phone, oblivious to Enzo standing in the dark watching him. He moved toward the car and Gino abruptly hung up and got out.

"Son! We missed you at dinner tonight. Your mother made manicotti."

Enzo gripped his father by the back of his shirt, catching him off guard and easily steering him to the illumination of the head-lights in front of the sedan.

"What're you doing? Get off me." Gino jerked out of his grasp, squaring off with Enzo.

He shoved the photo in his father's face. "What's this, Pop?" All of the anger he'd arrived with was back, plus some.

"Looks like me and your ma and the Sheas."

"Look closer." Gino grabbed for it and Enzo jerked it away. "Nope. It's not mine. It belongs to Mitch Shea." He was gratified when his father registered surprise. "What, did you think it was a secret? You look like a goddamn predator. Ella Shea looks pretty oblivious to me."

Gino looked unperturbed, which only pissed Enzo off more. "It's old news. What does it matter? Jesus Christ, Vincenzo. Get ahold of yourself." He turned to head into the garage.

Enzo grabbed him by the arm, pulling him back. "You're not going anywhere. Not until you tell me what happened. This is why you quit seeing them, right? This is why I couldn't see Blue anymore? So which was it—did Ma know you slept with her best friend? Or did you rape Ella Shea?"

Gino hit him. Stunned, Enzo reeled back, his eye throbbing. Holy shit, he hadn't seen that coming. He shook it off and came toward Gino, nose to nose, fists ready. He stood, rigid, using his height advantage to stare him down. His arm twitched to let fly but he couldn't. He couldn't hit his father.

"Go ahead." Gino glared at him. "You've been wanting to do it for weeks."

"I've been wanting to hit you a lot longer than that, you son of a bitch." He stepped back. "What happened? Why'd Blue's mom have to be carried home that night? Why was she *bleeding*?" Enzo's gut twisted, hearing his own words.

"I don't owe you an explanation. You were a kid. You're still an overdramatic little boy," Gino said, spitting the words.

"You owe me the truth. What did you do?"

"Nothing she wasn't asking for."

Enzo punched him, rocking Gino backward into his truck. He looked shocked.

"I quit. I'm done, Pop." He meant it.

"We're not even close to done here," his father bellowed, recovering and straightening up.

He lunged at his father, stopping inches away, the older man's cologne seeping into his nostrils. "*You* are done," Enzo growled. He drew back, out of reach as Gino grabbed at him. "Don't fucking touch me."

★   ★   ★

Enzo woke up Thursday morning certain of one thing. He couldn't marry Jillian.

★   ★   ★

He grabbed a cup of coffee and, not bothering to throw on shirt or shoes, followed Moon through the crabgrass and bird of paradise bushes. They emerged on his little section of beach, nestled into a point that jutted out onto the Gulf. He lay back on the sand, inhaling the salt air. He'd been avoiding the truth for a while.

It didn't matter if she made sense, if they made sense together. Jillian was amazing. But just because she was perfect didn't make her perfect for him. Long-awaited relief washed over him, the tension of forcing himself to be someone he wasn't finally released. He pressed a shaking hand over his eyes and then jerked it away in pain. He'd almost forgotten about the black eye from Gino. He had major fish to fry now because of his father, the first of which was figuring out how to talk to Blue about what happened the night Gino attacked her mum.

But first he had to get through today. Breaking up with Jillian was going to be ugly. He felt awful, knowing how upset she'd be. They never should have gotten engaged. He'd done it so he wouldn't lose her, but it would have been kinder to let her go months ago. He'd have to wait until their dinner plans this evening to see her; she was in court today.

He'd already group texted his brothers and told them he was finished with Gino and wouldn't be in. Ever. Marcello had texted back *Cool, see you tomorrow at the staff meeting.* Lately, he could count on Marcello to be a dick no matter what. He didn't get it. Salvi hadn't replied yet, which probably meant he was on the water. Matty hadn't answered either, which likely meant he'd just gone to bed as the sun came up. But Luca came through. *We'll miss you. We should all walk out on him.* It wasn't realistic to think any of the others could quit. They supplied too many restaurants and markets up and down the southwest Gulf Coast to run with a skeleton crew. A little voice nagged at Enzo that he wasn't really quitting either. He'd cultivated relationships with their clients. He had his brothers to think of. He had a house and a truck and a dog to feed. Bigger than any of that, he now had a son. He might hate Gino, but the idea of flaking on all of his responsibilities was terrifying. He'd have to formulate a plan, a way for his father to be held responsible for hurting Ella Shea.

Enzo was showered and dressed and ready to leave for Jillian's a full hour ahead of time. He wanted it done. He rang her bell at five minutes to eight. She opened the door, mascara wand in hand. "You're early! You're never early." She held the door open for him. "Oh my God, what happened to your eye?"

"Gino hit me." He stepped inside as she moved down the hallway, now wishing he wasn't early. He hated knowing he was about to hurt her.

"Are you serious?" she said over her shoulder, and he followed. "Why'd Gino hit you?"

"Because I called him out on his bullshit, running around behind my mom's back," he said. He stood awkwardly in her kitchen, not wanting to pull up a stool.

"Oh wow," she said, widening her eyes at him. She put the mascara away. "Did you put anything on that? How about some ice?"

He shook his head. "It's all right."

She stared at him. "You're acting really weird, Enzo. What's going on?"

"I—" He met her gaze. She'd turned him down the first time he'd asked her out. She'd needed to focus on law school and had no time to date. But then she'd changed her mind the next day and found him in the library, studying for his last final before graduation.

"Enzo?"

She'd broken up with him twice in six and a half years. He couldn't remember why. He'd apologized and she'd taken him back and things moved forward each time. The night they'd gotten engaged was almost the third time, but he'd proposed instead. He gripped the back of his neck, trying to find the words. "Jillian, I can't do this. I'm so sorry. We can't get married."

The color drained from her cheeks. "What? Why not?"

"I . . ." He shook his head. "I can't. I just can't. It's . . ."

She searched his eyes, her lower lip trembling. "You're really doing this?" she asked. "Less than three months from our wedding? I don't understand. Is this . . . this is because of your dad." She stared at him.

"No, it's not. That—it's got nothing to do with this."

"I don't know. I don't think you even know. Look at what's happened. You get in a huge fight with your father over him cheating and now you're breaking up with me," she said slowly. "Because you're afraid of being just like Gino." Her eyes welled up as she held his gaze.

"No. I'm *not*. You're connecting things that have nothing to do with each other."

"We're good together. Us, and our families, right? Your dad and my dad work well together, that's a partnership. Like ours," she pleaded her case.

He had to be misjudging what she was saying; she was upset, but she was always ethical. She couldn't be drawing any parallels to their fathers' working partnership and his and Jillian's romantic one—or lack of one. "Jillian, I've—I'm sorry, but I think I've known for a while that we shouldn't get married. It just doesn't feel right. I don't feel right."

"Because of Blue."

He frowned. "No. That's not it. Blue has nothing to do with this."

"You've been playing this game, Enzo, where you keep telling yourself you're not like Gino and you can have your cake and eat it too. You can have your *friendship*"—she put air quotes around the word—"with Blue—yes, I know more than you think I do—and your engagement to me and keep it all separate and legit, but it's not. You can't. You're lying to yourself." Her face was flushed red through her tanned skin.

"That's not it." His heart was pounding; she was wrong. This wasn't about Blue. It was about his life, his future. He wasn't meant to spend it with Jillian. "Listen, we're not right. You don't want to see that. Maybe you think it makes sense to get married since we've been together so long, but do you really want to tell our kids we got married because we'd already put in too much time?"

"You're twisting things," she said, her voice shaking. She glared at him. "Why did you agree? If we're so wrong for each other then why did you agree to get engaged?"

"Because I was afraid to lose you. But you won't be happy with me. I know that now. That stunt you pulled, introducing me to Jack Kelly? That wasn't you making a valuable business connection for me."

She shook her head. "What are you talking about?"

"I didn't need you to sell me on the idea of adding and running a cruise line. Why would you think that was necessary? All the talk about how much cleaner work it is, better hours, better pay. Why try so hard to convince me? Do you really want to marry me, Jillian? Do you want to spend the rest of your life with a fisherman? Do you? Because that's what I am."

"That's not all you are!" she blurted. "You're an engineer and you have so much potential—"

His heart dropped. He hadn't realized until now that he'd hoped he was wrong about her. He was crestfallen. "There it is. *All* I am. I'm not a fixer upper. I'm just me. I'm happy with that."

She moved closer to him. "I'm happy with that too, Enzo."

He'd come here feeling resigned and ready for it to be over. He was surprised how sad he suddenly felt.

"Let me ask you something," she said. "Bluebelle Shea. That's her name, right? That's who you were with at The Mariner a couple of Sundays ago." She searched his eyes.

It wasn't a question. He frowned at her. "What?" How did she know?

"You had lunch with her."

Dennis. Of course. He should have known nosy Dennis taking in that whole scene between him and Blue would come back to bite him. What did it even matter now? "Yes, I did."

"Tell me the truth this time. How long have you known she was back?"

He sighed. "Since we went to the ER for my eye. That was her. The nurse."

Jillian's sharp intake of breath jarred him. He didn't want to hurt her. He could have lied. But he was tired of pretending. He should have come clean about who Blue was the moment he saw her, with Jillian in the room.

"You . . . so you pretended not to know her? Why? Why would you. . . ." She stared at him. "There's only one reason I can think of. You love her. You're still in love with her."

"I should go." He took a step back, turning to leave.

She didn't move. Her tears finally spilled over and she reached for a tissue, looking away from him.

"Jillian—I'm sorry. I'm really sorry."

He didn't feel nearly as lighthearted pulling out of her drive-way as he had that morning. She was right. He was still in love with Blue. He'd been facing truths all day, why stop now? The way he felt about her had only intensified in the last ten years. There was no way he could change it. And there was no way he could be with her. Even if he took his family business out of the picture, which he'd taken a good first stab at, she was married; she was still thinking of going back to him. She'd had no trouble keeping things platonic since that stolen moment at the hospital.

He stopped at the hardware store on a whim on the way home before crossing onto the peninsula. On Live Oak Way, as soon as he'd passed Blue's cottage, he turned into the narrow strip of beach access parking on the opposite side of the Sheas' fence. Her house was dark. Enzo propped a hand on the fence and leaped over it.

Even in the moonlight, he could see all the work she and Murphy had done. The table and chairs on the patio had been painted, along with the glossy aqua bench under the willow tree. Hibiscus flowers dotted the back of the house, and large flower-ing potted plants decorated the corners of the patio. Enzo set the boxes of solar globe lights on the bench and got to work with his stepladder and the first strand, tossing it over a high branch at the entrance to the fairy garden trail and taking the old ones down in the process. He'd string them back and forth overhead, illumi-nating the village, and then he'd add more around the patio and firepit. They wouldn't come on right away; the solar panels had to soak up enough sunlight over the next day or two.

He was several yards into the grove of trees when he saw movement. He wasn't alone. A shadowy figure darted off the path and Enzo followed, peering into the foliage. "Hey!" He spoke in a loud whisper.

The small figure emerged, and he was shocked to see Sierra stepping carefully over the bluebell flowers back onto the path.

She stared up at him in the low light. "What are you doing here?" she whispered.

"What are *you* doing here?" He'd half wondered if the mysterious fairy village benefactor was Sofia, with the soft spot she held for Blue's mom. Or even Mitch Shea, though Enzo had struggled to imagine the gruff old fisherman painting fairy houses and erecting tiny, message-filled mailboxes.

Sierra held her arms out to her side and curtsied. "Fairy Garden Bandit at your service. But why are you here? Did you come to help?"

"I guess I did." He held up the light strand in his hands. "I wanted to brighten it up back here. Wait. Where's your car?"

"Chloe drops me off at the beach access," she pointed to the fence he'd just jumped. "She goes on an ice cream run and comes back. Plenty of time to do what I need to do. Let me help with that." She held a hand out.

He gave her an end, and they worked silently together, Sierra moving along the trail and handing the lights up to Enzo's outstretched hand until they reached the last house. They were halfway across the backyard with the third strand when the kitchen light went on. Sierra grabbed his arm and yanked him onto the ground with her. They stayed that way, unmoving, watching the kitchen window.

Sierra jerked, kicking her legs. "Oh my God, *ants*," she hissed. She slapped at her bare legs, trying to stay low to the ground.

Enzo got to his feet, crouching low, and motioned her to get to the edge of the grove of trees with him. He hoped they'd blend into the trees the way Sierra had earlier. They stood still and waited. When the kitchen light went out, Sierra ran over and grabbed the light strand they'd dropped, handing it to him. They hurriedly finished without a word.

Enzo helped Sierra over the fence, following silently. They stood near his truck waiting for her ride. She startled him from his thoughts. "Don't tell her it's me." A car passed by, illuminating them, and Sierra gasped. "Your eye! What the hell?"

"It's a long story. I won't tell her it's you. Don't tell her I was here either."

"Why are you here? What about your fiancée?"

"We broke up." It felt good to say it out loud.

"Oh." Sierra stared wide-eyed at him.

"What made you think of doing this?" he asked. He didn't want to answer any questions about Jillian. "The fairy garden thing. It's cool. They love it. I think it's even making a believer of Murphy."

"Maybe a little bit," she said, giggling softly. "Your kid's a little too wise for his years."

Enzo's eyes flooded with tears, startling him. He swallowed hard. *His* kid. Jesus.

Sierra beamed at him. She squeezed his arm. "Congratulations. And I'm playing Fairy Garden Bandit because she needs to stay. For her own sake, she needs to never go back to that asshole she was married to."

"Was?" He latched onto the word.

"Ugh," she groaned. "Is. He filed for divorce, though, so can't I say was?"

"Do you think she's staying?" Enzo's heart was in his throat.

"I hope so. I don't know." She shook her head. "He left, and then she couldn't pay her bills alone so she took Murph and came home. Fucking finally. Now he wants her back. But he's a— wait, she hasn't told you all this? You guys have spent some good chunks of time together lately."

Enzo ran a hand across the top of his head, pressing his lips together. She couldn't leave. Not again.

Sierra's tone grew softer. "She needs to stay," she repeated. "He's not good for her or Murphy. I don't think she's even told me all the crap he's done, but I do know it's bad. But it's like she's been brainwashed or just can't fully see it. She's only now starting to get some of her . . . confidence? Nerve? Some of herself back. I guess I'm painting the houses and leaving the little notes because I've tried talking to her, Chloe and I both have, and I can't tell if we're getting through. But maybe the messages will. I don't know."

"Maybe I should go talk to him." Enzo meant it. If Blue had been so trampled down that she couldn't stand up to him, he would. He'd relish the chance.

Sierra stared at him, eyes wide. "No. That's not—no. Let's not make this worse." Headlights swung into the parking area and a car pulled in beside them. "That's Chloe. It's been fun. Let's hope we can hang out again, next time with our girl, yeah?"

20

B LUE SAT IN THE PARKING lot of the bait store, summoning her nerve. She'd just come from the pawn shop. She tipped her head back, following the rusted post up to the large sign she'd parked under which bore the words *BAIT* and, in smaller letters, *fishing gear & tackle rental*. The shop itself had never had an actual name. It was sandwiched between Bliss Beach Boat Rentals and Anna's Sandwiches and looked every bit as old and neglected as it probably was. She doubted Jim Arden's wife would remember her, if she was even working today. Blue'd been a kid the last time she was here. If she wanted any answers to the things that didn't add up with Dale, she had two choices: talk to Dale's daughter Missy, if she could find her, or talk to Arden's wife.

The bell over the door jingled weakly, the scent of worms assaulting Blue's senses. She hung back near the fishing poles until the lone customer left. She set a small box of fishing lures by the register and the skinny, worn-out looking woman typed in the price without looking at the sticker—or her. Blue handed her a ten dollar bill.

"Three dollars and fifty-six cents is your change," Mrs. Arden said, counting the bills into Blue's hand. She glanced up and met her eyes and froze. "Bluebelle Shea."

"Yes." She was shocked—did she really look the same as she had when she was twelve or thirteen, the last time she'd been here? "Mrs. Arden?"

"Lord-a-mercy. I just about called you Ella. Bluebelle Shea, my goodness, but you could be your mother. You've come back to stay now?"

"I . . . uh. Thank you. I like hearing that I look like her. I'm back to stay, yes." If her trip to the pawn shop a half hour ago hadn't cemented that, she didn't know what did. "I'm glad you remember me."

"Child. Nobody around here can forget what happened to your poor mother." She wrapped both hands around Blue's, still on the countertop. "And not everyone blames your dad. Some do. But not us."

Blue's eyebrows went up. "Really?" Who was *us*? Maybe the Ardens had children she didn't know about.

"Jim and I know how things work here. You're on the inside or you're out. People like us," she said, nodding at Blue, then resting a hand over her own heart and looking toward the ceiling. "We ain't never been insiders. You know."

Mrs. Arden stared at her with such certainty. Feeling like an outsider in a town where their little bait shop had been a fixture for decades seemed an odd perspective for the woman to have, but Blue got her point. She hated to admit it, but Mrs. Arden was right to see a similarity between them. Her father—her little family—had become outsiders here the day her dad had been arrested for her mum's death. Or had it begun to happen two years earlier, the night they'd become enemies of the Castellaris? She summoned her nerve. "I was actually hoping to ask you about that. About your husband."

"Shoot. Go ahead. We don't mind." The woman moved quickly to the front door and flipped the sign to Closed, turning the lock. She was starting to creep Blue out, talking about her husband in the present tense, furtively looking over her shoulder and locking the door.

She dove in. "I'm wondering about Missy Bryant. I'm sorry to—"

"No, no sorries here. People think they'll make me mourn deeper by mentioning it—by saying her name or saying Jim's. Like they'll remind me of what happened. It don't work like that. He's always right here. Right. Here." She tapped her forehead aggressively. "At the front of my mind. He's part of me. There's no reminding me. It never goes away."

The woman's words hit Blue square in the chest. "Exactly. Always. With my mum, it's nice when someone mentions her." She took a deep breath. "Could you tell me what happened to Missy after . . . afterward?"

"She was arrested," Mrs. Arden said. "Her son was just a baby then, couldn'ta been more than a few months old. I heard a while back that her parents adopted him. Anyway, Missy went right from that jail cell to Oakhurst Facility for six months."

"And then?" Blue had heard Missy went to a psychiatric hospital for drug rehabilitation. Oakhurst was a county-run mental health facility. "After her six months, did she serve time in prison?"

"Bluebelle Shea." Mrs. Arden shook her head. "You're born and raised in Bliss, you understand better than that how it works here. Missy's father hired a Suncoast lawyer who got her six months at Oakhurst and that was that. Six months for my husband's life. Now listen," she said, leaning across the counter. "I ain't saying she didn't pay. She's still paying. That girl's life was ruined the day she took my Jim's. Every so often, she'll disappear from the beach for a while, and come back looking healthy and well. Until the next time. My sister works in food service at that posh Havenvale up in Orangetree, and she says she don't know why they bother to clear out Missy's room—they know she'll be back. Sometimes, just ain't no cure for folks like her."

She was floored. There was minimum sentencing time for all manslaughter charges, she knew that because of her dad. "I don't understand. How did she avoid jail time? How can her parents afford all those rehab stays at Havenvale?"

Mrs. Arden frowned at her. "Bluebelle, you really don't know? Dale Bryant is bought and paid for. The Castellaris own him. Just like they own half this town."

★　★　★

Enzo was waiting by the Yellowfin when Blue and Murphy walked out onto the docks Friday morning. She was dragging this morning; she'd slept fitfully, waking more tired than when she'd gone to bed. Now, her heart lifted, seeing him. As she got closer, she saw that he sported a deep purple and gray black eye. Murphy jogged the last bit to reach him, pointing at his face.

"Whoa, what happened to you?"

"I had a small accident."

"Does it hurt?" Murphy's voice reflected his fascination.

"Not much." He met Blue's gaze, behind Murphy. "Hey there."

"It looks sore," she told him. "Are you all right?" He looked great even with the shiner. In red and white board shorts and a white long-sleeved Reef shirt, he could be in one of those *Come to Florida* commercials. He smiled, and it made her smile too.

"I'm fine. I've got a free day and thought maybe I could fish with you guys again?"

"Yes!" Murphy exchanged a high five with him and boarded the boat.

Blue stayed back. "How do you have a free day?" She glanced at the Yellowfin. Murphy was ducking into the cabin with his backpack, Hook following him like a dog. "And what happened to your eye?"

"Gino hit me. I don't work for him anymore."

She covered her mouth with one hand. "Is that from the other night? What did he say when you showed him the photo?

You can't—what do you mean you don't work there anymore, it's your family's company."

"Let me fill you in on the water. We should get out there before the clouds burn off."

He was right. "I'm glad you're here," she said. "I'm sorry about your eye." She boarded, nervous about what he'd learned. She knew her mum had loved her dad. She'd been aware of it at a young age. They'd slow dance sometimes in the kitchen and she'd never thought anything of it until Enzo was over one evening and commented on it. His parents didn't do that. Neither had Sierra's. Blue told Murphy to start the engine, a habit now since Enzo had let him do it on Wednesday. They didn't speak until they were out of the channel and on the open water heading southwest.

Blue turned from the helm and faced him. "I'm not sure I'm ready to hear what your father said about the photo, but I have to know." She gritted her teeth, gripping the edge of the Nav panel.

"Blue, you know your mom. There was nothing mutual going on in that photo. Gino's an arrogant son of a bitch. He's never going to admit to any wrongdoing. He—" He frowned, looking at her but somehow through her.

When he didn't finish, Blue prompted, "He what?"

Enzo shrugged. "He blew it off. Said he didn't know what I was talking about."

"But you showed him the photo?"

"Yeah. I did."

He seemed off. Was he hiding something?

"You're passing it! Mom," Murphy yelled. He was in the cabin, keeping a lookout through the portholes. "You gotta turn around now, that was our spot," he called.

"He's good," Enzo remarked, impressed.

She made the course correction and the boat slowed, readying to turn. "Well, fishing's in his blood." She caught Enzo watching her intently. The other day, they'd both spent an abundance of energy avoiding eye contact, being careful not to infringe on each other's space. But now he was present, tuned in, meeting her eyes. "You seem different today. Did you have too much coffee?"

"I've had a lot of coffee," he admitted. "I'm starting to regret that decision. I was nervous."

"About skipping out on your dad?" She frowned, scrutinizing him.

The Nav system beeped three times, letting Blue know they'd reached their destination. This time she heard it and hit the corresponding prompts on the screen, idling down to a slow trawl.

He glanced toward the doorway to the cabin, where they could hear Murphy and Hook below, and then met Blue's eyes. "No. About seeing you. I broke things off with Jillian. We're not getting married." The muscle in his jaw pulsed and he held her gaze.

Her breath caught in her throat. "Why? What happened?"

"We never should have gotten engaged. We aren't right for each other. I knew that. And I—"

She searched his expression. He was holding back.

"I can't stop thinking about you, Blue. I don't think I ever got over losing you."

A starburst exploded in her chest. She reached up, cradling his cheek, careful not to touch the bruise above his cheekbone. Before she could lose her nerve she slipped her arms around his neck and kissed him.

He bent, his strong arms pulling her into him, holding her there. He slid one large, warm hand up to the nape of her neck, his fingers in her hair. Every single nerve was on fire under his touch, at the feel of him against her. His lips were soft, and when she touched the tip of her tongue to them they parted, his tongue skimming across her upper lip before his mouth covered hers. His palm at the small of her back moved, gliding over the bare skin under the hem of her T-shirt, and her eyes fluttered open and then closed again as he dipped his head and kissed her jawline and the hollow underneath it. She was freefalling, and she wasn't afraid. She'd never been afraid with him.

"Mom!" Murphy's footsteps coming out of the cabin broke them apart. Enzo turned abruptly toward the bow, hands on the wheel. Blue sank onto the seat behind her, her legs like noodles.

"Yeah, Murph?" She felt slightly drunk.

He pulled open the cooler panel on the deck where the bait-fish were. "Come on. Are you guys ready yet?"

"Yep. Coming." She gulped air. "Gotta go fish," she told Enzo.

He looked at her over his shoulder. "I'll be there in a minute." His cheeks flushed red and he gave her a one-sided grin and it took everything in her not to abandon her sense and climb him like a tree right in front of her son and God and the baitfish.

The rest of the day on the water was a study in restraint. Blue couldn't count the times she brushed by him, almost but not quite touching him, or how many accidental-on-purpose collisions they'd had, passing each other or reaching for the same pair of gloves or pliers. By the time they were back in the slip at the docks, she felt like her skin might throw sparks with one more touch. She followed Murphy and the cat up the dock toward dry land, Enzo behind her. He'd come by boat that morning, tied to the end of their other dock.

"Why don't you take Hook inside, Murph?" Blue suggested, hoping to walk with Enzo to his little aqua and red Sea Ray alone.

"That's okay. I wanna see your boat," Murph said to Enzo.

They stood on the dock while Murphy checked out the speedboat. "This is so cool! Do you water ski with this? You probably can't use it for fishing, but I bet it goes super fast!"

"You know what? I've never used her for water skiing. We could give that a try sometime if you want."

Murphy shrieked, his eyes wide. "Really? Can I, Mom?" He turned to Blue and she couldn't help laughing, his little face was so scrunched up with hope.

"Sure, your dad can teach you; he was great at it when we were kids."

"I'll get a tow rope and some skis," Enzo said, "and we'll go next weekend."

Murphy hugged him so fast and forcefully, Enzo was nearly knocked off the dock by his nine-year-old. He returned the hug, head tucked down toward his son's. Blue's throat swelled, her eyes burning with unshed tears, but she couldn't look away. She'd always wondered what it'd be like one day bringing Murphy home to meet Enzo. Nothing could've prepared her for this.

★ ★ ★

At Captain Crab's after dinner that night, Blue raised a toast to Sierra and Chloe's upcoming wedding. Murphy clinked his lemonade glass with them. Enzo's band was playing and he'd invited them, saving the table right in front of the stage for their foursome. Enzo, Salvi, and two other guys came out and began setting up. Murphy leaned over to Blue, speaking loudly enough for her to hear over the pop music playing through the PA system. "This is so cool, Mom. Thanks for letting me come."

She stared at him, speechless. Five weeks in Bliss and he was like a different kid. "You really like it here, don't you?"

"It's a lot better," he said simply. It made her happy and sad at the same time. How dismal must their existence have been in Tallahassee; it had taken Brent leaving and Aunt Eva dying to wake her up to her own life.

"Bluebelle Shea," Matteo Castellari spoke from behind her. She looked up to see him smiling at her.

"Matty!" Blue stood and gave him a quick hug, scooting over to make room. "Grab a chair, join us." She made introductions, focusing most on acquainting her son with his uncle Matteo. This was all new territory and it warmed her to her toes.

"I heard about your grandpa," Matty said. "My brother says your quick thinking saved his life. Nice work, kid."

"How are you doing?" she asked, thinking of their morning encounter here a week ago.

"Getting by. Enzo told you he quit the family?"

"What?" She stared at him, her eyes wide. "No, that's crazy. It sounded as if he'd be taking a break from work but—what do you mean?"

He shrugged and took a swallow of his drink. He lowered his speaking volume so only she could hear. "He got in a fight with fucking Gino. He told us he's done. I didn't believe it, but Marcello said he didn't even show up for the monthly staff meeting today. He's paving the way for the rest of us." He lifted a hand, signaling their server, and downed the rest of his drink.

Blue shook her head. "I don't think—he can't quit your family." She turned in her chair toward him and put a hand on his arm. "Hey. I've known you since you were born. I remember everything about you as a little kid. You've got to stop this." She nodded at the empty glass in front of him. "It's hurting you. Please, Matty, you've got to deal with whatever you're trying to drink away. You can't live like this, angry and drunk and hating your life. Maybe no one else will say it to you, but I will."

The overconfident swagger he wore thinned as his gaze moved from Blue to the empty tumbler. He didn't say a word.

The lead singer did a mic check, and Enzo positioned himself between Salvi and the drummer. Blue realized she saw him as front and center in his family—the eldest, his father's right-hand man. But here, as the bass player, he was clearly not the leader, but a vital piece of a whole. Maybe she'd had it wrong about his role in his family all this time. He and Salvi were on equal footing onstage, as they seemed to be in their day-to-day. Luca would perpetually be the baby, whether he liked it or not. As for Marcello, his CFO role in the business was more in line with the firstborn of a man like Gino Castellari, but at just thirteen months younger than Enzo, he'd always been right at Enzo's heels, even as a kid. But Gino's firstborn would always choose fishing or tearing apart engines over the intricacies of the company's financials. Each son had always known his place. Except for Matty, and maybe now Enzo too.

The band launched into their first number, an upbeat modern rock tune that the crowd seemed to love. Murphy cheered louder than all of them. Enzo was in his element playing on stage with Salvi and their bandmates.

Near the end of their hour-long set, the band stumbled, discordant notes coming through the speakers. Enzo stared, fixated, at something behind Blue. When she turned and saw Gino Castellari coming through the entrance, her stomach dropped like a stone. A younger man who could only be Marcello was with him.

Matty stood and put a hand on her shoulder, but his glowering gaze was fixed on his father. "Thanks, Blue." He headed toward Gino. Why was he even here? She'd only felt comfortable coming because Enzo'd said his father had never seen them play.

Sierra tapped Blue's leg. "Hey. Don't look."

Blue frowned at Sierra. "What?"

"I'm trying to tell you. Don't turn around and look. Not yet. But Jillian Josephson is at the bar. Okay, stretch or lean over for your purse or something. She's second from the end and she's been watching you since I noticed her a few minutes ago."

Blue reached for her purse and purposely knocked it off the back of her chair. She turned and picked it up, taking care to sweep a glance over the bar area. Jillian sat on her barstool looking like the lawyer version of a Victoria's Secret model—short skirt, long legs, heels Blue would break her neck in. Jillian met Blue's gaze coolly and held it until Blue turned back toward Sierra. She was shaking. Murphy was oblivious beside her. She grabbed Sierra's hand and squeezed. "We should go."

"Are you sure? You haven't done anything wrong, Blue. We don't have to leave."

Blue nodded quickly. "I know. I know that. But Gino's here too. I need to go. And Murphy doesn't need to end up in the middle of some ugly screaming match if Jillian decides to come over here."

On stage, the slightly mangled song ended and the lead singer said good night, thanking the crowd. "Good timing," Sierra said. "I don't know if you'd have gotten Murph to leave."

Blue nodded, dimly registering her friend's words. She followed Sierra, Chloe, and Murph through the crowd toward the door. As they approached the exit, she looked back and spotted Gino and four of his five sons on the side of the stage in a heated argument. Matteo turned, his gaze moving over the restaurant patrons and resting on Blue. And then Gino did the same, sending a chill up her spine. She froze, unable to look away.

◆ 21 ◆

Enzo stared at Gino and lost his place, fumbling the bass line in their last song. Of course. The one and only time his father would hear them play and he flubbed it. What the fuck was he doing here? Salvi turned the neck of his guitar toward Enzo to help him find his place and pick up the notes again. Enzo jerked his head toward the entrance. Salvi took one look and shrugged, shaking his head.

He was relieved to see Blue and her group gathering their things. He'd hoped to spend a little more time with her, even if it was with all of them, but with first Jillian showing up tonight and now Gino, he wanted her gone. She didn't need a front row seat for the storm he could feel coming.

Their singer, Andre, walked the stage with the mic, clueless, and wrapped things up with a flourish. He thanked the crowd and bid them good night, and the lights aimed at the stage went dark. Enzo unplugged, ignoring Gino's approach.

He stepped offstage and into his father's path. "I'm not doing this here," Enzo growled.

"Why?" Gino's scowl transformed his features. "You're ashamed of how you treat your family? You think you can just walk away from responsibility?"

"Why not?" Matteo interjected, at his brother's side now, with Salvi descending from the stage to join them. Matty leaned in toward Gino and left a cloud of sickly sweet liquor scent under Enzo's nose. "He's not your puppet anymore and neither am I."

Gino stepped close and jabbed a finger into Matty's chest. "Watch yourself, son."

"Or what?" Matty's voice grew louder. "Are you scared, Pops? What's gonna happen when Enzo finds out what you did to Blue's family? 'Cuz he's almost there. You wanna tell him? Or should I?" Matty turned, spotting Blue by the door. His father followed his gaze.

"Tell me. Matty, what the fuck happened? Tell me!" Enzo demanded. His heart thrummed in his chest like a drum; he was on a crumbling cliff with no way back.

Gino grabbed a fistful of Matteo's shirt, pulling him nose to nose. "I said—"

Matty shoved Gino back, but it lacked force. Gino kept hold of him. Enzo put an arm between the two just as Henry appeared with the bouncer who'd been stationed by the exit. The proprietor focused on Gino. "All right, fellas. Let's take this outside." Henry stepped back, and the much larger man with him ushered them toward the back door.

Enzo heard Salvi shouting before he got out the door to the alley. Salvi stood between Gino and Matteo, his outstretched palm on his father's chest, as he addressed Matty. "What the fuck are you talking about?"

The door slammed open once more, hitting the wall, as Marcello stormed out. "That's enough," he bellowed. He stood with Gino, staring down his brothers. "Get ahold of yourselves, for Christ's sake. We can talk this through at home like goddamned adults."

"Says Pops' mini-me," Salvi muttered.

"He's right," Enzo agreed, looking at Marcello. "Your head's so far up Gino's ass you can't even see reason anymore."

"Tell them, Pops," Matty said. Unhinged, he lunged around Salvi at Gino. "Motherfucker. Say it!"

Gino wrenched Salvi's hand off him and rushed Matteo, knocking him onto the asphalt. He stood over his son, fists clenched. "Get up."

Matty pulled himself to a sitting position, making no move to stand. Enzo offered him a hand but he waved it away. What had Gino done? And what had it done to his brother?

Enzo faced his father. "What did you do?"

"Nothing." Matty spoke from the ground behind them. "He did nothing. He's never going to say it. I was never allowed to. He heard Mitch Shea's distress call and we went home. He did nothing."

"But—you heard him? You—" Enzo stared down at Matty, reeling.

"We were close, we saw the *Shamrock*. We were *right there*. We could have saved Mrs. Shea. He let her die." He put his head in his hands and sobbed.

Enzo braced his hands on his thighs, sucking in air. Mitch Shea had told the truth. All these years, his stories in court about another boat nearby, everyone thinking he was just a lying drunk. But if he hadn't lied about there being a boat—"What else?" he asked, his voice barely audible. "What else did you do, Pops? Was Shea even drunk? Did you—what else did you do?" Jesus. What was his father truly capable of? Did he have the power to pull the right strings and have Blue's dad arrested on a false intoxication charge?

"I didn't know she was with him. Ella was—she should've been my—goddammit, if I'd known—" Gino's faced crumpled, his pained, tortured eyes bore into Enzo's, and the rest fell into place like the dropped blade of a guillotine.

"The other night," Enzo said. "Before that. The party. Matty and Luca were upstairs playing, they saw Blue's dad carry her mom out of your room, bleeding, crying. I—how *could* you? Why didn't she press charges?"

The alley was silent. Enzo's brothers and Gino stared at him—no, past him. Behind him. He turned around.

Blue stood in the open doorway, unmoving.

✦ 22 ✦

SHE COULDN'T BREATHE. NOW that it was out, Enzo's accusations floating in the air, she realized she wasn't even shocked. She'd known something awful had happened that night. She'd always known. Her feet moved of their own accord, taking her across the asphalt to face Gino. He stepped back. His dark eyes were glossy, his expression tortured, as if he had the right.

"You raped my mother." Blue clamped a hand over her mouth the moment the words left her tongue, her gut twisting.

Gino shook his head. "No. She—that's not what it was."

Blue took a deep breath. "Then what happened? Tell me."

The older man's entire demeanor shifted. He straightened up, his face stony, glaring at Blue. "I don't owe you a goddamned thing."

"But you do," she said softly. "You do. You owe it to my mum. You hurt her that night. My dad carried her all the way home, did you know that? My mum, my strong, vibrant mother who was always so full of life; I thought she was dying. You did that. And two years later you had a chance to save her. But you ignored the distress call. You could *see* them, and you let her drown." That got to him, she could see it. In some sick way, Gino thought he'd loved her mum.

"Don't say that. Your father should have saved her. We saw the Yellowfin, but I had no idea the signal was for Ella," he said angrily. "It's not my fault."

"It is." He'd ruined her family. He'd never know the kind of pain he'd caused the three of them.

He shook his head, his dark gaze boring into hers. "No."

An odd calm washed over her. "She was afraid of you." Blue saw that now with startling clarity. Pulling into the parking lot at Gulfside Market only to have her mum inexplicably change her mind and say she didn't need groceries after all. Dropping out of all their former social events, one by one, except for ones with just a few girlfriends. Her mum's newly adopted habit of adding baggy layers anytime she went out, even in the heat. "My mother was terrified of you."

Gino faltered, stepping backward as if she'd struck him. "No," he said, but his tone lacked all conviction. He suddenly looked much older than his years.

Enzo finally spoke, breaking the silence. "This isn't going away, Pop. I want you to know that. We—"

Gino cut him off, his son's words seeming to provide the fuel he needed. "Go ahead. Do your worst. You've got no proof of anything," he said. He turned and walked away. Marcello went after him, the two of them disappearing into the darkness. "Fucking traitor," Salvi murmured.

Enzo offered a hand again to Matteo and this time he took it.

Blue had promised Sierra she'd call when she needed a ride home, but now she sent a quick text that Enzo would drop her off. When Gino had locked eyes with her on her way out the door earlier, she knew she couldn't leave. Now, Enzo's hedging on the boat earlier today made sense. She couldn't be upset with him; how was he supposed to break it to her that his father had assaulted and possibly raped her mum? She had to go to the police; she wasn't sure she could convince them to do anything, not based on Gino's word versus his son's, but she had to try.

She and Enzo took Matteo home and helped him inside. Between his ongoing alcohol-soaked bender and his scraped-up arms from Gino knocking him down, he was a pathetic sight. In the foyer, he nearly fell as he bent to scoop up the fluffy white cat waiting for him. He hugged her, burying his face in her fur. "Hi, Ghost."

Blue sat with him at his kitchen table while he nursed a cup of black coffee. Enzo moved about the kitchen, putting a dish of cat food on the floor for Ghost, and then rifling through a mostly empty refrigerator, setting about dicing and frying a mountain of potatoes and sausage. She had a feeling he'd done this for his brother before.

"I don't blame you if you hate me," Matty said to her, his voice quiet. He stared down at his hands.

Blue sucked in air, overcome with emotion. She grabbed him and hugged him. Tight. His thin arms went around her and he hugged her back, and she felt him heave a jagged breath and then let it go—all of it, all at once, tortured sobs shaking him. She held on to him, patting his tangled hair, unable to speak.

After a while, Matty finally quieted, regaining control and wiping roughly at his eyes. Enzo put the food on the table and sat, leaning forward toward his brother.

"I'm sorry, Matty. I should have seen something was up, especially these last few weeks. Your drinking's never been this bad before. You used to at least show up for work. You never should've had to keep Gino's secrets."

Matty stood and left the kitchen without a word. Blue exchanged a glance with Enzo; she'd ask if he was okay, but it seemed none of them were.

He came back, setting an old, worn-looking, leather-bound notebook on the table.

"No," Enzo breathed, his stunned gaze moving from the book to his brother. "You've had it this whole time?"

"I took it because I was worried he'd destroy it. It's the captain's log from Gino's boat the night your mother drowned," Matty told Blue.

Enzo flipped through the pages, finding the date. "The coordinates are here, from dock to dock."

"I know it's not the worst of what he's done, but maybe it's a way to hold him responsible for some of it," Matty said.

Enzo handed it to her. "You should show your father. And then we need to take it to the police."

Blue frowned down at the book. "What if they act on it? Are you . . . you'll need to be prepared for that."

"I hope they act on it," Matteo said. "I hope it makes them question all the other lies he's told. I'll make a statement too if they'll let me."

★ ★ ★

Blue was on her way out of Gulfside Grocery with Murphy Saturday morning when she spotted Jillian at checkout, staring at her. She hated this. She wasn't the enemy.

Jillian caught up to them as she was loading the groceries into the van. "Blue."

She handed Murphy the keys. "Go ahead and start it, get the A/C going," she said, knowing it was the only way not to have him witness whatever was about to happen.

Jillian had the good grace to wait until Murphy shut the door. "I thought you should know, Enzo and I were together almost seven years before you came back. Our wedding is ten weeks and two days from today, and everything is planned. He doesn't love you. He doesn't even know you anymore."

Blue swallowed hard. Jesus. She fought the urge to look down, to melt into the concrete. She met Jillian's eyes. "You might be right. I'm sorry he broke things off with you. But I don't think this is about me."

Blue's response only seemed to anger her. "Whatever he thinks he's feeling will blow over. This is just Enzo having cold feet and using you as his excuse." She moved closer, her words cutting. "How do you think this is going to go, with him seeing me all the time at work? My firm still represents his family. Enzo's father still hates yours. There's no place for you here." She spun around and stormed away, leaving Blue speechless.

She didn't want to believe her. Jillian knew nothing about her, nothing about what she'd been through before landing back in Bliss. She wasn't going to be intimidated into running back to Brent. But what if she was right, at least partly? What if Enzo didn't really know what he wanted? None of this was fair to Murphy, and he was smack in the middle of it. Would her son be better off if she tried to keep things platonic with Enzo and avoid the risk of tangling up their hearts further?

She threw the rest of her groceries into the minivan and pulled out of the parking lot so fast they were almost hit; her right arm went out reflexively in front of Murphy's chest, and she cringed as the car she'd just cut off swerved and honked at her.

"Mom!" he protested. He leaned forward to see the man passing them, still honking. "Oh crap, he gave you the middle finger!"

She turned a wide-eyed stare on him and then faced the road. "Sorry."

"Who was that lady at the store? Why was she yelling at you?"

"You heard her?"

"Not really, but she looked super mad."

"She's a friend of a friend," Blue improvised. "It's not a big deal."

"Can we go back to Captain Crab's next time my—Enzo—my real dad plays?" Blue felt for him, watching him fumble with what to call Enzo. He didn't wait for an answer. "Remember when my stepdad got me guitar lessons?"

She gritted her teeth. "Yeah. I remember." Of course she remembered. It had been two years ago, and Brent had made him quit after the second lesson. "Y'know, we brought your guitar. Do you ever mess around on it, just for fun?"

He shook his head. "No, I sucked, remember? But maybe now that I'm older I could try again?"

One more reason why they couldn't go back. She and Murph had grown so accustomed to Brent constantly diminishing them, Blue could kick herself now for being blind to it when it was happening. What parent makes their eight-year-old quit music lessons for not being good enough—after two sessions? The longer she was here, the more she was realizing there had been countless little things just like that. How had she thought it was normal? "I think trying guitar lessons again would be a great idea. I bet it'd be a lot of fun. Let me ask around; you could start next week." Her son beamed at her.

Blue stewed in her thoughts the next couple of hours as she and Murph put groceries away, made lunch, and got a start on laundry. Thank goodness she'd been able to get Kai to do the fishing this weekend. She needed time to catch up around here. She'd hoped checking some of her busy work off her list would offer a distraction, but Gino's guilt and Jillian's biting words played on a vicious loop in her head all afternoon.

She and Murphy rode in silence for most of the fifteen-minute drive to meet their new therapist, Dr. Shannon Harbrough. She'd made the appointments to humor Sierra, but now she was glad she had. Murphy finally spoke as she turned into the office complex. "Cooper says therapy is for crazy people."

Blue laughed. "I'm sorry, Murph, that couldn't be further from the truth. Therapy is a healthy way for people to be able to talk about their feelings and what's bothering them."

"How's that supposed to help anything?"

She pulled into the parking spot, turning to face him. "It can help people figure out why they feel or act a certain way, and how to deal with it. I thought we could go in and meet Dr. Shannon together, and then maybe it would be nice if we each got to talk with her separately too for a while." The clinic had recommended they each have their own appointment, and Blue agreed; as much as she was struggling with the fallout from the last several years, Murphy had to be too.

He was quiet, digesting that. Then, "I've been better since we've been here, Mom. I'm trying to be good. Is this because I yelled at you the other day?"

Ugh. "Murph, you're almost ten years old. I feel like . . . do you want the whole truth?"

He raised his eyebrows, surprised. "I mean, I think so?"

"Oh honey," Blue said, hating the worry that crossed his features. "It's not because of anything you're doing or not doing. It's . . ." She frowned, thinking. "Every family is different. There are so many different ways a family can function and be healthy and happy; but the family we had in Tallahassee with your step-dad was not one of those." How could she explain it without trashing Brent? Somehow she just felt that'd make things worse, but was that true? Or was it only because he'd made sure she lacked the confidence to trust her own instincts?

She tried again. "I want to learn how to deal with my nervous and upset feelings when they happen. I don't know how to do that very well. And I want the therapist to help me figure out how to feel like I'm . . . capable. Smart. Strong enough to do things on my own," she admitted. "Therapy is different for everyone, but that's what I'm hoping it helps me with."

He nodded. "I'd like that. All that stuff you just said, maybe she can help me with that too."

Blue called Sierra when they got home. Shannon had asked who she relied on for support, and she'd instantly named Sierra. She needed some support right now; her therapy session had flown by much too fast and had been primarily spent discussing her time with Brent.

"I'm coming over," her friend said over the phone before Blue could even get through half of what had happened between last night and this morning. "We're out running errands, we'll be there in ten."

Blue greeted them at the door with a bright bouquet of flowers. She ushered the two women inside.

Sierra put her face near the blooms and inhaled. She passed them to Chloe. "Divine. What are these for?"

"They're for you. I was going to bring them to your wedding shower tomorrow, but you're here now. Come in, I just made lemonade." She led the way to the kitchen.

"You're going to the police, right?" Sierra asked when Blue had finished filling them in on what they'd missed last night.

"Yes. Matty let me take the captain's log. I want to show my dad that date before I take it to the Sheriff's Department. It validates what he's been saying for a decade about seeing a boat nearby."

Chloe spoke. "I wish there was a way to do something about the assault. I mean, Enzo's brothers witnessed your mom being carried out of Gino Castellari's bedroom, hurt. Can you get your dad to make a report?"

Blue sighed heavily. "I think my dad really can't deal with it. I know he did, in his own way, at the time. But he won't talk about it, and with his heart, I don't want to stress him. And Matty and Luca were little kids; would the police even allow their recollections to go on record? I'm not sure I'll ever know exactly what happened."

Sierra nodded, moving to the silverware drawer and taking out Ella's dragonfly stirrers that had lived there since they were kids. She set them on the counter with the lemonade pitcher and glasses. "I get that."

"Running into Jillian this morning makes me second guess everything," Blue continued. "Enzo was with her for seven years. He obviously loved her. Loves her," she corrected. "She's perfect for him. What if she's right? What if he's meant to be with her, and me being here just gave him an excuse to act on pre-wedding jitters? I don't want to be the reason he left her. He said they're not right together, but that sounds like some bullshit his father would say to one of his—"

"No," Sierra interrupted, pointing at Blue with a butter knife. "Take a breath. Right now. Good, slowly, take another one. Let it out, slowly."

"But—"

"No." She stomped her foot. "Stop it. He's not his father. You're not an excuse. Stop shouldering blame for everything, Blue. Trust that Enzo is a grown man and can make sound decisions. Now just—" Sierra put one hand up. "Give me a minute. Chill." She went around the other side of the kitchen nook counter, dropped to her knees, and began prying at a floorboard.

Chloe peered over the counter, staring at her. "Um, okay, I'm sorry," Chloe told Blue. "I have no control over what she does. Why are you destroying our friend's floor, love?"

Sierra grunted, getting her fingertips under one corner. "She knows why," she said, straining to pull up the board.

Blue knelt beside her and hooked her fingers under the other corner, helping. The board popped free.

"Have you gone back in here?" Sierra asked.

"Not since we were fourteen," Blue said. She peered down into the dark recessed area. "What about spiders? Or worse."

Sierra pointed the light from her phone into the hole. "I don't see any spiders. Reach in there and grab it."

Blue scoffed. "It was your idea. You reach in there."

"Fine." Sierra snaked her arm in. "Aha!" She pulled out a shoebox covered in cobwebs and set it on the floor between them.

Blue carefully lifted the lid, the corners beginning to crumble. "Oh! It's still here. We were so ridiculous." She pulled out two ancient raspberry wine coolers and set them on the kitchen floor.

"You stashed booze down there?" Chloe joined them on the floor.

"Of course. To drink while we wrote our Book of Love." Sierra carefully took out the only other item in the box, a purple satin scarf wrapped around a notebook.

"Book of Love?" Chloe asked. She picked up one of the wine coolers. "Doesn't look like you did much drinking."

Blue laughed. "We stole them but were too scared to drink them."

"Well, duh," Sierra said. "We were fourteen! Your parents would've grounded you forever. Here," she said, holding out the wrapped book reverently.

Blue carefully unwrapped the fabric from around an old three-hole notebook with kittens romping on the cover, giggling when she saw it. "I can't believe you remembered this. I'd forgotten all about it."

Sierra set it on the floor between their trio, flipping through page after page filled with drawings and school pictures and both their handwriting. "How could you forget? This is every single crush we ever had since kindergarten. Oh! Caleb Rowens in second grade." She wrinkled her nose. "I only liked him because of that *hair*." She made a sweeping motion across her forehead, rolling her eyes.

Blue laughed. "I think he was one of mine too." She turned a few pages. There was no format, simply a series of doodles, photos, magic marker hearts, names of boys, and, by sixth grade for Sierra, girls, each page decorated with little flowers and stars and more hearts.

"Look," Sierra said, flipping back. "Right here on your side of page one: EC."

Blue tipped her head. "In kindergarten," she murmured.

Sierra went through, stopping after another few pages. "EC again. Mrs. Landy's class; what was that, second grade?" She kept going, pausing and tapping her fingertip again. "EC. You wrote this on our fifth grade field trip, I remember because I doodled that bird on the bus."

"Enzo Castellari," Chloe said. "Why not his whole name, like," she leaned over, reading, "Albert Nowicki or Jesse Gilmore? Why just the initials?"

Sierra raised an eyebrow at Blue, but didn't answer for her.

"I was afraid I'd jinx it," she said softly. "So dumb. He was my best friend besides Sierra for so long, even before I fell in love with him. If I wrote his whole name, it'd never work out with us. I was superstitious. But I think it was jinxed to begin with."

"Okay, that is not why I wanted to show you this. Here's another, and here's one more. And right here, too, balloon letters with hearts inside; you were still writing his initials in here in eleventh grade." She looked up, meeting her friend's eyes.

Blue's eyes burned. She swallowed around the lump in her throat. "I remember."

"I think that's the last one. How many times did you write EC in the Book of Love, Blue?" Sierra counted each corner she'd just folded. "Six. You made this silent wish from kindergarten until you left Bliss."

Blue turned the book over. On the cardboard backing was a pink heart with EC inside of it. "Seven."

"I've made my point," Sierra said, rewrapping the book inside the scarf and putting everything back in the box. "Look, I'm not sure what's ahead for you; I know you aren't either. But don't tell me how perfect Jillian is for him. You've loved him your whole life."

◆ 23 ◆

Enzo's mother could not sit down. When he'd shown up in her kitchen Saturday morning, bearing fresh donuts from town and saying he wanted to talk, she'd launched into full-blown Chef Sofia mode, chopping vegetables and preparing him a proper breakfast.

"Ma, I'm not even hungry," he said. "Can you just—"

"You can't live on donuts, Vincenzo. What kind of breakfast is that?"

"I ate breakfast, I swear. They had the crullers this morning, your favorite. Come sit down."

Moon suddenly leaped up from the sunspot on the kitchen floor, happily wagging as the side door opened. His mother's sister Lorna patted his head, laughing. "Well, hello there! Vincenzo! Oh my goodness," she said, rushing over to hug him. "I've missed you! So handsome, look at you. Look at this face." She cupped his cheeks briefly, smiling. Aunt Lorna was the only person in the world he'd let get away with this crap.

"Ma's making us breakfast," he said. "You're just in time." He was outnumbered; there was no way he was escaping a second breakfast now that his aunt was here.

When they'd feasted on omelets and donuts and so much coffee Enzo was feeling jittery, he sat back, uncertain whether to bring up what he'd come to talk about in front of Aunt Lorna.

His mother moved to stand. "We have some shopping and a nail appointment, but you stay and finish, okay?"

"I need to talk to you about Pop," he blurted. If he didn't do it now, he'd lose his nerve. Or his father would be back if he tried later. It had to be now. "That's why I'm here. I can say it in front of Aunt Lorna or maybe we should go to the living room, it's up to you, but I need to talk to you, Ma."

His mother stood. "I'm sure we'll have time later. Tomorrow, maybe?"

He groaned, scrubbing a hand through his hair. "I—"

Aunt Lorna motioned his mother to sit back down, surprising him. "Sofia. When your son asks to talk to you, you should listen."

Sofia sat, meeting his eyes. "Is it bad?" she asked softly.

"You could say that."

"I'm not leaving," Aunt Lorna announced. She crossed her arms over her chest. Sofia nodded.

"All right," Enzo said, sighing. "There are some things you need to know about Pop. And also about Matty." He proceeded to fill her in, starting with the photo of Gino leering at Ella Shea. He slid it across the table to his mother.

She studied it, then looked up at him. "I know he had an affair with her."

"What? I'm not seeing that in this picture," Enzo said, thrown off kilter.

"Your father confessed it to me," she said, "after that awful night at our party. Mitch Shea walked in on them. She was my friend; I don't know how she could have done that to me."

Enzo shook his head. "That's not what happened, Ma. Not according to Blue's dad or even Matty or Luca, who were playing upstairs when she was carried out of your room. Why did she need to be carried? Why did you lie about being there when that happened?"

She shrugged. "I knew they'd had a scuffle, but it was over Ella, not business. It was just easier to say I was there, that it was nothing; if the town knew about your father's fling with her, the gossip would've hurt our business."

He shook his head, glancing at Aunt Lorna and then back at his mother. "I'm sorry, I have to say this. You knew about his affair with Nadine. I know for a fact there've been others. Mrs. Shea wasn't one of them. Pop hurt her, Ma. I think he was so used to getting any woman he wanted, that when Mrs. Shea didn't want him, he hurt her. He tried to take what he wanted."

Sofia balled up her fists on the table, her cheeks flushed with abrupt anger. "Shut your mouth, Vincenzo. Your father slipped up. He didn't mean for anything to happen with Ella, they just . . . couldn't help it. But he loves me. You make him sound terrible. Look around you. Look at the life he's given us!"

"Jesus. Do you really believe what you're saying? Ella Shea was your friend. We all knew her. You're telling me you believe she stabbed you in the back over *Pops*? Really? *Look* at him," he jabbed a finger at the photo on the table between them.

Sofia was silent, her eyes drifting to the photo of predatory Gino leering at Ella.

"He hurt her that night, so bad that she was bleeding when Luca and Matty watched Blue's dad carry her out. And then two years later, she drowned because Pop ignored Shea's distress call and lied about it—hell, for all I know, Shea wasn't even drinking that night. Blue says he was sober. What did Pops do, who'd he pay to make sure Shea served time for your friend's death, Ma? Turned out to be a great way to take over all his contracts. What the hell made him ruin Blue's father after she'd already lost her mom? Were you in on it too?"

Sofia slapped him. His cheek burned, the sound violently loud in the quiet kitchen. "Shut your mouth!" Sofia stood, her chair tipping over behind her. "Get out of my house."

Enzo reeled back, shocked. His mother was in denial; that didn't surprise him. But this, standing by a man like Gino in spite of everything . . . this was crushing. He'd come here today so

Sofia wouldn't be kept in the dark; he hadn't even gotten to bring up the impact all of this had had on Matty yet. He stood to leave, the remains of his family disintegrating before his eyes.

His mother looked away, covering a sob with one hand. Aunt Lorna pulled her into a hug and then drew back, staring eye to eye with Sofia, their noses nearly touching. "You know I love you. But if you send Vincenzo away like this, I go too."

Sofia leaned on the table, hanging her head. "What do you want me to say? He wasn't always like this. Mitch was your father's friend," she said, looking up at Enzo. "That was real. I think . . . I guess I've always thought he fell in love with Ella. And the more he loved Ella, the more he hated Mitch. But he just made it sound . . ." Her voice trailed off and she fell heavily into a chair, staring at the photo in front of her.

Enzo came around the table and hugged her and she held onto him. "How can I leave him?" Strangled anguish infused her words as her tears overflowed. "Everything we have is his. My name is on nothing. I'll have nothing. He'll make sure of that," she whispered.

Before Enzo could refute any of what she'd said, Lorna spoke. "Sofia, I'm a sixty-year-old widow living in a house the size of this kitchen. My poor husband, God rest his soul, was a good man, my kids are safe and loved and happy, and my conscience is clean. Money isn't everything. I've been telling you this for years."

As much as he pitied his mother, Enzo now saw a side of her he'd been blind to. She had some hard choices to make. He straightened up, leaving a hand on her shoulder for the moment. He finished what he came here to say. "Matteo's not well, Ma. I know this is hard to hear, but Pops hurt him too. Matty is struggling with alcohol, maybe drugs, I'm not sure. He's agreed to get help. We're all taking turns staying with him for a while." Almost all; Marcello had been out of touch since last night.

His mother gasped, her features twisted with fear. "I have to see him," she said, turning first to Aunt Lorna, then to Enzo. "I'm sorry. I've tried for so long to pretend everything's fine, but I know it isn't." She came around the table and hugged him. "Is he going to be okay?"

"I think so. He will be. None of us want you to worry, Ma."

"It's my job," she said.

♦ 24 ♦

Blue woke up early Sunday morning, planning to go to the Sheriff's Department. Her father had other plans. She was walking out the door with her purse and the captain's log when the nurse from her dad's cardiac rehab program called to say her dad was checking out of the hospital. "What?! He can't do that. He's supposed to have another week there."

"We've explained that to him. He insists he's leaving. We just thought you should know before he calls the cab company."

"Can you put him on please? Or—you know what, I'll call him on the way there. Would you just tell him to wait for me? If he really wants to leave, I'll bring him home."

"We don't recommend he leave yet—"

Blue threw a hand skyward in exasperation. "I don't recommend it either! I'll call him in a second. Just tell him to wait, please." She was glad Sierra and Chloe had taken Murphy home with them last night, but she hadn't planned on using her free time today to check her dad out early.

At Collier County General, Blue tried along with her dad's nurse to explain to him why he needed to finish the program to help get his strength back. It didn't work. The nurse left to gather his Against Medical Advice papers and discharge instructions, and Blue leaned on the computer cart, rolling her eyes at her father.

"You're being a little dramatic, Bluebelle. I'm fine."

"You're getting more therapy here than you will in the out-patient program. You're sure you won't just stay put?"

"I belong at home. The cat misses me," he grumbled.

She chuckled. "There are a couple of people there who might miss you too, you know." She glanced at the computer screen. An idea occurred to her, but she just as quickly wished it hadn't. She could lose her nursing license for looking up a family member's chart. He'd signed the release of information to her, so technically she was allowed access to his medical information, but as a daughter, not a hospital employee. But . . . if his chart was already on the screen, which happened to be in full view, was that different?

She knew it wasn't, even as she turned the cart toward her and tapped the keys. She navigated through the Cerner software program fields to her dad's past medical records. She filtered the time line, browsing through notes and diagnostic reports from years ago. Her dad hadn't sought medical care often in his life. She found the date her mum had died, though there was no reason she should have; her dad hadn't been treated here that night.

But he had. There was a CT scan of the brain to rule out concussion—which it had. Keeping an ear out for the rehab nurse's shoes on the linoleum, Blue skimmed the notes. The outrigger that had let go had hit her father in the head on its way to the water. There was no concussion, just a contusion. And a note referencing blood alcohol findings.

Blue backed out of the imaging field, reapplied the time line filter, and found lab results: her father's blood alcohol report showed as invalid. So he did have blood taken that night. As an ER nurse, she'd seen plenty of alcohol and drug screens. Invalid on a standard lab draw typically meant an insufficient quantity of blood. She clicked the triangle on the right of the screen to view the breakdown of the diagnostic: anyone who'd touched the specimen, from the draw to the processing, would be notated here. The blood was drawn during her father's short emergency room visit due to his head injury the night of her mum's drowning. The result was listed: *negative*.

Blue read it again, checking the name at the upper left of the screen, and then read it a third time, making sure she was seeing it correctly. A lab tech named Marcus Green had done the initial analysis. The chart showed an amendment after that by another tech, Scott Grandon, to change the final negative result to invalid. She snapped a photo of the screen.

"Hey. Are you supposed to do that?"

Her head jerked up at her dad's protest. "Do what? Shh."

She was about to return to the screen the nurse had left open when she had a thought. How far back did the records go? She couldn't leave this chart and search her mother's, not unless she really wanted to guarantee she'd lose her license, but . . . what if her dad had also been treated the night her mum had been hurt? Enzo said his brothers had heard shouting in Gino's bedroom right before her father got her mum out of there. What if they'd come here? What if her dad did bring her in, what if they'd tried to file a report? And if so, they'd certainly have made sure any scrapes or injury he'd sustained got checked. She changed the time line filter to two years earlier. No other medical reports came up. But a document flashed as available to view, date stamped July 5th at 3:23 AM that year. She opened it.

The document was an intake form for Ella Saoirse Shea. Her mother's name, birthdate, insurance information were all listed, and halfway down the page, she read: *Emergency contact: Mitchell Shea*. Beneath it on the next line bore the words: *Clinical diagnosis: sexual battery, adult.*

Her heart dropped. She snapped a photo of the screen and clicked through, hoping to stumble on something else—anything else—from that night, but there was nothing. The only reason it had come up was the link to her dad's name from her mum's chart. She backed out of the sections she'd opened and returned the chart to the way she'd found it.

Five minutes later, the nurse's discharge instructions filtered through a hazy shock that gripped her, as if spoken from the end of a long tunnel. Blue left to bring the car around and got her father loaded in; when she pulled into the driveway at home, she had no recollection of getting there. She'd just gotten him settled in his recliner when Sierra dropped Murphy off.

"Grandpa!" Blue's son burst through the front door, beaming. He crossed the room and leaned in to hug him but froze, pulling back. "I—uh, is it okay? Does that hurt?" He eyed his grandfather's chest. Two inches of the twelve-inch-long incision were visible above the collar of his shirt.

Mitch nodded. "Some. It'll heal. You gonna let me have my job back when I'm well enough?"

Murphy laughed. "It's your boat. Besides, Mom says she can't keep up this pace for long, so I'm pretty sure she doesn't want your job."

Blue laughed. "Some days are rougher than others, that's all. It's not easy."

"Yeah. But I miss it." He turned to Murphy. "I'd be in the ground if it wasn't for you, Murph."

"Dad!" Blue frowned, gaze moving to Murphy.

"What?" He looked at her. "It's true. I owe you my life, son." He reached out, and Murphy hugged him.

When her dad held out an arm to her, wrapping her into their welcome home embrace, Blue struggled to find the right words amid the numbness gripping her. She knew he could give her answers. He could help her bring charges against Gino, if it wasn't too late, for everything he'd done and failed to do. All she had to do was ask. That fresh scar below the notch in his collarbone walled off any possibility of her asking. She couldn't. "We missed you so much, Dad," she said simply.

His ruddy cheeks were damp when he let go, his eyes red-rimmed. Her father's tears were jarring—she hadn't seen him cry since the night her mum died. He cleared his throat. "I'm glad to be home."

An hour later, she followed the stone walkway up to Dale Bryant's house. He stepped out onto his front porch before she reached it. "Everything all right, Bluebelle?" He trotted down the steps, meeting her.

"Not really. I have some questions . . . I figured it'd be best to ask you first, before I head to the sheriff's office."

Dale held her gaze, poker faced. He nodded once. "Sure." He moved past her, toward the docks. She hurried to keep up, not thrilled about being alone on the docks with him, with what she aimed to ask about.

She stopped before they'd gone past the first slip, planting her butt on the built-in bench across from the pelican roost. She opened the folder she'd brought, looking up at Dale. "Want to sit?"

He grunted as he joined her on the bench. "How's the old man doing?"

"Good. Getting better. My dad's blood was taken the night of my mum's drowning. It's right here. Negative." She passed him the first paper, a printout of the screenshot she'd made. She rushed on. "This guy here, Scott Grandon, amended the result to invalid. I don't have the chart notes from that tech saying why, but I don't think it matters. I've been wondering all these years why my dad would say his blood was taken if it wasn't. So I started thinking about that Breathalyzer report you showed me. How could his blood test be negative for alcohol but the Breathalyzer be positive just an hour or so earlier?"

"It couldn't have been right," Dale answered. "Probably why the tech marked the blood sample invalid. Had to be wrong."

"But it was negative to begin with," Blue said.

Dale shrugged. "Don't see what you're gettin' at."

She was sure he did. "Okay. So, my dad also maintained that he'd seen a boat nearby when he put his distress call out, remember?" She pulled the log book for *Dollar and a Dream* from her bag and handed it to him, flipping it open. "Those are the route coordinates for Gino Castellari's boat the evening my mum died. Gino was aboard, with Matteo skippering for him."

Dale bent over the page, reading, and then frowned at Blue. "Huh. Not sure there's any way of knowing specifics on the timing. Castellari's boat could've been out of the area by then."

"Except they weren't. Matteo remembers, vividly. He heard the *Shamrock*'s distress call over the radio, heard my dad say man overboard on the *Shamrock*. Matteo argued with his father but Gino fled anyway, leaving my mother drowning, waiting for the Coast Guard. Dale." She said his name sharply, getting him to look at her again. She took a deep breath. "Matteo saw my father's boat. They were that close. Gino admitted to that Friday night in front of me and four of his sons. Bare minimum, that's six months under federal law. The exact amount of time my dad spent in jail for manslaughter."

Dale closed the book and handed it back to Blue. "Where'd you get this?"

"Matteo saved it. Since he was thirteen."

"I'd have to check on statute of limitations. Not sure if it's still prosecutable." He started to stand.

"There's no statute of limitations on sexual assault. Not when it's reported in the first seventy-two hours. Which it was."

He stared at her. "What—Bluebelle, where do you expect this to go? You think stirring all this up will go well for anyone?"

She laughed, a harsh, unfunny sound. "Wow." She shook her head. "So your first response to me bringing up assault isn't to ask what the hell I'm referring to or to say I'm crazy. You know what I'm stirring up, then. Castellari's Fourth of July party, two years before my mother died. You were there. Did you see my dad carry her out, bleeding and crying? Gino's sons did. That's the kind of thing you don't forget. Did you wonder what had happened to her? Did you even fucking care?" She drew in a ragged breath, angrily swiping away sudden tears.

Dale lurched forward, resting elbows on knees. "Jesus Christ," he whispered.

She didn't respond. She was shaking with anger.

"So your dad told you," he said.

She sucked in her breath. "No. But you just did."

He jerked his head, staring at her. "I didn't say shit. Even if your dad wanted to try to pursue it now, there's nothing to back up his word. There's no evidence."

She stared at her father's so-called friend. "There's an ER visit documenting that my mother was sexually assaulted that night. My dad took her in, tried to do the right thing. But why do I get the feeling there's no DNA on file, no records of the exam or anything incriminating? Is that why Gino was never charged?" She paused, thinking of her conversation with Jim Arden's widow. She jumped in with both feet—she had nothing to lose. "How many people has he had you pay off to lose and falsify evidence, Dale? Why do you do it? Is it because of Missy? To pay for her fancy lawyer and all her rehab stays?"

"Fuck's sake, Bluebelle." He stood, swaying on his feet, shell-shocked. "What're you doing? What do you want?"

She leveled her gaze on him, every muscle in her body tensed. "I want my dad's name cleared. I want the last ten years back. I *want* my mother back."

★   ★   ★

It was late when Blue pulled into the driveway after Sierra and Chloe's wedding shower. Judging from the loveliness of the event, their wedding was sure to be amazing. She'd put all her energy into being there and *on* for her best friend, in spite of her past doing its best to crush her the last few days. She was exhausted.

A deep voice came from the darkness as she started up the porch steps. "*Bluebelle.*" She spun around. Gino Castellari emerged from the shadows. She backed up, heart racing.

"We need to talk." He took one last pull from the cigar he held and flicked the butt at the ground, stepping on it. His deep-set eyes were hooded, unreadable.

She slipped a hand into her purse, fumbling for her phone.

"I wouldn't do that." He stepped closer, into the dim light cast from the porch light. "I'd like us to reach an understanding." He reached into his jacket.

She tried not to flinch. She forgot to breathe. Her gaze went to the fat envelope he held out to her. "I don't want it," she said. Her voice shook.

Gino wrapped one large hand around hers, pressing it into her hand. "I know about your son."

She jerked her hand back. "Enzo's son," she blurted.

"We don't know that. You need to leave, Bluebelle. This should help." He gestured at the envelope. Arrogance oozed from his pores; he thought he could buy her off.

"I don't want your money. I can't leave. This is my home."

He smiled, sending a chill up her spine. "Ah. But it isn't, now, is it? You don't belong here. Has anything gone right for you since coming back?" He lowered his voice, tipping his head in simulated concern. "Your father was doing fine until you showed up. How's his heart now?"

Blue seethed—she'd never hated anyone so much. "Stop it. Don't you talk about my dad," she hissed. Her eyes rolled to rest on the house in her periphery, where Murph and her dad were sleeping. She had to get inside, had to get away from this crazy, self-important man.

"Tell yourself whatever you need to. Everyone was better off without you. Think about that—and that." He nodded at the envelope she tried to thrust at him; he wouldn't take it. "You could buy your own place, free and clear, away from here.

There'd be enough left to pay off your dad's boats, his mortgage, all of his debts. Give him a clean start. I wonder, how does a single mother support herself and pay for her son's education on a nurse's salary? You want him to have a bright future, I assume. It's in there, paid for."

She couldn't help it. It was only an instant, but she saw it. Her father out from under all of his obligations. Her and Murphy flush, able to make decisions based on what was best, rather than what was cheapest. She shook her head, trying to clear it. His money had blood on it. She didn't want any part of it. She shouldn't even be entertaining what he was saying. She shoved the envelope into his chest and let go. "You can't pay me enough to leave my dad, to take my son away from his real father. I don't *want* it."

"That's fine. More in my pocket. But you're going to leave me alone. If you don't, I'll make sure your father's contracts all get dropped."

"You can't—"

He chuckled softly. "Yes I can. And don't count on Dale Bryant to suddenly want to clear his conscience. He needs me too much. I'd suggest you avoid any more visits over there."

When Blue had left Dale earlier today, she'd agreed to wait a day, just one day, before going to the police. He'd asked for time to think. She saw now what a mistake that had been.

Gino mistook her silence for agreement. "So, we're clear?"

"I want you to leave. I'm going inside now," she said, working to keep her voice level even though she could barely breathe. She completely understood her mum's fear of this man.

"Are we clear? Or should we go inside and talk about it with your father and Murphy?" He was loud, dropping the low tones now.

Blue's throat closed, her heart pounding in her temples. "Don't say his name," she said. "Don't talk about him. You don't know him, and you never will."

He closed the space between them, so close she could smell his cigar breath. "You'll want to make sure of that," he growled.

The front yard was suddenly illuminated. She glanced over her shoulder to see the large picture window brightly lit through the curtains. No—her dad couldn't handle this right now. But it wasn't her father who'd woken up; her heart lurched as she caught a glimpse of Murphy's face peering between the curtains. She turned back, ready to say whatever she had to make Gino Castellari leave, but he was already retreating. She never saw his car; she had no idea where he'd parked or how long he'd waited for her. Blue went inside, head spinning with impossible choices.

25

CASTELLARI AND SONS WAS business as usual Monday for everyone except the Castellaris. Gino and Marcello were conspicuously missing. Enzo rushed through the marina, bent on getting out on the water without any lip from his brother, but Marcello's office was empty along with their father's, and the conference room was dark.

Enzo called and checked in with Matteo while he and Salvi prepped the *Minnow*. Luca answered Matty's phone. "I don't think he's okay. I have class, I'm supposed to leave soon, but he can't be left alone like this. One of you needs to get over here."

Enzo hit speaker, setting the phone on the bow so Salvi could hear. "What's going on?"

"He's super restless. His stomach hurts. He can't sleep, doesn't wanna eat."

"Ugh," Enzo said. "I was hoping he'd be a little better today; he barely slept all night for me."

"I'll go," Salvi said. "Isn't it awesome that Marcello's part of this conversation? The way he's been taking shifts to look out for our brother like the rest of us? Oh wait. He's not," he growled, rolling his eyes at Enzo.

"I can come too. I'm thinking he may need more help than we can give him."

"What should I do?" Luca asked, his concern coming through the phone.

Enzo frowned. "Should I call and ask Blue? She hasn't answered any of my texts since Saturday, but she would for something like this for Matty. She'd tell us what to do."

"He's in withdrawal and it sounds like it's just getting worse," Salvi said. "I'm texting Maggie right now. She'll know if we should take him in."

Luca spoke. "Fuck, he just threw up. He's shaking. I gotta hang up. How do I help him?" Luca sounded frantic. "Should I call Ma?"

"No!" Both brothers answered at once.

"We're on the way," Enzo told him. "But—it'll take us twenty minutes to get to you."

"Maggie says to call an ambulance," Salvi directed. "We have to. We'll handle Ma and Pops later, just hang up and call 911, all right? We'll meet you at County."

"Got it." The call ended abruptly.

Four hours later, Enzo pulled back into the same parking spot at the marina. Spending the morning in the emergency room with his brothers, watching helplessly as Matty writhed in agony, had sapped all of his energy and goodwill. He wanted to kill his father for piling so much onto the most sensitive person in their family. He doubted he could've carried what Matteo had all those years, but keeping Gino's secrets had shaped Matty into the sick, dysfunctional bundle of trauma unmasked today in the ER. He'd probably been finding ways to numb and block his own conscience since the first time he'd gotten drunk or high.

Matty was now—thank God—safely admitted for the night and would be transferred to an inpatient recovery center tomorrow. Once whatever they'd pushed through his IV started to work and he became coherent, he'd agreed to the twenty-eight-day stay, and longer if necessary. Luca had gone directly from the hospital to pick up Ghost and bring him home until Matty was well.

Enzo strode through the marina to tuck the *Minnow* back in—he and Salvi had left her as she was when they raced to the hospital earlier. He stopped in his tracks passing Marcello's office; his brother was in. He opened the door without knocking, standing in the doorway, loath to move any closer. As angry as he was at Gino, he was nearly as upset with his brother.

Marcello's hands on the computer keyboard stilled and he met Enzo's eyes. "What's up?"

"What's up?" Enzo asked, incredulous. "Have you gotten any of our texts or calls?"

"I've been busy," Marcello said.

Enzo gritted his teeth together. "Yeah. Us too. If you gave two shits about Matty, you'd be acting like his brother."

Marcello hit the desk and stood. "Zo, with respect, shut the fuck up. You take care of Matty, I'll keep us above water. It's taken me months to figure out Pops' books and why the numbers are off. I don't have time right now to wipe our alcoholic baby brother's ass. He did this to himself."

He was taken aback. "He didn't do—you know what? Never mind. You think any addict *wants* to feel this way? Matty's in trouble. He's in the hospital. We'd all take care of you if you were ever in his shoes—"

"I wouldn't be," he shot back.

"Goddamn, when did you turn into such a dick?"

"Maybe when Pops pulled me into the middle of his embezzlement mess," Marcello spat, furious. "Maybe that's when."

Enzo was speechless.

"He's been padding expenses and cost reports, and he's got under-the-table deals with four of our biggest contract holders now, so I can't accurately track cash flow. He's been moving money to an offshore account, but even that doesn't account for all of it. I'm pretty sure the rest is just going to his girlfriends. He's got an apartment in Fort Myers. The numbers haven't made sense in months. I'm still working on how the fuck to fix this before the IRS catches on." Marcello dropped into his chair, holding his head against the heel of one palm. "Look. I didn't want to tell you. I'm dealing with it. We were with Hamish Josephson all morning, hashing it out."

"Hamish knows? Christ, does Jillian know?"

"I doubt it. He wouldn't even let the other senior partner in on it. We'll get it figured out."

Enzo shook his head. This explained a lot. "Holy shit," he breathed. "Is he—he's got to turn himself in. The company will fold. We—"

"Nope," Marcello shook his head. "That's not the play. Hamish has a plan. Pops isn't happy, but that's too fucking bad. I can't let him take the company down. We'll fix it. I'll get over to see Matty when I can." He sighed. "He'll be all right, won't he? He's gonna be okay?" Marcello asked earnestly, his face painted with worry.

Enzo was surprised and gratified at the relief that washed over him with Marcello's question. His brother hadn't shown an ounce of compassion or much of any human emotion in weeks, he'd been so absorbed in work. At least now it made sense. He nodded. "I think so. If he can stay in recovery, Matty might finally be okay for the first time in a long while."

26

Blue was just finishing dishes with Murphy after dinner Monday evening when the doorbell rang. He tossed his towel at her. "I'll get it!"

"No!" she cried.

He stopped and stared at her. "What, jeez, Mom."

"Sorry. Let me get it. It might be for me." If Gino was back, she was calling the police. She planned to head there anyway as soon as the dishes were done.

Blue pulled open the heavy front door and her heart dropped into her stomach. Brent stood on the front porch. She felt oddly disoriented, he was so completely out of context.

He stuck one hand in the pocket of his khakis. "Hi."

He could not be here. He didn't look mad . . . he didn't really look *anything*. He was wearing the navy blue button-down she'd bought him last Christmas. He looked shorter.

"Are you going to invite me in?" he asked.

Her brain had forgotten how to make words. "Um."

He waited, raising an eyebrow at her.

She heard Murphy come up behind her and cringed. Oh God. She didn't want to do this, any of it. And not with Murph here.

"Hello, Murphy. Did you get taller?" Brent leaned forward, peering inside through the screen.

"Uh, yeah, I think so. My pants are too short," Murph said. He looked down at his chili pepper swim trunks. "I mean, not these. But my jeans are too short now, so I think I did get taller." He stopped abruptly and drifted over so he was partially hidden behind Blue, the same as he had when he was two and afraid of everyone.

"Can I come in?" Brent asked again. Blue expected impatience in his tone, but it wasn't there.

What was she supposed to do? She pushed the door open. "Sure." She felt like those stupid girls in all the vampire movies, inviting the monster in.

He glanced around. "So this is your dad's place."

"Yes," she said. "Since before I was born. It was one of the first houses along this part of the Gulf. It's small, but I made a nice bedroom out of the sunroom for Murph—" She stopped. Why was she telling him this? Seeing him had instantly brought on a creeping anxiety and now she felt it spiraling up toward full-blown panic as he stood looking around the living room.

"Where are your suitcases?" Brent asked. "I'll help you pack your things."

Her heart pounded in her throat. "We're not coming back," she said, dismayed to hear her voice come out timid and weak. She was surprised to realize she meant it, despite how she sounded. There was no doubt left in her mind. She turned to Murphy. "Go back to the kitchen." He shook his head, his eyes glued to Brent.

"You're coming home," he said. "We talked about it. I told you I was flying down to get you."

Blue started to argue, but her dad spoke from the doorway behind her. "She said she's not going. They're staying here."

Blue met her dad's pale blue eyes briefly. "Brent," she said, her mind racing. "Let's go talk outside, okay?"

He stared stone-faced at her, completely unreadable. By now, the old Brent would've already had enough of this. "Sure."

She put a hand firmly on Murphy's chest. "Stay in here with Grandpa. I mean it." She went through the door after Brent.

"Mom!" The alarm in his tone pulled her back.

"It's fine. I'll be right in. Just give us a minute." She followed Brent past the red and orange zinnias she and Murph had planted in two large aqua flower pots she'd found at a yard sale. She'd thought they made the front porch look so inviting along with the new paint. She descended the steps after Brent, feeling like she was seeing everything through his eyes: the century-old beach-front cottage half the size of their Tallahassee house, the patchy grass in the yard so unlike the perfectly manicured lawn she'd left, the laid-back fishing village vibe that was nothing like life in the suburbs. Jesus. What if he tried to take Murphy? Could he? He was a cop. He knew the court system. Nothing had been estab-lished yet to prove Enzo was Murph's biological father. Brent had had no use for her son before, but would he use him to make her come back? She felt clammy, a wave of nausea hitting her hard.

He stopped in the yard and faced her. "So."

"Listen, I told you about my dad; he just had heart surgery. I'm not leaving. I tried to tell you."

She saw the muscle in his jaw clench and unclench. "And I told you that this whole little adventure was over. Your father looks fine to me."

She swallowed hard, struggling to breathe, her throat con-stricting around the jumble of words she wanted to shout at him.

"What do you need, Blue?" His tone was cajoling. "If you're really that concerned about your dad, maybe we can arrange for you to come back here in a couple of weeks. You could check on him, make sure he's okay."

A chill shot up her spine, catapulting her right back into their six years of marriage. This was conciliatory Brent, the way he always sounded when he apologized and promised everything would get better. His soothing demeanor, his controlled patience and stoic face only made her more nervous. There was no way he was letting her come back here once she left. "Brent, you left us. You wanted a divorce," she said, hating the quiver in her voice. "I know I didn't at first, but I think it's the best thing for all of us. I'd like you to leave now. Please."

He closed the space between them in two steps. "Enough," he said, the word a low growl, color rising in his cheeks. "I've tried to give you time, I've been patient, but I'm done. Go get your things."

"No. Go home, Brent. I don't want you here."

He gripped her upper arm, and she gasped at the biting pain, her other hand coming up to push him off. He grabbed her hand and twisted it toward him, staring at her naked ring finger. "Where's your ring!"

"You're hurting me," she said, trying to pull free from his grasp.

The front door clapped against the molding as her father came out. "Hey!" Mitch started down the steps toward them, his shoulders squared. His posture and quick stride had to hurt. He'd been hunched over, guarding his chest incision, since he'd come home yesterday.

Brent was so close to her she could smell the pine of his aftershave, the scent turning her stomach. "Do you know where you'd be if it wasn't for me? A high school dropout single mom with a bratty kid; who would've wanted you? Everything you had, everything you are, is because of me." He let go of her with a shove, and she stumbled backward.

Mitch stepped in front of her, facing Brent. "You need to leave. Get off my property. We're not telling you again." Mitch's tone was firm as he looked down on Brent from his height advantage.

Brent settled his cold stare at Blue's father. "Fuck off, old man. I know all about you, how you wouldn't let your teenage daughter come back home. She's not staying here." He stepped around Mitch Shea, starting toward the house.

Mitch grabbed the back of Brent's collar, jerking him back and grimacing in pain as he did so. Brent pulled away and hit the older man with the heel of his hand against his left shoulder, knocking him to the ground. Her dad grabbed at his chest.

"Dad!" Blue shrieked. She knelt beside him, searching his face, terrified.

"Stay down," Brent pointed at Mitch, standing over him. "Let's go," he told Blue. "Get your things."

She had to get help; if her years with Brent had taught her anything, it was that he was about to get a lot angrier than this. But she'd left her phone in the house. She looked worriedly at her dad. "Are you okay?"

He nodded. "Just. Wind knocked. Out—"

"Shh, all right, don't talk. Take some deep breaths if you can." She turned back toward Brent, planning to try to cajole and calm him, say what he needed to hear so he'd let her go inside on her own to pack, and she could get to her phone, but his hand clamped around her arm like a vise.

He dragged her to her feet and she cried out in pain, positive he'd break her arm. "Brent! Stop! Please!"

He pulled her toward the porch steps and she went, trying to keep her arm from twisting in his grasp, stabbing pain shooting out from where he squeezed her. She stumbled and he jerked her toward him and she shrieked, her arm on fire.

"Knock it off," he said. "God, Blue, always so dramatic. You could have made this easy, I didn't want to do it this way. Let's go." He started up the porch steps with her just as a squall of gravel flew into the air along the driveway.

Blue saw Enzo's truck through the dust: he was already out and coming across the lawn toward them. "Let go of her," he bellowed.

Brent pulled her against him, closing a hand around her neck. He jerked his service revolver from the back of his belt, holding it at his side. "Who the fuck is this?" he asked her. "A new boyfriend already?"

She tried to swallow but couldn't under his grip. She got an elbow into his side and Brent put his lips against her cheek, making her recoil. "You want to stop that now. Calm down, and I'll let go." He pointed the gun at Enzo. "Far enough, bud. What the hell did you make me walk into here, Blue?" He tightened his fingers at her throat and she choked out a strangled cough, her eyes burning with tears.

Blue's chest was about to burst, her heart racing as she struggled with short shallow breaths. Her pulse pounded behind her eyes. Where was Murphy? She hoped like crazy he was still in the house. The edges of her vision grew dark, as if she was in a tunnel. She closed her eyes, distantly hearing Enzo's voice and her father's. If she could just calm down, he'd let go. She could reason with him and get him to leave. But she knew that wasn't true. All these years, he'd had her believing that she was the cause of his temper; if she'd just listen to him, do what he expected of her, he wouldn't have to get angry. But he was always angry.

Blue used the strength she had left and limply brought her hand up to Brent's wrist, patting it. His vise-like grip loosened just enough and she whispered, "I'll go."

He opened his fingers and she bent forward, coughing. He pulled her toward the porch steps and Blue threw all her weight in the opposite direction. She fell onto the walkway, taking Brent with her. She got to her hands and knees and scrambled away from him, expecting his hand to close around her leg and yank her back at any moment.

She made it over to Mitch and turned in time to see Enzo wrench the handgun out of Brent's grasp. He pinned his arms behind him and pushed him onto his knees. Sirens sounded in the distance and Blue prayed they were somehow coming here. Her dad helped her up and she brushed herself off. Her knees were bleeding and her throat felt raw.

She met her husband's infuriated stare from where she was. "It's over," she said, ignoring the pain when she spoke. "I don't love you, Brent. I didn't deserve the way you treated me. Neither did Murphy." The sirens sounded like they were heading straight toward Live Oak Way. "We're staying here, and you're going back to Tallahassee. Or maybe to jail."

He laughed. "It won't happen. I'm one of theirs. They'll take my word over yours."

"I doubt it," Mitch said, nodding toward the house. "Not with it all on video."

On the other side of the living room window, Murphy stood with Blue's phone pointed at the front yard. The sirens screamed closer, but the first car that rolled into the driveway was not a squad car; it was Dale Bryant's old Lincoln. He climbed out, gun drawn, his Collier County Sheriff's Department badge clipped to his belt. For a moment, Blue held her breath—was he here as her father's friend, or Gino Castellari's right hand, ready to shut her and her dad up for good?

"I heard your boy's 911 call over dispatch on my radio," he told Blue. "So we've got what? Domestic dispute, disgruntled estranged husband acting a fool, tryin' to force you back home?"

Murphy came out on the porch at the sight of Dale in their yard. "He strangled my mom," he called, his voice hitching with tears, "and hit my grandpa." He took a faltering step toward them but stopped, clearly terrified of Brent.

"Huh. So assault and battery then. Times two, looks like," Dale said, as a Sheriff's Department squad car tore into the driveway.

When Brent had been handcuffed and loaded into the back of the squad car and the two responding officers had taken their statements, Dale hung back. He stood in the shade of the willow, talking with Mitch.

Blue hugged her son. "Thank you, Murph," she said. "For staying inside, for getting help, for recording. You're pretty amazing."

He pointed at her neck. "Does it hurt? You're all red. Are you really okay, Mom?"

Blue touched it gingerly, wincing. She was already sore. "Yeah. I will be." She looked at Enzo. "Are *you* okay? You could have been shot."

"I'm fine, don't worry. I'm glad Murphy called me," he said. "Maybe you should get checked out. Your dad too."

Mitch approached, leaving Dale hanging back, on his phone. He grabbed Enzo's hand, shaking it. "You saved her life. Thank you," Mitch said, his voice gruff. "He was killing her."

Enzo's dark eyes were wide; Blue could see he'd assumed her father hated him as much as Gino hated the Sheas. Enzo covered the older man's hand with his. "I didn't do much, sir. Blue saved herself."

"She's tough, like her mum."

"Like you," she said, hugging her dad. "Go inside and rest; go with him, Murph. I'll be in in a minute to check your incision and make sure everything's all right."

When they'd gone, Enzo spoke. "I've gotta say it. Our son is one amazing kid. You've done an incredible job, by yourself from what I can see. Brent was lucky to have you. He was lucky to have a stepson as great as Murph. Your husband's a fucking idiot."

Her eyes filled with tears in a rush at the words *our son*. She looked skyward, blinking fast. She couldn't cry. If she started now she'd never stop. "Don't call him that. Don't call him my husband. The sooner he's not, the better I'll feel."

"Mom!" Murphy yelled from the porch.

Blue's heart raced. Her dad. If his surgical site was hurt, she'd kill Brent. "I'm coming!"

"He's okay. But he's going out to smoke," Murphy said, pointing toward the backyard. "I told him you'd be mad."

"*Go*. Good luck with that," Enzo told her, opening his truck door.

"Hold on." Dale joined them, addressing Blue. "I talked to your dad. I'm headed in for a sit-down with my chief and the undersheriff. Gonna tell 'em everything I've done for Gino Castellari. You should probably go in and make your own statement; take the book you showed me."

Blue was stunned. "But—Dale, are you sure?"

A cloud crossed his features, a split-second glimpse of what this would cost him. He scowled and kicked the crab grass. "Your parents filed a report the night of that party. She went through the whole deal in the ER. It was standard ops right up to when Gino had me make sure forensics lost the evidence; he paid off a tech at the hospital too. County won't prosecute without some kinda proof. Same shit happened the night your poor mom drowned. Gino made it go the way he wanted and—you gotta understand something, Bluebelle." He took a deep breath, locking eyes with her. "He hates your dad like nothin' I've ever seen. Wasn't always like that. But after that night, after he found out your parents tried to press charges, everything changed. He's, uh—well, he's used to folks lookin' at him a certain way. After that night, he'd of done anything, used anyone, to ruin Mitch's life. Hell, he did. Me sayin' sorry for my part in it don't bring your mom back, I know that."

She was silent. She'd never been so sick over learning the truth. "Dale—thank you. What about Missy?"

He sighed heavily, mouth turned down. "Well. She'll still have her mother while I'm . . . away. There's no point anyway in keeping this up. Can't help someone who doesn't wanna be helped."

Dale got in his car and left without another word. She watched him go, unmoving, until Enzo spoke quietly at her side.

"I'll go with you to talk to the police. If that'd help. Or it can just be you and your dad. Matty will want to make a statement too, as soon as he's doing better." He briefly filled her in on where he'd spent the morning.

"I'm so sorry. I'm sorry I didn't answer your texts; I just . . . I think I need things to settle down a little." It was a cop-out, she knew; she wasn't going to get into all the ways Jillian had made her doubt what she and Enzo might have. Not now. "I really hope Matty will be okay."

"He will be. Blue." Enzo searched her eyes, his gaze dropping to her neck where Brent had hurt her. "Are you okay?"

"Yeah. I am now." She hugged him, exhausted, like she'd just run a marathon.

He kissed her temple. "Go take care of your dad."

After she'd watched him leave, Blue went around the side of the house and sat beside her dad on the garden bench. He was lighting his second cigarette off the almost finished first.

"Dad—"

"Bluebelle," he said, talking around the cigarette in his mouth. "I need a smoke. After all that, I just do. I'm gonna sit out here and have one. I'll try to make it my last. That's all I can promise."

She looked up, exhaling her frustration. "Oh my goodness!" Someone had strung lights across the backyard and through the grove of trees, the soft glow twinkling in the darkening twilight. She laughed, catching sight of Murphy out of the corner of her eye. He stood on the patio staring upward.

"The Fairy Garden Bandit struck again," Blue said.

Murphy and Hook sprinted down the path into the grove of trees. She didn't have to wonder for long whether their anonymous benefactor had done anything else. "Mom! You have to see this!"

Blue followed the trail around the little curve, finding Murphy in front of a beautifully painted, turquoise-colored fairy cottage with a matching mailbox. He turned in a slow circle and Blue stopped and copied him. All around them, bits of multicolored light glinted in the last of the daylight: their bandit had somehow attached dozens of dime-sized colored mirror tiles to the tree trunks along the path, creating a glimmering walkway all the way through the fairy village. Murphy gently moved the cluster of bluebell flowers off the path before he knelt on the cedar, taking care not to crush them.

Blue's hand flew to her neck where Brent had choked her. Her mum's words echoed in her head, the fairy lore she'd heard her entire childhood, the lessons in the bluebells. She hadn't been crushed; she was here, whole, a survivor. Her mum was still with her, even now. Blue's heart was full. She knelt down beside Murphy.

He opened the turquoise mailbox and handed her a tiny, folded square of paper. She read:

> *"Miss Bluebelle and young Sir Murphy,*
> *A final message:*
> *Love is the whole thing. We are only pieces. —Rumi"*

Murphy turned a worried expression toward her. "A final message?"

She tipped her head. "I guess so."

"But—why? There are still things in here that need to be painted! Why are they quitting?"

"Well," she said, thinking aloud, "we can take over. Maybe we don't need the bandit anymore. And the quote—"

"I get the quote. I think I know what this one means." He took it from her, reading it aloud. "*Love is the whole thing. We are only pieces.* Like a puzzle. It means we're all pieces and the puzzle needs all the pieces to be whole."

27

ENZO WAS SITTING ON his deck, looking out over the choppy black water of the Gulf, when Blue's car pulled into his driveway just after ten that night. His heart leapt; he'd hoped she'd call or text, but he hadn't expected her to come over. He was on his feet, grinning at her as she greeted Moon on the bottom step, petting him and scratching the happy dog around the ears.

"Well, hello there. What a cutie."

"Aw, thanks," Enzo said.

She laughed. "I was talking to your dog, but okay. You're pretty cute too." She came the rest of the way up.

"This is Moon," Enzo said. "He's your best friend for life now that you've petted him." There was a barrier between them. He'd felt it that afternoon as he was leaving, an invisible line that hadn't been there before. "Let's talk inside." In his living room, he sat beside her on the couch.

She faced him. "I talked with Jillian yesterday. I mean, she mostly talked. I have to ask you something. A few things."

Enzo was stunned. "What the hell? Where? What did she say?"

"She caught me at the grocery store. She really hates me. She says you're using me as an excuse and you just have cold feet and you don't know what you want." She stopped, taking a deep breath and wincing. Even in the dim light, Enzo saw there were dark red, finger-shaped marks around the curve of her neck that hadn't had time yet to change to bruises.

"None of that is true," he said. "Jillian's just lashing out."

"I don't know. I'm not sure you even really know."

"Blue. Give me some credit. We just—"

She stood, feeling the coffee table against the backs of her legs.

He sighed. "She's angry at me. She's taking it out on you, which isn't fair. It's easier for her to believe we aren't permanently broken up or that it's someone else's fault."

Blue's gaze dropped for a moment to his mouth and Enzo's heart skipped a beat, tripping forward at a faster pace. "I need to know how you really feel," she said. "What you really want. Jillian said we don't even know each other anymore."

He leaned forward, his knees touching her legs, and looked up at her. "I know you, Blue. I always have. And what I don't know now, I'll learn."

She drifted closer and he slid a hand up her arm, gently pulling her into his space. She stood between his knees, searching his eyes.

"Blue." His voice was low. "I don't want to be with anyone but you. I never have."

She combed her fingertips lightly through the black waves behind his temples. He leaned into her hand and closed his eyes. "I always felt like there was a piece of me missing," Blue said, her voice quiet. "I thought it was my mum. When I came home, I thought I'd find it, but my mum's never left me. I carry her with me. It wasn't her." She traced a finger along his jaw. "It's you, Enz."

Enzo's heartbeat thumped in his throat. He stood, lightly cradling her cheek, taking care to avoid her neck. He slid his thumb across her bottom lip and bent his head and kissed her, softly, gently, his lips brushing against hers. That night on the docks when they were seventeen and dreaming of their future, he couldn't have imagined they'd be torn apart before it could happen. Since then, he'd never let himself believe he'd hold her again. Now, Blue melted into him and he covered her mouth with his, parting her lips and kissing her. His hands moved over her waist and hips and she responded, wrapping one leg tightly around his. He groaned, holding her to him, and Blue planted kisses along his neck, each movement, each minute shift incredible and excruciating. She bit the side of his neck and he inhaled sharply.

He'd resisted, he'd tried so hard to avoid losing himself in her again. But she was the air he breathed, the blood running through his veins. She'd always been. He had no choice.

Blue pressed Enzo's palm over her racing heart, her chest rising and falling rapidly. "I don't want to wait anymore," she whispered. She touched the corner of his mouth and it went up in a half smile and he captured her hand, kissing her fingertips.

He took her by the hand, moving backwards, only taking his gaze from hers long enough to stop and kiss her as they went. In his bedroom, Enzo brushed his lips over her cheekbone, and then her jawline, his fingertips hovering over the bruised skin of her neck but not touching her there. He spoke, his voice quiet, thick. "Does it hurt?"

Blue placed her hand over his and guided it to the side of her neck that Brent hadn't injured. She closed her eyes as Enzo caressed her skin, his fingertips at the nape of her neck. "It doesn't hurt here. You won't hurt me, Enz," she said softly.

★   ★   ★

He wrapped her in his arms and she was home, safe, loved, as Enzo touched her, her heart and mind and every nerve in her body aching with need and longing. She was spinning, weightless, soaring through urgency and sensation, her body lit from within. He was warm and firm and gentle and real under her hands, his strong arms pulling her into him, tighter, closer, until there was no space left between them and Blue gasped, flying and falling, coming undone and bringing him with her.

Later, when her eyes drifted sleepily open, the sky outside his window was a black canvas painted with stars. She rested her cheek against his chest, tucked into the safe circle of his arm around her, his heartbeat her own.

Enzo stirred. He traced lazy figure eights onto her skin, his eyes half closed. "Stay with me, Blue."

She could think of nothing better.

28

BLUE BREATHED IN THE salt air under the rose-colored sky, a light breeze lifting the white wedding canopy beside her and making the hem of her turquoise dress flutter around her calves. Palm fronds and calla lilies climbed the bamboo trellises, interspersed with pink roses matching the bouquets Sierra and Chloe carried as they approached the minister. The light from the sunset over the Gulf cast a warm glow over the smiling couple.

Blue's gaze moved to her son in the second row between Enzo and her father, Rita beside Mitch. She'd taken Murphy and her dad suit shopping, and her son had chosen a charcoal gray, Mitch going with navy. Side by side, grandfather and grandson, she saw the resemblance, but it was obvious he was Enzo Castellari's son.

Enzo caught her eye and winked, and her knees noodled for a moment. His black hair was freshly cut, the top button of his crisp white shirt left undone under his black suit jacket. He'd picked the three of them up that afternoon in a high-end, polished black SUV instead of his truck, simply saying it was his other car.

He'd shaken his head when she'd suggested they arrive separately. "I'm not sneaking around. I've wasted too much time already."

It had been five days since Brent had staged his ambush on her front lawn; three days since he was arraigned and released back home to Tallahassee, fined and sentenced to anger management courses and community service.

After Dale had come clean with his superiors, and Blue and her dad followed up the next day, filling in details with the captain's log and the photos from her father's hospital chart, Gino Castellari had gone in Wednesday of his own accord for questioning before he could be arrested in public. Hamish Josephson was with him. Enzo had given her minimal details, but she knew Gino's arraignment was that morning. She was avoiding asking the outcome as long as possible.

On Thursday, Blue and her dad had officially hired Kai to work full time on the Yellowfin, which she'd calculated would double their catch and also allow a return to direct distribution, with more manpower, meaning they could add more contracts. She'd also convinced Mitch to raise his per pound rate significantly while still staying competitive. Her father had been undercutting himself for years. He was a great fisherman but not so great with business finances.

Sierra's veil floated behind her on a soft gust of warm air as she reached the altar. She handed over the bouquet for Blue to hold while she took her vows. Blue's eyes welled up and she kissed Sierra's cheek. "I'm so happy for you," she whispered, feeling a tear slip from the corner of one eye. Sierra grinned and swiped it away.

"Me too," she said. "I'm so glad you stayed." She turned toward her bride.

Chloe and Sierra linked hands and faced the minister, who opened a book and slid the ribbon bookmark to one side. She read:

"May this marriage be blessed. May this marriage be as sweet as milk and honey. May this marriage be as intoxicating as old wine. May this marriage be full of laughter and every day a paradise. May this marriage be a seal of compassion for here and hereafter."

The words resonated in Blue; she knew them. She'd read them before, when she was puzzling through that very first fairy garden quote. The minister closed the book and set it down, the cover confirming her suspicions. It was Sierra. Sierra had been secretly working in their fairy garden all these weeks, repairing and painting and penning notes with quotes meant to help guide her back to her life. Quotes from Rumi, the same as the lovely, lyrical Rumi reading during their vows. Of course it was Sierra. Like Enzo, she was always there when Blue needed her.

Later, after dinner and wine and watching Murphy splashing with Chloe's nephew in the waves at the shore, their pantlegs rolled up but still soaked, Enzo put his lips near her ear and asked her dance. Blue took his offered hand. The wedding guests were slowly saying their goodbyes under the pavilion. She slid a hand inside his jacket, her palm opening on his back as he held her in his arms, conforming his body to hers, leading them over the dance floor effortlessly.

She gazed up at him. "You're a good dancer."

"I've got a good partner."

She smiled, resting her head against his collarbone. She couldn't believe so much had changed in such a short time.

The band announced their last song. Enzo stepped back, raising their linked hands above them, and pulled Blue into a twirl under his arm, bringing her back into him. He turned them in a circle and dipped her, making her laugh. "All right, you've had lessons," she giggled as he pulled her upright.

He shrugged. "Matty taught me."

She stared at him, incredulous. "I can't even imagine. How is he? Is he doing any better?"

"He's working through the program, going to groups. He really likes his therapist there. He got a letter from Lucinda Key for an art job that might still be an option when he's better and ready. He seems . . . different. Hopeful."

Her heart swelled. "That's amazing. I'm so glad. And . . . Gino? What happened this morning?" She couldn't avoid the topic forever.

He frowned down at her. "Let's just enjoy the evening."

She sighed. "Enz. No matter what happens, my dad and I finally have answers. It's all out in the open, no more secrets. It's okay, you can tell me."

"They released him on bond. There will be a trial; word is, Hamish Josephson isn't worried." He rolled his eyes. "There's more; Ma is taking over the business for a while. It's all in her name now."

She narrowed her eyes. "I feel like I'm missing something."

He nodded. "Jillian's dad's an arrogant prick, of course he'd tell Gino not to worry. But we all think he'll be convicted on both charges—for the assault on your mom and his failure to respond to your dad's distress call. The prosecuting attorney says it's open and shut, with the evidence that's come out, thanks to you and Matty and Dale. Castellari and Sons now belongs solely to my mother. Marcello basically corrected everything Gino'd done with the company finances, closed the offshore shell accounts, cut off the girlfriends—that was fun. But," he said, scowling, "Pops kept a percentage of shares, so he still holds a seat on the board; I lost that vote."

She pressed her lips together. "That makes me feel better." She nearly added a *sorry*, but didn't, proud that she'd stopped herself in time.

He tipped his head, searching her eyes. "Blue. I don't want to talk about them. Have I told you today how much I've missed you?" He ducked his head, nuzzling her neck near her ear and sending delicious tingles through her. "Because I did. Every minute for ten years."

He unnerved her. She wasn't accustomed to the focus being on her, not in a good way. She supposed that's what her weekly therapy sessions were for. "You might have mentioned it," she said, her cheeks flushing. "I feel like I missed so much of your life. I want to hear all of it, everything, including the Castellari brother dance lessons."

He held her gaze. "I have something for you." He loosened his arms around her, and she saw that he'd guided them away from the thinning crowd as they danced. They were closer to the water now, the rose-colored sky streaked with gold. Enzo pulled a small black box from inside his jacket and handed it to her.

"What is this?"

"Something I've been meaning to give you since we were fifteen."

She opened the box. A thin gold band was displayed on the black satin.

"I bought it for you that summer, before everything changed. We were kids, I knew we were too young, but I bought it anyway with my fishing money. It's not the real—"

Blue wrapped her arms around him and hugged him, pressing her face into his neck. Her throat was thick with tears; she drew in a hitching breath. "You're unbelievable," she said, half laughing, half crying. She let go enough to meet Enzo's own tear-filled eyes.

He took the ring and slipped it onto her finger, bringing her hand to his lips and kissing her palm. "It's just a placeholder. But it's always belonged to you; my heart's always been yours. One more thing," he said, handing the box back to her. "Something I added today."

Where the ring had been was a small white corner of paper tucked into the satin. Blue pulled it out, unfolding a square of paper like the ones from her fairy garden. She read: *For those who love with heart and soul there is no such thing as separation.* —*Rumi*

She stared up at him, unable to speak, barely able to breathe.

"I love you, Blue. Nothing can change that."

She kissed him. When her tears had slowed enough for her to talk, she cradled his face in her hands, smiling. "I love you too, Enzo. Always." She gasped. "Was it you, then? The Fairy Garden Bandit?"

He laughed softly. "I can't take Sierra's credit. I just strung the lights. And borrowed her book," he said, nodding at the quote in Blue's hand.

"I have a feeling we still have a lot to learn about each other."

"So much. We should start right away," he said. "Now that you're really home."

"I am really home." She gazed into his eyes, the tiny flecks of green against brown bright in the waning light, the same as they'd been years earlier, before their world tipped over. She'd given him her heart that night, and he'd kept it safe for her all this time.

ACKNOWLEDGMENTS

I MET MY HUSBAND at the A&P grocery store in Detroit when I was six years old. We were in line for the movie booth with a bunch of other kids at the front of the store. For a couple of quarters, we'd get to watch a short cartoon while his mom and my grandma shopped. We figure we must've spent hundreds of Saturday mornings together for years growing up, though neither of us remembers the other. We discovered our shared past when we met again—I was seventeen then and he was nineteen. He is still my best friend, the love of my life, and the best man I know. It seems important to include my own little story here, within the pages of a story that required my entire heart and soul to write.

I am forever grateful to the people who made it possible for this book to happen. Frances Black's unwavering support and belief in my voice, my writing, has been an incredible gift. She provided me with keen insight and feedback and championed this book without hesitation, securing the best possible publishing home for it with Alcove Press.

Alcove Press senior editor Faith Black Ross was instrumental in shaping this manuscript into the story I'd always hoped it could become; she saw the forest when I could only see the trees in front of me. She offered me crucial, detailed guidance and notes, and the fact that she had enough faith in the bones of this story to do so was unexpected and greatly appreciated.

I had the pleasure of meeting Alcove Press publisher Matt Martz in 2022. Getting to shake the hand of the publisher himself was surreal and wonderful. It's difficult to adequately express my gratitude for the opportunity to have my words become an Alcove Press novel. The entire Alcove team is fantastic. I'd be lost without their help, from early questions to marketing and everything in between. Thank you so much to Madeline Rathle, Dulce Botello, Rebecca Nelson, the copy editors, cover and design artists, and all involved in bringing this book to life.

Huge, heartfelt thanks to Sherry Rummler, new friend, prolific author, and early reader of Unbreaking Blue. I could not have asked for a greater reaction to this story. I love how much you loved it! And a big thank you to good friend, fellow Michigander, and prolific author Darci Hannah for being so certain Sherry and I should meet. I'll always be one of your first fans from way back!

To my sweet friend and concert wife Ann, thank you for reading these pages in their early form, even while you were dealing with one of the most difficult challenges of your life. To my good friend and other mother to my kids, Rocsana, thank you for your constant support and kindness. I love you both.

I owe my sailor dad major thanks for all those days, nights, and weekends spent on his boats out on the water in Michigan and Florida. I learned so much more than I realized, which was, I am certain, always your intention. I owe my mom thanks for my love of writing and storytelling. I am grateful to both my parents for dancing in the kitchen and showing me what two people in love look like through the years.

Thank you, Julie. You like to say I'm your favorite sister; you're my first and forever friend in addition to being my sister. There are fragments of you in Blue and in Luca, perhaps more than you'll realize. These characters would not be as fully formed as they are without the inspiration I borrowed to write them. You are so much stronger than you know.

Thank you, Joe, for always believing in me, and for the spark of the idea that became this book. Thank you, Katy, Joey, and Halle, for being you and being mine. I couldn't imagine what it'd be like having kids, but if I could have written it, it still wouldn't be as amazing as the real thing. Being your mom is the joy and privilege of my life.

And thank you, wonderful reader. I hope some small part of this story stays with you.